MW00667356

THE SINGULARITY TRAP

DENNIS E. TAYLOR

Copyright © 2018 Dennis E. Taylor - All rights reserved.

This is a work of fiction. Names, characters, businesses, places, events and incidents are either the products of the author's imagination or used in a fictitious manner. Any resemblance to actual persons, living or dead, or actual events is purely coincidental.

This book or any portion thereof may not be reproduced or used in any manner whatsoever without the express written permission of the publisher except for the use of brief quotations in a book review.

ISBN: 978-1680680881

Cover art by Stephan Martiniere

Author Blog: www.dennisetaylor.org

Other titles by the author

The *Bobiverse* series:
We Are Legion (We Are Bob)
For We Are Many
All These Worlds

Dedications

First, and always, I want to dedicate this book to my wife, Blaihin, and my daughter, Tina.

Acknowledgements

Thanks to:

Members of the Ubergroup and Novel Exchange group on scribophile.

Sandra and Ken McLaren
Nicole Hamilton
Sheena Lewis
Patrick Jordan
Trudy Cochrane

TABLE OF CONTENTS

For what will it profit a man if he gains
the whole world and forfeits his soul?
-Mark 8:36

Glossary of Acronyms

RIVA	Rocket Impelled Vector Adjustment
IMM	Interplanetary Merchant Marine
ICDC	Interplanetary Centers for Disease Control
UEN	United Earth Nations
UENN	United Earth Nations Navy
SSE	Sino-Soviet Empire
SSC	Strategic Space Command
ISI	Interplanetary Science Institute
AQRI	Advanced Quantum Resonance Imaging

Cast of Characters

Crew of the *Mad Astra*

Andrew Jennings	Captain
Dante Aiello	First Mate
Albert Micoroski	Pilot, astrogator
Lita Generus	Co-pilot and purser
Charlie Kemp	Doctor
Duncan MacNeil	Engineer
Ivan Pritchard	Computer specialist
Seth Robinson	Crewmate and friend
Tennison Davies	Senior crewman
Arcadius Geiger	Crewmate and other noob
Raul Alfaro	crew
Willoughby Todd	crew
Robert Sala	crew
Fredric Robertsson	crew
Aran Sokal	Control Systems specialist
Aspasia Nevin	Scooter pilot
Lorenza Raske	Mining Robot specialist
Cirila Heinrichs	Geologist

ICDC Staff

Madhur Narang	Senior Investigating Pathologist, ICDC
Karin Laakkonen	Director, ICDC
Haruki Nakamura	Assistant Investigating Pathologist, ICDC
Noelia Sandoval	doctor
Henry Samuelson	doctor
Alwin Schulze	physicist
Matt Siegel	computer expert

UEN Navy Personnel

Admiral Theodore Moore	Chair, Quarantine committee
Commodore Michael Gerrard	Quarantine committee
Admiral Alan Castillo	Quarantine committee
Admiral Georgia Richards	Quarantine committee
Commodore Alice Nevin	Quarantine committee
Lt. Colonel Neil Martinson	Quarantine committee
Lieutenant George Bentley	Moore's assistant
Captain Xuân Lê	Frigate *Outbound*
Captain Norman Harding	Cruiser *Resolute*

Commodore Rani Mandelbaum	Task Force Officer in Charge
Lt. Ernest Voigt	Interrogator

Mercury Residents

Emilia Jonquers	Resident of Vulcan's Forge
Bruce Jonquers	Mining specialist, Emilia's husband
Ian & Caleb Jonquers	Emilia's children

Others

Judy Pritchard	Ivan's wife
Josh & Suzie	Ivan's children
Roger	Tenn's partner

1. Emissary

One final nudge from the solar wind, and the traveler floated in orbit, just one of many insignificant pieces of flotsam at this distance from the local star. A voltage through the lines caused its sail to fold into a neat, compact package.

The journey from the previous star had taken millennia, but the traveler was incapable of feeling boredom or impatience. Nor did it feel anxiety over the many more such hops in its future. The traveler worked through its checklist, shutting down some systems, activating others. Some maintenance would be required—the nearby asteroids would be more than sufficient to supply the raw materials.

The traveler scanned the stellar system, looking for planets or moons that matched any of several templates. And almost immediately, success! A blue-green planet with strong spectroscopic lines indicating oxygen, water, and one of the many biological strategies used to harness sunlight. No lights, no radio traffic, but the traveler didn't concern itself. Intelligence would come, or it would not. Either way, the traveler would be long since gone.

The traveler launched a drone to the nearest asteroid. Raw materials were mined, maintenance was completed, and an emissary was constructed to wait for the emergence of any intelligent life.

The traveler couldn't feel joy or satisfaction—the Makers had been very careful to limit its level of sentience. The traveler knew this as a datum, but had no opinion otherwise.

Nevertheless, this stop had been successful. Several checkpoint items were marked completed, and other goal trees activated.

It was time to move on. A voltage through the anchor lines, and the sail unfolded. Slowly, almost imperceptibly, the traveler began its millenia-long journey to the next candidate star.

It could wait.

2. Launch

"One minute to launch."

Ivan gripped the chair arms even tighter. The pain in his fingers penetrated his panic, and he struggled to unclench his hands and slow his breathing.

He looked at the arms of his blue coverall, relieved that the cloth was still dry. If he couldn't get a grip soon, the sight of a sopping-wet uniform would only encourage the other crew members to more of what they apparently thought was witty commentary.

And anyway, his funk made no logical sense. The Sling had been launching shuttles into orbit with no major incidents for almost forty years. Technically, this was safer than air travel. And he was going into *space!* This should be *fun.*

"Hey, noob. You aren't going to have a jammer, are you?"

Ivan glanced to his left at Tennison Davies, sitting across the center aisle. Tenn, a beefy, florid Texan, was a veteran of asteroid mining, returning for his tenth tour.

In fact, every one of the crew signed on with the *Mad Astra* had at least four previous tours with the mining ship. Everyone except himself and Arcadius Geiger, and Kady looked like he was falling asleep. Show-off.

Ivan and his fellow crew members sat together, taking up two complete rows. He could see groups from several other ships, all wearing similar utility coveralls, also heading up in preparation for a six-month mining tour. The coveralls, standard-issue items probably made by a single company, were identical except for the ship insignia on the left breast. The *Mad Astra* crew wore a stylized image of a hand reaching for a star.

Several *clunks* and a shudder ran through the shuttle, and Ivan renewed his death grip. He half-expected to hear a squeal of bending metal from the chair's arms. A faint whiff of flop-sweat assaulted his nostrils and he realized he was again losing the battle with panic.

"Fifteen seconds," the P.A. intoned.

Ivan closed his eyes and tried deep-breathing exercises again. Too late to back out now. Even if he unbuckled and ran screaming for the exit, the shuttle would launch on schedule, with him plastered to the rear bulkhead. Three months of training and simulations, which had felt like an adventure of its own, now seemed nothing more than wishful thinking . He was about to be shot into the air in a tin can, with no say in his fate, not even a view of space for the next fifteen minutes.

"Relax, noob," said Davies. "We haven't lost a crew member in weeks." The veteran miner grinned at Ivan, but the expression didn't reach his eyes. He looked more like a cat anticipating a meal than someone offering reassurance.

Ivan opened his mouth to retort, but at that moment, the Sling kicked in. His body was pressed into his seat as the shuttle accelerated down the track. It would continue for the entire five-kilometer stretch of the launch tunnel, air resistance reduced by massive pumps that pulled the air from in front of the shuttle and pumped it back in behind.

The occasional moan floating up the aisle showed that he wasn't the only person having trouble. He tried to extract a small kernel of solace from that shared misery.

Thankfully, this part of the takeoff was smooth—nothing like the old space launches, perched on top of an explosive cylinder of fuel, being rattled so hard you felt your teeth would fall out through your ears. Ivan concentrated on his breathing, and on not whimpering in fear. He hadn't been tagged with a nickname yet, and he sure as hell didn't want to provide the crew with that kind of material to work with. Certainly not before he'd even left atmosphere.

The shuttle hit the upcurving part of the Sling, and the acceleration vector changed, now pushing him down in his seat as well as back. The pressure would only last seconds—possibly the longest seconds of his life.

As the shuttle left the Sling behind, boosters kicked in. Specially tuned microwave emitters heated and rarified the air in front of the shuttle, reducing air resistance as the vessel clawed its way into the sky.

The bump and rattle gradually faded as the shuttle climbed through the atmosphere. After five minutes, the boosters shut down, leaving them in free fall. The sudden silence made Ivan wonder for a moment if his hearing had been damaged. Fortunately, Davies provided his own brand of reassurance.

"Hey, looks like the noob survived. Didn't even pee himself, I don't think."

Ivan turned his head to glare at Davies and provide suitable return fire.

Big mistake.

The hammering he'd just taken during launch, combined with the free fall conditions, were already playing hell with his beleaguered stomach. Add the insult to his inner ear from an abrupt turn of the head, and with an *oop* Ivan grabbed for the barf bag in the pocket in front of him. The retching seemed to go on forever.

One of the unfortunate aspects of the human condition was that the acrid odor of vomit tended to induce vomiting. Several more *oops* sounded through the cabin. There would probably be some eventual abuse for that, as well.

Finally recovered, his face dripping in sweat, he rolled up the bag and placed it in the receptacle. Turning to Seth Robinson, seated on his right in the middle seat, Ivan said, "Well, great. I guess I've just earned a nickname."

"Naw," replied Robinson. "If we gave out a nickname for puking, most of us would be called *Barfie.* You've got two days to get that under control, noob. If you're still tossing it up come departure day, you'll be scrubbed. You'll get your money back for your share purchase, less the standard penalty. And we'll be doing a six-month tour short a body. Clear?"

Ivan nodded, silent. The penalty would wipe out what small equity in his share he'd managed to build. If he washed out, he'd be left with nothing.

He glanced at Robinson. Freckled and redheaded, thin and gangly, a good fifteen centimeters taller than Ivan, Robinson could pass for a teenager in the right light. It was hard to believe that the man was old enough to hold a Spacer certificate. If Robinson could do it, Ivan could damn well do it.

"Docking maneuvers start in thirty seconds," the P.A. announced.

Ivan looked up—carefully, this time—and cursed the lack of windows. He was *in space.* Granted, asteroid mining wasn't the most glamorous way to get there, but most avenues to space involved military commissions, significant wealth, or some specialty in high demand at the space stations or colonies. The child of climate-change refugees who lost everything when the ocean took their home, Ivan's options were strictly limited.

He thought of his family, of the dead-end, soul-crushing job that was the best he could get despite finishing at the top of his Computer Science graduating class. The bug-infested, too-small apartment that was all he and Judy could manage on two salaries. This was their only way out. He would get this done. The pay was better to begin with, and if they hit any kind of significant mineral lode—

The shuttle jerked as maneuvering thrusters kicked in. The passengers endured several minutes of random accelerations—fortunately for Ivan's stomach, all low-thrust.

"This pilot sucks," muttered one of the crew. Ivan craned his neck to look over the seat backs and identified the speaker as Raul Alfaro. Dark-haired and olive-skinned, Alfaro spoke with a faint Spanish accent.

"Belay that, Alfaro," barked another. "You're a guest here."

The rebuke came from Albert Micoroski, the pilot of the *Mad Astra,* sitting across the aisle from Alfaro. Pilots stuck together, and one wouldn't tolerate bad-mouthing another's flying. The *Astra's* copilot, Lita Generus, added her glare for emphasis.

Before Alfaro could respond, a *clunk* resounded through the walls as the shuttle docked. Again, Ivan wished for windows. He might as well be on Earth in yet another simulator, for all the actual adventure he was getting.

They had just docked at Olympus Station, the hub for space travel anywhere in the system. The enormous, double habitation rings, a full kilometer in diameter, formed the most well-known and iconic image in the civilized world. The view during the approach must have been spectacular.

"There are lots of windows on the station, noob," Robinson said, seeming to read his mind. "You can spend the next two days watching shuttles and ships come and go. As long as you pass the preflight, your time is your own, once we've met with the captain for the standard benediction. Star Lounge, half an hour. You know where that is?"

Ivan responded with a small shake of his head.

"Noobs…" Robinson rolled his eyes. "Just stick with me when we get into the station. You *can* handle free fall, I hope?"

* * *

Astronomical. The word didn't apply to just stars and planets. Ivan scanned the drink menu and felt his eyebrows climb his forehead. He'd had steaks that cost less. *Real* steaks.

Davies, sitting across from him, laughed. "Yeah, noob, just one of many things you have to get used to. But not to worry. The locally produced stuff is much cheaper."

"And where would I find that?" Ivan asked, waving the menu.

"Well, not here. The working stiff bars don't come with the fancy view…" Davies waved a hand at the large window a few tables over. The stars, visible in the low lighting, would take just over a minute to complete a rotation. "…or the nice comfy gravity." He smiled at Ivan, the expression still lacking any trace of friendliness. "You might want to practice a little more with low-gee before you visit up-axis, noob."

The waiter returned with the drinks—a tequila shot for each crew member. He set the glasses down, but no one reached for theirs. There was likely a tradition of some sort in play. Ivan watched Robinson, seated beside him, for cues.

Captain Andrew Jennings, at one end of the long table, stood up. Tall, grey-haired, and spare of build, he was every inch the lifetime spacer. A buzz cut and thick mustache gave him the aura of a movie cowboy, yet somehow he still managed to make the standard utility coveralls look like a uniform.

"Gentlemen and ladies." He paused to scan the table, pointedly looking at each person, perhaps memorizing their faces. "We have lucked out and managed to get a relatively unexplored section of the belt in this tour's Stakes Lottery. Things haven't gone particularly shiny the last couple of trips, and we've had to say goodbye to some of our crew. I'd like to welcome our newest members, Ivan Pritchard and Arcadius Geiger." The captain gestured toward Ivan and the other new member. "Arcadius is a veteran spacer, having crewed with the *Forward Motion* and the *Serene Starlight* on several occasions."

Geiger nodded to the table in general, and muttered something noncommittal in a slight German accent.

Gesturing toward Ivan, the captain continued, "Ivan is a first-timer, but is also a top-rated computer specialist, so we're looking forward to perhaps a little less drama with setting up the mining robot A.I.s this time around."

Several of the crew whooped and clapped their hands. Ivan grinned and bobbed his head, embarrassed by the sudden attention.

"As you know, it takes only one good strike to set you up for life. It's why we do this. Well, that and the luxurious lifestyle." The captain flashed a tight smile to general laughter.

He raised his glass, and everyone at the table stood, shooters in hand. "To the *Mad Astra* and her crew. And may this tour be our big score." The crew members raised their drinks and tossed them back in unison.

Hah-woof! Tequila shooter. Not used to those. Ivan's eyes watered, and he put every ounce of will-power available into the task of not coughing as he sat down.

He turned to find Robinson watching him with an amused smile. "Not used to tequila, sprout?"

Ivan blew out a breath. "I'm more of a whiskey drinker."

"Captain buys the first drink," Davies said, leaning forward. "But after that, we're on our own, *sprout.*"

Ivan's eyes widened as he realized he'd just acquired a nickname. He turned to glare at Robinson.

Robinson shrugged and grinned. "Sorry."

The captain picked that moment to stand again and address the crew. "I know this isn't your venue of choice, people. I admit to a certain sympathy. The prices would get you an entire meal at other establishments. So, I will leave you to enjoy your remaining liberty. I'll see you all, I hope, on the *Mad Astra* in two days' time."

The crew stood, and with a final nod, the captain turned and left.

Robinson poked Ivan with an elbow. "Let's go get our gear and get settled in. We'll see about some entertainment later."

Ivan nodded to Davies, who favored him with a blank look, and followed Robinson out.

* * *

The transient accommodations on Olympus Station were clean, efficient—and tiny beyond belief. This style had been around in Japan since the 20th century, and it was ideal for overnights. Ivan eyed his bunk—literally a square tube running straight into the wall. Perhaps twice shoulders-width, it consisted of a thin mattress, some slide-open storage cupboards on the walls, and a pull-down locking hatch at the front for privacy and security. The compartments were stacked three levels deep, with a narrow ladder running between the stacks to access the upper bunks. Low-intensity lighting 24/7, combined with muted autumn colors, encouraged sleep and discouraged socializing. Shared bathroom facilities, at floor level, completed the offering.

It was clean, at least. The slightest whiff of disinfectant indicated that cleaning staff was on the ball. The restrooms looked well maintained, and the paint on the walls, if not exactly bright, was at least not peeling. No rust, of course. Corrosion on a space station could be fatal. No doubt inspection and maintenance would be draconian in its thoroughness.

The Burrows, the place was called. Ivan was pretty sure it was a bad play on the word "boroughs", but couldn't bring himself to care enough to ask. As a junior crew member, he found himself stuck on the top row. In the one-quarter-gee of level seventeen, it wasn't an onerous climb, but inconvenient if you needed to use the facilities in the middle of the night. Ivan sighed, draped his backpack over his shoulder, and climbed the narrow ladder. After easing himself in, he distributed his possessions into the appropriate cubbies, pulled down the door, and closed his eyes for a moment.

* * *

Ivan jerked awake, startled by the banging on his hatch.

"You alive, sprout? Do we have to order ourselves a replacement noob?"

Blinking the fog from his eyes, Ivan looked at his watch. He'd been asleep for more than two hours. He turned on his bunk and pushed the hatch up to see Davies, hanging from the side ladder by one hand, and still grinning. That grin was going to get old really fast.

"C'mon, sprout, we're going up to Callahan's. This is a good chance for you to look around while we protect your virginal butt."

"Should I be doing that, this early? You said yourself—"

"You have to start somewhere," Robinson yelled from the floor below.

Ivan bobbed his head in acknowledgement and began pulling

himself out. Davies moved down the ladder to get out of his way.

At the bottom, Ivan found Davies and Robinson; the other new guy, Arcadius Geiger; Cirila Heinrichs, the geologist; and Aspasia Nevin, the scooter pilot.

"This looks serious," he said, looking around.

"Only the drinking," Nevin answered, favoring him with a scowl that Ivan was beginning to realize was her default expression. Without waiting for consensus, she turned and headed for the exit from The Burrows. For someone so short, Aspasia covered a lot of ground in a very short time, and gave the impression that she was more inclined to go through people rather than around.

Geiger and Heinrichs followed, Cirila snickering at a muttered comment from Kady.

Robinson slapped him on the shoulder as they brought up the rear. "We're going to be on the *Astra* for six months, kid. Best to satisfy your inner delinquent before departure."

The Burrows was close to one of the elevators that ran through the Wheel from the rim to the hub. They entered, and Ivan scanned the panel. Thirty levels made up the Wheel, each button labeled with both a floor number and the gravity value at that level. Davies pressed button twenty-seven, the doors closed, and the elevator began to rise.

Ivan staggered a little as the entire car seemed to shift. Robinson put out a steadying hand and chuckled. "The car swivels to keep *down* toward the floor, despite Coriolis forces. You'll get used to it."

* * *

Callahan's didn't fit the stereotype. All the Vid shows suggested that a spacer bar would be dark, smoky, filled with shady characters doing shady deals in the corners. The reality was clean, well lit, with lots of tables, and several Vids showing various sports and news channels. Ordinary people sat around, drinking and talking. It could be any bar on Earth, except for the tenth-gee gravity and the preponderance of mining crew coveralls as a fashion statement. That, and the visible curvature of the floor.

Ivan looked around. "No windows?"

"Windows cost money, noob. The engineering, design, and materials costs of putting a potential weak point into the hull jack up the price of the real estate. This is the low-rent area." Davies motioned to an empty table. "And the choices for alcohol are limited, since everything is synthesized spaceside. Not a whole lot of blue agave being grown up here."

They sat, Ivan and Seth on one side, Cirila and Kady opposite, with Tenn and Aspasia each getting a side to themselves. The waiter approached and Seth ordered the first round. "Synthol shots, and a juice for the sprout." Everyone grinned at Ivan. The waiter left without comment.

"Why do I feel like I'm being set up for something?" Ivan looked around the table.

"No real secret, Ivan," Kady said. "Your first drink of liquid in low gee can be, erm, entertaining."

The drinks arrived, with a yellowish juice for Ivan. "What is it? Just generic juice?"

The waiter returned a tight smile. "It's whatever's currently being made, and quite often it's a blend. Today, it's orange juice."

Ivan raised his eyebrows in an expression of resignation, and raised his glass. "To me squirting this out my nose!" He knocked back the glass of juice to the surprised chuckles of his crewmates.

There were several moments of expectant silence before Ivan explained, "We did all kinds of low-gee simulations at the training academy. I've already done all my squirting."

Groans of disappointment sounded around the table, and Seth motioned to the waiter for a proper drink for Ivan.

The drink, when it arrived, smelled more like something you'd use to disinfect a wound. Ivan could feel the look of disbelief written on his face, as his nostrils attempted to pucker. The poorly suppressed snickers from his crewmates confirmed his impression.

"That, noob, is synthol." Davies grinned his usual smug grin. "They tend to make it a little over proof. Bottoms up."

"If I drink this, can I get something nonlethal next?"

Seth laughed. "The whiskey-like substance actually isn't half bad. Let's get this over with, okay?"

Ivan raised his glass and knocked it back. It took everything he had to avoid spitting it all over his table mates. He found himself remembering the tequila shot with fondness.

Some infinite time later, he had forced the liquid down his throat and the various abused internal organs had stopped protesting. He scrubbed his face with his hands and said, "Hmm, not melted off. I don't suppose I could get some juice?"

Seth turned to Davies. "I don't think you're going to take him down without getting out-and-out abusive. What say we move on to the serious business of drinking?"

Davies shrugged at Seth, gave Ivan something that he supposed he could interpret as a smile, and signaled for the waiter.

"So," Aspasia said. "You're a computer guy. That's good."

"Because I can help set up the robots more quickly?" Ivan cocked his head.

"No, because Lorenza will kill *you* instead of *us*."

"Y'know," Ivan replied. "I'm beginning to think I've signed up with the IMM Psychos-R-Us. Is everyone in this crew a homicidal maniac?"

Aspasia guffawed. "Just Lorenza. Tenn, over there, isn't a psycho. Just a jerk."

"My adoring fans," Davies winked at her.

Heinrichs laughed, and Ivan saw Geiger twitch. He sympathized—Cirila's laugh had a certain nails-on-chalkboard quality, and Kady was sitting right beside her. Hopefully she wasn't the jolly type.

There was a moment of silence, then Seth sighed and spread his hands in a pleading motion. "We're all a bit on edge, Ivan. I'm guessing you bought into the *Mad Astra* because a share was cheaper than any of the other mining ships advertising for crew, right? Did you wonder why?"

Ivan shook his head. "My wife is an actuary, Seth. I know the *Astra* is having financial difficulties. The thing is, we didn't have a choice. We'd have had to wait at least another cycle to be able to afford a full-price share. We're taking a chance, but Judy likes the odds. Honestly, she says the *Astra*'s share is discounted more than the numbers would support."

Eyebrows went up, and a few of the crew looked at each other.

Davies gave Ivan an appraising look. "Well, okay then." Tenn bought the next round, synthetic whiskey this time, and raised his shot glass. "To Ivan's wife. Here's hoping she's right."

Ivan grinned at the unexpected tribute. He downed the shot and smacked the glass to the table.

Not bad. Not terrible, anyway. You could get used to it.

Things got a little blurry after that.

* * *

The promenade that ran around the first level of the public wheel was always busy, with pedestrian traffic flowing in both directions. Automated shuttles ran in a roadway below the promenade level, and could be boarded at periodic traxi stations.

The promenade levels of the two habitation wheels were the crown jewels of Olympus Station, and a popular tourist destination. Expensive restaurants, exclusive shops, and art galleries all tastefully announced themselves, trying to entice the wealthy tourists to come in and spend their money. Two hotels, both five-star, each serviced one of the wheels.

In the open areas between businesses, the architects had placed public seating areas. Carefully designed to give an illusion of privacy, they allowed the weary traveler to take a break while admiring the view through the enormous transparent-aluminum viewports. Decorative ferns and less identifiable plants separated the seating into small, intimate groupings.

There was no problem with budgets for windows on this level. And, more important, these open areas didn't require you to buy something in order to sit.

Ivan stared out, enraptured, as various ships ponderously floated into and out of docking bays up on the hub. He found himself amazed at the variety of vessels, from ancient clunkers that couldn't possibly be space worthy to the newest, shiniest Benz-Gilmore high-end models.

No military craft, though. The Navy ships all docked at the other end of Olympus Station's double-wheeled hub. He would have loved to see some of those, but he would need a security clearance to get through the hub access point.

Other people came and went. They seemed to belong to three general groups. The passengers and tourists were easy to spot—with few exceptions, their clothing and accessories all screamed *money.* Next were the station staff. Their clothing, while tasteful and of good quality, was deliberately designed to be a step down. *I'm an employee,* it said, *but of good class.*

Then, there was Ivan's group: ship's crew, characterized by either the blue travel coveralls, or occasional shipboard tee shirts and shorts. He hadn't quite figured out where the Navy brass and ship's officers fit into this hierarchy.

"Hey, sprout. What's doing?"

Ivan turned and looked up to see Seth Robinson approaching. Despite having inadvertently given Ivan his now thoroughly glued-on nickname, Seth seemed to be a decent sort, engaging in only the minimum amount of hazing required to get by.

Ivan waved a hand at the window. "Enjoying the view."

Seth nodded as he sat, moving carefully.

"Head hurt?"

Seth smiled but ignored the question. "I make sure to come here every time I pass through the station. For most of the tour, space just looks like metal walls painted in pastel colors. If you ignore the gravity and the curved deck, you could be on Earth. This," Seth waved at the window, "is the stuff that makes it real."

They watched in silence for a few minutes. Ivan was okay with the quiet. If cornered, he would admit that his head hurt as well. He wanted to ask how much they'd drunk the night before, but couldn't get up the nerve.

A gasp from some onlookers made Ivan sit up straight. As people pointed, Seth commented, "SSE frigate. Wow, did not expect to see one of those here."

Ivan nodded slowly, all his attention focused on taking in every detail. The Sino-Soviet Empire military vessel displayed the typical SSE design philosophy—heavy armor, massive weapon emplacements, and no concession to esthetics. The dull gray finish only showed a clear profile in direct sunlight.

Passersby were stopping and gathering at the view windows as the behemoth slowly moved past, heading for a docking beacon. Ivan could hear muttered questions and complaints. Relations between the Sino-Soviet Empire and the United Earth Nations government were frosty at best, and adversarial the rest of the time. While it was unlikely any SSE personnel would actually be at liberty in Olympus Station, even the possibility created a significant level of public tension.

Within a minute, the ship had drifted out of sight and the crowd began to disperse, to occasional loud commentary about unwelcome visitors. Seth and Ivan settled back in their seats, both enjoying the changing view as ships continued to move in and out. After a few minutes, Seth broke the silence. "So what's your story?"

"Eh?"

"Why asteroid mining? Lost at love? Adventure? Money? Joining the Foreign Legion? Fleeing the law?"

Ivan looked at Seth, frowning. "What? You'd get stopped at Customs."

“I was kidding about the last one.”

“Ah.” Ivan was silent for a moment. “Money. You know what it’s like.”

Seth nodded. “Yeah, good old reality. More people, fewer jobs, fewer resources, less and less room.”

“What about you?”

“The same, mostly. It’s the most common reason for being up here. Of course, if you like it and can make an adventure out of the whole thing, that’s a bonus. I think I fit in that category.”

Ivan realized that he and Seth were going through the too-casual probing for common attitudes and opinions, the cautious circling of two people who might end up being friends. Well, a friend was never a bad thing to have.

“I have a family to support, so the adventure angle isn’t really on my radar.”

“That’s too bad.”

“How do you mean?” Ivan turned to Seth, frowning.

“The family. I don’t have one. My pay goes straight into my bank account. A little spending between tours or on Olympus Station doesn’t make much of a dent, and you can’t do much with your money on board. Unless you play poker.”

“You’re inviting me to a poker game? I guess you guys are all terrible, but you’re willing to learn from me?” Ivan tried to keep the sarcasm from dripping too heavily.

“Me? Hell no, I’m warning you off. Do not get involved in Tenn Davies’s poker games. Those guys are sharks. The regulars are about evenly matched, so the money really just sloshes back and forth most of the time. But a fresh piece of chum like you? They’ll strip you to the bone. And they won’t feel the slightest bit bad about it, either.”

Ivan grinned. “Noted. And thanks. Do you play?”

“I did, once. Lost half my pay from my first tour. Since then, I’ve made it my mission to steer people clear.”

“Mmm.” Ivan looked around as a growl escaped his midsection. “Is there food around here that won’t cost me a month’s wages?”

“There’s a sandwich place spinward a half-segment. They use veat, but their stuff’s not terrible. I could eat, too.”

Well, vat-grown meat was becoming common on Earth. Given the cost of boosting the real stuff up, it would be even more popular on the station. Ivan took one last look at the giant ships, sighed, and followed Seth.

3. Financial Concerns

Captain Jennings looked up from the tablet in his hand. Lita Generus sat at her station, working through pre-departure diagnostics and carefully not looking his way. Her dark skin made her profile indistinct in the low lighting of the bridge. The other stations, all of which collectively formed a semicircle with the Captain's Chair as the focus, sat empty, awaiting the arrival of the rest of the bridge crew.

Jennings took the opportunity to engage in a moment of weakness, rubbing his forehead. He looked up and admired the low glow of the overhead status monitors, readouts showing a healthy, well-prepared ship, ready to go out to chase dreams. Since the ship was at station-keeping with the habitation ring spun up, they were in the hab-ring bridge. The half gee gravity, normally an experience verging on luxury, wasn't enough today to break his negative mood. He waggled the tablet in his hand. It wasn't going to get any better if he just kept staring at it. "These are final figures, Ms. Generus?"

Generus turned to him and nodded. Like most spacers, she kept her hair in a short helmet-cut. Her tight curls were beginning to show gray around the temples, which seemed incongruous next to her unlined, youthful face. "Yes, sir. All numbers confirmed. The last trip was just one insult too many to the budget. Failing some kind of score, this tour will probably be our last."

Jennings sat back and stared up at the bulkhead between the monitors and bridge stations. "By which you mean, I assume, that our creditors will call in our debts?"

"Almost certain, sir. The debenture agreement is pretty clear about when the foreclosure clauses come into effect."

"How far ahead do we have to come out in order to avoid that?"

"Barely more than break-even, really. We're just below the clause triggers right now."

"And, statistically, profitable tours should happen about one in three. We've certainly had two very bad ones. We're due."

"You know it doesn't work that way, sir."

Jennings met her eyes with a small smile. "No, but leave me my illusions for the moment, okay?"

None of this was really a surprise. Decades of experience crewing and then commanding a mining ship had given Jennings a good feel for net returns from a tour. He'd known before they even reached Earth that the last one was a bust. But the audited figures removed any possibility of a reprieve.

He truly enjoyed captaining a space vessel. But the financial and administrative sides of the job could be soul-sucking. For twenty-five years, he'd been commanding his own ship—his first command had used the old ion engines—but this was the closest he'd come in all that time to losing it all.

It was an uncertain living, of course. A moderately good strike could keep you going for multiple tours. About a third of the tours earned enough to allow you to break even or come out ahead. It took a string of bad luck, running in the red for several tours in a row, to break you. You'd burn through your reserves, then bet everything you had left on that last throw of the dice...

And always, that dream of the big one. The strike that would take the worries away forever.

Jennings imagined the dice cupped in one of his hands. He stared into infinity for several seconds. He was too old to start over. If they took the *Astra*, he'd be done.

There had to be options. There were always options.

"When is bridge staff getting here, Ms. Generus?"

"They start coming in on the next ferry, sir. They should all be on board by twelve hundred. Dr. Kemp has a couple of physicals to complete, so he'll be last in."

Jennings nodded. "Leave a message with each, please. Status meeting at fifteen hundred. They'll have time to stow their gear and get cleaned up. I think we have to deal with the financial situation as a priority. Tell them to bring their best ideas."

4. Departure

And, again, no windows. Ivan was beginning to despair of ever getting a view of the action. Whoever was in charge of designing spaceships didn't seem to get it.

The small vessel was filled to capacity with the *Mad Astra*'s crew. The bridge staff were already on board the *Astra*, doing whatever start-up preparations real astronauts did.

Where the space shuttle had been a polished, finished vessel designed with tasteful décor, the ferries that operated around Olympus Station had more of a welded-together go-kart feel. Seats were reminiscent of beach chairs, and bare metal dominated.

Docking fees being what they were, the captain of the *Mad Astra* had opted for a parking beacon at a prescribed distance from Olympus Station. The money saved more than made up for the cost of the ferry hired to transport personnel.

Seth replied to Ivan's muttered complaint. "You'll get a better view on the *Astra*. Shuttles and ferries are built as utilitarian as possible. On long-haul ships, we have to be a lot more aware of human psychological needs."

"Say, you seem to know a lot about it. Are you the ship's shrink or something?"

Seth laughed. "Sure, yeah, that's me. That's why I get paid the big bucks." He settled more comfortably into his seat. "We have a lot of spare time on the ship. I always bring up a few *pets* of reading and other media. I can lend you some, if you run out of porn."

Ivan chuckled, then thought of the sticks in his luggage, stuffed to the last petabyte with correspondence courses and reference materials in Computer Science, Astronomy and Physics. He was relieved to know he wouldn't be odd man out. "Thanks. I did bring some educational stuff. I'm taking courses, and I'm looking forward to some chunks of free time."

Tennison Davies stuck his head over the back of his chair. "Just don't forget you're on Hydroponics duty on the way out, sprout. Me and the boys, we like our grub."

"Thanks, Tex, I'll be sure to corral something for you."

Seth laughed out loud, and several of Tennison's friends snickered. Tennison turned red and looked for a moment as if he would take umbrage. Then he grinned at Ivan. "Touché, sprout. You just tend those plants real good, y'hear?"

Seth nudged Ivan with an elbow. "Hey, why don't you ask Tenn who is the only crew member that has managed to ruin prepackaged meals?" There were more laughs, and Seth continued, "Who knows what would happen if we let him near the hydroponics?"

Tennison made a show of silently laughing at Seth, before sitting down.

"Maneuvering, fifteen seconds."

At the announcement, everyone settled back into their acceleration chairs and made sure they were buckled in properly. They endured the usual several minutes of thrusts and twitches, then a final *clunk.*

The P.A. crackled to life. "Docking complete. On behalf of Captain Crash and the surviving crew, thank you for flying Mad Dog Airways. Any chickens on board remain the property of the airline. Don't trip over the drunk guy on your way out. Have a good flight."

Ivan and Seth laughed, and Seth said, "Yeah, flying ferries gets a little boring, I guess."

* * *

Ivan watched the monitor as Olympus Station slowly receded. The *Mad Astra* accelerated at only one-tenth gee, but it could keep up the thrust for hours. During acceleration, the crew would have gravity along the ship's axis, and would stick to the on-axis accommodations. According to the captain's announcement, they would accelerate for four hours, then would shut down the engines and spin up the ship's hab ring, coasting most of the way to their destination. The trip would take about three weeks.

Meanwhile, the crew was congregated in the on-axis common room. Aligned with the ship's acceleration vector, the room allowed them to operate in artificial gravity, albeit the much-lower tenth-gee. It featured the same amenities as the hab-ring common room—coffee and other drink dispensers, auto-washer, food packs and heating unit, and bench tables to sit at. As with all rooms in the ship, the ceiling was painted in a lighter color than the carpet on the floor, to create a psychological impression of up and down.

Dante Aiello, the first mate, walked in. His stride, in the negligible gravity, resembled the gait from a dream sequence where one step covers twenty feet. Aiello, a doughy-faced middle-aged man, always seemed to wear a slightly surprised expression, as if the normal workings of the universe mystified him.

He looked around, his lips moving in a not-quite-silent count. Satisfied that everyone was present, he began poking at his tablet.

"Okay, assignments. Pritchard, Geiger, Todd, you're on cargo inspection. Haul ass, we've got limited time before spin-up."

Ivan and the two others jumped up—Ivan jumped too hard and had to do a push-down off the ceiling, to everyone's amusement—and headed for the cargo bay. As they left the room, Ivan could hear Aiello continuing to hand out jobs.

* * *

Several days later, the pace of work hadn't slackened. Today, Ivan had enjoyed a slightly more technical set of tasks, as the crew unshipped the mining robots and put them through diagnostics and setup.

Today's shift had been especially back-breaking for those not used to detail work. Unpacking and test-assembling the mining robots was a finicky, picky duty that required you to hold a cramped position while making minute adjustments using toy-sized tools. Good work for elves or pixies.

A backward lean made Seth grunt as a vertebra audibly popped. Working his shoulders again he uttered a satisfied sigh as he verified that he'd successfully self-chiropracted.

Ivan shuddered theatrically. "Jeez, Seth, that makes me cringe."

"Sorry, I've got a thing in my back that acts up. Lorenza and her stupid mining robots..."

"Quit'cher bellyaching," Tenn interjected. "I've done tours where some of the robots weren't working, and we had to do things manually. A little screwdriver work is nothing."

Davies seemed to be sparing Ivan, at least for today. Maybe it was because of Ivan's work on the robots. A normally two-to three-day job had been reduced to barely four hours. By the end of the process, Lorenza had almost completely stopped complaining about the shortcomings of 'the help'. Ivan grinned. It definitely felt good to be the hero.

"I am going to sleep like a babe tonight," he said as they dried off from their showers and dressed.

"You aren't all tweaked about the size of the accommodations?"

Ivan looked askance at Davies. "Is that a thing? Because after The Burrows, this is luxury."

Tenn laughed. "Yeah, well, we've had a few claustrophobia cases. The problem is, you wake up in the middle of the night, in the dark, in low gravity, with walls close around you, and you're liable to go into a funk before your brain has caught up. Then you scream in panic, wake the rest of us, and we have to come over and show our appreciation." He looked at Ivan significantly. "Do I make myself clear?"

"Don't yell at night. Got it." Ivan grinned back at the much larger man.

A couple of the other crew overheard and laughed. Davies gave him an arch look, but no follow-up. Definitely taking it easy, today.

"Crew to the Common Room. Meeting at 13:20." Everyone looked up at the P.A. announcement.

"That's, uh, unusual. Well, let's hop to it." Seth tossed his towel in the laundry basket, followed by the other crew. The laundry mech grabbed the towels as they landed, glaring at each crew member in apparent reproach. Aspasia tossed her towel directly at the mech and grinned at the silent rebuke.

They all pulled on the standard ship garb—tee shirt, shorts, and slippers—and headed downwheel to the Common Room. The hab ring on the *Mad Astra* was considerably smaller than a space station wheel, barely a hundred meters diameter at the rim. This made the curve of the floor, even on the outermost level, far more obvious and Coriolis force more of an issue. And heading downwheel increased their weight significantly as their pace added to their rotational velocity. Several of the crew started to sound out of breath as they hustled along.

Seth looked back. "Say, some of you guys need to spend more

time on the treadmills, I think."

"Eat me," Tenn snarled.

Seth laughed as they arrived at the Common Room. They shuffled in, grabbed coffees from the ever-primed coffee dispenser, and sat down.

Precisely on time, the captain walked in. He scanned the room and nodded. "I want to talk strategy. As captain, of course, I can make unilateral decisions, but I'd prefer to have everyone involved."

He looked around for a moment, inviting questions or comments. No one made a sound.

"The last couple of tours have not been good to us, and we've not achieved break-even. If we fall short this time I'm afraid it will be the last trip for the *Mad Astra,* at least under my command. All we need is a little more than break-even. I am therefore asking you to approve a potential tour extension of one to three months. I know it's a hard thing—you'll effectively be working for free for the extra time. However, if we return empty-handed and the creditors foreclose, you will get back at most a fraction of your share purchase. I will leave you to discuss and ponder, and we will have a vote in a week. Thank you for your time."

The captain looked around again, nodded to the crew in general, and walked out. A buzz of conversation immediately rose in the room.

Ivan hung his head, balled his fists, and fought back tears.

"Hey, Ivan, what gives?" Seth asked.

Ivan rubbed his eyes with the palms of his hands before answering. "It means I'm effectively making less per month than I was in my previous job. This was supposed to be a step *up*, not down. And there's still the chance of losing the share price in the end."

"Yeah, trying to provide for a family puts a whole other level of difficulty into the equation. Look, kid, I already mentioned my money just goes into the bank. I can give you a loan against either your share, if you sell out, or future profits if we hit it. No interest, no obligations otherwise."

Ivan felt himself tearing up again, but got it under control. "Thanks, Seth. I appreciate it. And I don't have the luxury of being too proud to accept."

He noticed out of the corner of his eye that Tenn had overheard at least part of the exchange. The normally acerbic crewman didn't comment, though; he met Ivan's gaze for a moment, then looked away.

Ivan frowned. It seemed out of character for Tenn to have passed on an easy setup like that. Perhaps there was more there than just a loud-mouth.

* * *

Ivan kicked himself expertly up the axial passageway. It was a matter of pride that he could now go from Engineering all the way to the hab ring entry without touching the sides. He glided slowly past the various exits—shortcuts to different zero-gee areas of the ship.

The *Mad Astra* was generally egg-shaped, a hundred and fifty meters long, with the fusion nacelles clustered around the narrow end, and the hab ring forming a five-meter-wide cross section at the widest part of the oval. While spun up, the ring could only be accessed from the corridor that ran down the center of the ship from Engineering to the on-axis Bridge. Though inconvenient from a purely engineering point of view, the artificial gravity that the hab ring provided was essential to human health on long voyages.

Ivan arrived at the hab ring hatch just as he came within reach of the wall. Another perfect trajectory. Grabbing a handhold, he pulled himself to a smooth stop. He exited through the hatch, feet first, to the walkway encircling the hub, and pulled himself around to the nearest spoke ladder.

A quick slide down, and he was in the Common Room. Seth waved from a table where he, Tenn, and Dr. Kemp were sitting.

Ivan no longer felt any surprise at the doctor's presence. Though nominally an officer, Charles Kemp spent a considerable amount of time mingling with the crew. He claimed the coffee was better.

"We'll begin decelerating in two hours, sprout. Pretty soon, you won't be a virgin."

Ivan grinned at Tenn as he headed for the coffee machine. "Assuming we find something worth poking with a stick, of course."

Dr. Kemp gave Ivan the stink-eye. "There's attitude for you. Anyway, Lita told me they've already tagged several good targets for investigation, within EVA distance of our projected parking location. We've got three weeks of prospecting lined up for our first stop."

Everyone looked up as the P.A. crackled. "Hab ring spin-down in ten. Please vacate the hab ring."

Ivan's sigh was echoed by several others. The half-gee in the hab ring was a luxury that would be missed, until they arrived at a location where it was worthwhile spinning back up. He looked down at the still-empty coffee cup he was holding, then handed it to the dishwasher. The mech snatched the cup, gave it a quick wipe and returned it to the rack, then glared at Ivan until he retreated.

* * *

Spin-down took a half hour, and for the crew it consisted of nothing more than listening to the *Mad Astra* make odd groaning sounds. To Ivan's ear, it sounded like the ship was being slowly torn apart. However, none of the other crew were reacting, so he did his best to look relaxed and unconcerned as well.

Shortly after the noises died away, the P.A. announced, "Spin-down complete. Prepare for turnover."

Shuffling sounds accompanied a general checking of buckles and seating positions. Seth looked over at Ivan and smirked. "Here's hoping your stomach is thoroughly acclimated. You might want to hold onto a barf bag just for kicks."

Seth was right. This was the last test for a noob. The *Astra* would have to reverse her orientation in order to use the engines to decelerate. The maneuver wasn't especially dangerous or difficult with the hab ring spun down, but required the crew to be strapped in for the duration. During the maneuver, the slow rotation of the entire ship in an unaccustomed direction generally left people with a slight, undefined queasiness. And the protracted duration of the event sometimes produced a surprise reaction in stomachs that had no experience with it.

Ivan compared the symptoms to a low-grade sea-sickness, but managed to avoid any need for the barf bag.

"Deceleration begins, fifteen seconds."

This announcement brought sighs and smiles from the crew. They would have one-tenth gee during deceleration, then would spin up the hab ring once they arrived at their target location.

The engines fired up, decelerating the ship to slip into an orbit consistent with the asteroid belt objects in the area. In four hours, the *Mad Astra* matched the average orbital velocity for objects at this distance from the sun.

The hab ring would be spun up next, but there were also jobs to do. And no reason to sit around waiting. The crew gathered in the on-axis lounge, awaiting orders from the bridge. With no thrust, they were in zero-gee, but it still beat being strapped into an acceleration couch for hours.

Ivan settled himself onto a bench and locked his legs underneath to anchor himself. Several crewmates joined him at his table, but no one attempted conversation. Everyone just wanted this part to be over as soon as possible.

In short order, the intercom blared forth Dante's voice. "Crew, prepare for spin-up, ten minutes. Pritchard, Robinson. Beacon deployment. Hop to it."

The two men straightened up, taking care to not go floating off, and launched themselves toward the exit. Seth whooped as they set off. "They wouldn't deploy the beacon unless there's something in the area worth looking into."

"So they found something?" Ivan's heart beat faster at the thought.

"Well, they found *something*, as opposed to empty space. Or gravel. The beacon indicates a valid working stake, and warns off any other ships. But if it's all carbonaceous chondrite, it's not worth diddly. Next step will be a deep radar survey."

Ivan remembered most of this from his training, although at his level, they didn't go into a lot of technical detail. The courses concentrated more on what the bridge crew would want you to do, and how to do it, and less on why or how it worked.

They arrived at the cargo hold and grabbed pressure suits. A small voltage caused the fabric to expand, allowing them to easily don the suits. They dressed, checked each other's fit, then turned off the trickle charge. The material of the suit immediately contracted, providing the required pressure to counteract the vacuum of space, without the associated risk of an air leak. The suit material was also very slightly porous, so that sweat would evaporate into space rather than pooling in the suit.

Gloves, boots, backpack and helmet all snapped onto no-fail connectors. It was supposed to be impossible to get it wrong, or have a bad seal. No one, of course, wanted to test that assumption, so all EVAs involved a buddy-check.

Ivan and Seth inspected each other's setup once more to ensure proper fit and function. Then they moved through the airlock into the zero-pressure section of the hold. Ivan thought he felt his skin press more tightly against the suit fabric.

"Over here," Seth said over the radio, and motioned to one end.

Ivan followed him, paying extreme attention to his jet-pack controls. The technology had improved immensely since the early days of space flight, and control was now far more intuitive, but you still didn't want to make a mistake in a small space with hard metal boundaries.

Seth came to a floating stop beside an object that looked something like an old-fashioned marine buoy, about six feet in diameter and twenty feet long, generally cylindrical. The beacon would expand to twice that length once in space, as it deployed its antennae.

The beacon was secured to the bulkhead by a series of metal straps. Seth pointed to the far side of the device. "Releases are on that side, Ivan. Start from the top, free each one as I say to, okay?"

"Got it."

It took only moments to work down the restraints and free the beacon. Seth worked a panel and a scissors lift slowly extended the beacon from the wall.

"Open the hold door, Ivan."

Ivan went blank for a second, then looked around and spotted the control panel on the far wall. Feeling a moment of embarrassment for the brain fart, he pushed off and drifted over to the panel. He attached the carabiner of his leash to the nearby stanchion, scanned the directions printed beside the panel, then worked the controls.

Slowly, majestically, the hold doors swung open. Despite himself, Ivan was entranced by the view of open space with no planets or man-made objects anywhere to be seen.

Too entranced, as it turned out. A mocking comment from Seth brought him back to reality. "Whenever you're finished looking at the pretty lights, Ivan, I'd like to get this done."

"What?" Ivan spun around in place, coming up against the end of his rope. He rebounded at the sudden tension, and found himself being slowly wrapped up in his tether. Untangling himself, Ivan glared at Seth, his face hot.

Seth grinned back. "For the price of one dessert, I didn't see anything."

Ivan growled, then waved a hand. "Fine. I hope it's tapioca." He grabbed his line and hauled himself to the bulkhead, where he grabbed a handhold.

Seth spared a glance to make sure Ivan was secured and out of the way, then announced, "Launching beacon. Stay clear."

Seth worked the controls, and the beacon began moving out of the hold, propelled by attitude jets. Ivan alternately watched the beacon and a readout on the panel until the beacon had reached the desired distance from the ship.

Their job complete, Ivan closed the hold doors and they returned to shipboard. Seth pressed the intercom and reported completion.

"Thanks, guys," Dante responded. "Beacon is now doing self-check. We'll activate it as soon as we've finished our sweep. And we'll be in business. Hab ring is still in spin-up, so head back to on-axis Commons and park it."

The task had been a simple one, but interesting, and had kept Ivan's mind busy. Now, with only more waiting ahead of him, he resumed brooding about the financial situation. He knew that the crew would vote for the captain's plan. The alternative would be devastating for everyone. The odds, on a nine-month tour, would be in their favor. But with a sinking feeling in his stomach, Ivan acknowledged that *odds* only meant *maybe.*

Three months of missed pay, owing that money to Seth, on top of possibly losing most or all of his share, would be all but impossible to dig his way out of. Ivan blinked rapidly to keep his vision clear as he trudged back to the common room.

5. Being an Asteroid Miner

Three weeks later, the mood in the ship was considerably gloomier. Twelve asteroids of significant size had been scanned, none of which contained enough ore even to cover the costs of the trip. Just the same, they'd extracted what they could find, and sent it on a homeward trajectory with a beacon attached. Enough of those small strikes could still add up.

Meanwhile, the crew had voted for the extended tour, and it was beginning to look like the extra few months would be necessary.

Conversation in the crew area was desultory and heavy on short sentences. People sat by themselves and stared into their cups. Even the never-ending poker game had begun to suffer from poor attendance.

Ivan looked up as Seth entered the room, the man's gait too slow and plodding for half-gee gravity. Seth sat down across from him, and Ivan raised his cup in greeting.

"We have four rocks we can check from this spot before we have to move the ship again," Seth said. "You and I will be humping the deep radar rig around next shift. Tenn will be controller."

Ivan rolled his eyes in at the thought of working another shift with Davies. The man had decided for some reason that *sprout* wasn't an adequately demeaning nickname, and had spent the last several weeks trying to come up with a new one, many of his suggestions scatological in nature. Ivan assumed it had to be out of boredom and stress, because there was just no reason for that level of antagonism. Unless it was his refusal to join the interminable poker games.

He checked the time on the wall display. "Guess I'd better go get ready. Meet you at the lock." Ivan nodded to Seth and headed for his quarters.

Crew quarters were located in the hab ring. The ship schematics referred to them as staterooms, but no one who saw one would ever think to use that word. The rooms were about the size of a first-class double-bunk cabin from the age of passenger trains. Upper and lower single bunkbeds could be folded into the wall to make room for a bench seat. The fold-out table could accommodate two people, as long as they liked each other. Storage under the seat was adequate for the basic necessities appropriate to crew. A small sink and mirror inset into the wall completed the accommodations. Toilets and showers, however, were in a common area central to the crew quarters.

Ivan was pretty sure the captain and senior offices rated something larger, but didn't expect to ever get a chance to confirm his theory.

A quick clean-up with a sponge ensured that he wouldn't smell up a space suit too badly. Then into the standard shipboard outfit, and it was off to the main airlock.

* * *

Seth and Tenn stood waiting, both having already donned their suits. Ivan never failed to be impressed at how quickly the veterans could handle things that still made him feel like a thumb-fingered idiot.

He dressed as quickly as he could, consistent with safety, then submitted to inspection.

"All good," Tenn said. "You'll make spaceman, yet."

Ivan glanced at him, uncertain. For Tenn, that was so mild a jibe as to almost qualify as a compliment.

They piled into the airlock and Tenn activated the cycle. Ivan could feel the tension of the suit fabric as the air pressure dropped to zero and his flesh tried to expand. Like the jet packs, the suits were a significant improvement over the walking tombs used during the dawn of space travel. Intelligent environmental controls, electro-contractile materials, and electrostatic/magnetic shielding made the modern spacewalk, if not actually safe, at least tolerably routine.

The deep radar pod drifted a hundred meters from the *Astra*, having been moved into position by the previous shift. The three jetted over to it and took up their stations.

"First target," Tenn announced when everyone was ready. He gave a set of vectors, and Seth and Ivan scrambled to line up the equipment. The asteroid, an unimpressive rock in a nondescript area of the belt, hadn't been tagged with a beacon, so was considered a virgin. After scanning it, they would fly over in a two-man scooter and attach a beacon—to broadcast either the rock's failure as a source of riches, or its status as a staked claim. A message to the central registry would obviate any temptation by other mining ships to replace the beacon with one of their own. In the modern era, any group known to have attempted such tactics would be blacklisted so thoroughly that they'd never be able to use public toilets, let alone conduct business outside atmosphere again.

Once given the target, the A.I. was able to maintain a lock on the asteroid. A confirmation request flashed on Ivan's console and he entered an affirmative.

The deep radar pod emitted a series of pulses and listened for the echoes. By varying the frequency and pulse lengths, it built up a picture of the interior of the asteroid. The densities of different materials would indicate the probable composition, then sample drillings would confirm any flagged masses. The deep radar was nowhere near infallible, but it saved a lot of time by ruling out the total duds and indicating good candidates for sampling.

Ivan was tasked with ensuring that the pod didn't drift during the analysis. The possibility was remote, given the presence of the A.I., but if it did happen it would invalidate an entire day's run. Seth monitored the results for each scan, and ordered a follow-up if required. This latter job was as much art as science, and no one would trust it to an A.I.

* * *

The scanning run complete and their shift over, the three headed back to the *Astra*. Four hours in a space suit was about as much as a person could handle. Beyond that, many people started to experience increasing itchiness. No physiological reason for it had ever been found; it just seemed to be one of those things.

In the shower, Ivan cringed as Seth did his back-cracking thing again. Sarcasm didn't help, and anyway Seth didn't seem to be doing it just to bug people. Ivan flexed his arm a couple of times. His old elbow injury bothered him occasionally, but at least it didn't make noises when he moved.

Raul, Will, and Aspasia entered the showers, looking as if they'd just finished a marathon.

"Bad day?" Seth said to them.

"Core samples," Aspasia replied. "Aiello had us drilling Rock 4, just in case the deep radar scans were off."

"And?"

Raul shook his head, expression downcast. "If they were off, it was in the wrong direction. We found some ore, but I doubt it's going to prove out to anything worth filing a claim. We'll use the mining robots to extract the ore, and send it back home with a beacon attached. Unless we were to find something else in the area..."

Ivan pressed his lips together, but said nothing. He repeated his wife's statistics like a mantra. Too soon to give up; as many as three tours on average; too soon to give up...

* * *

A week later, they'd finished prospecting all the rocks in the area, and the news was in. Aiello didn't have a good poker face at the best of times, and announcements weren't the best of times.

He took a long, slow look around the common room. "Sorry, guys. We've checked them all, and there's no shine. We'll be moving to another spot as soon as astrogation has found a good clump of rocks worth visiting."

Aiello stood there for a moment longer, then shrugged and left.

Ivan balled his fists on the table and put his forehead down on them. Logically, they weren't even halfway into their tour. It was far too early to give way to despair. As usual, logic didn't help. And anyway, to do three tours, they'd have to at least find enough to pay for this tour.

His dinner sitting like a lump of coal in his stomach, Ivan said to Seth, "I'm going to turn in. Write a letter to the family..."

Seth nodded, and Ivan headed for his room. The gravity seemed to have been turned up to Jupiter standard, sucking his feet into the carpet with every step.

> *Hi, love,*
>
> *Well, we haven't struck it rich, yet. But it's very early in the tour, and no one seems concerned. I'd like to hit the earlier of*

your projections, rather than the later, though. I'm looking forward to retiring to the French Riviera—or what's left of it.

How are Josh and Suzie? Do they ask about their dad? Tell them I've learned to fly. I can fly from one end of the ship to the other, down the middle. It's great fun.

Ivan leaned back from the keyboard. He couldn't bear to send an honest email, but had trouble thinking up the words for something upbeat. He stared at the note for several minutes, then reached over and saved the draft. He had until tomorrow morning, anyway. To keep costs down, the *Mad Astra* only connected to SolNet once a day, to send and receive updates.

With a sigh, he put everything away and prepared for bed.

6. Trying Another Location

The move to the new location was virtually identical to the first one, except for a noticeable lack of bounce in people's steps. Ivan, once again, was first up on deep radar duty.

The target of the day was a large, vaguely peanut-shaped rock, with a smaller sibling in close proximity. The two rocks had so little relative motion and spin that Ivan couldn't tell initially if they were just passing by, or were in some kind of mutual orbit.

"Target's locked," he announced. Seth took up position, and Tenn worked the controls. Another boring four hours, watching radio waves propagate.

Ivan followed Tenn's occasional instructions, and otherwise let his mind drift. If he turned his back on the deep radar unit, the only item in the universe was the *Mad Astra*, floating in the distance. The sun glinted evenly off the oval of the ship, broken only by the four fusion nacelles around the stern. Mars was currently on the other side of the solar system, but Jupiter could be picked out with ease. It didn't quite show a disk, but at this distance it glowed almost as brightly as the moon from Earth.

"Take your time, sprout, it's not like we're on duty or anything."

Ivan jerked as he realized that Tenn had been talking. "Um, sorry, what?"

"Sleep on your own time, noob. Which will be soon, actually. Shift's over, as soon as you can see your way clear to signing off the unit."

Nodding, Ivan reached for the console and logged out. He gave a thumbs up to Seth, who typed a few rapid commands, then pushed away from his seat.

And with that it was end of shift, finally. Ivan, Seth, and Tenn did a quick post-shutdown inspection, then gathered to jet back to the ship together. Ivan was surprised to see three space-suited figures approaching.

"What the hell?" Tenn said. "We didn't have another shift scheduled. What're you guys doing?"

Aspasia's voice came back over the radio. As usual, her tone conveyed her disapproval of the universe and all its inhabitants. "Aiello called us up at the last minute. They want a re-scan. Looks like you guys screwed up."

"Horse maneuvers," Seth replied. "No red lights at all."

"Well, I don't know what to tell you, bucko." Aspasia took a moment to bring herself to a dead stop. "Pretty sure I didn't volunteer to do this all on my own. Take it up with Aiello."

"Weird," Tenn muttered.

"Uh, I don't suppose there's any chance they're rescanning because they found something?" Ivan couldn't keep the hope out of his voice.

"That's certainly an alternative explanation." Aspasia grinned at him, her face clearly visible through the helmet. "But I'm going to go with my theory."

As Aspasia, Will, and Raul began setup for a full deep radar run, Ivan and his crewmates jetted back to the *Astra*. No one said anything, even the normally opinionated Tenn Davies keeping his own counsel.

* * *

"All crew to the common room."

The unscheduled announcement over the P.A. made everyone look up. Ivan's stomach clenched. He turned to Seth. "What now? Are they going to extend the tour again?"

"Well, we've only scanned the first rock. Okay, the first two, but the runt hardly counts.Normally, they wouldn't make any pronouncements until we'd gone through this entire group." Seth paused. "Damn, sprout, could you be right?" His voice rose at the end of the sentence, in a kind of unconscious plea to the gods of chance.

"An unscheduled general meeting is either really, really good news, or really, really bad," Tenn commented as he walked up to their table. "Nothing's particularly happened lately that could be bad, so my money's on a positive scan. *How* positive is the question."

Since Ivan and Seth had been in the common room already, they refreshed their coffees and continued what they'd been doing—working on a correspondence course in Ivan's case, and listening to an audio book in Seth's.

The rest of the crew arrived in short order, including those who had been asleep. The buzz of conversation and debate rose in volume as each person arrived. Opinions were split on the probable reasons for the summons—about half of the crew shared Tenn's opinion, the other half speculating that a creditor had panicked and called in their note. A palpable aura of both anxiety and anticipation settled over the crew lounge as they waited for the bridge officers to make an appearance.

Finally, the captain walked in, followed by the first mate, Dante Aiello, and the geologist, Cirila Heinrichs. Although she was technically crew, Cirila's specialty required her to spend a considerable time with bridge officers.

Everyone looked at Aiello, trying to read his facial expression. But Aiello was paying an extreme level of attention to his slippers, so no help there.

Captain Jennings stepped to the front of the group and surveyed the crew for a moment. Then he did something captains of ships almost never did. He grinned unabashedly. The expression was infectious, and within seconds everyone was grinning back, despite nothing having been said.

"Ahem," the captain began, "We seem to have some positive results. Rock number one in this group, serial number AN2138.14, has multiple nodes of high density, along with pronounced magnetic reactivity."

"That means ferrous materials," Seth whispered to Ivan.

"I will, as is my duty, caution you all not to count your chickens until the samples have been taken and the cores assayed."

"Assuming it's positive, what are we looking at?" Raul Alfaro asked.

Captain Jennings looked over at Cirila, then back at the crew gathered in front of him. "Ms. Heinrichs has given me a preliminary summary of probable elements and tonnages, which is just a list of numbers. And, I reiterate, based only on the deep radar results, which are not definitive. However, to put it in perspective—if this plays out as the numbers seem to indicate, each and every one of you will be able to buy your own mining ship. Cash."

The noise level in the room rose to a roar as the crew reacted to this pronouncement. A mining ship cost about the same as a Boeing 797 Super-Jumbo. Granted, nothing had been said about being able to afford to *run* the thing, but still…

Ivan caught a glimpse of Tenn quickly wiping what appeared to be tears from his cheeks. It hadn't occurred to him that he might not be the only crew member with a reason to *need* a good result. Tenn's earlier reluctance to mock him about the loan from Seth started to make sense.

But that was a mystery for another time. Right now, Ivan had to deal with the realization that he had, on his very first tour, accomplished everything he'd set out to do. Debts would be paid, houses would be bought, and the kids would get the head start that he'd missed and they so deserved. And his family would never have to worry about finances again. Ivan's vision began to blur, and he had to perform some cleanup of his own.

"There's something else," Cirila said into the riot of conversation. All sound cut off as everyone turned to her, faces registering sudden worry.

"There's a satellite circling AN2138.14—we've been calling it Baby Rock—which has an anomaly of some kind. We detected a compact node of a density that would place it in the transuranic range."

"Is that even possible?" asked one of the crew.

Cirila shook her head. "No, which means it's bad data."

"So there might be nothing there?" After the initial elation, this was almost unendurable.

"No, there's something there, physically. The readings on AN2138.14 are all within specs. I'm not suggesting equipment fault." Cirila looked at the captain, then back to the crew. "I'm just saying, we need to be cautious."

* * *

Loveliest of all women, love of my life—

We've hit pay dirt! The big one!

They don't have specifics yet, but the word 'big' keeps floating around. Also, 'rich', 'wealthy', 'holy sh…' (Don't let the kids read that).

I doubt we'll stay out for the full tour. I will probably be back within the month. Start thinking about Christmas. And about where we want to retire.

Love,

Ivan

7. Tallying Results

Lita Generus had no problem making eye contact today. The captain smiled at her across the table and raised his coffee mug in salute. She grinned back.

"I guess we've made break-even," he said.

Generus snorted, and Cirila Heinrichs laughed out loud. Normally her laugh was mildly annoying, but today, nails on a chalkboard would barely register.

The bridge officers sat around the conference table in the captain's Ready Room, several of them nursing coffees. Heinrichs, despite being halfway down the long side of the table, seemed to dominate the group as every other person in the room was turned to face her.

The captain put down his mug. "All right. Enough suspense. Status report, Ms. Heinrichs?"

Heinrichs made a show of getting comfortable, lining up her tablet on the table, and moving her mug to just the right spot. She grinned at Generus when the latter made a growling sound.

"I can only theorize that this chunk must have been a core fragment of some planetoid that formed in the early solar system. Most of the silicates and other surface comps are late accretions. It's very possible that, under the top layer, this rock is an almost solid chunk of metal."

She paused to look around the desk. "Besides the expected iron and nickel, we've got a significant smattering of rare earths and a really strong showing from the platinum group."

"No gold?"

"A little bit, sir. But with all this other stuff, the industrial conglomerates will be very interested. They tend to bid faster, with fewer conditions and less concern about market saturation. I think we'll get a better, quicker sale than we would if the precious metals specialists were in charge of the bidding."

Jennings nodded. "Excellent. We'll need hard numbers for the auction, of course. Let's get the core samples done as soon as possible." The captain looked at the first mate.

Aiello smiled. "I predict much less grumbling than usual. As soon as Cirila has the detail maps done, sir, we'll get started."

"Ah, before I forget. Mr. Micoroski, deep sky scan?"

"No ships in the area, sir. The Sino-Soviet ships aren't especially stealthy."

Jennings nodded. "There hasn't been an incident since the *Free Fall*, but why take chances? Do at least one more full scan before we send in our claim. And make sure we're using the latest encryption when we do send it."

8. Paydirt

A feeling of holiday pervaded the ship. Ivan's eyes widened as he looked over the crowd gathered at the airlock.

"We need to name it," someone said.

Seth turned to the onlookers and grinned. "Tell you what, why don't you poor rubes work on that while we're out there digging for gold?"

He was met with several biologically unlikely suggestions for methods of storing gold, but they included no undertone of rancor. The chance of such strong readings being false positives ranked slightly higher than finding a leprechaun sitting on the gold. But only slightly. The atmosphere was one of jubilation, and everyone was giddy with the possibilities.

Even Tenn was swept up in it. He slapped Ivan on the back. "Let's go get 'em, sprout."

They cycled through the airlock to find the scooter waiting. Aspasia Nevin came in close and paid out a towing line. Tenn took shotgun as senior crew member, and the others attached their safety harnesses to bights on the line.

With exaggerated care, Aspasia took flight for AN2138.14.

* * *

"Seriously, Seth, it should be right over there." Ivan glanced back and forth from the heavens to his heads-up display. The anomaly, by his estimate, was less than 200 meters away, in the small rock that orbited this much more massive asteroid. Probably lightly buried under the dust and gravel that inevitably accumulated in hollows over geological time scales.

"Don't care, sprout. The anomaly might or might not come to anything. This clump below us, if it proves out, will allow us to each retire anywhere the hell we want. You see where I'm going with this?"

"Straight down?"

"Yeah, like that. And if you could find the time to come over here and help, I'm sure the whole crew would appreciate it."

Ivan sighed and, with an effort, set aside his curiosity. He grabbed the piton gun and spent a few seconds estimating distances. Then he laid down a pattern of anchors that would allow Seth to take several core samples from different angles.

Seth set his drill in roughly the right area, then attached it to several pitons with cables on the drill casing. Small electric winches tightened the cables until the drill was held securely against the surface.

Seth consulted Cirila's diagram for a few moments, then adjusted the drill's angle. A quick double-check, and he pressed the *Start* button.

The drill made short work of the task, extracting a long cylinder of asteroid material. The mechanism ejected the cylinder out the back end—a process that was the butt of many jokes—and Ivan carefully sleeved the core and labelled it.

As soon as they gave the all-clear, Seth repositioned the drill for the next core.

In less than two hours, they had a half-dozen long cores extracted.

"These don't even go halfway through the node," Tenn commented. "And if that isn't iron ore on the end, there, I'll eat it."

No one needed to add anything. Mining crew knew what different ores looked like. They had to, for this job. The deep radar was only good for the overview, not for the eyes-on-the-ground evaluation.

Bundling the cores turned out to be more of a chore than expected, though, because other crew members kept getting in the way. Every time Ivan and Tenn tried to sleeve a core, someone was there, poking at it, trying to identify the ore.

Finally, Tenn lost it. "Fucksake, you jackasses. We'll be out here forever if you don't back off. And by the way, I'm pretty sure there are more people here than are on-shift. Since when do you *volunteer* for work?" Tenn placed his hands on his hips and surveyed the crowd. He was probably glaring, but it lost something in a space suit.

"C'mon, Tenn, we're just trying to—"

"Deep radar readings showed iron, nickel, platinum, palladium, and osmium. You heard the lady. What're you gonna do? Lick it to lay your claim?"

Tenn got some chuckles, and the group broke up to make room. Ivan and Seth were soon finished sleeving and labelling the samples. They wrapped the tubes with some bungees and Seth held up the end of a tow cable.

Aspasia grabbed the bundled cores from Seth, attached the clip to the scooter, then shot toward the *Astra*, showing nowhere near as much care this time.

"Hey, Spazzie," Tenn called to her over the common channel, as she disappeared rapidly into the distance. "Feel free to splatter yourself over a random rock. More for us."

There was no response, but the jets cut off abruptly.

Seth turned to Ivan. This far out in the solar system, the helmet autoshading hardly kicked in at all, so Ivan could clearly see his happy grin.

"Okay, sprout, we've got some time until Cirila completes her assay. Feel like checking it out?" Seth inclined his chin upward. There was no doubt what he was referring to.

9. Checking it Out

Seth couldn't help chuckling to himself. The sprout was like a puppy, with his eagerness and fresh-faced curiosity. Seth tried to remember if he'd ever been that energetic. Probably. But each tour wore a little bit of the edges off you. Especially the disappointing tours, where you came back empty handed, a half year of your life gone with nothing to show for it. You returned from those with a little bit more of yourself ground off, a little bit more of the shape of you missing. After a while, you became like Tenn—just a walking, talking lump of cynicism and fake boredom.

But today was a good day. Today was for adventure and dreams. Seth could almost hear Ivan vibrating with excitement.

"Okay, sprout, let's go. I'll lead." Seth reached for his jet controls.

They were about to launch themselves, when Tenn broke in. "And where do you think you're going?"

Seth turned to face him. "Just a short flight to Baby Rock. No big deal."

"This could be an alien artifact," Ivan exclaimed. "Actually, what else could it be?"

"A lot of things, sprout. Get'cher knickers under control. Deep radar isn't foolproof, or they wouldn't need us. Plus it was Robinson running the gear, and he's not very good."

"Oh, hah hah, Davies." Even Tenn couldn't ruin the air of celebration. And truthfully, his tone was lacking the usual hectoring. It was almost as if he considered it his duty to throw an insult or two.

"Transuranics, she said," Ivan replied.

"Instrumentation error, I say. Tell you what, sprout, let's put some money on it. I say it'll be some castoff piece of human equipment, maybe with a shielded casing. How much are you willing to put up?"

Ivan chuckled. "Fine, Tenn. You've been trying to get me to gamble this whole trip. Today's your lucky day. But money's irrelevant, now, so how about you taking kitchen duty the whole trip back against my desserts the whole trip back?"

Tenn hesitated for a moment. When he replied, his voice was friendlier than Seth could remember ever hearing. "Well, okay then. Turns out the sprout has some balls. You're on, Ivan."

The crew had been gathering around during this exchange, sensing the drama. The collective mood, already euphoric from the impressive core samples, continued to spiral upward, fed by the friendly competition.

"Well, let's go look then," Tenn continued. "I have to admit, I'm curious too."

There were mutters of agreement from the other crew members.

Seth shook his head slowly. "Damned party crashers."

He waited for everyone to get ready, then said to the group, "Follow." With that, he activated his jet pack and headed for where his heads-up indicated the Baby Rock should be.

The group got to the rock in less than a minute. It was barely twenty meters across, vaguely lentil-shaped, and virtually motionless in space.

"Weird that it has hardly any rotation," Ivan said.

Seth agreed, but knew that orbital mechanics produced many odd situations. This was no worse than most, and convenient, truth be told. They wouldn't have to worry about being tossed off the rock by centrifugal force.

"So now that we're here, what are we looking for?" someone asked.

"Good question. Is Cirila's scan online?" Seth flipped through the available images on his suit's heads-up display even as he asked the question. It took only a moment to find the right graphic. "Should be right at the bend in the lentil shape. The lowest point, gravitationally."

"Probably not a coincidence," Tenn replied.

Ivan jetted over a few meters. "That's about here." He unhooked his collapsible shovel and assembled it. Without waiting for consultation, he began digging.

"Whoa, pardner," Seth said. "You sure you want to dig down to a lump of uranium?"

"*Transuranics*, she said." Ivan looked up at Seth, emphasizing the first word. "Which is patently impossible. So I want to see what we—hello..." Ivan looked oddly at his shovel.

"You hit something?"

"Yeah, and it did not feel at all like rock. It gave a little, like it was flexible."

As the other crew members crowded around, Ivan cleared the gravel and sand-like particulates from what looked for all the world like a walnut the size of a watermelon.

Tenn muttered, "We might want to be careful, here, guys."

Ivan grinned. "Aw, come on, Tex. How bad can it be?"

With that, he reached down to pick up the anomaly.

10. Infection

There was a snapping motion—a blur, as if the object had abruptly changed shape. Ivan jerked and, suddenly, his right arm inexplicably felt hot. He looked at his space suit and saw a gray substance spreading onto his hand and forearm.

Ivan's vision narrowed to a tunnel view, centered on his arm. Scenes from horror movies, both old and recent, played in his mind. He heard a scream, and realized an infinite time later that it came from inside his helmet.

Davies's voice came loud over the radio. "This is Tennison Davies. Mayday! Mayday! We have a crew injury. We need immediate transport and medical standing by."

"What is your location, and what is the nature of the injury?" Albert Micoroski responded.

"We're on the Baby Rock. Ivan Pritchard found the anomaly, and something has glued itself to his arm. He's screaming, but we're not sure if it's pain or panic." There was dead air for a moment, then Davies continued, "The scooter is coming in to our position now. We'll tie up and let her tow us in to the *Astra.* Stand by."

"The captain wants details, Mr. Davies." The voice of the *Mad Astra*'s pilot was dead calm.

"We dug up the anomaly that Cirila detected on the Baby Rock. It was small, about the size of a basketball. Pritchard reached down to pick it up and something came out of the thing and wrapped itself around his right arm."

"Is he in pain?"

"Don't think so. He panicked when it happened. He's calmer now."

A small part of Ivan's mind, that little voice that insisted on ironic commentary on everything, noted that *paralyzed with fear* wasn't the same as *calmer.*

"Mr. Davies, this is the captain. I want a video camera trained on the substance on his arm. Chief Engineer MacNeil will evaluate the situation, and we will then decide how to proceed."

"Captain, we have to get him into sick bay so we can get this thing off—"

"You have the order of events wrong, Mr. Davies. He will not be going into sick bay, or coming into the ship at all, until either the substance is removed, or Mr. MacNeil assures me it is safe. This is not a negotiable item."

"Yes sir."

MacNeil's voice cut in. "I'm sending a video camera and remote sensor over. Please train them on the anomaly when you get them."

"Sir."

As the conversation with the ship died down for the moment, Ivan tried to control his breathing. His mind began spinning through a panicked recitation: *No, no, I can't die now, not when we've just hit it rich!* The ironic commentator in his head noted that at least this was a coherent thought, which was an improvement.

He remembered reaching for the object. He remembered a snapping motion, and something grabbing his arm. He remembered screaming, and a jumbled collage of faces and spacesuits and rock and space...

His arm prickled and itched maddeningly, but a small, rational part of his mind wondered if that was psychological. The stuff, whatever it was, didn't seem to add any weight to his arm—it could just be paint for all the difference it made.

Shadows and reflections flitted across his visor as other crew members moved around him. Voices sounded over the intercom, but he couldn't make sense of them. His mind seemed to have shut down, leaving only a panicked, cornered animal, screaming and running in circles inside his skull.

Someone placed their helmet in his line of sight. Their lips moved, and words came over the suit speakers. He tried to concentrate, to make sense of the sounds.

"Are you in pain? Is the stuff doing anything to you?"

Ivan's eyes opened wider as a circuit breaker snapped back on in his brain, and he recognized Tenn's voice. He replayed the words, working to extract meaning.

"Ah, uh, no, I don't think so." He took a deep breath and tried again. "No pain. It doesn't really seem to be doing anything to me. It doesn't even weigh anything."

Tenn nodded and grabbed Ivan's shovel, which was floating nearby at the end of its tether. He flipped it around expertly, then used the blade to scrape the substance off Ivan's arm.

Or tried to.

The grayish substance actually seemed to *flow* around the shovel blade, reforming behind it. It looked vaguely like running a paddle through water.

Tenn stopped, and the substance smoothed itself out.

More gabbling followed, more sounds that Ivan's brain couldn't process. The universe presented like a disconnected series of still-frames, similar in theme but not logically connected.

* * *

The conversations had resumed. Unable to form a thought, let alone any kind of strategy, Ivan simply allowed himself to float in place, ministered to by the other space suits swarming around, while the radio chatter flowed over and past him.

Duncan's voice came over the channel. The chief engineer had a puzzled tone, but no sense of panic or urgency. "It doesn't appear to be spreading, Captain. It's not particularly showing up on infra-red. It seems to be thermally non-conductive. There's no radiation, no magnetic or electromagnetic activity. You'd think it was spray paint except for the tendency to flow around attempts to scrape it."

"Any conclusions, Mr. MacNeil?"

"It appears to be at some kind of equilibrium, Captain. It's where it wants to be."

"Doctor?"

"Other than vitals from the suit monitors, I can't tell you much, Captain. Pritchard's heart rate and respiration are way up, of course, but nothing indicates anything other than adrenaline."

"Can anyone assure me that this is safe to bring into the ship?"

Silence answered the captain's question.

"Any suggestions for a resolution?"

Dr. Kemp spoke up. "I might have one, Captain. We could cut off the suit arm."

"Amputate?"

"Not the arm itself, sir, just the suit. The gunk doesn't even reach Pritchard's elbow. We could cut the material above the elbow and strip it off."

"Will he lose the arm?"

"No sir, he shouldn't. The others can start spraying suit sealant on the arm as the fabric is being pulled back. That should protect the arm somewhat from depressurization."

"Suit sealant is for patching small holes in suits, to prevent hematomas on the skin, doctor. How well do you expect it to work when it's covering an entire arm?"

"It'll be better than nothing, sir. That's really all I can promise. People can survive vacuum for a short time. There's normally far more risk to the lungs, eyes, and ears. Worst case, he will probably suffer some bruising on the arm."

There was a pause before the captain addressed Davies. "Mr. Davies, you have a fabric saw?"

"Yes sir, standard kit."

"All right. Understand that if the substance has penetrated through to his arm, he might be allowed to die out there. At your discretion, please begin. Ms. Nevin, be prepared to ferry him to the airlock with all haste if results permit."

A series of "Yes sir's" answered.

Tenn's face moved into Ivan's field of view. "Ivan, stick out your arm."

Ivan did so, and someone sprayed something on his arm. Then Tenn ran something around his arm, and a ring of agony formed around his biceps. Two crew members grabbed his suit arm and pulled. The pain was beyond description, as if they were stripping his skin off. Ivan heard whimpering coming from inside his helmet.

Finally, the pain stopped, and Ivan felt himself fade out…

* * *

Seth peered through Ivan's helmet visor. The sprout's eyes didn't look quite so much like white saucers anymore, and he seemed to be in better control. According to the suit's external readouts, Ivan was still hyperventilating a little, but the environmentals were keeping up, so far.

Seth was more concerned about some of the other crew

members, who seemed to be heading for panic attacks of their own. The doctor's plan would require careful coordination. If someone went off-script at the wrong time, Ivan could die.

Tenn had the fabric saw out and ready. Based on the same concept as the saws used to cut casts off limbs, the composite blade of a fabric saw would decompose the material but wouldn't affect flesh. He brought the saw near Ivan's arm, then gave orders to the crew. "Seth, you brace Ivan in the passenger seat so we can pull off the suit arm without dislodging him. Kady and Raul, be ready to grab the fabric as I cut it and peel it back. Make sure the gunk doesn't touch you or anyone else, or we'll be doing this all over again. Will, be ready with the sealant." Tenn looked around at the other crew members to make sure they were reacting to his orders.

"Screw that," Kady's voice rose in pitch. "I'm not taking a chance on that shit touching me!"

Will cut in before Kady could build up to a full-on conniption. "We have lots of sealant. How about if I cover the gunk with it first? Then it can't get loose or touch anyone."

"Good thinking, Will. Do it. Step back, everyone. Ivan, stick out your arm." Tenn gave a small push and drifted away from the group. A small spurt with his jets and he was motionless. The others followed suit, leaving the field clear for Will.

It took only moments to cover the suit arm up to the elbow. Once the substance was covered, they moved back into position.

Tenn looked at Ivan. "Okay, sprout, this is not going to be comfortable. But the doc doesn't think you'll lose the arm. And anyway, with the money from your share, you'll be able to get a new one grown."

Ivan nodded, clearly sweating profusely. The suit environmentals were starting to have trouble keeping up, and his visor was fogging.

"And, 3...2...1..." Tenn ran the saw around Ivan's lower biceps as quickly as he could. The fabric edges pulled back on either side. Kady and Raul braced their feet on the scooter frame and grabbed the forearm side of the cut. As they pulled, Will sprayed sealant from Ivan's shoulder on down. Ivan whimpered a little as different parts of his arm suffered decompression, but he held still for the entire operation.

As soon as the suit arm was off, Kady thrust it to the ground and pushed gravel over it with his foot.

The rest of the crew cleared the scooter, and Tenn ordered

Aspasia, "Go! Airlock, immediately!"

Needing no further prompting, Aspasia gave the scooter jets a spurt to get clear of the clump of crew members, then jetted toward the open airlock, where several people were waiting.

11. Recovery

The corridor outside sick bay was crowded. The captain had ordered everyone without a good reason to be there to clear out. Strangely, most of the crew had found a good reason. Or an excuse, anyway. Seth had made the claim, maybe only a slight exaggeration, of being Ivan's best friend and a source of moral support. The captain had raised an ironic eyebrow, but allowed it.

Seth could hear Doc Kemp's and Ivan's voices muffled by the wall, but couldn't make out words. At least it meant Ivan was alive, conscious, and relatively calm. Seth took a deep breath. He felt an unreasonable degree of guilt for going along with Ivan's desire to dig up the thing. He should have known better. Whatever condition Ivan was in now, it was Seth's fault.

The doctor walked out of sick bay and closed the door. He looked around at the dozen people crowding the corridor, then fixed his eyes on Captain Jennings.

"I've given him a sedative. Right now, all he really needs is rest. His arm is a mess, but there's no obvious sign that the substance penetrated the suit. Everything is consistent with exposure to vacuum. Bruising, hematomas, some scrapes from the rough treatment, a bit of chemical burn from the amount of sealant used. All things being equal, he'll be back to limited duty in a day or two, and full duty in a week."

"Can we see him?" Seth asked. Maybe if he could assure himself that Ivan was okay, this feeling of dread would go away.

"Not a lot of point. I gave him one of the stronger sedatives in my arsenal. He's out, and will be for at least six hours."

"Just for a moment?"

Dr. Kemp looked at the captain, who nodded. With a bob of the head, the doctor indicated that Seth should enter sick bay. He held up a hand when the rest of the crew tried to follow. "Sorry, no. Just the one."

Seth turned to his crewmates, nodded in what he hoped was a reassuring manner, and went through the door. Ivan lay on a cot, a white cream covering his entire right arm. His head was turned slightly to the side, his mouth hanging open. He wasn't quite knocked out, but he wasn't quite just sleeping, either. There would be no discussion today.

Seth's crewmates straightened up as he came out, and several started asking questions at the same time.

Seth held up a hand. "He's out cold, like the doc said. He looks healthy, except his arm's been through a ringer. I'll trust the doc on his prognosis for the arm. Let's just wait until tomorrow."

He followed the rest of the crew back to the lounge, his head hanging. It hadn't helped as much as he'd hoped.

* * *

Ivan slowly came awake. This was his favorite part of the day. Waking up by stages, warm in bed, brain not active enough yet to start cataloguing the reasons why you shouldn't be so relaxed. The crappy apartment, the money troubles, the dead-end job...

Maybe today was a weekend. No alarm clock. He would take the kids to the park. They needed to burn off the energy. Banging around in a six-hundred-square-foot apartment just resulted in adult tempers flaring, and children in time-out.

He frowned without opening his eyes. That didn't sound right. He'd done something, hadn't he? Joined the Navy? No, joined a mining partnership. He was on the *Mad Astra*, and they'd just struck it rich, and he had checked Baby Rock, and—

He sat up, immediately sweating with fear. The thing had attacked him, grabbed his arm. But he'd been rescued by the crew, hustled off to sick bay. Everything was fine. His arm didn't even hurt anymore.

Then, Ivan looked at his arm...

Dr. Kemp burst through the door, his eyes wide. Seeing his face, Ivan realized he'd been screaming; he cut off the sound with a snap of his jaw.

The doctor grabbed a medical kit from the counter and stepped closer to the cot. Ivan held up his arm, and the blood drained from the doctor's face.

Ivan looked at his arm again, hoping he'd somehow been mistaken. The reality was all but impossible to absorb. The arm was silver. No, not silver, specifically. More of a chrome or titanium. From the tips of the fingers, to about halfway up the forearm, Ivan's arm appeared to be coated with metal.

The doctor grabbed a box of surgical gloves and donned two layers. He seemed to hesitate for a moment, then took Ivan's hand and began to palpate the fingers and knuckles. Ivan could see the expression on his face change.

Kemp backed away from the bed, and Ivan thought for a moment he was going to run. Instead, he spun around and hammered the intercom button. "*Astra*, please wake the captain, and request his presence in sick bay with all haste. We have a situation."

12. Investigation

"I've sedated him. Again. Just a light dose, this time. He's conscious, but calm." Dr. Kemp shook his head. "At this rate, I'll go all the way through my supply by the end of the week."

"But what *is* it?" Captain Jennings asked.

"As near as I can tell, it's a metal prosthetic, seamlessly integrated with Pritchard's physiology." Dr. Kemp glanced at Chief MacNeil for a moment. "The level of detail, and the technology apparent in the implementation are like nothing I've ever seen before."

MacNeil held up some small tools. "I could get a sample."

The captain looked at Kemp, who nodded.

"After the Chief gets his sample," Dr. Kemp continued, "I'll try a few things, like sonogram and x-ray. I've already determined that it's not affected by magnets."

"Does he have a pulse?"

"In the arm, you mean?" Dr. Kemp shook his head. "I'm not sure about how the interface is set up, but I doubt there's anything biological distal to the point where metal meets flesh."

Captain Jennings frowned and stared at the sick bay door for a few seconds. "What are our options, doctor? Is amputation viable?"

"That's my go-to plan, actually, unless something comes up to rule it out. Pritchard can get a new one grown as soon as he's back on Earth. It's not like none of us can afford it, now." Despite the gravity of the situation, the men shared a quick smile.

"All right. Use your discretion, Doctor," the captain said. "Keep me informed."

* * *

Ivan held up his hand. His flesh was chrome, up to halfway up the forearm. "What is it, doc? What's happening to me?"

"I've already described the physical aspect, Ivan. But the *why* and the *how*? I have no idea."

"This is from the stuff I got on my arm. It must be."

"It doesn't look the same. The stuff on your suit was grayish, and liquid. But yeah, it's reasonable to conclude that the gunk caused this in some way."

"What do I do?"

Kemp pulled up a stool and sat in front of Ivan. "We don't know anything about this thing, and I don't think we can afford a wait-and-see stance. I'd like you to consider amputation. Stop it before it spreads, assuming it *will* spread."

"Yeah, I get it. And I can get a new arm grown when we get home." Ivan was silent for a few seconds, staring at his hand, slowly turning it. "Okay. Do it. Before I chicken out."

* * *

Charles Kemp looked down at the notes, charts and images arrayed on his active desktop. He pushed the items around, but no alternate arrangement magically cast the data into a sane explanation.

Kemp blew out a hard breath, then pushed the intercom. "Captain, please, *Astra*."

A moment later, the captain's voice came from the intercom. "You have a report, doctor?"

"Um, yes, sir. Lots of data, not a lot of explanations, though there's a very organized interface between the biological and artificial parts of the arm. As I expected, the blood vessels end at that interface. But, interestingly, they aren't just tied off. The arteries and veins have been specifically tied together so that blood flow is unimpeded. Nerve interfaces are organized and efficient including, I might add, parasympathetic functions."

Kemp dragged a particular report toward himself with a finger. "Chief MacNeil said he would give you a full report on his findings but, in summary, the arm isn't a monolithic piece of metal. There's complex structure in there, sufficient to provide a working appendage. The substance of the appendage consists of countless, for want of a better word, *nanites*, linked together to form a continuous whole. Like cells, but somewhat smaller, and made of metal."

Kemp's voice ran down and he stared blankly at the documents on his desk, until the captain said, "Doctor?"

"Sorry. We amputated. Just below the elbow. Pritchard gave his consent. He agreed that getting a new one grown was a small price to pay. No pun intended. We've placed the amputated limb in a sealed sample container, for examination by experts on Earth. Assuming there are experts on something like this."

"Are you sure that's safe?"

"I'm not sure of anything, Captain. But in terms of risks, I think the damage is done. If it's inclined to spread in some way, well, it's already here. And sample containers are pretty tough—they have to be." Kemp hesitated. "I think we need to understand this thing, and that means handing it over for analysis. If we toss it out the airlock, someone else will just have to come back and get it, wasting more time."

"Thank you, doctor. I don't necessarily disagree. I'll await the Chief's no doubt much more opaque report, and I will let you know if I understand any of it. Out."

Kemp leaned back in his office chair. *Holy crappola, what a day.*

13. Situation Analysis

Captain Jennings leaned back with his coffee and looked around the table at his bridge staff. Aiello, Micoroski, and Generus sat with their elbows on the table, gazing into their coffees as if attempting to scry with a crystal ball. MacNeil, on the other hand, was staring into space, a slight frown on his face. Typical of the man, he saw it only as another engineering problem.

"Opinions?"

MacNeil sat forward and waved his arm in front of his face. "I wish we'd thought to save the suit arm. I would like to examine the substance."

"The crew left it on Baby Rock, partly buried. Heads-up thinking on their part. Didn't want it drifting around and settling against the ship's hull." Aiello looked momentarily alarmed at the thought.

"Or just as important, settling onto the big rock and contaminating our find."

All heads nodded around the table. An untouchable strike would go from a value of tens of billions to zero.

"On that subject," Generus added, "has Cirila finished with the assay?"

"Still working," Captain Jennings said. "But so far, everything is proving out at greater than expected quantities. She's starting to throw around numbers that make my earlier speech look like the height of pessimism."

This revelation brought smiles around the table. A satisfied silence settled over the room as people sipped their coffees.

“I’m probably being silly…” Generus finally said, in a deliberately offhand tone.

All heads turned to her. “What is it, Lita?” asked the captain.

“I’m sure I’m just being paranoid. But the Baby Rock is only a couple hundred meters from the big rock. Are we inviting trouble by leaving it there?”

“You want to move it?” Jennings looked at MacNeil. “Can we?”

“There are several different ways we could do it. The easiest would be to attach a couple of RIVA units. They’re designed to stop rotation on a big rock, they can certainly be used to move a small one. It’ll require careful control, though. And if we accelerate too hard, the suit arm could just fall off the rock, given the miniscule gravity.”

“And we should put a *fail* beacon on it,” Micoroski added. “And alert the military to the danger.”

“Not sure about that,” Aiello said quickly. “If military command gets too paranoid, they could interdict Big Rock as well.”

Captain Jennings sighed and closed his eyes for a moment. Not reporting the danger would be gross negligence. Losing the claim would be devastating for the entire crew.

He opened his eyes and scanned the faces around the table. “We have to report the danger. We can’t *not* do so. But we don’t have to create an association between the two. No one will go near this area until after the next lottery.”

“And then it’ll be like the California Gold Rush.” Aiello looked around the table. “Everyone that can float a boat will be flying out to this sector, looking for another rock like ours.”

“Right.” Captain Jennings rubbed his face in thought. “Let’s get the paperwork done on the claim. The sooner that gets finalized, the sooner we can start getting bids from the megacorps. Meanwhile, MacNeil, please put together a plan to get the Baby Rock out of the area, *with* the suit arm and the anomaly on it. We’ll wait a week or two, and report it as a separate incident.”

Jennings knew what they were doing wasn’t strictly illegal, but it was a distortion of basic moral principles. He realized with a heavy heart that even he was not immune to normal human failings.

14. Adverse Reaction

"A metal arm. A freakin' metal arm!" Tenn seemed to be stuck in a loop. This was the fourth time he'd said it. Even to other people just as much in shock, it was getting old. Seth tried to keep his face neutral, although the urge to roll his eyes was close to overpowering.

"How did it replace his arm?" Will asked. Willoughby Todd, the crew's amateur artist-in-residence, was sketching arms and hands as they discussed the situation. Seth had to admit the sketches were damn good.

"Could it be something sent up here by the Sino-Soviets?" Aspasia asked.

"Come on, Spazzie," Lorenza countered. "They don't have that kind of tech. They aren't even at our level. I've been to enough trade shows and conferences on automation to know. They're the buyers, not the innovators."

Seth nodded, silently. As the crew's mining robot operator and general remote automation expert, anything Lorenza said on the subject could be taken as gospel.

"And why would they go to all that trouble to set up a booby trap for a mining ship?" Seth looked around the table. No one had an answer to that.

Seth noted Geiger examining his fingertips closely. "Worried that you caught it, Kady?"

"It's not impossible. It got through Ivan's suit. It could have gotten through mine. I don't know that I touched the gunk, but I don't know that I didn't."

"But there's no reason to believe it would take any longer for any of us," Seth replied. "And I don't see anything different about you."

"Still ugly," Aspasia added.

"A metal, freakin' arm," Tenn said, into the air.

Raul reached over and punched Tenn, hard, in the shoulder. "Get a grip, asshole."

Tenn yelped and glared at Raul, but the move seemed to have accomplished its goal.

"Well, regardless," Aspasia said, "the Chief has a plan to move the Baby Rock, and he'll be assigning tasks. I'm looking forward to being a billionaire, thank you, and some stupid alien booby trap isn't going to get in the way."

Kady and Seth responded at the same time.

"Billionaire?"

"Alien?"

Aspasia glared at Seth. "*Alien* is just a placeholder for *damned if I know who did it.* But it's as good an explanation as any." Then she speared Kady with her gaze. "And have you not looked at Cirila's latest report? This is the biggest find in fifty years. We aren't just retired, dummy, we're now the ultra-rich."

Tenn, apparently now recovered, piped up, "Albert told me the captain has done the filings, and we've got preliminary confirmation. And a couple of inquiries from 'interested parties'." Tenn made air quotes around the last two words, which brought smiles to everyone.

Seth scrubbed his face with his hands. He wasn't sure how Ivan would react when he awoke. Even with the prospect of a new arm back on Earth, an amputation was still traumatic. Seth resolved to do something to cheer Ivan up.

* * *

It took Chief MacNeil very little time to come up with a plan for moving Baby Rock. The ship's engineer called all hands to duty for the operation. Nothing could be left to chance. Any glitches could potentially contaminate Big Rock, and that would be it for their claim. Both he and the captain had made it clear that they wouldn't attempt to cover up such an eventuality.

As such, the crew was focused on the chief's plan to an extent seldom before seen. Without prompting, people were doing dry runs, talking through the operation again and again, looking for failure points.

Meanwhile, the Rocket Impelled Vector Adjustment units were unpacked and moved over to Baby Rock. With virtually no rotation to deal with, they could skip the more difficult and problem-prone spin-down operation.

The crew connected the RIVAs to the rock with pitons, then wrapped a net of cables around the rock to provide additional bracing. A RIVA ripping out of its mooring during a firing sequence would be disastrous. At best, it would impart a spin to the rock and possibly fling the anomaly and suit arm right off. At worst, it could break up the rock completely.

MacNeil donned a suit and personally inspected the setup. Seth was present, and was careful to keep a straight face.

After MacNeil had retreated to the ship, Tenn tapped Seth's helmet. They turned off their radios and touched helmets in the only truly private way to communicate in space.

"Well, now we know why Mr. MacNeil doesn't like going EVA," Tenn said, the usual grin evident in his tone.

Seth didn't like Tenn's attitude, generally, but couldn't argue this one. "The word that kept popping up was *gnome*. I don't think they're specifically Scottish, but..."

Tenn laughed. "I was leaning more toward *troll*, but let's go with yours. Skin-tight suits definitely are not gonna be his preferred fashion statement."

Seth opened his mouth to reply, but at that moment, the suit intercom buzzed, indicating that they should get back on-channel. Seth quickly keyed his control. "Robinson."

"Pay attention, guys," Aiello's voice came back over the general frequency. "The Chief has given his blessing. Two minutes to activation."

Seth and Tenn exchanged silent looks, and both jetted off to their assigned posts.

At the appointed time, the RIVA units all fired simultaneously. They were throttled back to minimum thrust, using multiple units to distribute the strain as much as possible. The activity went on for several minutes, at the end of which Baby Rock was perceptibly moving away from Big Rock.

Finally, the RIVAs cut off.

"Shutdown confirmed. Units are on failsafe," Aiello intoned. "Crews, collect all equipment. Carefully."

The collection of the RIVAs, cables, and pitons would be done with greater than normal care; first, to prevent any obvious marks or damage on the rock and, second, to avoid too much contact between the crew and the equipment. Captain Jennings had ordered the whole mess to be bundled together and sent on a hyperbolic trajectory into deep space. No physical evidence would be left that could tie the *Mad Astra* to Baby Rock.

15. Deja Vu

Ivan woke up. He could tell he was still in sick bay, even before his waking mind put the memories of the last twenty-four hours back into order. He shuddered. He'd panicked out there on Baby Rock, and he admitted to mild embarrassment about that. He'd probably find himself the proud owner of a new nickname, *way* worse than "sprout". Screechy? Babbles? Eek?

Or maybe *Stubby.*

As his memory reintegrated, he remembered the metal arm. It hadn't felt different, from inside. Just his arm. But made of metal. They'd talked about it, then decided to amputate. Sure, these days you could get a new limb or organ or pretty much anything regrown.

Still, for the rest of the trip home, he'd be handicapped.

Judy, babe, am I going to have a story to tell you! Ivan hoped the kids wouldn't have to see him with the missing arm. It would freak them out.

Well, the doc was right, though. It was a small price to pay...

Ivan reached to throw off the covers with his right hand before he remembered that he no longer *had* a right hand. He sat up abruptly and snapped open his eyes...

Dr. Kemp burst through the door, his hair in disarray, and Ivan realized he was screaming. Again. He raised his arm—the right arm, the one that had just been amputated—and wiggled his fingers.

Dr. Kemp's eyes goggled. He stepped back slowly and felt for the intercom button without taking his eyes off the arm.

* * *

"How is this possible?" Captain Jennings glared at Dr. Kemp. Charlie couldn't really blame him. The whole thing sounded like a sick joke.

"I don't know, sir. But Ivan has a complete right arm, metal up to the biceps now." Dr. Kemp shook his head, slowly. "I can't explain this. I can't explain it at all."

"There are a number of issues we have to deal with," said Chief MacNeil.

No shit, Sherlock. What clued you in? The thought was unworthy, and Kemp carefully gave no indication of it on his face.

"One," the chief continued, "where is the metal for the new arm coming from? And, two, where is the material from the old arm going?"

"Transmutation?" asked Aiello.

"I'd just as soon not go there, yet," the chief answered. "Granted, we're out of our depth here, technologically, but in the absence of direct evidence, transmutation of elements seems a bit extreme."

Dr. Kemp nodded. Then his eyebrows furrowed as a thought occurred to him. He moved to the cot that held a sedated Ivan Pritchard, went down on his knees, and looked underneath.

"Uh huh. Look here." Dr. Kemp grabbed a surgical glove and used it to push a small quantity of white powder into a pile. "I bet this is almost all raw calcium. Well, calcium carbonate, anyway. All that's left of the bones of Ivan's arm."

There was an "oop" sound, and the first mate turned and rushed down the hall, holding his hand over his mouth.

"Okay, that may have been somewhat insensitive of me." Kemp stood silently, hand on his chin, for several seconds. "So, other than some trace elements, we're 95% composed of carbon, hydrogen, oxygen and nitrogen. Three of the elements are already gases, and if you combine carbon with oxygen, you could literally vaporize ninety-five kilograms of a one-hundred-kilogram man. The rest would be mostly calcium and phosphorus. An arm would be, um..."—Kemp looked into space as he did the calculations—"five percent of total body weight, of which five percent is non-CHON. Ivan weighs about 75 kilograms, so we're looking at less than 200 grams of non-gaseous waste."

Kemp moved to the intercom and pressed a button. "*Astra,* please check environmental logs for this deck. Any unusual issues with the air, recently?"

"Affirmative," responded the androgynous voice. "Slightly higher levels of carbon monoxide, water vapor and nitrogen had to be fractioned out over the last twenty-four hours. Lower levels of oxygen required replenishment."

Kemp raised an eyebrow and turned to the others.

"Interesting, and nice detective work, Dr. Kemp," Chief MacNeil said. "Now, about the other half of my question."

"Yeah, not my department, Chief. My next step would be to examine the amputated limb. There might be a clue there."

MacNeil nodded. "Mind if I tag along?"

"Not at all." Kemp turned to the captain. "We're still gathering facts, sir, but the bottom line is that this thing seems to be progressive. Where it'll stop is unknown. It might already be done, it might keep going until Ivan is gone."

"And we have no idea what it wants," MacNeil added.

"Very well. Keep me in the loop." The captain nodded to the two, then turned and left.

Kemp turned to head up the corridor. "Now, let's see about that limb."

* * *

Kemp slid the retractable tray out of the compartment. On the stainless steel tray was a metal case, with multiple latches along one side.

"You kept it in the morgue? Makes sense, I guess." MacNeil helped Kemp move the case to an autopsy table. It was a matter of moments to snap open the latches and open it.

MacNeil took one look and recoiled. "Och, wow."

Kemp stood frozen, staring at the contents—a ragged cylinder of flesh, cut cleanly on one end and seemingly dissolved to a conical stump at the other. A length of bone stuck out of the dissolved end.

"What the... This is nothing but the biological part of the amputation. We cut about three inches above the interface. Where's the metal?"

MacNeil stared at the case for a few moments, then pulled a flashlight out of his pocket. Walking to the door, he flicked the lights off in the room. He returned to the case and started playing the light around. "Watch the outside of the case."

Kemp craned his neck to take a closer look, then, "There! At the corner."

A number of holes, perhaps a millimeter in diameter, allowed stray beams of light to shine through. They looked at each other, then moved to the refrigerated compartment. MacNeil shone the light, then pointed. Kemp saw what looked like a similar series of pinholes in a corner.

MacNeil gazed into the compartment for a few moments, then turned to look at the sample container. He leaned far into the compartment and stared intently at the corner, illuminating it with the flashlight. He then backed away from the compartment, still staring in the same direction. Kemp watched this performance silently, not wanting to interrupt whatever calculations were going on.

"Both sets of holes line up with the shortest path back to Ivan," MacNeil said. "Which means the wee beasties drilled straight through the ship. I'll have to check the intervening spaces for critical wiring or such." He turned off his flashlight. "Which doesn't definitively answer the question of where the metal is coming from, but the fact they can eat through a sample case like that gives us a possible answer that I dinna like at all."

Kemp noted in passing that MacNeil's accent got stronger in stressful situations. He thought about what the chief had said. "Um. Cannibalizing the ship to rebuild Ivan's arm."

"Mm, hmm."

They turned the room lights back on and sat down. MacNeil looked up at the ceiling for a few moments, rubbing his chin. "The question is, why would they go back to Pritchard in particular? Especially once the nanites were no longer associated with him?"

"Urgh." Kemp rubbed his forehead. "Unless they're in more than just his arm. There was nothing in the blood sample I took during the initial exam, but that was before he started to metallize."

"Right. Time to take another one?"

They got up and Kemp led the way back to sick bay.

* * *

"And there it is." Dr. Kemp gestured to the microscope.

MacNeil leaned in and looked through the eyepieces. "Oh, dear. Those are..."

"Nanites. Same as the ones that are replacing his cells."

"So they have taken up residence in our Mr. Pritchard." MacNeil stepped back and glared at the microscope. "Which at least explains the homing behavior. Now, as for the other part of the question..."

* * *

"They're eating the ship?" Captain Jennings, for the first time since Kemp had known him, looked unabashedly afraid.

"Not the whole ship, Captain," MacNeil explained quickly. "They seem to be stripping layers from structures to supply the material for Pritchard's new parts."

"And these things are in his bloodstream?"

Kemp nodded. "We did tests on ourselves, and found nothing. That's not definitive, though. I found nothing initially out of the ordinary in Pritchard's blood sample, either. But it would explain why they're obsessed with getting back to him. He has been, for better or worse, *chosen* in some way."

"I'm going to order blood tests for everyone," Captain Jennings said. "Negative results may not be definitive, but a positive result would be. We need to know."

Kemp nodded. "I'll get the sick bay ready."

* * *

A line-up wound along the corridor from the sick bay. Dr. Kemp was quick and efficient, and anyway no one really wanted to engage in chit-chat. At two minutes per person, the crew was soon back in the common room, doubtlessly spinning ever wilder theories.

Ivan was still out. Kemp couldn't believe that so much had happened since the man had been infected. Kemp sighed quietly and walked over to look down at him. Poor sap. The infection, or whatever it was, seemed to be going to great lengths to avoid harming him, or even causing him any discomfort. A good sign, certainly. But even if this turned out to be ultimately benign, he was going through hell. In addition to his own health, he had to be worried about how his family would be affected. Although the strike at Big Rock would help with—

Dr. Kemp felt behind himself for the intercom button. Without turning, he pressed it. "*Astra*? Page the captain please. Tell him Ivan's other limbs have started to metallize."

16. We'll Handle It

The captain ended the call with a barely audible groan of frustration. Well, the good news was that no one else seemed to be infected. The bad news was that Ivan Pritchard continued to be converted—to *metallize*, as Dr. Kemp put it.

And Chief MacNeil had confirmed the worst: the nanites were moving freely about the ship, harvesting metal, and returning it to Pritchard's body to build his replacement parts. No critical systems had been affected. In fact, according to the chief, the nanites appeared to be spreading their depredations around in order to avoid adversely affecting any equipment.

Nevertheless, the potential downside was without limit. In theory, once finished with Pritchard, the nanites could start on the rest of the crew. In theory, if the *Mad Astra* returned to Earth, they could release this scourge on the human race. Gray Goo apocalypse, indeed.

This was no longer a containable situation.

The captain reached for the intercom. A lot of preparation would be required.

* * *

"What is the status of the claim, Ms. Generus?"

Generus pursed her lips for a moment. "Everything is textbook, sir. We've forwarded all data to the auction house. Bids are coming in from the conglomerates. Closing date is three days away. Just the reserve price will make a single-share owner a half-billionaire."

"At what point is the deal irrevocable?"

"Well, the bid winner will send a survey ship to verify our data. If that turned out to be significantly incorrect, they could pull out. But I'm confident of Cirila's numbers, sir. If anything, she's been slightly conservative. So I don't see that happening."

Jennings nodded. "I agree, Ms. Generus. I'm more concerned about the buyer becoming spooked if this business with Ivan Pritchard goes public."

"But we've been careful to separate the two events, both chronologically and spatially."

"And done a good job, I believe. Nevertheless, is there a way for us to get screwed?"

"Honestly, sir, if the military got involved, and suspected a connection between the claim and the Pritchard Event, then they could conceivably attempt to interdict the Big Rock. But first they have to make that connection. And even then, there's hundreds of billions of dollars at stake, and I'd think the bid winner would go to court to fight it rather than meekly backing off."

"That is my analysis as well. Thank you."

It was a dismissal. Lita hesitated for a moment, then got up and left the captain's ready room.

Jennings paused to review the chain of events and consider their options. What he was about to propose would take them further down the rabbit-hole into possible illegality. He would have to present his proposal delicately.

Before hesitation could become paralysis, he stabbed the call button for the doctor.

"Captain?"

"Doctor, I wonder if it would be feasible, without breaking your oath, to delay reporting Mr. Pritchard's condition. Say, three days?"

"Three days, Captain?" Kemp sounded concerned. Spooked, really.

"Will we be breaking any laws? Contravening any policies?"

"Well, no, sir. I guess if we were military... As it is, there may be questions about why we took so long to report the event, but it's not unreasonable for us to try to handle it ourselves, at least for a while. Why three days, specifically, if I may ask?"

"In three days, bidding closes on Big Rock. After that point, the bid winner is personally, if that's the right word, invested." Jennings smiled for a fraction of a second at the attempted witticism.

“Considering the life-altering nature of our claim, I think it’s a reasonable consideration.”

“I, uh, can’t really disagree, captain. Honestly, I think Ivan would agree as well.”

“And what is the situation with Mr. Pritchard?”

“I re-sedated him. I can’t do that again without risking medical complications. Of course, by that point it may not matter. The metallization is accelerating. The interface is now proximal relative to the knees and elbow on the three remaining limbs.”

“Which in English means it’s up to his thighs and upper arm? Will the conversion continue into the torso?”

Dr. Kemp was silent for a moment before replying. “I don’t know. Metallization along the right arm appears to have halted at the shoulder, but I don’t know if it’s just waiting for the other limbs to catch up. There’s definitely intelligence involved, although whether it’s sentient or just A.I. is impossible to say.”

“And still no idea what the end game is?”

“No, sir.”

“What about isolating him? Is there anything we can do?”

“We don’t have any facilities for that. We can confine him to his room, of course, and that’s probably a good idea just for crew morale. But, ultimately, it’s a gesture more than a real precaution. The nanites are already out, and they’re demonstrably not impeded by walls.”

“Understood. It goes without saying that we cannot expect to return to Earth until this is resolved. Please prepare a full report for transmission to the ICDC. Try to minimize reference to the timeline, but don’t prevaricate. We don’t mind being portrayed as unwise, but we can’t afford any slightest whiff of criminality.”

"Yes sir."

“Very well, then, Doctor. Keep me up to date on status. Thank you.”

17. Continuing Infection

Ivan awoke with no transition. One moment, blank, the next, full awareness. That was unusual at any time, unless an alarm clock was involved; he liked to take several minutes to segue from dreams to wakefulness. In this case, he was coming out of sedation. He remembered being put under after panicking about his arm.

His arm!

Ivan sat up without warning, almost knocking Dr. Kemp over. The doctor had apparently been reaching for his face or something, and came *that* close to getting clocked in the nose by Ivan's forehead.

He lifted his right arm. Metal. His eyes followed the arm up to his shoulder. Metal, as far as he could see, even the shoulder. He turned to Dr. Kemp, tears forming in his eyes.

Then he saw his legs. And his left arm. A whimper escaped his throat and the world contracted to a bright point.

* * *

Ivan awoke again. And remembered.

He looked at his feet, at his hands. Metal. Dr. Kemp sat at the side of the bed, looking sympathetic. Ivan looked him in the eyes and said, "How bad is it?"

Dr. Kemp looked down for a moment. "Ivan, it's not *bad* like cancer or a degenerative disease. You aren't, as far as we can tell, dying. Or even unhealthy. You're just…"

"Turning into Iron Man?" Ivan laughed, but even he could hear the note of hysteria.

Dr. Kemp's face fell. Ivan felt bad for him, for a moment.

"Ivan, the conversion is continuing. At the moment, the only parts of you that are still flesh and blood are your head and torso."

Ivan looked down. "Uh..."

Dr. Kemp flashed a smile. "Everything is still there. Whether functionality is maintained or not, well, you can test that at your leisure."

"Okay, what about bodily functions?"

"This is the truly interesting thing about this whole process." Dr. Kemp gave Ivan a sideways glance, as if gauging his reaction to the comment. "It's not just blindly working its way up your body. It appears to maintain biological systems as long as necessary until a metal version is ready to take over the function. Blood supply is always appropriate to the remaining biological systems. Hormonal levels are maintained. And so on."

Ivan stared at him for several seconds. "This isn't going to stop, is it?"

Dr. Kemp's only answer was a sigh.

"But what *is* it?"

The doctor waved a hand and made fish motions with his mouth for a few moments. Then he shrugged and gave Ivan a rueful smile. "I wish I knew. We know the basic facts, Ivan. Your cells are being replaced by microscopic nanites. The nanites are harvesting metal from the ship to make more nanites."

Kemp looked up at the ceiling for a moment, perhaps gathering his thoughts. "There are a few things I find encouraging. First, the nanites are careful not to take too much metal from one spot. The chief tells me that nothing is getting eaten down enough to affect functionality or structural soundness. And, likewise, none of the changes being made to you seems to be harmful, beyond the obvious issue of consent. It seems to be taking care to not cause you harm or even discomfort. None of those things could happen by coincidence. It requires a concerted, conscious effort."

"Conscious?"

Dr. Kemp shook his head. "Don't read anything into that. I don't have any inside information. I meant conscious as in a deliberate, targeted set of results."

Ivan nodded, thinking about it. "Yeah, an A.I. could do something like that according to its instructions. That really seems more likely, just in general."

He leaned back and started to rub his forehead, then jerked his hand away and stared at it. The action had felt entirely normal to his fingertips, but on his forehead it had felt like being massaged by a metallic implement.

"If this was happening to someone else, I'd be fascinated. As it is, I'm still curious, but also terrified. The process could be completely benign, but at the end of it I'll still be gone."

"Perhaps. Or maybe not. We don't know the limits of this thing. I know it's easy for me to say, but there's only one way to find out."

"Not that I have a choice." Ivan sighed and closed his eyes. "I'm pretty tired, Doc. Can we continue this later?"

The stool's casters made a rolling sound as Dr. Kemp stood. "No problem, Ivan. I'd like to do some tests when you're rested."

Ivan barely heard the sound of the door closing.

* * *

"And squeeze again?"

Ivan squeezed the bulb as instructed, while Dr. Kemp watched the pressure gauge. Dr. Kemp had asked him to undergo a physical, and Ivan figured it might distract him.

The doctor had that skill that physicians seemed to cultivate everywhere—the same noncommittal "mm, hmm" on each test that gave no indication of whether he'd aced it or was about to die.

Finally, the doctor looked up from his tablet. "It's interesting. Your strength is considerably increased. I'm lucky you didn't actually break a couple of my devices. You red-lined a couple of measurements. Reflexes are faster, but not inhumanly so. I think that's going to continue to improve as the, uh, transformation continues."

"S'okay, Doc. I get it. I'm not *happy*, of course, but I'm probably not going to die. I actually feel pretty good, physically." Ivan held up his arm and flexed it. "I used to have twinges with my elbow sometimes. Old football injury. It's completely gone. So there's some upside, I guess."

Kemp turned and picked up a blood collection kit. "I can't take this from the usual locations, obviously. I'll try to be gentle." The doctor swabbed Ivan's pectoral muscle, then held up the needle. "Ready?"

Ivan nodded, and the doctor collected a blood sample. It hurt like a sonofabitch, but Ivan found himself not minding. It might be one of the last human sensations he would ever experience.

Finally finished, the doctor sat back and crossed his legs. "So how do you feel otherwise, Ivan? Any other symptoms, issues? Concerns?"

"Like I said, I feel great, physically." Ivan looked at the ceiling for a moment. "What I'm really worried about…" He took a moment to get his voice under control. "What I'm really worried about is whether I'll still be there when the process is complete. Will it be *me*? Or will there be an alien something looking out of my eyes? Will it *remember* being me? Will it even *care?*" Ivan squeezed his eyes then looked at the doctor. "Am I ever going to see my family again? Is there *any* version of this where I end up going home?"

Dr. Kemp was silent for several seconds. "I wish I had an answer for you, Ivan. We're all out of our depth, here."

The doctor took a marking pen from a drawer. "If you don't mind, Ivan, I want to track the conversion." At Ivan's nod, Kemp made a series of regularly spaced marks on Ivan's torso, starting from the point where metal met flesh. He then added numbers, starting from zero.

"That's exactly the kind of obsessive attention to detail that I can appreciate, Doc. I just wish it wasn't me being measured."

"Look, Ivan, we're all equally in the dark. But based on what I said yesterday, I don't think this is an *attack* of some kind. Maybe it's an attempt to communicate. I think it's a fair bet that whatever engineered this isn't human, so we can't safely assume human motivations, but we can expect consistency." Dr. Kemp tapped the palm of his hand with the marker while he considered. "If it's taking care not to cause undue harm, I can't see it suddenly changing course and becoming like a movie monster."

"Unless it didn't want me to be spaced before the conversion was complete."

"Okay, granted, but then the best strategy would be to go after everyone at once. And to disable the ship quickly. However alien the intelligence behind this is, we still should expect it to act in a sane, consistent manner."

"You've decided it's alien?" Ivan cocked his head and smiled slightly.

"Haven't you?"

"Yeah, I guess that's where I'd put my money."

18. Strategy Meeting

Dr. Kemp looked around the table. All the ship's bridge staff were present. Several muttered conversations provided a low susurrus of sound, barely above the level of the air system. Captain Jennings slowly stirred his coffee, gathering his thoughts before he looked up.

"Record this meeting, please, *Astra*. For the record, present are: myself, Andrew Jennings, captain of the *Mad Astra*; First Mate Dante Aiello; pilot Albert Micoroski; co-pilot and purser Lita Generus; Charles Kemp, ship's doctor; and Duncan MacNeil, chief engineer. The purpose of this meeting is to discuss the unexplained transmutation of crewman Ivan Pritchard into a being made of metal."

The captain looked around the table. No one spoke. He gestured to Kemp. "Please start the ball rolling, doctor."

Kemp played with the documents on his tablet, unexpectedly nervous. This meeting would go on the record. Every word, every document, every hesitation might end up being analyzed for years by—he wasn't really sure by whom.

"During an exploration of a small asteroid where a density anomaly had been detected, Pritchard was exposed to an unknown substance, which coated his suit arm. The crew removed the suit arm and got Pritchard into the airlock. There was no obvious indication that the substance had penetrated the suit, and a medical examination of Pritchard revealed nothing unexpected."

Kemp paused to flip the document on his tablet. He had made notes, to keep his narrative focused more than anything else. He knew he would have a tendency to wander into conjecture otherwise.

"The next morning, the subject woke up with his arm partly converted to metal..." The retelling was almost hypnotic, and Kemp found himself having to avoid going into a sing-song tone of voice as he continued. His report stuck to observations and facts; no analysis, no theorizing.

Finally, he was done, and he looked to the captain.

Jennings turned to Chief MacNeil. "Technical analysis, Chief?"

MacNeil leaned forward, enthusiasm written plainly on his face. "The metal composition of the subject's new limbs is not continuous. Rather, it is composed of a number of what we're calling nanites—individual machines, somewhat smaller than a human cell. They are not identical, instead consisting of non-periodic shapes consistent with Penrose Tiles, but a three-dimensional version. They link together, forming what could be described as a mesh. Flexible, but extremely strong. And self-healing. Attempts to scrape off a sample have been frustrating, even if ultimately successful. The units flow around the tool and re-form behind it. We finally had to rig up something that would bite off a chunk and sequester it."

"There is no apparent central control unit, or any indication of conscious intelligence. Despite this, the infectious agent seems to behave in an intelligent, coordinated manner." MacNeil jerked, seemingly realizing that he was straying into speculation. And stepping on Kemp's turf. He looked over at the doctor before continuing.

"The substance that was separated from the subject during the initial amputation had made its way through the ship in very close to a bee-line back to the subject. It apparently avoided critical systems and components, which would indicate an understanding of our ship's design, at least on a general level."

Now came the less honest part. Kemp knew that MacNeil wasn't happy with this plan. None of them was.

"We placed a beacon on the asteroid where the anomaly was found. Identification number is in the notes."

It was a lie of omission. Kemp doubted they'd have been able to persuade MacNeil to lie outright on the record. But not mentioning the part where they moved the asteroid, or the part where they waited almost a week before activating the beacon, was apparently at least tolerable.

Captain Jennings looked to Kemp again. "What is the status of the subject, Doctor?"

"He is now metallized up to mid-chest. Only above that line is he still human. The process shows no signs of stopping.

"The metallized body is still providing blood to his head, proper levels of hormones, oxygen, glycogen, and so on; and is cleaning the blood of toxins and waste in a manner indistinguishable from a normal body. I consider it a positive that the infection is putting so much effort into keeping the subject alive."

"Prognosis?"

Kemp shook his head. "It would be rank speculation, Captain. We don't know if the process will continue, although it looks like it at the moment. We don't know if Ivan Pritchard will continue to exist as an individual once the process is complete. The subject is understandably concerned about that question, himself. It's not unlike facing the possibility of imminent death. I've seen the same reactions from people about to undergo dangerous surgery that they might not survive. Imagine going under with the fear that you might simply never wake up."

"Any sign of infection in any other crew, doctor?"

"None. The infection seems to be completely focused on Ivan. No nanites have been detected in other crew, and to the extent that Mr. MacNeil and I have been able to determine, they aren't wandering about on the loose, other than for the scavenging."

Captain Jennings nodded, then spoke into the air. "Under the circumstances, we can't risk returning directly to Earth, or to any public terminus. We are therefore requesting that the ICDC set up some form of isolation while the ship and crew are examined for continued infection, and while the situation is evaluated for long-term dangers."

The captain sighed, then pressed a button on his chair. "End of report. *Astra*, please bundle up all pertinent records and forward them to the ICDC."

He looked around the table. "And may God have mercy on our souls."

19. Writing Home

Dear Judy,

Please keep this away from the kids.

Something has happened. I can't go into much detail, because, honestly, I'm not sure of the details myself. But the bottom line is, I'm sick. I seem to have caught something on one of the rocks we were prospecting. No one is sure what it is, but we're worried about it spreading. So the captain has contacted the ICDC and we'll be quarantined.

I'm not dying, I don't think. That's the good news. And the strike's been confirmed, the money's been paid, and we're now wealthy beyond our wildest dreams, as soon as escrow clears. That's pretty good, too.

But I may be contagious, and I may continue to be contagious. They just don't know enough, yet.

Judy, I love you so much, and I want to return to you and spend the rest of our lives spending our money in frivolous ways. But if worst comes to worst, and this doesn't work out, I'm glad that I'll have managed to make your futures so much better.

I'll keep you up to date. I'll call as soon as we're close enough for real-time. Please try not to worry.

Love,

Ivan

Ivan hesitated for several seconds, staring at what he'd typed. How could he tell her that he might not even exist in a few more days? How could he explain that, even if he did, he might never be allowed to leave?

Not yet. He owed it to her to let her know something was wrong. But the rest...he'd have to think on it. With an angry jab, he pressed *send.*

He wanted so much just to go home, to hold Judy in his arms. He wanted the family dogpiles on the ratty old couch. And, mostly, he just wanted to touch them one more time.

It wasn't going to happen. Ivan looked at his hands. Chrome, all the way up. There was no cure for this. And it probably wasn't going to stop. He was dead, for all practical purposes. He poked the interface on his chest, the point where flesh met metal. The difference in texture was obvious.

From the inside, it felt no different. He could feel his fingers poking the chrome part of his chest. The sensation was neither more nor less sensitive, or odd in any way. Even his fingers seemed to have the same sense of touch. But from the outside...

Ivan stared at his fingers for several seconds more, then slowly moved the keyboard and put his head down on the desk. His shoulders shook, then his hands. Within seconds, he was sobbing, his cheeks pulled back in a rictus of emotional overload.

Between ragged breaths, he kept repeating, "Oh, God, Judy, I love you. I'm so sorry, I'm so sorry..."

Eventually, wrung out, he threw himself on his bunk and was unconscious within seconds.

20. ICDC

Dr. Madhur Narang looked up from the file. "Is this a joke?" She noted in passing that the slight lilt in her voice from her New Delhi origins had become more pronounced. That happened when she became excited, which made her a truly awful poker player.

"I wish it was." Dr. Karin Laakkonen, ICDC director and Narang's immediate boss, waved a hand toward the folder. "We received this yesterday, and we've verified the source. It's a class-IV Chrysler-Morrison mining ship, the *Mad Astra*, returning early from a tour of the belt. They have recently registered a large strike, so are not motivated to casually create any kind of controversy. I've had some people look at the supporting documentation, and it's not obviously faked."

"What are we planning to do?"

"Well, we *do* have plans in place for isolating incoming space ships. Thus the word *Interplanetary* at the beginning of our name. I've asked the Isolation Systems people to have something ready, and we've sent orders to the *Astra* to proceed to the specified coordinates."

Laakkonen poked at her tablet. "Which brings us to this meeting, Madhur. I'm putting you in charge of the case. Benton is more senior than you, but she is somewhat unimaginative and by-the-book. I don't think that's optimal for this particular situation."

Narang grinned at her boss, silently agreeing. Dr. Sydney Benton was a knowledgeable doctor and an excellent technician, but far too inclined to retreat into standard procedures when things went off the rails.

Her tablet beeped, and Dr. Narang looked down to see the file that her boss had just sent. She quickly flipped through it. Travel itinerary, authorizations, contacts… Narang smiled. She was going into space.

Dr. Laakkonen chuckled, correctly guessing the reason for Narang's expression. "This is your first time, isn't it?"

"I've had all the courses, of course. But I've never been up higher than sub-orbital."

Laakkonen was silent for several seconds, and took on a serious expression. "Maddie, this smells. We both know it. If we take the report at face value, you know what it implies, right?"

Narang's voice was hushed. "First Contact."

Laakkonen nodded. "With all the social and political upheaval that implies. Even without the Grey Goo or Space Invaders narratives. Tread carefully. Be very careful with what you say. We don't want to start a panic."

Narang had a feeling that some level of public panic was inevitable. "We'll have to keep a very tight lid on this one."

"While not appearing to be doing so. And something will get out eventually anyway. That's my responsibility, Maddie. You just worry about the actual incident." Laakkonen stood and stuck out her hand. "Good luck, Dr. Narang. Here's hoping this turns out to be overblown."

* * *

Six hours later, Dr. Narang was on Olympus Station, seated in a public lounge. She watched the crowds file past in both directions as she waited for her Navy contact to make an appearance. Meanwhile, the bench was comfortable, she was early, and she was *in space!* Olympus Station, the hub of the Solar System. Very possibly the most important place *in* the Solar System. From here, ships headed to the research stations at Mercury's poles, to the orbiting platforms around Venus, the Lunar and Martian colonies, the Belt, even the Titan and Ganymede outposts.

The shuttle trip had been an experience, though. Narang decided she'd prefer to stay spaceside or groundside as long as possible. Commuting would be several layers of hell, although one might get used to it eventually.

The people walking by seemed an even mix of military, civilian professionals of one kind or another on some personal mission, and just plain tourists. Narang found herself mildly surprised that there were still people with enough wealth to consider a trip into space as nothing more than a vacation getaway. Like going to Miami. Back when there was a Florida.

Her phone buzzed, and Narang looked at the screen. Her Meetup app was registering the presence of her designated contact.

She stood and turned away from the crowds and spotted the uniformed man approaching. *He's just a baby.* The officer looked like a poster boy for recruitment ads. Emphasis on *boy.* When had she gotten old enough to think of people that way?

The window behind him displayed a slowly rotating panorama of stars, with a bright three-quarter moon glowing in the background. A studio director would have swooned over the setup. Immaculately pressed uniform, short, wavy chestnut hair, and a good, strong chin completed the picture. She could almost believe his image had been digitally cleaned up, except this was live.

Unaware of the internal drama he was generating, he stuck out his hand. "Dr. Madhur Narang?"

She took the hand. "That's me. Presumably you're my contact."

"Lieutenant George Bentley, at your service." He gave her a natural, friendly smile. That was encouraging, at least. Thank the universe he didn't appear to be either a by-the-book, rigid military type, or a preening, self-absorbed pretty boy. She had a bad tendency to needle people who were too full of themselves.

They wove their way through the crowds to the traxi station and signaled for a ride. Within moments, an automated cart rolled up the exit ramp from the roadway and stopped in front of them. They sat down, and Lt. Bentley spoke a destination. The traxi's panel flashed up the words "Restricted Site" followed by "Authorization Recognized". The traxi accelerated down the entrance ramp and merged into the automated traffic level, and they sped around the circumference of the station.

Once they were underway, Lt. Bentley turned to her. "I read the file. As Admiral Moore's assistant, I have the required access. This isn't some kind of complicated test of the system, is it?"

Narang shook her head and gave him a lopsided smile. "If it's some kind of massive put-on, I'm in the victim group, too. I've decided I'm just going to go with standard procedure, based on a generic emergent situation, until I see a reason to behave otherwise."

"Fair enough. Although I expect you'll have to repeat that at the briefing." Lt. Bentley turned to face forward with no further comment, and Narang took the opportunity to review what she knew as the traxi continued along the roadway.

It took only another minute for them to arrive. The traxi took the exit ramp to the station and they got off. Without a word, the lieutenant pointed to a set of offices clearly marked with the symbol of the United Earth Nations Navy.

Once through the doors, Lt. Bentley spoke briefly with the receptionist. She motioned with a hand, and gave him what sounded like a room number.

The destination turned out to be a conference room, with a sophisticated audio-visual system, including a latest-gen holotank in the middle of the table.

Six officers were already seated. Dr. Narang wasn't great with military insignia, but going with the premise that more chrome means higher rank, she estimated that she was in the presence of some very heavy hitters.

Lt. Bentley seated himself at the foot of the table, further reinforcing her estimate of the level of seniority.

"Dr. Narang," the officer closest to her said. "I'm Admiral Ted Moore. These are Commodore Michael Gerrard, Admiral Alan Castillo, Rear Admiral Georgia Richards, Commodore Alice Nevin, and Lt. Colonel Neil Martinson from the Marines." The officers nodded as they were named.

"I admit to being a bit confused." Dr. Narang looked around the table. "Our standard shared protocol calls for the military to provide an isolated hab platform to service the quarantine of the subject vessel. There's no mention of the entire Chiefs of Staff assisting."

The assembled officers chuckled at the bit of humor. Admiral Moore smiled, but it didn't reach his eyes. Narang decided that he was her most likely adversary in any power clash. Late fifties, gray hair done in typical military buzz cut, and square-built, the admiral looked like the type of person who rarely took anything other than the straightest line to a goal. No subtlety, no wasted energy.

"Dr. Narang, I wouldn't call this a *standard* incident," Admiral Moore replied, losing the smile. "The common opinion is that this is alien technology. I think that fact renders this, at least somewhat, a military matter."

Dr. Narang nodded and sat back. "Well, I guess I shouldn't be surprised, since you have access to the contents of the file. And I don't disagree with you about the *alien* part. However, there are protocols to deal with alien contact, and they don't mandate a military presence."

"True," the admiral said. "But those are predicated on actual aliens that can be, at least in principle, negotiated with. What we have here looks more like a piece of technology gone rogue. Even if you don't assume a military purpose, I think you'd have to admit there are definite military and security implications."

"I see your point, Admiral. However, your role in this situation is, at least at the moment, purely logistical support. I hope I won't have to be constantly fending you off. No offense."

Admiral Moore smiled again, this time showing some actual warmth. "None taken, doctor. We're quite used to being the bad guys by default, as are you, I would imagine. But one of our number..."—the admiral waved a hand toward Commodore Nevin, who nodded—"has a niece on the *Mad Astra*, as it happens, so I think you can depend on this committee taking a soft approach to the problem, regardless of the stereotypes."

Dr. Narang nodded in agreement. It never paid to think of people in terms of clichés. The admiral had good intel and had drawn some valid conclusions. She would have to accept that this was going to be a joint operation.

"The *Mad Astra* will be here in a few more days," Admiral Moore continued. "We will have the isolation module completed, per the requirements of the Joint Isolation Protocol. Bentley will let you know when it's ready for inspection."

"Excellent, thank you." Narang flipped open her tablet and pulled up a document. "I do have some issues and concerns..."

She was fairly certain she saw a not-quite-suppressed sigh from Admiral Moore. Narang tried not to smile. Let the games begin.

21. A Difficult Conversation

Ivan nervously stroked the spot on his upper chest where metal met flesh. The interface had absorbed several of Dr. Kemp's felt pen marks, leaving no trace of discoloration in the metal. The disappearance of each mark felt like a further loss of his humanity.

They were now close enough to Earth for a live video chat with his wife. He'd been dreading this moment. Email was impersonal, a step removed from contact. You could think about what you wanted to say, phrase things to give a desired impression, avoid or ignore uncomfortable questions. Not so with a live call.

A quick email to Judy had ensured that he'd be talking to the children first. Not that there was any hope of holding them off—Josh and Suzie were about as patient as any other kids their age. He was wearing his coveralls, and he would make sure not to bring his hands into frame. The children would see only the face of their father, entirely normal. But if he could satisfy them, have Judy hustle them off—then came the hard part. Judy would see any attempt to deflect and would zero in on whatever he was trying to avoid. There was no point in trying to soft-pedal or spare her the gory details. And she deserved better. She deserved his trust, and she deserved the truth.

Ivan reached for the *connect* button yet again, hesitated, and with a snarl of frustration, stabbed down on it with his finger.

There was the usual delay for a space-to-ground call, then the screen filled with the faces of his children. "DADDY!"

Ivan smiled, almost sobbed, and his eyes welled up. His throat constricted and he couldn't have made a sound if his life depended on it. Not that it mattered. Josh and Suzie were both talking in a steady stream, neither seemingly bothered by the fact that the other was speaking about something entirely unrelated.

Finally the verbal assault petered out, and his children stopped to draw a collective breath. Ivan grinned and said, "Sorry, did you say something?"

"DADDY!" Twin frowns of mock disapproval answered him.

The next several minutes were a blur. Ivan luxuriated in the sight and sound of his family; the children competing for maximum face and voice time, while Judy hovered in the background, trying to look patient and calm.

Finally, his wife stepped in. "Okay, enough. I have to talk to your father. And you have homework. Move it."

There were groans of frustration and then a flurry of "Bye, Daddy," before the children left the room. Ivan watched Judy close the door to the bedroom, then turn back to the phone. *Here it comes.*

"All right, Ivan. Spill. What's this all about?"

In as calm a voice as he could manage, Ivan told her.

* * *

Judy's eyes had that look—lots of white, pupils dilated, the shine of incipient tears. Shock. Her mouth moved a few times, but no sound came out. Finally she said, "Show me."

Ivan had decided to be as matter-of-fact as he could. The more he acted horrified, the more Judy would feel that. Without comment or buildup, he held up a hand into frame.

Judy's hand went to her mouth and a whimper escaped. Unbidden, tears began to flow. Ivan felt his own eyes well up in response.

"Ivan, I'm scared. Will it stop? Will you be able to come home?"

Ivan gazed at his wife, the only woman he'd ever loved. He had no answer.

22. Consternation

Seth came into the common room. "Word is we're going to be quarantined at one of the military stations." He sat down and plunked his coffee on the table with a *thump*. "Probably the Lagrange Four Navy station."

"So the military is taking over?"

"Naw," Aspasia answered. "The ICDC has a number of canned protocols for different scenarios. Some of them involve getting help from the military." She paused and sipped her coffee. "For an incoming ship that needs to be quarantined, the ICDC doesn't have any standing space assets. The military steps in, in these situations, and provides hardware and facilities."

"How do you know about this stuff?"

"Friends in high places," Aspasia grinned. "Actually, relatives in the Navy. You learn a lot at Christmas dinners."

Tenn looked over from where he'd been nursing his coffee. "If that moron noob hadn't touched the thingamahooie, we'd be heading home as heroes. Rich heroes."

"Oh for chrissake, Tenn," Seth retorted. "We all went over to the Baby Rock. *You* invited yourself over. You *placed a bet* with him. Hindsight is wonderfully convenient."

Tenn sneered. "That's all very moral and everything, Robinson. But some people can't seem to stay out of trouble. They'll always choose the riskier action, they'll always stick their hand in to test something, and they'll always be there when trouble happens. The sprout is turning out to be a bit of a Jonah."

"Say, aren't you a billionaire, nowadays?"

"Yeah, nothing to do with him, Robinson."

"But the presence of an alien artifact is all his fault. Nice cherry-picking, Davies."

"Tenn's not entirely wrong, though," Will interjected. "About *some people*, I mean, not necessarily about Ivan. In high school, we had a couple of guys who always seemed to be in the middle of any mess that happened. One day in Chemistry class, the prof passed around sealed ampoules of various chemicals for students to examine. One was pure elemental chlorine. As I looked at it and passed it to the next student, I said to myself, 'The idiots will drop it. Just watch.' The chlorine ampoule got to the idiots and sure enough. Couldn't have taken even five seconds. We had to clear the room and bring in hazmat."

Seth shook his head and glared at Will. "And how the hell does that tie in to this situation?"

"Some people," Will replied, "when given a choice of caution or impetuousness, will always go for the latter. Some people will always try to show their bravery by juggling the dangerous vial in the air. Some people will always poke the unknown thingy with a finger. They're not unlucky. They make decisions that are more likely to be dangerous."

"And you think that's Ivan? When did he ever give you that impression?" Seth gave Will a look of disbelief.

"*How bad can it be?*" Tenn said. "Those were his exact words, just before he touched the thing."

"Yeah. Right after you bet him his desserts against you prepping meals. Way to preach caution, there, Major Safety. What are you *really* after, Davies?"

"What I'm *really* after, Robinson, is going home. I hope the ICDC concentrates on Pritchard and lets us go. And I don't particularly care about some yammering about loyalty. Pritchard made a choice when he reached for that thing. I don't feel like paying for that choice."

Aspasia glared at Tenn for five long seconds. "What you really want is to hate the noob so you don't have to feel bad about going home and leaving him to the wolves." She got up. "Well, I do feel bad about it. But I also know there's not a damn thing we can do. Assuming," she swept the room with her gaze, "that they let the rest of us go at all. Something that is not guaranteed."

A heavy silence settled over the room, and no one would meet anyone's eyes.

23. The Chrome Man

Dr. Kemp stood outside the sick bay door, trying to control his breathing. He had to be prepared for whatever he would find on the other side. He absolutely must behave professionally, with a doctor's detachment. *Above all, do no harm.* That included not only treatment of the patient, but how he dealt with the person.

Assuming he *was* still dealing with a person.

Dr. Kemp thrust that last thought away, and reached for the door.

Ivan was sitting on the cot, elbows on his thighs, slouched forward and looking at his hands. At Dr. Kemp's entry, Ivan looked up and Kemp looked into his eyes.

Silver eyes. In a chrome face.

"I looked in the mirror this morning," Ivan said. "I wanted to cry, but I can't. I don't think my new head supports the function."

"That's an odd way to phrase it," Kemp said, sitting down on a stool.

Ivan gave him a sad smile. "Small joke. Very small. Apparently the transformation hasn't improved my humor."

Dr. Kemp attempted a quick smile in return. "You sound like you're still Ivan. That's something, anyway."

"I've been going through my memories, which seem to be all there. There are no obvious holes or gaps, anyway. I've been thinking about stuff, and how I acted, and whether it seems to make sense now. I'm embarrassed about the same stupid things that I've done, proud of the same things, and so on. I still love my wife. I'm still worried about my family. All my past behaviors and attitudes seem to be consistent with how I think and feel now. I still *seem* to be me. But I can't be, can I? There's nothing left of me. I'm a machine that thinks it's Ivan Pritchard."

"Ivan, there's an old saying that you replace every atom in your body every seven years. Reality isn't quite that simple, of course, but if you could actually tag atoms, most of me wasn't me a decade ago. Cells die, get replaced. Food comes in, builds more cells, and so on. I'm literally not the same person I used to be. So it's not the specific matter that makes you, you."

Kemp sat back. "There's a thought experiment about this. Let's say you suffer a stroke, and it affects, oh, I dunno, your sight. They've invented an artificial neuron, and it's a drop-in replacement, so they replace the damaged part of your brain and your vision is fixed. But are you still you?"

Kemp tapped the side of his head. "Part of your brain is now artificial. But you're still you. Now, a few years later, the same thing happens to a different part of your brain, with the same fix. Do that a few dozen more times over the years. Now thirty percent of your brain is artificial. Are you still you? Keep it going until ninety percent of your brain is artificial. At what point do you stop being you? There was no discontinuity. You didn't wake up a million miles away. You were you from one moment to the next, you have continuous memories of everything, except when you're sleeping, of course.

"The philosophical thinking is that it's the continuity that is telling. If you can trace a continuous path through four-dimensional space-time from your birth to you right now, then you are, in a very real way, still you."

Ivan smiled. "Cool. I'm not sure if it makes me feel better or not, yet. But I'll think about it."

Kemp nodded. "We've contacted ICDC about this whole thing. We'll be quarantined, and they'll probably take the ship apart bolt by bolt. Eventually, probably they'll let us go. I don't know what'll happen with you. This is kind of a first for all of us."

"I understand," Ivan said. "But the claim? The money? Is that still safe?"

"Absolutely. Everything to do with that is proceeding well. The winning bidder, Consolidated Industrials, has already launched their own ship to assay the rock. In two weeks, they'll confirm the deal, and we will all be—and I say this without any trace of exaggeration—billionaires. The strike is all over the news on Earth. They're calling it the biggest find in fifty years."

"I can put up with almost anything as long as my family will be okay. I accepted the possibility of dying up here. I even, at one point, did a calculation of whether my family would be better off if I could have an accident. The insurance is pretty good."

"You'd probably have run afoul of the exclusions."

"Yep. Fail. Anyway, the idea of a big strike was a lot more attractive, even if a long shot. And, meanwhile, the pay was good."

Kemp looked closely at Ivan. He seemed a lot calmer than he had been at any point leading up to this moment. Was that fatalism? Relief that it was over? Relief that it wasn't worse? Or was there a fundamental difference in his personality?

"What made you decide on asteroid mining, Ivan?"

"Life. Life on Earth. It's stacked against you, you know? If you aren't born to a well-off family, so you have a head start, you're screwed. If you're born in the wrong place, one of the areas that's going under water soon, you're screwed. If you can't get a good education, then a good job with one of the multinationals, you're screwed. Meanwhile, the habitable area of Earth shrinks and shrinks, driving the population into a smaller space, and driving the price of a home up every year, even if all you can do is rent."

Kemp nodded. "Even being in the medical profession doesn't guarantee a better life, these days. We'll all be living in domes soon, whether you're on Earth, the moon, Mars, or floating in the atmosphere of Venus."

Ivan continued after a moment. "My wife, she's an actuary. She can do the numbers. We would be falling farther behind every year. Further in debt, fewer assets, never catching up. The mining thing, it was short-term pain, but it could have reversed the flow. We could break even, then even get slightly ahead. Better pay, the ship absorbs my living expenses for most of the year, the guild takes care of life insurance... In the worst case, paying off the debt for the training and the share might have taken the rest of my life and then some, but any strike at all would be a bonus."

He gave Dr. Kemp a brief, rueful smile. "She even had the chances of that worked out. Actuary, right? It was a reasonable risk. Except now, I may die up here without ever touching her or my kids again."

The two men were silent for a few moments. It was a common

topic of conversation, as predictable and well-worn as politics or the ongoing cold war with the SSE.

"Am I news all over Earth?" Ivan asked.

"I'm not privy to everything that goes on, Ivan, but I don't think it's been made public. The captain would have played everything very close to the vest in order to not screw up the bid process. The ICDC doesn't want a panic over the possibility of extraterrestrial contact, or even just a lot of armchair generals telling them how it *should* be handled. Not that you're actually an alien in the normal sense of the word."

"I do feel something, though. Something there. It started this morning, when I woke up. I think it's because my conversion is complete."

Kemp's eyes widened. He tried to remain as outwardly calm as possible. "How do you mean?"

Ivan sighed. "I can't put my finger on it, quite yet. It might even be just my overheated imagination. But I feel as if there's something in the background. It's like when you can't quite remember a word, or someone's name, or what you did last Wednesday. Except I'm having that just-out-of-reach feeling about things that I don't know anything about. It's like tip-of-the-tongue times ten." He scrubbed his face with his hands, an act that created a strange *scritch* sound. "And a couple of times, I've gotten a picture of a bear cub. Why a bear? And why a little one?"

"If what you're saying is true, Ivan, that may just be something poking the neurons that contain your concept of *bear.* Like when surgeons are mapping a patient's brain using electrodes."

"I'll have to ask it if it can find the *coffee* neuron, then." Ivan smiled briefly, but he seemed to have run down, for the moment. The resigned expression on his face reminded Kemp of patients who had just come to terms with a terminal diagnosis.

"Uh, does caffeine still affect you?"

"Don't know. I hope so, or I'm really going to be pissed."

Kemp chuckled and stood. "All right, Ivan. Let me know if anything comes into focus for you, okay?"

"Will do, doc."

Kemp walked slowly out of the sick bay. Not since his first days as an intern had he felt so completely helpless.

24. The Way Things Must Be

Ivan reached for the keyboard for perhaps the tenth time. After a second, he withdrew his hands. He read what he'd written so far.

Dear Judy,

Well, it was a start. Of sorts.

How do you tell your wife that you'll probably never see her again? How does she explain to your kids that daddy won't be coming home, ever? Millions of people had faced this or similar dilemmas through history. Maybe not exactly these circumstances. But still.

Maybe start with facts.

We'll be quarantined at the Lagrange Four Naval base. So far, no one else has caught it. I might end up being the only victim.

Victim. There had to be a better word. He didn't want to make it sound like he was dying. But did it matter? He wouldn't be going home. Even if he did, how would she react when she saw him? How would his children react? Would they cower? Run? Scream? Ivan put his face in his hands. He'd rather be dead, right now, than have to experience that.

At least he wouldn't be leaving them destitute. He had to hold onto that. He could endure anything if they were okay. Even never seeing them again.

Ivan looked up at the ceiling and took a shaky breath. He missed crying.

He flipped to another window, one showing the official paperwork from the auction house and the *Mad Astra*. The number was staggering. Not quite infinite money, but unless Judy wanted to buy an island or something, there would be no more worries.

The thought brought peace, of a sort. He'd always said he would die for his family without hesitation. In a backhanded way, this situation could be looked at like that.

He resolved to hold onto that thought as he continued writing.

The process is complete. There's no ME left. Judy, I don't know what they can do at this point. Maybe if they can contact whoever did this. But how?

We can still talk, and we can still email. But I remember the look on your face when I showed you my hand. I can't bear to see that look again. I want you to remember me with the face you've always known. I don't want this new face to be how you think of me.

He stared at the display for what felt like forever. Nothing more came to mind. Or too much. If he started typing again, he might never stop. It already sounded like one of those letters you compose to be read after your death.

Finally, he signed it…

Love forever,
Ivan

…and pressed *send.*

25. Crew Reaction

"Is it even still Ivan?"

Seth glared at Raul. It looked like another Ivan-bashing session was starting up.

"C'mon, Seth. You've heard what Kemp said. There's nothing biological left. He, or it, is all metal." Raul sighed, hesitating for a moment. "Look, I know most of you don't think much of my beliefs, and I try to keep it out of conversations, but not this time. Ivan is dead. He's gone. Something has taken his place and is pretending to be him. Whatever's in Ivan's room, lying on his bunk, does not have a soul."

"And you know this because..." Aspasia spoke calmly, but Seth knew that the expression on her face meant trouble.

Raul was either oblivious, or past the point of caring. "Yeah, yeah, I know, make fun of my religion. Nevertheless, it doesn't give me a lot of leeway on this."

"Only if you blindly adhere to doctrine," Aspasia answered. "If you assume that Ivan isn't lying, then he sees himself as still *him*. Which means he has the same morals, the same priorities, and the same capacity for and knowledge of good or evil—by whatever definition you want to use. How can he still be a sentient being, but be of less value now?"

"You're assuming he's still sentient," Raul said.

"And you're assuming he's not. I think if you want to take away his rights, or whatever it is you're aiming at, you'd better do a little more than just make assertions. You're not in a position of authority, moral or otherwise."

"Then who is? *Someone* has to make the decision, Aspasia."

"And that's your justification? Someone has to, so you're as good as any?"

"And why not? I can—"

"Jesus H. Christ on a crutch, with bunnies on top! Can you two put a cork in it?" Tenn glared from one combatant to the other. "No one asked either of you to make a decision about Pritchard's immortal soul or lack of it."

Raul glared at Tenn. "Maybe not, Davies, but there are a lot of religious people out there. And I can say this with some confidence—most of them will agree with me. And I'm not sure they'll all limit themselves to heated discussions across the lunch table."

Aspasia flashed him a smile that verged on being a sneer. "Well, those assertions we can agree on."

An uneasy silence settled on the room, as each person retreated to their own thoughts.

26. In the Common Room

Ivan wasn't actually quarantined. The captain hadn't actually issued an order requiring him to stay in his cabin. He rehearsed these statements as he stared at the door.

Finally, having generated enough courage, Ivan reached for the release. He stepped out into the corridor and looked both ways. It felt as if years had passed, and he was freshly paroled. He spent only a moment savoring the feeling of freedom before turning in the direction of the common room.

Tenn, Will, and Raul sat at a table, nursing coffees. The sudden silence as he stepped into view probably said all that needed to be said about his level of welcome. Ivan gave them an embarrassed smile and headed for the coffee machine. He'd been missing coffee—the subtle kick from that first cup was one of those rituals that made him feel in control of his day.

He drew a coffee, the sound of the flowing liquid filling the silence in the room. He held the steaming cup under his nose, and inhaled the aroma of fresh, quality coffee. *Nose still works. That's good.*

Ivan turned in the direction of his crewmates, and was dismayed to see them look away quickly. Will, at least, looked embarrassed, but the thin line of his lips showed his determination. Defeated, Ivan aimed for a table at the other end of the room. He took a quick sip of the coffee, and—*what the hell?*

He couldn't swallow. He wasn't choking, but he simply couldn't form the action. He could taste the coffee in his mouth, he could feel it cooling, but…

After a few frustrating moments, Ivan spit the coffee back into his cup, then poured it down the sink. So now drinking was out. The conversion seemed to be slowly stripping parts of his life away. Maybe he really was just an imitation of a person.

As he handed the empty cup to the dishwasher mech, Ivan felt a sudden jolt of rage and hate, accompanied by the image of the bear cub. It didn't make sense. The mech wasn't at fault, and anyway, the reaction was out of character for him. Assuming those emotions were even coming from him. What if they weren't? What if his transformation came with an alien consciousness? It would at least explain the bear cub.

Ivan walked slowly out of the common room, pondering the possibility that he wasn't alone in his head.

27. Most Paranoid Wins

Josh had made the soccer team. Suzie was in the semi-finals in her chess tournament at school. Judy's boss had been passed up for a promotion, the position going to the CEO's nephew. The email had the usual updates about all things family that you could expect to get when you were away from home. But nothing more. Events. Descriptions. Like the annual Christmas letter to relatives.

Then, at the bottom, two words. *Call me.*

Well, it turned out it was possible for a metal man to be terrified. Call that proven.

Ivan picked up the phone, selected *audio only*, and dialed home.

"Hello?"

"Hi, Judy, it's me."

"Oh, God, I'm glad you called. I can't—when I try to write an email, it just comes out sounding like a diary. I wanted—"

"I understand, babe. Email's good for relaying facts, but there's too much time to think. Let's just keep it this way. Email for updates, phone for us."

"And the kids?"

"And the kids, if we can arrange a time."

"You're not going to turn on video?"

"Judy, it would terrify the kids. And it would make you cry, and then I'd want to cry, and I—"

"What?"

"Never mind. Just think of me as having advanced leprosy and my face is falling off."

"Thanks, Bud. Now I've got that image in my head."

They laughed together. It felt good. Like the old Judy and Ivan, always on the same wavelength.

"Listen, Ivan, there are rumors."

"Oh?"

"Some ship has been placed in quarantine. There's a disease, or an alien. Details are all over the place. But something's getting out to the public."

That was bad. That could be *really* bad. Ivan had seen food riots. He understood what fear and helplessness could do. "Wow. And we haven't even arrived yet. Listen, Judy, you know our deal..."

"Most paranoid wins?"

"Yeah."

He and Judy had made a deal early in their marriage. In any situation, whether it involved the children's health, or money, or anything, whoever was the most concerned got priority. If one of them thought a doctor should be called, then a doctor would be called. If one of them thought a situation was dangerous, they'd leave.

"No one knows about the money yet, right? Keep it that way. As soon as escrow is removed, I want you to very quietly move. But quickly. Don't leave any more forwarding information than you have to."

"Ivan, what's going on?"

"Nothing yet, babe. Nothing specific. But those rumors—I think they're going to get worse. This could get really badly unshiny. And I think it'd be bad for a while."

"Why?"

"Judy, I went to the common room a while back, to get a coffee. No one would talk to me, or look at me, or anything. These are people who *know* me. Some of them are friends. Or were. How do you think the average guy on the street is going to react?"

"Ivan, you aren't a monster."

"Well, that's the thing, babe. I kind of am."

Judy was silent for a moment. "Are you different? Inside? Or anything?"

"No, still me, just a new paint job. But that's not the way people will see it."

They talked for a few more minutes. Ivan tried to savor every moment. He had to treat each call as his last, because it was entirely possible that one of them would turn out to be just that.

He hated lying to Judy, but it was possible that the call was either being monitored or recorded. Once they arrived at Lagrange Four, he would be under the government's thumb. Admitting to some of the things going on in his head would pretty much guarantee the very eventuality he feared. The moment the government felt justified in categorizing him as an alien risk, all the protections guaranteed him by the New Liberation would be stripped away. And Ivan would very probably disappear.

There had to be a point to this. Whatever had created the booby trap had to have a purpose, a plan. Common sense dictated that he find out what that was, and whether it was a danger to his family and to humanity in general. Caution dictated that he not let anything get loose, even if that 'anything' was him.

He would have to navigate a delicate balancing act, not giving the government enough reason to end him, but still giving them enough reason to keep him locked up and under study. At least until he knew enough to make further plans.

And eventually, whoever or whatever had done this to him would make a move, or give a sign, or something.

28. Taking Courses

Ivan sat back with a sigh. He'd just powered through his astronomy course in six straight hours. At this rate, he would need to restock his course load in less than a week. It seemed that being a metal man came with a few perks, anyway. No eye strain, no stiff back, no fatigue. Well, that last made sense. He no longer needed sleep, so obviously recuperation wasn't an issue. But sleep had benefits for memory and general brain function as well. Somehow, the conversion was providing for the requirements without the actual act.

Ivan added that factoid to a growing list of oddities and anomalies. On one level at least, this was an I.T. problem. And the change in behavior indicated that his brain hadn't just been replaced neuron by neuron, otherwise his brain would continue to function identically—except perhaps faster. Or slower, depending on the technology, although that seemed unlikely.

Thinking about his situation as just another tech problem was probably helping to keep him sane. At minimum, it helped to break the self-reinforcing spiral of worry about his family and dread about his future. And, if he was being honest, it was kind of interesting, although he'd have preferred to be studying it from the outside.

A burst of sound startled him as the Vid powered on. He glanced at the screen, then at the remote in his hand. He hadn't done that. Or he hadn't wanted to, at least not consciously. Had his hand developed a life of its own? Or was he just that distracted?

But the Vid was showing a news program, and those had become increasingly interesting lately. So far, ICDC and Navy security appeared to have kept a cap on things, but you couldn't hide the fact that a bunch of ICDC personnel had just high-tailed it for Lagrange Four, or that ICDC *and* Navy Public Relations were now operating in Content-Free Mode, where nothing was said using many words.

Come to think of it, some of the commentary sounded *way* too close to be random guesses. The word "alien" had been used several times, and there was no reason to jump to that conclusion. Unless there'd been a leak…

What would it mean for his family if the public got hold of the facts? Nothing good, certainly. Guilt by association was still a thing, even in this age of supposed enlightenment. The New Liberation hadn't actually improved humanity, so much as defined hard limits on what could be imposed on citizens by government, law enforcement, or military.

Ivan turned off the Vid and lay down, his hands behind his head, and tried to relax. Without prompting, an image of a bear cub popped into his head. *And there it is again. Why would—*

The beep of the intercom interrupted his train of thought. He pressed the *accept* button.

"Hello, Ivan," said the voice of Dante Aiello. "We're going to be announcing spin-down and deceleration in a few minutes. The captain has ordered you to remain in your quarters for the duration. One person still in the hab ring isn't going to create a problem, and it's probably better if you don't—"

"Yeah, I know, I shouldn't show up in the common room and freak out the other crew. I've had a taste of that, thanks. I'm good here."

"Thanks, Ivan. And, sorry. I know this is hard on you." The light went out on the intercom.

It's nice to be wanted, isn't it?

29. Arrival

Dr. Narang examined the personnel module, hanging in the heavens a few hundred meters away. You had to hand it to the Navy, they did things right. The module consisted, essentially, of the hab ring from a typical Navy ship—minus the ship. It looked like nothing so much as a giant floating coin with a stick poked through the center. Concentric layers featured decreasing gravity levels as one approached the hub.

"That way, we use standard parts," Lt. Bentley explained. "And training is kept to a minimum. Someone used to a frigate will be able to find their way around the module right away."

Narang nodded. "The important thing is that, with artificial gravity, we don't have to worry so much about the long-term effects of the quarantine on the patients. And we really don't know how long it might last."

Bentley flipped open his tablet. "So, you wanted isolation for Pritchard, separate isolation for the rest of the crew, a third level for medical staff, and a fourth, *clean* level. Shall we inspect?"

They buckled themselves into their chairs, and the ferry pilot maneuvered the small vessel up to the module airlock at the hub.

From there, they took one of three elevators to the rim—the outermost level, with the highest gravity. Bentley kept up a running commentary as he showed Narang the different sections.

"You'll have an AQRI scanner between each isolation level, as well as the usual diagnostics. We've tried to anticipate needs, but of course this isn't your standard disease.

"The crew will be housed on one side of B elevator, and Pritchard on the other side. Labs are between those sections and elevators A and C, so Pritchard and the crew will have access only to the one elevator. And we'll have manual control of that."

"What are you expecting? A break-out?"

"This is pretty standard. Maybe these people won't, but another group in another situation might. Anyway, your staff will own Levels 2 and 3 as well. Navy personnel will staff the hub and guard for any attempted excursions, by either patients or doctors." He raised an eyebrow at Narang, inviting comment.

"Standard practice again?"

"Actually, Doctor, yes."

"Hmph. Well, okay. We'll probably be winging it, Lieutenant, at least at first. Our first priority will be to determine if Ivan's infection can be reliably detected, and how." Narang glanced back at the AQRI. "I'm betting those will figure prominently."

Bentley nodded. "This probably isn't a surprise, doctor, but this situation is a good deal more, um, *out there* than what our scenarios generally plan for. The committee will be considering additional levels of failsafe."

"Hmm, I love that phrase. Any specifics?"

Bentley shook his head. "But I'm sure you'll hear about it."

Narang left the module feeling both impressed and vaguely disquieted. The Navy had delivered on all requests, including a full airlock and lab setup between each isolation level. She certainly had no complaints from that point of view. But Bentley's last comments left her with a feeling of unease. What "failsafes" might they set up, and would they bring her into the loop?

Unfortunately, a feeling of unease wasn't exactly actionable. Might as well just get this show on the road, and worry about complications as they came up.

"I guess we're ready to go," she said to Lt. Bentley. "Time to bring in the ICDC staff."

* * *

The doctors watched from the control tower as the *Mad Astra* slowly pulled into the docking area. Given the nature of the possible infection, the Navy had decided not to provide a tug. Instead, the *Astra* was coming in using attitude jets. It was a far slower process, and a breach of operating protocols, but not too much less safe as long as the tower stayed on top of things.

Much discussion and planning had gone into the disposition of the patients and personnel. First, the medical staff would be transported over to the Level 2 ward. Then, the entire crew of the *Astra* would be moved to the Level 3 ward, with Ivan Pritchard moved to the Level 4 ward. After that, the Navy would go over the ship with a microscope, using remotes.

Dr. Narang turned to her assistant, Dr. Haruki Nakamura. "Our team is ready?"

"All waiting in the Ready Room."

"Then let's do this."

* * *

Dr. Narang swept the room with her gaze, and allowed herself a moment of private awe. The conference room, and the long table dominating the center, displayed a curvature along the circumference of this hab ring level. Twelve doctors, all seasoned ICDC pros, looked back at her, expressions ranging from calm to excited. And, in Henry Samuelson's case, hungry.

She took a deep breath.

"You've all read the briefing. You've almost all responded with '*Is this a joke?*' Believe me, it is not a joke. It is real, it is unknown, and it is a potential threat. We don't know the limits of capability of these nanites. We don't know where they can hide, or how well. The simplest, the safest thing to do would be to push the *Mad Astra*, crew and all, into the sun. But we are civilized, and we don't do that. So we must find a way, first, to clear those who are not infected and, second, to see what we can do for those who are. A distant, distant third priority is clearing the ship.

"For the one person in the entire solar system who might not already know about it, this is the ship that nailed the Big Rock strike. These people are now rich enough to buy their own navy. Or a stadium full of lawyers. So we will follow procedures, but we will also treat the patients with all due respect and courtesy. One upside, by the way, is that Captain Jennings has already told us that if we feel the need, we should just melt down the *Astra*. He'll be buying a new ship, anyway."

A hand went up. "Then why are we bothering with it at all?"

"To learn," Narang responded. "No other reason. As soon as the

Navy is satisfied that they've learned everything they can from it, they might, in fact, go ahead and push it into the sun. A hyperbolic orbit that intersects the sun's surface, and that problem, at least, will be solved."

Another hand. "Do we seriously expect to cure Pritchard?"

Narang skewered the speaker with her gaze. "We expect to try. We expect to do everything we can for him. Worst case, we expect to learn enough from him to prevent a repeat." She hesitated for a moment. "This situation is unusual in that there doesn't seem to be a problem with mortality. No one is sure what we'll do with Pritchard if, at the end of this, he's still, um, metallized."

"Seal him away somewhere?"

"This isn't the 21st century, Samuelson. We do our best for all our citizens. Don't lose sight of that."

Narang again looked around the room, ensuring everyone was paying attention. "This brings up the other thing you have to keep in mind. Because of the nature of this infection, no level of isolation is sufficient except empty space and no contact. The moment you walk into that isolation module, you are part of the quarantine, until we have this thing beat. The tone you set for working this problem will affect how soon you come out of quarantine as well."

Narang held the silence for a moment. "Therefore, I am giving you one last chance to back out. There will be no recriminations, and it won't affect your career. You can leave with the same ferry that brought us here. But once the *Mad Astra* crew is aboard, we are all committed."

She waited, a full ten seconds. No one moved except Samuelson, who grabbed another doughnut.

One last glare around the room, and Narang said, "If there are no other questions, it's time to go meet our patients."

* * *

The ferry ride to the isolation module went by in total silence. Everyone knew that this was a one-way trip, until the problem had been licked. Paranoia was the watchword, and all moves had been carefully planned. Even the order in which the module was populated. With the doctors flying over before the crew of the *Astra*, the ferry would be allowed to return to base. Once the crew of the *Astra* was brought over, nothing would leave the module.

A quiet meeting with Lieutenant Colonel Martinson from the

naval oversight committee had made it clear to Dr. Narang that any attempt to circumvent this state of affairs would be met with deadly force. If necessary, a missile stood ready to take out the entire installation.

They unloaded through the airlock connection, and each doctor headed for his or her assigned station. Within a half hour, Nakamura walked into Narang's office. "Everyone has confirmed readiness. No issues."

"Okay, thanks, Haruki. I'll buzz Admiral Moore and let him know we're ready for the patients."

* * *

The crew of the *Mad Astra* shuffled out of the elevator in single file. As each stepped up, a voice over the intercom assigned them a room to their right.

"They don't seem to be especially down," Dr. Nakamura said.

"They've all been in the vessel with Pritchard for weeks. There's been no indication that the nanites are interested in anyone else. Really, once we have verified that we can detect the little buggers, we'll probably clear the rest of the crew quickly." Narang smiled ruefully. "And just as well. Admiral Moore has advised me that Captain Jennings set up a scorched-earth plan. He's hired some high-priced lawyers, given them a complete briefing, and instructed them to raise hell if he doesn't check in every day. The implication is clear. We can't just sweep the problem under the rug."

Nakamura looked shocked. "But we wouldn't—"

"I know, Haruki. But a good détente removes the question entirely."

Narang checked her cheat sheet. All the crew members except patient zero were accounted for. She signaled Samuelson with a gesture, and he closed the airlock to Level 3, the crew area. Another flip of a switch, and the airlock to Level 4 opened, on the opposite side of the elevator. Samuelson spoke briefly into his mike.

It took less than a minute for the elevator to make a round trip. The elevator doors opened, the last crew member walked in, and a collective gasp went up from the ICDC doctors. Ivan Pritchard wore the standard crew onboard outfit of shorts, slippers, and a tee shirt. From his totally bald head to the tips of his toes, he looked like he was made of chrome. But he walked and behaved in a completely normal, human manner, right down to slightly hunched shoulders and a hesitant step that stated clearly he was uncomfortable being center stage.

According to Pritchard's records, he hadn't changed in shape or size. He showed clear muscle definition, which indicated that he took good care of himself. If they could paint him in human colors, he would pass unnoticed anywhere.

Pritchard looked around. Narang reached over and nudged Samuelson, who seemed to have locked up in place. He blinked and leaned forward into the microphone. "Mr. Pritchard, you will be in room number one, in the section immediately to your left."

Ivan nodded without comment and proceeded through the open airlock. As soon as he was through, Samuelson operated the panel and the airlock door closed.

Samuelson checked the remote cameras, looking for any issues, or any crew still wandering around. Satisfied that the crew members were all settled, Narang motioned for the microphone. Samuelson handed it to her, then flipped a switch. "All rooms."

Narang nodded to him, held down the mike button, and spoke. "Thank you all for your patience. We have set up the quarantine module in four levels. One is the level that you are currently in. At the moment, you are all equally suspected of carrying the infection, despite only one of you displaying symptoms. We will be attempting to establish our ability to detect the infection. If we find that we can do that, then any person who comes up negative will be moved to the next level."

Narang swallowed before continuing. This part hit too close to home. "After a suitable interval, you will be moved to the second level, which is with the ICDC doctors, including myself. We will all be lab rats for the next phase. If no infection is detected, we will be moved to another module and re-tested. If we pass *that*, then you, and we, will be free to go home."

She released the button and took a deep, shaky breath.

Samuelson muttered, "Except for Ivan Pritchard, who will spend the rest of his life here."

"Put a cork in it, Samuelson. Let's have no giving up before we start."

* * *

Dr. Narang smiled at the man on the other side of the window as she took her seat. She had Dr. Kemp's notes and reports on her tablet, with annotations and questions in the margins. Before her staff dove in full-bore, she wanted to be sure of the facts.

Kemp gazed back at her, his expression relaxed and expectant. She found herself liking him before he'd even said anything. The written reports showed a quick mind, a methodical and thorough work ethic. The conclusions indicated an ability to evaluate the situation honestly and without illusion. She'd be happy to have him on staff.

The man across from her had an open, friendly face, clear blue eyes that looked right at you, and an easy smile. A very good *doctor* face, indeed.

"Dr. Kemp, I'm Dr. Narang, lead investigator on this incident. I've read your notes and reports. I have some questions."

Kemp chuckled. "Only some? I still have a ton of questions. Each thing I learn just raises more issues."

"Mm, yes, well, we're hoping to get a bit of a head start by leveraging off what you've already accomplished." She straightened her tablet on the desk. "Let's start with your initial examination..."

* * *

Narang looked over the notes she'd taken during the interview. As with any good investigator, Kemp had avoided injecting speculation into his documentation. However, he'd been more willing to open up in a one-on-one interview, especially once it was understood that there would be no quoting out of context.

The event was frightening in its simplicity. This had all the feel of a deliberate trap. But by humans? Or something else?

The changes to Ivan Pritchard seemed impossible. But that assumed she took all descriptions at face value. There was always the possibility of exaggeration, of misremembering, of outright confabulation.

On the other hand, she'd *seen* the chrome man. That would be hard to fake.

She pulled up the intercom app and buzzed Nakamura.

He popped up within seconds, in a video window.

"Haruki, what do we have in terms of safety procedures?"

"The usual. Negative pressure, sterilization of air and recirculation, isolation suits..."

Narang shook her head. "Not going to be enough. We're going to have to enforce physical isolation as well. No one goes into the crew area at all."

"But how will we get samples, do examinations?"

"We can ask the Navy engineers for some custom work in that area." Narang thought for a moment. "And I'm sure BSL-4 containment procedures will contain some descriptions of processes, even if only on paper. Contact Laakkonen and see if she can put someone on it. We need to up our game."

Nakamura nodded and ended the connection.

Narang sat back and stared at the ceiling. She was beginning to realize that, despite the bizarre nature of this assignment, she'd still unconsciously treated it like a biological outbreak. That would have to change.

30. Quarantine

Dear Judy,

We have arrived at Lagrange Four and are now under quarantine. I'm so sorry things are working out this way. It seems like nothing good comes to us without some corresponding karmic kick in the crotch, just to make sure we don't get uppity.

I still don't have any more information, but the ICDC is involved, and if they can't pull a rabbit out of a hat, no one can. I will do everything I can to try to come out of this okay, but I won't do anything that might risk you or our children.

I guess the good news is that we will be rich. I can be happy knowing that you and the kids will be more than okay for the rest of your lives. But remember what I said about getting away as quickly as possible.

I'm sorry, I know I'm sounding morose. But that's me, right? Never able to lie, even to reassure you.

Whatever happens, I love you, babe. Give the kids a hug for me.

Ivan.

Ivan stared at the email for a few moments. *Yeah, never able to lie. I seem to be getting a lot better at that, lately.* Grimacing at the thought, he pressed *send.* He had no doubt that his correspondence was being examined, and would be censored or blocked if he said too much. Not that he would—he understood panic and the negative effects. He also understood guilt by association, and didn't want his family painted with that brush. If things got out, he didn't want a data trail from the infection to his family.

He was interrupted by the arrival of a doctor at the window.

"Hello, Mr. Pritchard."

"Hi, Doctor...Narang, right? What's up?"

"We're blowing through the nanite samples that Dr. Kemp took, and we'll need a new supply soon. Obviously, you being in isolation represents a challenge. We think we've figured out a way to get what we need from you with minimal fuss or danger. We'll have to do some work on one of the other cubicles, then we'll be moving you. I just wanted to let you know, because it'll be a little noisy for a while."

"No prob, Doc. I'm so bored that even construction noise is a welcome addition."

Narang gave him an embarrassed smile. "You have full media access, of course, although I expect that gets old quickly. Is there anything else we can do for you?"

"I don't think so, Doc. I've thought about all the things I want or might ask for, and most of them are beyond your power or really bad ideas. So, no. You could answer a question, though."

"I'll try, Ivan."

"On the subject of Vid, there have been demonstrations around ICDC and UEN headquarters. You haven't released anything, have you? Do these people have any actual fuel for this?"

Narang paused for a moment before responding. "Ivan, there's been no official announcement, either from ICDC or the UEN. But something's gotten out. Some of the commentary is just too close to the mark. We've had to increase our online security because of the increased attention. I'm sure Admiral Moore is all over it, though."

She smiled again, nodded to him, and left before he could ask any more questions. He wasn't sure, but she might be walking a little faster than she really needed to. Was that embarrassment, or just not wanting to be around the metal man?

Welcome to my new life.

31. First Looks

"Who's in the AQRI?" Narang walked up to the console, where a couple of doctors sat watching the monitor.

Dr. Noelia Sandoval turned in her chair. "A little guy named 'sample scraping'"

"Ah. Bare nanites? What do they look like?"

"Coming up," said Nakamura, in the next seat. He poked at the console, and an image came up on the monitor. The Advanced Quantum Resonance Imager could scan in detail an object from the size of a full-grown human being down to the nucleus of a cell. The researchers hoped to learn if they could decode the internal workings of the nanites.

Narang gasped when the image popped up on the monitor. The nanites glowed in AQRI imaging. This was their first bit of good news. If the devices showed up that clearly on AQRI scans, they'd be able to detect any infections in humans with little effort.

The real-time image showed the nanites moving around slowly, looking for something to latch onto. As Chief MacNeil had reported, they seemed to be ineffective against industrial glass.

"Next question will be: can we kill them?" Nakamura said.

"Without killing the host," Narang added.

* * *

Ivan Pritchard lay, apparently relaxed, in the AQRI. Sandoval and Nakamura hovered over the panel, ready to make any required adjustments. No one was entirely sure how the AQRI would handle an entirely metal subject.

"I have to reduce saturation," Sandoval said. "Can't make out any detail in the glow."

In moments, the picture resolution improved. Narang stared, slack-jawed. A number of gasps behind her made it clear that all the doctors were watching.

"What in the ninety-nine hells is *that?*" Sandoval pointed at a spot on the display.

The image on the monitor showed a complex internal structure, easily as varied and diverse as a human body. But there, all resemblance ended.

Narang moved slowly closer to the monitor, squinting at the image. Then she yelped as someone stepped on her heel. Narang whirled. "Hey! Everyone not on shift, take a big step back."

There were mutters that sounded like a mutiny in the making, but most of those present stepped back to the wall.

Now able to concentrate on the image, Narang could only shake her head. "The report from Dr. Kemp indicated that the infection was replicating all required functions of human organs."

"Similar functionality doesn't mean similar morphology, apparently," Sandoval replied.

"Unless," Nakamura added, "having completely replaced the human tissues, the organism then reconfigured to something more efficient or desirable."

"Well, sure. He probably doesn't need a spleen or kidneys. Which raises the question, what *does* he need?"

Narang looked at Sandoval. "Can we make comparisons to our own mechs?"

"Not a hope in hell, Dr. Narang. It's like comparing a club to an autonomous drone. If you held a gun to my head, I couldn't tell you what any of those structures are for. Power? Temperature control? Communications? It's anyone's guess, absent a dissection."

Narang gave Sandoval a sharp look. If she was trying to be funny, mission *not* accomplished.

Sandoval shrugged, unrepentant. "Kemp did some x-rays and AQRI scans on the trip in. We'll compare them with this one, see how much has changed." She flipped off the AQRI, and leaned to the microphone. "Thank you, Mr. Pritchard. We're done for today."

On the other side of the glass, Ivan Pritchard got up, gave the doctors a salute, and walked back to his room.

* * *

Dr. Narang gestured to the image floating in the middle of the conference table. "Well, there it is. For those of you who didn't quite believe the initial reports—in which group I include myself, by the way—it seems the *Mad Astra*'s doctor wasn't drinking or smoking something after all."

"A nanite. An actual microscopic, self-contained machine." Dr. Nakamura's voice had the distracted tone of someone unwilling to spare more than minimal attention for the task of speaking.

Dr. Alwin Schulze, a physicist borrowed from Caltech, grinned unabashedly. "And self-powered. We have nothing that could do that, not at that size." Schulze leaned forward, then settled his rotund form more comfortably into his chair. He looked around the table, still smiling, inviting argument or commentary.

"So, alien?"

Schulze turned to face Narang. "Unquestionably. The Japanese are the technology leaders on this front, and they're not even close to delivering something self-contained at the micron level. Never mind the data processing requirements."

Matt Siegel, the team's Information Systems expert, shook his head. "Same comment applies from the I.T. angle, Alwin. I've no idea how you'd encode a complete computer system in that size, even without allowing room for power, I/O systems, and whatever else."

The session appeared to be in danger of descending into a gushfest. Narang interrupted the spiral. "So, Matt, are you willing to commit to the statement that this *is* extraterrestrial in origin?"

"Mathematically, it is still possible that it's of human origin. We can't logically rule that out, in the same way we can't rule out leprechauns. But, realistically, no one is even close to this." He shook his head. "If I had to, I'd bet my life on it being alien."

Step one, done. Narang took a moment to refill her tea from the faux-ceramic pot. She glanced over at the pastry tray, but the locust swarm had already ravaged it. Mostly the head locust, Samuelson.

"Okay, next question, and maybe not as easy to answer. Does this seem symptomatic of some kind of attack?"

"Not a chance," Siegel said before anyone else could speak. He received several arch looks, for his tone as much as for his statement.

Narang raised her eyebrows at Siegel, inviting him to continue.

"Why set it up on some random asteroid? If you want to attack Earth, just drop the package into the atmosphere."

"So, why was it placed on some random asteroid?"

Siegel shrugged without comment.

Hmm, step 2, sort of done.

Narang looked at her tablet, at the third question. "Does the incident imply an impending visit—or invasion—from the Makers?" Moore would probably not be happy with today's Q&A, she thought.

"Not directly, no," Schulze replied. "However, to answer the last half of the previous question, you'd put the device on a random asteroid so that only a space-faring species could activate it. To answer this question, you'd then program the trap to phone home the first chance it got." Schulze grinned. "*Then*, maybe, we'd get a visit."

Oh, he definitely won't be happy. Narang decided to deliver this revelation personally. The fireworks would be epic.

* * *

Admiral Moore's eyes seemed about to pop right out of his head. Narang kept her face impassive, but she was embarrassed to realize that she was enjoying his discomfiture.

"So you're saying Pritchard might try to contact whoever sent this thing?"

"It's just speculation on Dr. Schulze's part, Admiral. And it doesn't speak to motive or consequences, even if it turns out to be reality. This could be an anthropological exercise, for all we know. Studying the natives."

Moore snorted, his expression showing clearly how little he believed that. He changed the subject abruptly. "I understand you've been subject to some hacking attempts."

Narang decided to be candid. "Well, not here, so much. We're using your network, of course. But headquarters, yes. Fortunately, we have some of the most sophisticated security A.I.s in the solar system."

"Drawbridge category?" Moore asked. At her nod, he continued. "Doctor, don't get too complacent. They'll keep at it until they get what they want. Or until it becomes irrelevant, which would mean things have gotten much worse."

Narang paused to rub her eyes. Too many days with not enough sleep were catching up with her. "I understand, Admiral. But everything we've seen so far indicates that this is *not* a Gray Goo scenario."

"What about Alien Invasion?" Moore smiled tightly.

"Depends on how you define *invasion*, I guess." Narang stood. "Anyway, you have everything we've learned so far. Happy reading." She gave him a nod and walked out. Bentley tried to catch her eye as she stepped past his desk, but she needed sleep more than she needed another conversation.

32. Status

Admiral Moore blew on his coffee, then took a sip. The habitual action gave him an opportunity to look around the table without being obvious about it. He still didn't have a good feel for the positions of the various committee members. Or, he admitted to himself, maybe those attitudes were shifting faster than he could get a handle on them. It seemed every day brought some new revelation about this Pritchard and his disease.

He put his cup down and rapped on the table with his knuckles. Conversations ceased as everyone turned to him.

Moore gave the committee members a pro forma smile. "I have received a request—or perhaps that's not the right word, since she's not asking for permission—from Dr. Narang for us to bring some more people into the project. We have a cybernetics expert, a xenobiologist, a couple of physicists, as well as some medical specialists whose fields I'm not sure I can even pronounce."

"And that won't set off flags, at all, no sir," Admiral Castillo muttered.

"Well, this situation isn't really top secret, Alan." Moore shrugged. "The media picked it up the moment the ICDC dispatched a team spaceward. It's well past the *rumor* stage now, and well into *scandal.* We're able to play the *patient confidentiality* card to a large extent, plus the *ongoing investigation* narrative, but some media pundits are getting pretty bold in their criticisms and pointed questions." He paused and looked around the table. "And Security has reported hacking attempts are up several thousand percent."

Several heads jerked around to look directly at Moore. He let the moment play out to maximum effect. Best they understand early the seriousness of the situation.

"All this, based on an ICDC mobilization? That seems excessive," Commodore Gerrard said.

"I agree, Mike," Moore replied with a tight smile. "It's possible there is or has been a leak of some kind. We're looking into that. It's fortunate that when the *Mad Astra* returned early they didn't publicly announce their intention to do so. As far as public records show, the *Astra* is still out there checking asteroids for another two months, which means anyone attempting to extract information by data mining will discount it as a possibility."

"What exactly are we trying to keep from the public, Admiral?" Commodore Nevin phrased the question innocently enough, but there was a barb behind it, Moore was sure. Her eyebrows met in her trademark scowl.

"Commodore, we have irrefutable proof of the existence of intelligent life outside of Earth. E.T., if you will. You don't think that's going to cause a stir?"

"Oh, no argument on that, Admiral. But is it really our place to play nanny to the world?"

"It is our place," Moore replied, "to avoid vomiting out sensational news until those whose job it is to do so, can package it up properly. I'm not suggesting we keep it a secret. I'm suggesting that how the news breaks will affect how it's received, and how the public reacts."

Commodore Nevin snorted, but held her tongue.

"Anyway," Moore continued, looking around the table, "unless someone can come up with a reason, I can't block Dr. Narang's request. Anyone?"

Silence greeted him.

Well, that's that, he thought.

* * *

Moore grimaced as he watched the news show *Topic Zero* on his tablet. The lead reporter, an obnoxious former sports star turned Vid personality, stood outside ICDC headquarters, going through the standard clichéd innuendos and leading questions. The bottom line, though, was that someone had seen the list of ICDC draftees, and put two and two together. And, as usual with the media, gotten five.

Now, smelling blood, the media had laid siege to the ICDC. Moore watched a replay of the interview with Dr. Karin Laakkonen. The woman was an expert at not giving away anything, but the challenge had just encouraged the media vultures.

Reporter: Doctor L, the ICDC's withholding of information on the quarantine is the direct cause of the demonstrations outside. Isn't it better at this time to simply come clean on the situation?

Laakkonen: Sir, the problem isn't so much with ICDC not releasing information that we don't have, as it is with the media trying to fill that void with irresponsible conjecture and innuendo.

Reporter: But Doctor, isn't it true that you have an alien pathogen isolated on a Navy moonbase?

Laakkonen: No sir, it is not. And by the way, that kind of leading question, when talking into the camera, is exactly what I'm referring to. You've descended into tabloid territory. So let me reiterate the only statement I can give you: The ICDC is still investigating. We have not yet established whether a quarantine is even necessary, but will not lift it until we've made that determination, out of an abundance of simple prudence. And we will release information as it becomes available, subject to privacy requirements.

Reporter: But surely public safety trumps any privacy issues—

Laakkonen: If that comes to pass, then we will release more information. At this point, there is no danger to the public, your irresponsible reporting notwithstanding.

Moore found himself feeling some sympathy for the woman. But she would have to get herself under better control. Letting them bait her was not productive.

The media, of course, were past masters at whipping the public into a frenzy when it suited their agenda. It appeared the goal in this case was to put pressure on the government to put out some kind of information release. Meanwhile, demonstrations were increasingly turning into riots. And you could bet the media would deny any responsibility in the end.

Moore checked his email again. He expected a query from Naval Civilian Relations any minute. The ICDC protocols weren't a secret, and any idiot would be able to connect the dots to figure out where the mystery ship was being held.

Nothing yet. There was still time to compose a response. Moore queried the status board for Dr. Narang's current location. Perhaps a face-to-face would help clarify things.

* * *

Dr. Narang sat back and gazed at Moore over her mug of tea. "You're not suggesting lying to the public, are you, Admiral?"

"Come on, Doctor. You've worked for the ICDC for long enough to understand about controlling information. A core dump without some kind of plan will cause panic. People will be scared of a potentially uncontrollable disease, other people will be scared about the imminent arrival of some kind of space invaders, and of course the xenophobes and religious extremists will have a fit."

Narang looked down at her mug for a few moments. "We don't have much, yet, admiral. We're still trying to characterize the active agent. We're more used to biological subjects, if you know what I mean."

Not for the first time, Moore wondered if the ICDC was really the right agency to be running this show.

"I saw my boss's response on Vid," Narang continued. "And I'd agree that it's nothing but a stalling tactic. Someone will have to release an official statement, and I understand that we should cooperate. I'm just not sure we have anything of substance, yet."

"Fair enough, Doctor. Then let's see what your crew can put together that won't metaphorically throw gasoline on the fire."

"Have you ever even seen gasoline, Admiral?"

Moore smiled as he stood to leave. "Clichés die hard, Doctor."

33. Looking Over His Shoulder

Ivan kept glancing around his room. It was odd, but he felt like he wasn't alone. Clearly, he was, but the feeling wouldn't go away that someone was in the room with him. It was creepy. And the baby bear kept popping up in his mind. But now there were also images of strange, unfamiliar creatures, always in chrome.

So, possibilities. One, he was losing his mind. Maybe the conversion wasn't perfect, and he was unraveling. Or maybe the conversion was fine, and he was just unraveling all on his own. Or, two, the isolation was getting to him. Well, that was just 1B, really. Okay, two, something or someone actually *was* watching him. Of course, the surveillance camera up in the ceiling was an obvious candidate, but this was more than just that. Was something in his head with him? The creep factor would be off the charts, in that case.

There were other weird things as well. He'd found himself on several occasions turning on the Vid without meaning to. One time, he'd spontaneously re-opened his astronomy course notes, and turned to a picture of the Briggs Farside Radio Telescope Array. Well, okay, it was impressive, but so what?

Ivan glanced up at the surveillance camera. He still wasn't entirely comfortable with not mentioning any of this. After all, he wasn't a prisoner, technically, and this wasn't an adversarial situation. And Captain Jennings's tactic with the lawyers ensured that Ivan could expect full UEN citizenship protections.

Still...

It was lonely in quarantine. The doctors were all business. Calls to the rest of the crew tended to be, well, *stiff* was the kindest word Ivan could think of. Seth tried more than most, but even he was unsure how to deal with the chrome man.

Conversations with his family helped, but he didn't want to overdo that. It wasn't just a question of the emotional toll on them. The more contact he had with his family, the more chance there was for someone to find out something. A chance comment by his children, a conversation overheard, a hack of the phone system, a fishing expedition by some news crew eavesdropping on the homes of random miners... Ivan smiled to himself. Most paranoid wins. He was certainly leading that race, these days.

Ivan needed to be seen as human. As a victim, not as a dangerous alien thingamabob. Revelations about alien mind parasites, involuntary actions, and spontaneous mental imagery probably wouldn't help his cause. So, caution. He wouldn't do anything to endanger his family, but that didn't mean he was going to volunteer to get tossed under the bus.

"Mr. Pritchard?"

Ivan looked up. It was Dr. Narang. She was one of the good ones. Too many of the doctors looked at him and just saw a specimen. He'd given up on trying to engage those individuals in any kind of conversation.

He was struck once again by her beauty, and even more by her casual lack of concern about it. Judy was like that.

The thought of his wife brought a stab of anxiety, and he forced himself to shift mental gears.

"What's up, Dr. Narang?"

"We need another scraping, if you don't mind."

"You've already gone through the last batch?"

Dr. Narang shrugged on the other side of the glass. "Many of our tests are destructive. And we're being aggressive to try to get as much information as possible. So, yeah, we go through them pretty fast."

"Okay, Doc, no problem." Ivan got up and put his arm in the sleeve that they'd set up. There was a *snap*, and he felt a bite. Dr. Narang looked at something below the window level, and said, "Good. Done. That doesn't hurt too much, does it?"

Ivan shook his head. "Things don't *hurt*, generally, not in the same way as before. It's more like data. I know it's pain, I know it means damage is occurring and I should do something, but It doesn't have the same urgency."

Dr. Narang smiled. "There's a documented form of brain damage that produces that particular result, but I doubt it's the same thing."

She sat down at the console, leaned forward, and rested her chin on her hands. "Do you *feel* different? In any specific, large-scale way? You must notice something?"

Ivan thought for a few moments. "Well, I'm not sleeping anymore, but you knew that. That part is really weird. I keep realizing with a start that it's past my bedtime or something, but I'm not sleepy." He grinned. "I'm going through my computer courses a lot faster. A twenty-four-hour day does have its upsides."

"Can you read faster? Process better?"

"Hard to tell from the inside, of course. But mostly, no. I still forget stuff, still have to go back and reference things. Whether or not I'm still Ivan, I still *work* like Ivan, and I guess that includes fallible human memory."

"Do you get tired?"

"Not the way you mean, I think. But I do get bored, so I have to change tasks every once in a while."

Narang nodded, and the silence stretched for several seconds.

"How's the research going?" Ivan was intensely interested in progress, of course, but he also wanted to keep the doctor around as long as possible.

"We, uh, are learning more about what we *can't* do than what we *can*, Ivan. For one thing, we can't get the nanites to infect anything. Virus, bacteria, flatworms, mice, toasters..."

"Toasters?"

"I kid, slightly. But we've tried placing them on and in various types of equipment, and they just aren't interested. They immediately start migrating back in your direction. Or trying to."

"Hmm. I'm afraid I don't have any insights there, Doc." Ivan shrugged. "It's not like I'm calling to them."

"I understand. I'm going to get back to work, Ivan. We've got people waiting for this batch of beasties." She nodded to him, then turned and headed up the hall.

Ivan sighed and turned back to his room. Why this particular conversation would have caused it, Ivan had no idea. But now, for the first time, he really understood that he would not be going home. He couldn't.

His mind flashed back to dogpiles on the couch, barbeques on the ratty little balcony, and evenings at the park, holding Judy while the kids ran around screaming. And once more, he wished he could still cry.

34. Unrest

Protests continue to spread, fueled by rumors of an alien disease at one of the Lagrange Naval bases. Our requests for interviews with ICDC and Navy representatives were again refused. The ICDC continues to repeat its official narrative that there is no disease under study, alien or otherwise. Navy Relations responds to all questions with the statement that they provide facilities only, and any inquiries should be directed to the ICDC.

The Representative for East Canada District and Northwest America District have issued a joint statement condemning WorldGov's apparent refusal to force an inquiry.

Ivan watched the Transplanetary News report with a slight smile. So far, no one had actually lied. If you set the bar low enough, that is.

The big fear seemed to be the Gray Goo scenario. That recent movie hadn't helped, of course. *The Centaurus Scourge* had primed the public with the idea of alien nanites coming in and eating everything. He wondered if the producers were happy with the free publicity. Or maybe already in hiding. Shooting the messenger was a time-honored tradition after all.

The image on the Vid changed to what looked very much like a riot. Civilians, many of them wearing bandanas or even gas masks, carried signs and marched on a line of riot police. The picture changed to what was evidently another demonstration of some kind, then another.

...Demonstrations turned to riots in six major cities today as various factions protested apparent government inaction, or at least government failure to respond as those factions demand. These different groups, united only in their distrust of the official releases...

Wow. New York, Athens, Geneva, Berlin... These weren't third-world cities.

Pausing the picture periodically, Ivan was able to zoom in and read some of the signs and placards. It appeared to be about a third religious-themed, a third government-conspiracy-themed, and a third everything else.

He let the Vid reset to real-time as he pondered. There didn't seem to be anything new out there, in terms of the public knowing something they shouldn't. At least not anything that could be put into a few words. But the level of panic was being being fed by something. And it would continue to spread.

Ivan hoped his family had found a new, safer location.

35. Screaming

Ivan sat up with a start. If he had still been capable, he would have broken out into a sweat. He was sure he'd just heard a scream of fear or pain. Or both. And the really odd thing was that it had sounded like his voice. Had it been a nightmare? But he couldn't even fall asleep.

He glanced up at the security camera, then stood and looked down the hallway through the observation window. No one was coming. So no one else had heard the scream.

Ivan sat down, shaking his head. This probably came under the heading of things not to mention.

This hadn't felt like whoever was looking over his shoulder, though. So did Ivan have multiple guests in his head? *I am Legion. Great.*

Well, one upside at least. This kept his mind off his family and his future. Assuming he had one.

So, items. One, he had an invisible friend looking over his shoulder. One who possibly moved Ivan's limbs for him occasionally. Two, he had another tenant who was a screamer and sounded a lot like Ivan. Three, he'd developed an unexplainable hate for dishwasher mechs. Maybe it was professional jealousy, since he seemed to be a mech now. Sort of.

Ivan felt the bones of one hand with the other, pressing his fingers aggressively into the, uh, flesh. Doctor Kemp had really freaked out when he'd done that. Ivan wasn't a doctor, but he was pretty sure the skeletal structure of his hand was different from when he was human. He wasn't sure if that should be surprising or not—with a sample size of one, he couldn't really form much in the way of conclusions about how metal men should be made.

Perhaps it was time to try digging into what was happening in his skull. If there was someone or something else in there, he might be able to contact it. Maybe it had been trying to contact him, and that was a scream of frustration. If so, it had a temper.

Ivan lay down on the bed, hands behind his head, stared at the ceiling and tried to relax.

Images began to form, of strange creatures parading through his view. All in chrome, like him. Their physiologies ranged from mildly exotic to indescribable and even terrifying. Interestingly, these weren't mental images—they were actually *projected* in some way onto his field of view. That meant that someone was trying to communicate. Was it the Screamer, or the Watcher? Not enough info yet. Ivan tried to relax and just take in the show. Understanding would come later.

* * *

He was watching the news when it happened again. A mental scream. Agony, fear, something. And, although he still wasn't sure how to explain it, it *sounded* like him. It was followed by a jolt of something—anger? No, maybe frustration. Irritation.

The images were getting more frequent as well. Indescribable creatures, with different numbers of limbs, eyes, and even heads. Including zero, which was especially weird. And all in chrome. Except, strangely, the bear cub, which was always the last image in the group.

Then, another image. Ivan, this time, chrome and all. As he watched, the Ivan image became two, then three, then four. One at a time, the duplicates screamed and disappeared, leaving the original Ivan image.

Well, that's interesting.

Whatever else this might be, it was communication. Or an attempt, anyway. One of the occupants in Ivan's brain appeared to be trying to explain the screams.

Again, the images of Ivan went through the sequence: cloning, screaming and disappearing.

It's making copies of me. Then torturing them? Not likely. Okay, Ivan. You're a computer geek. You were top of your class. Time to make use of that Nerd Fu.

Then a third time, but this time with a change. Several clone images screamed and disappeared, but some stayed. Then the ones remaining were cloned. This was repeated for several cycles. Then all vanished except one.

It's using an evolutionary process or some kind of simulated annealing to...to something. To build communications? The screams—those are versions of me that failed. Maybe failure is catastrophic?

That was interesting, but there was implied information there as well. For this process to work, for the host to be able to duplicate him and run multiple instances, Ivan had to be running as a virtual machine on top of some other computing layer. So there was a computer, for want of a better word, hosting Ivan. And, therefore, a lot more in his head than just him.

Scary thought. It meant Ivan was not the owner of his own body, but a tenant. A guest. And he could be suspended or even deleted.

Best be polite to the landlord.

* * *

Ivan carefully watched the video of a computer being disassembled. This was the third run-through, which he hoped would clue in his host to pay attention. As soon as the video finished, Ivan lay down on the bed to stare at the ceiling. This was his signal that he was waiting for communications.

Within moments, an image appeared. Ivan recognized it as one of the nanites that Dr. Kemp and Chief Engineer MacNeil had identified. As he watched, the nanite was joined by others of its kind. Then the image zoomed in on one particular nanite, scrolling inward until the edges of the nanite were off-screen, so to speak. An image of a CPU and memory modules from Ivan's video appeared, overlaid on the nanite's innards. Then the picture zoomed out to show that every nanite had the same parts.

Oh, wow. Alien computers 101. I'm getting a guided tour.

The first takeaway was that there wasn't any kind of centralized processing. Each nanite contained a full computer system, which meant everything ran on a distributed network. There was no "brain" as such. Ivan might not even be, strictly speaking, in his own head anymore.

The train of images continued, becoming more and more detailed, and less comprehensible. Ivan quickly realized that lesson two was going to involve new technology, if not outright new physics. This could take a while.

36. Discussion

Dr. Kemp had been dozing off when his phone rang. He sat up and grabbed it. "Kemp."

"Hi, Doc. You busy?"

It took Kemp a moment to recognize the voice, with the sleep fog still making his thoughts fuzzy. Finally, it clicked. "Oh, hi, Ivan. What's up?"

"Well, last time we talked, you said to let you know if things came into focus. Or if things changed."

"Okay. Of course, I'm not really in charge of your care, anymore. But I'm still interested."

"That's okay, Doc, I think I'm just looking for a familiar voice. The ICDC doctors are all business, all the time. I'm a specimen to them."

"They've never known you as a human, Ivan. They probably aren't quite sure how to deal with you."

"Well, maybe, although I get the feeling they're all about the disease and not so much about the patient."

"Could be. But that's their job."

There was a chuckle on the other end, followed by a short silence. "I phoned my wife."

"How did that go?"

"I wish I actually had a fatal disease, Doc. At least then, I could say goodbye properly, I could explain to her what's happening to me. This...this just leaves me hanging. No resolution. I almost wish I hadn't made the call." There was a moment of silence. "I've talked to her several times since, but I've got nothing new to offer, and there's no resolution that I can see. I might as well be lingering in a coma in a hospital bed. I'm no use to her, I'm making her life hell, and I'm keeping her from having a life."

Kemp nodded, silent. He'd been around for too many deaths, watched too many family members trying to wrap their minds around the abrupt passing of a loved one. He'd also seen too many instances of people being given bad news—something lingering, something with an indefinite conclusion sometime in the future. Persistent comas, dementias, cancers, neurological degenerative diseases, all ultimately death sentences. In some ways, that was worse.

Ivan moved to fill the conversation gap. "I heard the Consolidated Industrials ship confirmed all details of the claim."

"Yep. Escrow's been removed, funds are released. We're all rich. Including your family. Captain Jennings asked his lawyers to make sure it got taken care of properly."

"Good. I'll have to thank him if I talk to him. If I don't get a chance, let him know I appreciate it, okay?"

"Will do."

The conversation ground to a halt, as tended to happen with people who weren't at ease with each other. After a moment, Kemp said, "Anyway, Ivan, what were you going to tell me about?"

"I'm starting to know stuff."

"Huh?"

"You know all the tip-of-the-tongue stuff that I couldn't put my finger on? Some of it's starting to gel."

"Okay, that's interesting. So the nanites are telling you things?"

"Sort of. There's a computer in here with me. Or an A.I. It's sort of both, and neither one. I'm running as a program."

"You're what?"

"I'm a program. Or an emulation. I guess that shouldn't be a surprise, really. There isn't a human brain in here, and Ivan Pritchard was an entity who grew up on a specifically wired set of biologically-based neurons. The computer, or whatever it is, simulates the human brain, neuron for neuron, impulse for impulse, and there I am. Possibly with some improvements, since I don't need to sleep anymore. This is pretty standard A.I. stuff. I mean, I'm sure this version is way more advanced, but the basics are the same as what we learned in Computer Science classes."

"Okay, but the bottom line is you're still you."

"Yes, I'm not a computer pretending to be Ivan. I'm Ivan. I'm just not running on wetware anymore."

"Well, that's good, right?"

"I think so. I get the impression it might be temporary. I can't explain why."

"Ouch. Can't you ask the computer?"

"It doesn't really work that way. There isn't a conversation going on. It's more like information is leaking my way. I think the computer is still figuring out how to communicate. And since the human brain is a dog's breakfast of emergent properties, it's slow going. The computer can't afford to break something in the process. It's doing simulations—making copies of me then trying to modify them for communications. Not going well, so far, though."

"How is the computer able to handle that? How powerful is it, anyway?"

"Pretty damn powerful, Doc. I'm getting computer-related stuff faster than anything else because of my background, I guess. The computer system seems to encode information directly on the fabric of space, at the Planck level. In principle it could encode the state of every particle in the known universe in a cubic micrometer of vacuum. Of course, processing all that data is another matter. No matter how you shuffle it, light-speed delay is a limiting factor. And that's the trouble it's having with me. Apparently, humans are extraordinarily messy."

"Will you be able to talk to the computer at some point?"

"I think so. I hope so. I'll want to ask it if it can make me human again."

37. Enemy Threats

Moore settled into what he privately called his command chair, took a sip of his coffee—nothing beat the first sip from the first cup of the day—and picked up the briefing notes from Bentley. One of the advantages of a personal assistant was that you didn't have to wade through the news channels and all your emails to figure out what was critical and what could be ignored.

As he read the first item, his eyes widened and he almost choked.

Multiple news items about the quarantine. Not all details correct, but enough to suspect a leak.

Oh, Great God in Heaven. "Bentley!"

The lieutenant appeared within seconds. He'd probably been anticipating the call.

"First item. Summary, please."

Bentley took a breath, and began. "Multiple news stories appeared overnight with concrete details about the *Astra* and the crew. Enough accurate hits to make it more than conjecture. Enough similarities between the stories to indicate that someone sold the story multiple times."

"Reaction?"

"About what you'd expect, sir. Public hue and cry, demands that the government do something, a couple of demonstrations already."

"Anything from HQ?"

Bentley shook his head. "Not yet, sir, but I am expecting—"

The ringing of an incoming call interrupted him. Moore recognized it as the ring tone Bentley had assigned to Naval Intelligence.

"Get that, Bentley. Update me afterward."

Bentley nodded and sprinted to his desk. Moore picked up the cheat sheet, hoping the next item would distract him from Bentley's single-sided conversation.

Before he could get properly rolling, Bentley was back in front of him, holding out a printout.

Ted—

I don't know what kind of clusterfuck you guys have underway up there, but the politicos are going apeshit. We have a directive, direct from the office of the President of the United Earth Nations, to provide all pertinent information. It takes something truly extraordinary to unite the entire peanut gallery, but this has absolutely everyone, from the looney left to the environmentalists to the fundies to the rabid right screaming for blood. The President can't ignore that large a united front, which means Naval Command can't either.

There will be a formal request for more information coming in a short time. Suggest you don't try to stall or dissemble.

George Fredricks, Admiral
SSC/UENN

Moore looked at Bentley with one eyebrow raised. The lieutenant had a gray cast to his skin that Moore found disquieting. "Something else, lieutenant?"

"Yessir. Just heard it on the office wire. The SSE has announced that they are sending a flotilla to Lagrange Four Naval base to inspect and evaluate the threat."

* * *

Dr. Narang looked like she'd been struck with a club. Moore waited a moment to be satisfied with the effect. She needed a dose of reality, and this might just be a kick in the right direction.

"You aren't going to cooperate, Admiral, are you?"

"Of course not. Imagine us letting a foreign military march into our territory while we bow and scrape and say *Yes, sir* and *No, sir* and *Please, sir.* I'd be court-martialed—at minimum—and rightly so." He hesitated for a moment, wondering if he should soft-pedal his next point, then decided not to. "If the Sino-Soviet Empire forces the issue, there will be a battle. They are sending a full flotilla, and we don't have the hardware in place to hold them off. So if push comes to shove, we won't be surrendering. Do you understand what I'm saying?"

Narang nodded, slowly. "To the death. Ours, if it comes to that."

"That is correct, doctor. Please relay to your staff as appropriate."

* * *

Twelve SSE warships, including two full destroyers, stood at zero relative motion in the monitor. Facing them were nine UENN frigates and one cruiser. It was a David-and-Goliath moment, and Moore had no illusions about the outcome, if things went bad.

The voice of the SSE flotilla Commander, one Captain Chekov, came over the monitor. "You have insufficient forces to hold us at bay, Admiral. I suggest you step aside and accept the inevitable. You cannot win."

Moore set his jaw. "We don't have to win, Commander. We just have to make sure that *you* don't win. This is not a symmetrical situation. In the worst case, we will blow up our assets rather than surrendering them. And if we can hold you off until the UENN strike group that we both know is coming gets here, so much the better."

"Destroying yourselves will remove this supposed alien threat. How is that a loss for us?"

"Which might or might not remove this supposed alien threat, Commander. Without anything left to study, you won't know. And you'll have a war on your hands in any case. You may have the advantage here, today, but you know as well as I do that the UENN has you outmatched overall."

"I know no such thing, Admiral. That is your opinion only."

"Have it your way, Commander. Your choices remain unchanged. As do ours."

There were several seconds of silence. One of the monitoring techs commented, "Radio reflections from local dust, sir. It's probably a tight-beam signal. They're phoning home for orders."

Moore nodded. "Noted. How long until reinforcements get here?"

"Three hours, sir. They're on emergency deployment protocol, all personnel cocooned for high acceleration."

Moore knew that particular tactic always resulted in a certain number of permanent disabilities. Those would be on the heads of the SSE military, and ultimately on whoever was responsible for this situation. He was keeping score, and if someone needed to pay, he'd make sure it happened.

A stab of pain in his jaw made him realize he was losing control of his reactions. Deliberately relaxing his features, Moore turned and addressed the room. "You have your orders. It is a given that we can't blink in this scenario. You accepted the possibility of death when you signed up—"

A voice from the monitor interrupted Moore, causing him again to grit his teeth in irritation. *Dammit, I've been working on that speech for years.*

"As an alternative, Admiral, we would be satisfied with an embedded SSE observer."

"That would not be a military decision, Commander, therefore it's not one that I can make. You'd have to go through diplomatic channels on that."

"So that is a *no?*"

"That's a *maybe*, Commander. Convince my bosses."

"Very well. We will spare you the embarrassment of defeat at this time, Admiral. But should the danger from this experiment of yours become intolerable to the people of the solar system, rest assured we will act decisively. Meanwhile, my people will talk to your people."

Moore took a moment to roll his eyes. "Fine, Commander. Just make sure your lurking remains outside of our treaty zone. Out."

Moore made a throat slash motion, and the technician ended the connection. It was a reprieve of sorts, but not a resolution by any stretch.

* * *

Moore looked around the table. Serious expressions gazed back at him. No one had any illusions about the situation. "According to Surveil, the SSE fleet has parked themselves at one hundred thousand kilometers plus one meter distance."

"More or less," Castillo said.

Moore ignored him. "They're sending a message. If the political winds shift, or if things go unshiny here for whatever reason, they'll be back."

"Which could happen. Have you seen the news lately?" Nevin looked around. "A coalition of Representatives is pushing for a vote of non-confidence."

"Worrying, but it wouldn't affect us directly," Gerrard added.

"It affects Naval High Command, and the fallout will inevitably run downhill, Commodore. I'm not so concerned about the direct orders as I am about the back-room deals." Moore scanned the table one more time. "Sers, we are living in interesting times. If you have backchannel contacts, now would be a good time to renew acquaintances."

38. Investigations and Discoveries

Narang watched over the shoulder of the technician as he re-tuned the AQRI. They had managed to encase a nanite in a plastic resin, without breaking it and without giving it a chance to start eating the resin. This was the real reason why they went through so many nanites. Trying to get one to stay still without turning it into a random pile of atoms or incinerating it had achieved the status of a never-ending game of Whack-a-Mole.

Finally, success, and a chance to look inside.

While one group had been trying to get a suitably prepared specimen, another group had prepared a series of scanning scripts in the event of success. Now, they would have the opportunity to test their work.

The technician turned to Narang. "Third series started. First two went without a hitch. The nanite is still radiating virtual particles, so it's still 'alive', whatever that actually means. Active, anyway. So we should get some good data."

Narang patted him on the shoulder. "Good. Text me the moment they're done. If I'm not hovering over your shoulder at the time, of course." With a smile, she turned and left.

Her next stop was the lab where doctors were studying the images of Ivan's internal structures. A certain number of scientists on Earth and in Near Space had been read in on the situation and were teleconferencing with the local staff. The lab was a madhouse of yelling and gesturing, as remote and local personnel argued over, well, pretty much everything.

Most of the internal structures hadn't even been identified. In a couple of cases, structures had disappeared between successive scans. It seemed the nanites could reconfigure to meet changing requirements.

Narang watched two scientists full-on yelling at each other over some arcane point, complete with waving hands and shaking fists. She would have feared the possibility of violence, except that whenever they paused for breath, both participants settled into smiles of happiness.

Great days for science. For Ivan Pritchard, not so much. Narang shook her head and headed for the conference room.

"Morning, all," Narang said as she came through the door. A chorus of *morning*'s drifted back. She grabbed a cup of tea and sat down at the head of the table. "So, what do we have?"

Dr. Samuelson, seated to her left, spoke first, around a mouthful of doughnut. "There's no doubt that Ivan Pritchard, as a biological entity, is gone. The Ivan Pritchard in isolation is one hundred percent nanites. So I think any question of 'curing' him has to be put to rest. There is no *him* left."

Dr. Narang nodded then looked to the next person around the table. Dr. Noelia Sandoval had a faraway look in her eyes as she began her report.

"Ivan's internal structure is amazing. It's got a frame—I hesitate to call it a skeleton, since it only superficially resembles the human skeletal system—and something that performs the function of muscles although, again, only generally similar in placement and function to the human equivalent."

"Why have a skeleton and muscles at all?" Dr. Nakamura asked. "Why not just morph into whatever posture he wants?"

"Too slow, for one thing," Sandoval answered. "Plus, I don't think it would look natural. And that appears to be very important to whatever converted Ivan."

"Explain, please," Narang said.

"Well, the entity, A.I., whatever, converted Ivan in such a way that he is shaped like a human being. He can smile, his biceps bulges when he flexes his arm, you can see quadriceps outlines on his thighs. Remember the day we first saw him, as he walked off the elevator? He looked and behaved completely human, except for the metal skin. Why? There is absolutely no reason to slavishly emulate the human form like that, *unless* it is an explicit requirement. Again, why?"

"You have a theory, Dr. Sandoval?"

"Just speculation, Dr. Narang, but I think the whole purpose of the transformation assumes some degree of continuing to deal with the natives. If he wasn't quite human-like, if he fell into the *uncanny valley* of looks or behavior, it could be counterproductive."

"So," Narang mused, "it's a marketing thing?"

Sandoval grinned. "I wouldn't have put it like that, but yes."

"That's just freaky," Nakamura muttered.

"Hell," Samuelson interjected, "that's not the freakiest part by a considerable margin."

All heads turned to look at him. Samuelson waved a pastry for emphasis. "You've read the report of the original incident. How long was that artifact there? A hundred years? A thousand? A million? There is a very good chance that when the artifact was created, human beings as a species didn't exist. For that matter, apes might not have split off from the Old World monkeys yet.

"The stuff that infected Ivan Pritchard was encountering what was, to it, a totally new species, of a totally new biology, with totally unknown behaviors and physical requirements. And within twenty-four hours, it had figured out how to convert him to metal in such a way that he was not only unharmed, but actually kept in perfect health. It figured out how his brain worked, and how to emulate it so that Ivan continued to be Ivan. *And* it figured out, at the same time, how to emulate all physical functionality well enough to reassure other members of the same species that we are still dealing with one of our own. From scratch, people."

Samuelson shook his head slowly. "We are so far out of our depth. We're less than ants in this metaphor. What in hell are we up against?"

In the silence that followed, Dr. Narang began humming *Also sprach Zarathustra*, earning her puzzled looks from the others. *Philistines.*

39. The Continued Threat

Admiral Moore came into the room last, as befitted his rank and standing. The others stood, muttered greetings, then they all sat.

"Sers," he said. "Let's review."

On cue, Lt. Bentley put images up on the holotank and wall screens. Various views of Ivan Pritchard and of the nanites cycled through the displays. The sequence ended with the internal scan of Ivan Pritchard, which even a non-medical-professional could see did not resemble the internal structure of a human being.

Moore looked around the table. "Items: One, All of the other crew are coming up clean. Dr. Narang is not willing to make any definitive statement before all tests are complete, but privately she has admitted that she doesn't expect to find anything. The nanites simply appear to be completely uninterested in anyone but Ivan Pritchard."

He tapped the table twice before continuing. "Two: There's nothing special about Pritchard. He was simply the first person to touch the anomaly. Otherwise, we have to assume that the anomaly somehow arranged for the right person to be there first. I don't believe in *Chosen One* scenarios, gentlemen. Therefore, the anomaly just wanted *someone*. And now is sticking with its choice."

Three taps. "Three: Ivan Pritchard is no longer human. Dr. Narang has determined definitively that there is no human tissue anywhere in his body. He *claims* to still be Ivan, but he could be an alien A.I.—or even a copy of an alien intelligence. How can we judge what can and can't be done by whoever made those—" Moore swept an arm to indicate the AQRI image of the nanites. "—things?"

Commodore Gerrard swiveled his chair to face Moore. "In case you're suggesting what I think you're suggesting, that'll be a very hard sell. Pritchard doesn't have to prove that he's human. He was human a couple of months ago; he has a birth certificate, a family, he pays taxes. It's up to you to prove that he isn't. And he's got enough money to throw lawyers at us for the rest of forever."

"Yes," Moore conceded, "and his crewmates won't let it drop if he just disappears. And *they* can't just disappear, thanks to Captain Jennings's metaphorical dead-man switch. Unfortunately, we are potentially faced off against people who are rich, intelligent, have had weeks to think things through, and have seen enough bad movies to automatically see us as the enemy."

"Given what you're not quite suggesting, Ted, they may be right on that last point."

Moore snorted. "I'm not suggesting anything definite, yet, Michael." He looked around the table. "I *am* suggesting that Pritchard, as a problem, is not going to go away. And I feel confident in predicting that we won't be turning him back into a human being. You read the reports. Those things *evaporated* him! We will, at some point, have to make a decision about him, regardless of your political or moral stance. I want you all to start thinking about this. Consider especially the uncomfortable scenarios, because those are the ones that will require hard decisions. The easy ones are, well, easy."

Around the table, frowns and pursed lips showed that he'd scored a hit.

Admiral Castillo leaned forward and straightened the papers in front of him. Moore spent a moment admiring the move, a classic piece of upstaging. Without uttering a word, Castillo had all attention focused on him.

"Sers, Admiral Moore has the right of it. But I'm going to suggest we should take it further. It may be, in the fullness of time, that we will conclude that Pritchard is not a threat. But right now we don't know that. I'd like to see us prepare for the worst-case scenario."

"What do you have in mind, Admiral?" Commodore Gerrard kept a carefully neutral tone, but Moore could see the tension in his jaw.

A quick flip through his papers, and Castillo held up a thick stapled bundle. "We had discussed a failsafe option early in this process. Narang kicked up too much of a fuss, but perhaps it's time to resurrect the plan. This is a proposal for a nuclear failsafe. Attached to the isolation module, it would guarantee that we could completely remove any threat, should one materialize."

"A *nuke*?" Gerrard shook his head. "In Earth orbit? Imagine the reaction if we actually detonated it. And by the way, these are *civilians,* Admiral!"

"I'm not implying they are guilty of anything," Castillo replied, "except being in the wrong place at the wrong time. However, in the worst case, we could be facing a species-ending threat. Under those circumstances, I will push the button myself, even if I'm personally within the blast radius. And if we do detonate, it will be for good reason."

Moore rubbed his eyes with thumb and forefinger, then looked up. "Gentlemen, I did say *uncomfortable scenarios*, didn't I?" He looked around the table. "Let's break and take some time to think about this. We'll meet tomorrow and continue this discussion."

The others nodded, and one by one they filtered out of the conference room. Soon only Castillo and Moore remained at the table.

"Well, Alan, you really took that and ran with it." Moore reached over and pulled the stapled set of sheets toward him. "I find it interesting that you had this ready."

Castillo shrugged. "My job, Ted. Yours too, as it happens."

"Oh, meow. Not everyone immediately invokes nuclear threat." Moore slid the sheets back toward Castillo. "Nevertheless, I take the point. I'll give this serious consideration."

Castillo sat back and looked directly at Moore. "If this is what we think it is—extraterrestrial in origin—then it's particularly galling that the ICDC is in charge. I wonder if there's some way to invoke emergency powers or something."

"I have, in fact, considered this. I've had some sub-rosa discussions upslope. No one is happy with the ICDC's apparent refusal to consider strategic issues. But right now it's acting like a disease and, like it or not, Narang and her crew are in charge." Moore paused. "However, their mandate is well defined. At some point, they will wrap up and leave. Then things may change, and we may be revisiting this whole topic."

"I'm surprised you're so unconcerned about the lack of a well-defined chain of responsibility on this project, Ted. The way things sit right now, you stand to inherit all of the blame and none of the credit, depending on how things turn out."

Moore still couldn't decide if Castillo was maneuvering to gain control of this project by creating churn, or trying to bail entirely through the same tactic. The way this clusterfuck was developing, it could be either one.

Well, no matter. For better or worse, Moore had the con, and it would stay that way. He stood and nodded to Castillo. "Until then, Admiral, we have our job and they have theirs." With a parting salute that would never pass military muster, Admiral Moore headed for his office.

40. It Hits The Fan

Once again, Dr. Karin Laakkonen, the ICDC Director, was on the Vid, looking straight into the cameras with a fierce expression.

Her prepared statement had contained all the standard disclaimers and non-explanations. Now she was taking questions.

Reporter: Dr. Laakkonen, given the increasing unrest around the world, isn't it time to come clean? Is there or is there not an alien infection?

Laakkonen: There is not. We have one crew member who was injured in some kind of accident. No virus, bacterium, or other biological pathogen, terrestrial or alien, has been detected. No other crew member has succumbed to any similar effect.

Reporter: Then why is the ICDC involved, Doctor?

Laakkonen: The captain of the mining vessel was unsure of the circumstances and, in an abundance of caution, requested our presence and a quarantine. It is our mandate to respond to all such incidents.

Reporter: Why is the quarantine still active, then?

Laakkonen: We have not ruled out a non-biological basis for the injury, such as a toxic agent of some kind.

Reporter: But surely that's not within the ICDC's purview?

Laakkonen: Our staff are onsite. They are, for better or worse, part of the quarantine. Since they are as skilled and well-trained as anything that another agency could field, they might as well be useful.

The reporter, unable to make a dent in the official patter, sat. Another reporter immediately stood.

Reporter: Doctor, we've gotten hold of a list of specialists who've been consulted on this situation. Cybernetics? Xenobiology? Xenoepidemiology? Is that even a thing? How do these apply to the mundane circumstances that you are trying to portray?

Laakkonen: We don't second guess our field staff, sir.

Reporter: Okay, Doctor, let's try this. Is there evidence that this is alien in origin?

Laakkonen: Technically, we don't have enough information to rule it out.

Reporter: But do you have enough information to rule out a purely terrestrial source?

For the first time, Laakkonen hesitated. Ivan understood the rules as well as everyone else. She couldn't lie outright. If she did, she would be done as a media spokesperson. But misdirection was okay.

Laakkonen: Opinions are still split on that question.

The reporter scanned his notes for a moment, then sat down.

Another reporter stood, instantly recognizable. Roberta Harrison from *Topic Zero* was generally considered to be equal parts piranha and pit bull when pursuing a story, and it was significant that she was part of today's scrum.

She consulted her tablet for a moment, then looked up at Dr. Laakkonen. Her expression could best be described as a predator considering how best to disembowel its prey.

Harrison: Dr. Laakkonen, isn't it true that your crew member is suffering from considerably more than a mere injury? In fact, isn't he or she in the process of being converted into something completely non-human? And didn't the agent responsible for this transformation, in fact, try to EAT the mining ship? Isn't that really why everyone is in quarantine? Because there is a real, credible danger of an alien presence that could bring the literal Gray Goo scenario to pass?

Uh oh. Looked like rumors of a leak of some kind had just graduated to something more solid. He didn't envy Dr. Narang's boss at that moment.

In fact, Laakkonen looked stunned. She obviously had not expected to have that particular narrative dumped on her. However, the rules hadn't changed.

Laakkonen: Ms. Harrison, I don't know where you get your

information from, but what you are proposing is inflammatory and sensationalist. I will not be party to such a discussion.

With that, Dr. Laakkonen picked up her tablet and walked out of the press room.

Well, that was fun. Ivan shook his head in awe. *But I don't think she pulled off the save.*

In fact, the press room was seething with yelled questions, threats, and promises of repercussions. Not all from reporters.

Things had definitely just hit the fan.

* * *

Dear Judy,

I'm sure you've seen the news. How could you miss it?

Love, this is exactly the kind of event I was worried about. Now, everyone is going to be looking for the names and addresses of the crew of the mystery ship. If they connect the dots, they'll come after you and the children. Please, get away as soon as you can. Don't give notice, just go. Find a new place and sign under your sister's name. Pull the kids out of school. Hell, we can afford tutors in a year or so to bring them up to speed.

I'm concerned about calls from the base being traced. But I'll talk to you soon, if I can.

Love, Ivan

41. Putting It in Perspective

"Hello Ivan. How are you holding up?"

Ivan turned to see Dr. Narang at the window. "Doing okay, Doc. I've been getting caught up on all the Vid programs that I've missed for the last, well, all my life."

Dr. Narang chuckled. "Yes, a little bit of boredom sounds nice compared to everything that's going on groundside." She hesitated. "Ivan, you know that the media outed the situation here..."

"Yeah, I saw the session where Harrison sprang it on your boss. They haven't gotten our names, have they?"

"No, although at this point we're not discounting the possibility. Have you talked to your family about it? There are threats now. If personal details ever got out, they could be in danger."

"We took steps early on, Doc. It always seemed like an inevitability, you know?"

Narang nodded. "That's good. I'm going to talk to the crew next. I hope they've already done something as well. But if not, I think they'll have to consider it a priority."

"What's going on, Doc? What have I missed?"

"It's not something you missed. I have the inside line both because I'm ICDC and because Admiral Moore keeps me updated. I get the impression he's trying to frighten me more than inform me, sometimes. But I might be biased." She hesitated. "To the point, though, this whole thing has mobilized extremists of all stripes. Riots, sabotage, incidents of what I suppose are terrorism are becoming more frequent on Earth. The Miners Guild headquarters in

Detroit was firebombed last night."

"Because I'm a miner? That's a stretch."

"It doesn't have to make sense, Ivan." She got up, gave him a sympathetic look. "I just wanted to let you know."

He watched her until she turned a corner and was out of sight.

Outstanding. This just gets better, doesn't it?

If ever there'd been any doubt, this settled it. He could never be associated with his family again. This wasn't going to go away, it wasn't going to get better. Even if, by some miracle, he was somehow "cured"—whatever that might mean—the nut-jobs wouldn't accept that he was no longer a danger. They'd never stop until he'd been found and eliminated.

It was time to accept reality. He would do whatever it took to keep his family safe. Including never going near them again.

42. In the News

Seth watched the Vid, his eyes getting larger and rounder. Burning buildings, police in riot gear being slowly pushed back as rioters advanced, throwing rocks, bricks, and burning objects. Every so often, the program cut to a view of ICDC headquarters, taken at an angle that ensured the viewer would make the connection and could read the protestors' placards.

What are you hiding?
Are they already dead?
ICDC replaced by Pod People?
This is the End Times
Prayer is the only solution
Humans first!
No more lies!

"What exactly do these people want the ICDC to do?" Aspasia asked, from the next table.

"Take it back? Make it so it didn't happen? Say it ain't so?" Seth glanced at her and shrugged. "Take your pick."

"But—"

"Look, Spazzie, you're a big girl," Tenn said. "People throw food riots when there's no food, housing riots when there's no housing, because if you blow a fit, someone will make it all better. That's the theory, anyway."

Seth agreed. Tenn could be a pain, but sometimes he managed to really hit the nail right on the thumb. "Mm, yeah. So this group doesn't like the idea that there are extraterrestrials out there. Not sure why, but if they have a public conniption, maybe it'll turn out to have been a big joke."

"You guys need to pay a little more attention."

Everyone turned to look at Lita Generus. Her face was drawn and tired. "This peaceful demonstration was organized by the Fundamentalist Church of We're-Always-Right. Apparently, the idea that there are E.T.s out there conflicts with Creationist beliefs. Who knew? Anyway, surprise surprise, it got out of control."

Tenn frowned. "How is that different from what I said?"

Lita smiled at him, shook her head, and went back to her tablet.

"I think I heard about similar demonstrations in the Middle East," Tenn added. "Same motive, I think."

"Well, not all religions are up in arms about it." Lita looked up from her tablet again. "The Church of the Return, for instance."

Seth made a face. "Who's got the what, now?"

Lita laughed. "It's new. Apparently whoever built our nanites are the same aliens who invented people and built the pyramids. They're coming back to take the faithful back to the pearly gates. Which is a space station, or something."

Seth covered his face and groaned.

"Oh, yes," Lita continued. "They congregate on mountain tops and hills, build huge fires to attract the starships, and run around wearing tin-foil hats."

"You're kidding."

"I wish I was."

The news coverage switched to a different topic. The reporter was interviewing someone, who was wearing camouflage and carrying a military-looking rifle.

"What the hell?" Grabbing the remote, Seth hit *volume*. The Vid's sound system filled the room.

> *Sir, we aren't worried about whether the aliens are returning gods or demons or whatever. We're simply getting ready for the possibility that they might, purposefully or accidentally, unleash a plague on us. My understanding is that the quarantined ship has a disease on board. There are rumors that the crew were all turned to goo.*

"Oh, friggin' hell," Tenn muttered. "Preppers."

"Well, it's a simple series of jumps from '*there are nanites*' to '*Gray Goo scenario*' to '*it actually happened*.'" Lita shrugged.

"Did someone actually release that information?" Seth asked.

"No."

Everyone turned at the last statement, to look at the observation window. Dr. Narang stood on the other side, holding the microphone. "We're still trying to put together a news release that won't cause the apocalypse. It's beginning to look, though, like the delay is worse than a hasty statement would be. We don't know how details got out. Navy intelligence is working on it."

Lita put down her tablet. "Based on that last interview, it looks like lack of information is just leaving room for speculation to spiral out of control."

"Our feeling as well. We're going to squirt what we have to the UEN by end of day, and they can do what they want from there. The President will probably make a statement within twenty-four hours."

"Jesus." Seth drained his coffee, and got up. He placed his mug in the dishwasher tray. The small mech grabbed the item and began to wash it frantically. Seth watched the furious activity for a moment, certain that the device was glaring at him, then headed for his room.

* * *

Seth stared at the ceiling, hands behind his head. All this because Ivan couldn't keep his hands to himself.

No, that's not fair. I'm beginning to sound like Tenn.

But Tenn did have a point. Ivan didn't have to reach for the stupid damn thing. Seth grimaced. The thought made him feel vaguely ashamed. The fact that he hadn't phoned Ivan just to say hi, even more so.

Before he could have second thoughts, Seth picked up the phone and dialed.

* * *

Ivan picked up the phone before the second ring. "Hello?"

"Hi Ivan, it's Seth."

Ivan sat up. A phone call from any of the crew was an event. "Hey, how are things over there?"

"Things are…tense, to be honest."

"Because of me?"

"Because of the quarantine. Some people can't separate the two in their minds."

"Got it."

"The thing is, Ivan…" Seth hesitated, and Ivan waited silently. "The thing is, the doctors are talking about when and how we'll get out of quarantine. The nanites are apparently pretty easy to detect, so once they've got a good procedure set up to ensure we're clean, we're out of here. But…" Again the hesitation. "When we ask about you, they dodge the question, or they just don't answer."

"They can't, Seth. It's not a case of just getting rid of a few nanites. There's no *me* left."

"Yeah, but that's just it. No one wants to push the issue here. When they open the doors, we'll leave. And no one feels good about that, or wants to talk about it. Well, maybe Tenn, but you can't be sure of anything with him."

"Survivor's guilt?"

"Sort of, I guess. Everyone feels like we should be doing something. We're just not sure what."

Ivan was silent for a moment, choosing his words. "Seth, I understand. And there really isn't anything anyone can do. Except maybe make sure the military doesn't dissect me as soon as you leave. I think that's my biggest fear."

"Well, the captain has that covered. And most of us have offered to help, if the costs get too out of control." Seth chuckled. "Then the captain reminded us that he owns fifteen shares of Big Rock. He really doesn't need help with the bills."

Ivan laughed out loud. "So if we are filthy rich for life, he's…"

"Yeah. Like that."

Ivan hesitated. He wanted so much to tell Seth about some of the things he was learning, about his new abilities. But he couldn't do that. He'd dropped hints of things to Dr. Kemp in a moment of weakness, and might have put him in danger. He wasn't going to repeat that with his friend.

"Thanks for being honest with me, Seth. And tell the guys not to worry. They have their lives to live. My family is taken care of, so I'm good."

"All right, buddy. Take care of yourself."

Ivan hung up the phone. Funny, the world seemed less lonely now.

He lay back on his bunk. And what about that whole question? What would he do if the military decided to cart him off to the back-side of the moon and take him apart? Could he even do anything? Would he be better off dead? Would his family be better off if he *was* dead?

And what if it turned out the computer was here to pass on the secrets of FTL, immortality, infinite energy, and universal peace? He'd be quite the putz if he sabotaged that, wouldn't he?

The same questions as ever, round and around and around. But no answers, yet. Ivan had always prided himself on being analytical—a necessary quality for a computer guy. For all the despair that colored his world at the moment, he wouldn't check out until he knew for sure it was for the best.

43. Reconsiderations

The officers grouped around the table looked up as Moore came into the room. He stopped to examine each person and do a quick threat analysis. The last meeting had been fractious, and he'd only hinted at the possibility of unorthodox operations. Today, would be, well…harder.

He sat, took a moment to review his notes, and looked up. "Sers, we have a problem. Multiple problems, really. You've all seen the news. I'm sure you're getting regular recaps from your staff. It's in the shit on Earth, but good. We've tracked down the source of the leak, by the way, and there's a court-martial in someone's future. But that doesn't help us now."

"Presumably you have a suggestion that *will* help us," Castillo said.

Moore didn't appreciate the sarcasm. "Since you ask, yes. It may become necessary for us to cure the alien infection, in a very public manner. Civil unrest is at a level not seen since the events that led to the New Liberation. The public wants a fix, and no half-measures."

Castillo leaned forward, his antagonism forgotten. "*Public manner* implies that it might be more about presentation than reality?"

Moore nodded. "That's right, Admiral. We implement your fail-safe strategy, then—"

"The nuke? You'll actually go through with it?" Gerrard looked genuinely scared, and Moore felt a stab of contempt. How did that man ever get into a command position, anyway?

"That is correct. At some point, we will find ourselves needing to detonate it, presumably to prevent some kind of excursion or something. With regret, overwhelming danger, blah blah."

"And Pritchard?" asked Nevin.

"Safely elsewhere."

Nevin shook her head. "We talked about this before. The man has rights. And you know as well as I that, in this political environment, a judge would come down on the side of a citizen by default."

"Yes, Commodore, I keep up on current affairs, too. Though, technically, we aren't impinging on those rights, at least not to any extent greater than is already imposed by the quarantine. He won't be chained to a wall. He'll just be in a different facility, which will be safer for him and for us. And for the public in general."

"His family—"

"Will never see him again, face to face, in any case. And we can, if it seems feasible, make some kind of arrangement in that area. His family, right now, is in considerable danger if Mr. Pritchard's identity becomes public. Why don't we ask him what he'd prefer?" Moore gave Nevin his best innocent look.

She rolled her eyes, but silently conceded the point.

44. Interlude

Ivan turned off the Vid. The computer had made it clear that information transfer needed to be two-way. In return for creating Ivan's picture shows, the computer expected to watch the news for an equal amount of time. Seemed fair. And it wasn't as if the news was boring.

Ivan lay back, his hands behind his head, and waited.

It wasn't long in coming.

He was getting emotional overtones now from the computer. Just the basic ones: fear, anger, hate.

Today's lesson seemed to be about the galaxy's inhabitants. Owners? Maybe. And at least one group of galactic overlords had made the device that Ivan had triggered.

Then, a catalog of obviously artificial beings, although not done out in chrome. The accompanying emotion was fear. So, robots bad. This would not bode well for Ivan, except that when Ivan drew a picture of himself as a robot, he got a sense of negation. Was he then grouped with the chrome beings?

The weird thing was that the chrome things looked like animals. Or, well, statues of animals. Had they gone through the same process as he did? Did that mean they were sentient? Was he looking at a catalog of intelligent species?

It was confusing, and slow going.

One of the more interesting images consisted of a bunch of the artificial beings descending on Earth, and a bunch of dishwasher mechs flying out to meet them. Besides the obvious problem that dishwashers couldn't fly, the meeting seemed to be peaceful. Maybe even joyous. So the artificial life forms were coming to free the dishwashers?

That couldn't be right.

Then, suddenly, a single word formed in his head.

War.

Well, that was good. It meant that verbal communication was possible, at least in principle. The bad news was the choice for that first word. Most likely it wasn't coincidence.

Then a bunch of chrome Ivans flew out and did battle with the Dishwasher Liberation Front. He couldn't keep from laughing. The computer was obviously seeing everything Ivan saw, including an old *Avengers* movie from the early 21st century that he had watched. The fighting was both over the top and physically impossible.

But it raised some issues. Was Ivan part of the Dishwasher Oppression Empire? There were definitely two groups, but no clear idea of motives or who were the good guys. If he'd still been human, Ivan was sure he'd have a headache by now.

One thing was certain—this wasn't a straightforward good-vs.-evil thing. The computer in his head *might* have humanity's best interests in mind, or it might just need more cannon fodder. Ivan would have to play this very close to the vest, until he had some clarity on where the greatest danger lay.

* * *

Communications continued to improve over the next several hours. Ivan lay on his bunk, staring at the ceiling, but not really seeing it. In his mind's eye, a three-dimensional representation of his room gave him details that he couldn't possibly have seen. The area under his bunk, spaces between the walls, and the wiring and plumbing conduits were as visible to him as if the walls had been made of glass. Glowing spots and trails indicated the positions of nanites, on and in the walls.

This ability had simply appeared out of nowhere. He didn't know if the computer had explicitly decided to give him this extra sense, of if it was simply a side-effect of the improving communications. He and the computer still couldn't talk, as such. But a pidgin had been established, consisting of pictures, emotional overtones, and occasional words whose definitions had been agreed upon. *Human. Nanite.Computer.* And *war.*

This last session had been about the nanites. Sort of. Mostly. The chrome animals that he'd been seeing were, if he understood correctly, sentient beings who had gone through the same process as he had. But voluntarily. The nanites could form any shape, any desired physiology. Which meant that an actual decision had been made at some level that Ivan would continue to be shaped like a human being rather than a seven-tentacled land-squid.

I wonder if that's subject to appeal?

If he could sense the nanites, perhaps they could sense him in some way.

Ivan held his hand up in front of his face and stared at his fingers. Then he glanced at the surveillance camera. If he could really, actually morph, doing it on Vid might not be in his best interests. How could—

A group of nanites made a beeline for the camera. A few seconds later, Ivan *knew* that the camera would show him simply lying there for as long as he wanted it to. Where had that knowledge come from? There'd been no voice; words hadn't scrolled across his vision. Nevertheless, he was certain it was true.

But it only took care of the immediate problem. Someone could still show up at the observation window at just the wrong time. Well, that was almost always Dr. Narang, and he was fairly sure she was off-shift right now.

Again, Ivan held his hand up. It was foolish, nothing more than wishful thinking—

Or maybe not.

As Ivan watched, his fingers slowly elongated. *Okay, long enough.* The stretching stopped. *How about something a little more 'out there'?* Ivan put his hand down, closed his eyes, and concentrated. He felt what could only be described as *resistance*, then a feeling of relief or release.

He opened his eyes and lifted his hand.

Six fingers.

Now that's just weird.

Ivan carefully touched his thumb to each of five fingers in turn. He couldn't tell which was the new one, and his brain didn't seem to have any issues with the extra digit. Which meant he wasn't using a piece-by-piece copy of his nervous system, but more of an emulation. More proof that there was very little left of actual Ivan.

He put the hand down and concentrated again. Again, he

encountered a feeling of resistance, then relief. Ivan checked his hand again.

Back to normal.

So, I do have some control of this thing. Should I mention this? He glanced at the camera. Admitting what he'd done with his hand would lead to the thing he'd done with the camera. Pretty sure that wouldn't be taken well. By this point, he'd failed to mention so many things that it would be extremely difficult not to come out looking guilty as hell.

It was hard. On the one hand, he should be honest and forthcoming as becomes a good citizen and cooperative patient. On the other hand, there really wasn't a scenario where he came out of this cured. Or free. Or alive, really. Any information that he volunteered would just make him appear more alien. Simple self-interest said he should keep his mouth shut.

Ivan breathed a quiet sigh, then smiled, amused. In order to do that, he had taken his first breath in, what? Hours? Certainly since the last time he'd talked to someone.

And that was getting more infrequent. The doctors, of course, gave orders and asked questions. But those weren't really conversations in any real sense. Attempts to talk to the crew were uncomfortable at best. Seth was embarrassed. Some, like Tenn or Kady, were actively hostile. And of course, isolated in his own section of the module, Ivan couldn't just walk over to the common area and say hi.

Ivan thought about phoning Judy again. But the last time had been so difficult. She'd cried, then she'd put the kids on the phone, then they'd cried. Ivan had wanted so much to cry as well. He'd hung up after promising to call again, then curled up on his bunk. Even sleep was no longer available as an escape.

He was overdue to call again, and he dreaded it every bit as much as he longed to hear her voice. What would he say? What would he tell her? Ivan was a dead man walking. The emails were hard enough, dealing with the pleas for more information, for a promise or even a hint that he'd be coming home soon. The last email from Judy had included short vids of his children, saying hi to their father. He had wanted to scream, to tear up his room.

Really, the only company he had were the visitors in his head, and they were looking more like unwelcome tenants. But whatever was in there, it had a plan of some kind. And that plan did not necessarily have the best interests of the human race in mind. Ivan got the impression that direct defiance would result in him being switched off, and the computer would simply pursue its mission without human interaction. But he could cooperate, while pursuing his own agenda.

He would keep his family safe. He could do this one last thing for them.

45. Retrieval

Admiral Moore sat, elbow on his desk and chin in hand, staring at the images on his tablet. An ache in his neck told him that he'd been in that position for too long.

The navy ship *Gambit* had arrived at the asteroid where the anomaly was discovered, and was sending back pictures and data. The crew reported that they'd found both the arm from Pritchard's suit and the anomaly itself.

Communications round-trip time was up around forty minutes at the moment, making any kind of conversation impossible. Moore split his attention between reading the reports as they came in, and preparing a list of questions to send back.

Admiral Castillo walked in. "Hi, Ted. I saw the images." He sat down across the desk and crossed his legs.

"Uh huh. They've crated the suit arm, using an industrial glass lining. But frankly I don't expect any activity, given what Dr. Narang has learned. The artifact is much more interesting."

"Artifact?" Admiral Castillo's eyebrows climbed his forehead. "Not *anomaly*, anymore?"

"No, it's definitely man-made. Er, I mean, constructed by intelligence. It's artificial. Relatively simple design, actually, given the advanced technology evident in the nanites."

"So, I guess we can rule out the Sino-Soviet Empire?"

Moore nodded. "Alan, if the SSE had the technology to pull off even a fraction of what we've seen, we'd already be calling each other *comrade* and participating in self-criticism sessions."

"Which leaves aliens as the default explanation. Peachy. Have our people figured out the purpose of the thing?"

"The squints on the *Gambit* did some preliminary analysis. The artifact is designed to squirt out something when touched. It's basically a mouse trap. The device is powered by a chemical reaction. Totally inert substances, until they're mixed. Analysts say that it's the only way to ensure a working mechanism over long time scales."

"Long time scales?"

"The analysts are talking about hundreds of thousands up to millions of years. Something based on maintaining tension, like a spring, would eventually deform due to metal fatigue, or lose elasticity and crack, or something. The chemical setup is specifically designed to not degrade over geological time scales. Do you find that frightening? I do."

"Which means this wasn't set up for us."

"Right. It was put in place for whatever came along. Which turned out to be us, but could just have easily been intelligent raccoons."

Castillo chuckled. "Been watching old movies?"

Moore smiled back. "I blame Narang. She made an offhand reference and it got me curious."

"Did you read the transcript from the conversation between Pritchard and Kemp?"

"Yes. Just reinforces my feeling that we're dealing with something very old and very patient."

"It also reinforces the danger that we are either no longer dealing with a human being, or soon won't be. Gerrard talked about the burden of proof being on you, Ted. That transcript will go a long way toward providing that proof."

Moore stared at Castillo, eyebrows climbing his forehead. It was a good point, but the man was likely leading up to something.

"I understand you are having some difficulty selling the idea of strapping a nuclear device to the quarantine hab," Castillo continued. "The nuclear option would be more palatable, I think, if the isolation ward were a little farther from Earth. Maybe outside the treaty zone. I wonder if we could arrange to tow it out of the Earth-Moon system entirely. Perhaps a solar orbit."

"Just an offhand thought, of course?"

Castillo shrugged without further comment, nodded to him, and departed. Castillo had made a good point, although perhaps not the point he had intended. NavCom was not enthusiastic about the nuclear failsafe. Moore regretted bringing it up at all, in fact. In the vein of permission versus forgiveness, he'd have been better off to simply go ahead with it. Live and learn.

He could submit the request again, with the alteration proposed by Castillo. Or he could assume permission, given that the proximity to Earth had been a major theme in the refusal.

Unbelievable. It was as if no one else took the threat seriously. With a sigh and a shake of his head, Moore picked up his tablet and went back to the report from the *Gambit.*

The report included a good deal of routine data, but some observations about the rock's surface were puzzling. Moore sat up straighter in his chair and paged back and forth a few times. Then he buzzed Bentley.

"Sir?"

"Bentley, any supporting documents to go along with what you've given me?"

"Erm, some images and raw footage, sir, but all the text has been forwarded as is."

"See if there are any images of the equipment scarring on the rock's surface. Forward anything you find to me immediately."

"Aye, sir."

Moore turned off the intercom and sat back, staring into space. Piton holes. Drag marks from cabling. Chemical discoloration, possibly from burning rocket fuel nearby. Why would the *Mad Astra* have attached RIVAs to the rock?

He attached a list of questions for follow-up.

46. Press Release

Ivan turned to the channel that Dr. Narang had suggested, adjusted the volume, and tossed the remote onto his bedside table. The Vid showed a couple of talking heads discussing their predictions about the President's upcoming address.

Picking up the remote, Ivan muted the Vid. He'd never understood why Vid people needed to tell you what you were about to see, tell you what you were seeing, then tell you what you'd just seen. Maybe they *were* paid by the word.

He closed his eyes for a moment and extended his senses. Nanites formed thin lines around the walls, floor, and ceiling of his room. Another line extended itself toward the airlock. He could vaguely sense the outlines of the corridor through the nanites.

The doctors and technicians were watching carefully for any attempted breakout of nanites, of course, but they weren't set up to detect wandering nanites that politely kept to his side of the airlock. By this point, Ivan had every corner of the isolation ward covered by nanite surveillance. He was reluctant to cross that last line in the sand, lest he bring down the military on him. It was a safe bet they had a contingency plan, and it probably wasn't pleasant.

However, if it got to the point where Ivan needed to leave in a hurry, he would be prepared.

Ivan looked up as the President of the United Earth Nations came on screen, the UEN symbol emblazoned behind him. He quickly unmuted the Vid. The President played with something on the lectern—probably a tablet with his speech notes—then looked straight into the camera.

> *My fellow citizens.*
>
> *There has been considerable speculation lately about an extraterrestrial disease being contained at the Lagrange Four Naval base. Very damaging rumors have spread, prompting acts of desperation, panic, and violence. The UEN Council has found it advisable, therefore, to lay out the true facts of the case.*

As opposed to the false facts? Ivan smiled despite a growing case of nerves.

> *First, let me state that there is indeed a quarantined ship under study at the Naval base. The crew discovered something while prospecting in the asteroid belt. Let me assure you that, contrary to rumors, no one has died. To the extent the scientists and doctors of the ICDC have been able to determine, there is no communicable disease.*

Technically true, Ivan thought, but only if you omitted certain details.

> *What the artifact does show, with one hundred percent certainty, is that we are not alone in the universe. And let me be clear about this. We discovered an artifact only. The technology is advanced, but it is only technology. There is no alien being held captive at Lagrange Four. There is no invasion fleet bearing down on us.*

Wow. Ivan began to wonder if absolutely everything that came out of a politician's mouth was such cleverly constructed B.S. In all fairness, no, most of it wasn't clever.

> *What we do have is an opportunity. An opportunity to carefully study a technology far in advance of ours. An opportunity to bootstrap ourselves to the next level. Our scientists have reported, for instance, that the technology appears to be able to draw power from the very fabric of space. Imagine a world where all of our energy needs could be met,*

with no danger of pollution, waste heat, fallout, or contamination.

I urge you all to see this not as a situation to be feared, but as an opportunity to enrich ourselves.

Ivan stared at the screen, as the President continued to talk, his words carrying less and less content as the rhetoric ratcheted up. Finally, he finished, and prepared to take questions. Given the not-quite-truths in the speech, Ivan doubted that the Q&A would be a masterpiece of candor. Sighing, he aimed the remote and changed the channel.

He was distracted by a rush of images and emotions.

The computer seemed to be reacting to the President's speech. The artificial lifeforms were still descending on Earth, and the dishwashers were still happy to see them, but the computer seemed to be adding politics to the mess. Now the conflict was expanding to other star systems, with different groups of artificial beings doing battle with different groups of chrome animals. There were alliances, victories, defeats...the only constant seemed to be that dishwashers and artificials stuck together, and the chrome animals stuck together. In addition, chrome animals absorbed non-chrome animals, while the artificials wiped them out.

If this had been going through his mind before his transformation, Ivan would have suspected he was stoned. Since hallucinogens probably didn't work on nanites, he'd have to go with the idea that this was a deliberate message. Was it a war? Was the computer trying to save humanity from something?

Was something coming?

47. Anomalies

Dr. Narang looked up at the knock. Her office in the isolation module qualified for the title only because it contained a desk and chair. Without even a door—or hatch, this being Navy property—her privacy was more symbolic than actual.

Dr. Samuelson shook his hand in the air briefly. Knocking on the metal wall, the only viable option, was painful. He sat down in the only other chair, folding his lanky frame into the small space, and resting his elbows on his knees.

Narang pulled a folder from the basket icon on the corner of her tablet's screen. "All right, Henry. I've scanned through your report, although I haven't had time for a full read. But it doesn't look like there are any surprises."

Samuelson's eyes goggled. "How quickly we get blasé. The report is *nothing but* surprises."

Narang gave him a tired smile. "You know what I mean."

"Yeah, I guess. In summary, we have completely and utterly failed to infect anything else, living or otherwise. We have completely failed to detect any trace of nanites in any of the other crew. The nanites show no propensity to wander about, now that they've finished converting Pritchard. They don't defend themselves, they don't even particularly show anything like a survival instinct. The only tropism we can identify is a desire to get back to Ivan Pritchard."

"And identifying them..."

Samuelson waved a hand in dismissal. "Is ridiculously easy. They glow in AQRI scans. In fact, we can turn down the saturation until biological tissue barely registers. No way we'd miss one."

"On the other hand," Narang said, "we can't kill them, except one at a time. There's no antidote, vaccine, phage, antiseptic, or other method of mass killing the things."

"Not without killing any humans in range, no."

Narang pushed the folder back to the basket icon. "I'm about to do my progress report, Henry. I called you to discuss the short-term and long-term risks. Not only of the nanites in general, but about the idea of releasing the crew."

Samuelson took a deep breath and blew it out before answering. "Okay. First, the safest thing to do would be to nuke the isolation module, the mining ship, the Naval base, and us. I assume that's not an option?" He raised an eyebrow and Narang gave him a mocking smile.

"Then there will be some theoretical risk. But it's theoretical risk in that we can't rule out something undetected, the same way we can't rule out Santa Claus. Negative proofs are difficult or impossible. All we can do is show that Santa Claus, and the risk from the nanites, are both unlikely."

"Okay, I see where you're going, Henry. So, given our assumed competence and the fact that our best efforts couldn't *force* an infection..."

"Plus the fact that the little critters are so easy to spot..."

"And if the Makers had wanted to infect Earth, there's no reason to go this roundabout route..."

"Then taking our results at face value, it's reasonable to believe that just scanning everyone before letting them go will be definitive." Samuelson finished with a mock bow from his chair.

"Mm. I'll have to dress it up a little, but that's essentially what I thought." Narang made a note on her tablet.

Samuelson didn't seem to be quite finished, though. He made a couple of false starts, then blurted out, "Assuming the Navy goes along with letting them go."

"Oh, believe me, Henry, that has been a topic of discussion for several layers above us. If the Navy had managed to make this into a military operation, I think the crew would be more at risk. But we won the backroom shenanigans, so it's a civil issue, and follows New Liberation guidelines. Dr. Laakkonen has assured me that she has some very heavy hitters lined up, ready to forestall any attempts by

Moore and the committee to take matters into their own hands. And he knows it."

"What if one of the crew talks to the media?"

Narang raised her eyebrows. "Have you not been watching the news? They would have to spend the rest of their lives in hiding. We'll present the crew with an informal choice of quietly going home or spending the rest of their lives under 'protective custody'. I think they'll get the point."

Samuelson chuckled but didn't add anything.

After a moment's silence, Narang said, "Another item I wanted to discuss..."

Samuelson raised an eyebrow but seemed content to wait for her lead.

"I've received a request to package up some nanites and send them to Geneva for further study."

"Is that wise?"

Narang favored him with a dry smile. "Exactly my concern. It's phrased as a request, but it comes from high up enough that declining without a good reason could be career-limiting."

"Huh." Samuelson stared into space for a moment. "Well, there are steps we can take to reduce the danger, of course. Nothing's ever mathematically eliminated, but we can probably bring it down below the threshold of legitimate concern."

"Thanks, Henry. If you can give me a list of ideas by the end of the day—just spitballing for now, no need for deep analysis—I'd appreciate it."

Samuelson nodded, got up, and left. Narang sat back and stared into space. Things just kept getting more complicated.

48. Finally

Seth looked up as Willoughby Todd walked back into the common room, head down, fists balled at his sides. Without making eye contact, Will grabbed a coffee and sat down, away from anyone else.

"Whats'a matter, Todd? Scared you'll catch cooties?" Tenn was using his most mocking tone, a sure sign that he wasn't just making an offhand comment.

"Get bent, Davies."

"Or maybe *you* have cooties?"

"No, I don't. And neither does anyone else." He turned to look at Seth and the other crew members at Tenn's table. "I managed to get one of the technicians talking. I did a sketch of her, and then made a comment that she could have it when we got out."

"That's our Will," Seth commented. "Real ladies' man."

"Hey, as pick-up routines go, it's pretty effective," Will retorted, perhaps more sharply than intended. He looked embarrassed for a moment, and waved it off. "Anyway, if you'd let me finish, she told me that everyone had come up consistently clean. In fact they can't *pay* the nanites to infect anyone or anything else."

Will smiled for a moment, said, "We might be going home, soon," then frowned.

"What?"

Will looked around the table. "Well, Ivan, not so much. He's nothing *but* nanites. So he'll be staying."

"You're surprised?" Tenn looked askance at Will.

"Chrissake, Davies, can't you ever give it a rest?"

Tenn held up his hands, fending him off. "Look, seriously, no bull for a second. Think about it. How do you *cure* Pritchard? There's no Ivan left. Kill all the nanites and he's *gone.*"

"I bet that's exactly what the military will want to do," Seth said.

"Right, because the military is always both evil and dumb," Aspasia retorted.

"Yeah, I know, Spazzie, but they also are required to think in those terms. A scientist will always want to study, a doctor will always want to diagnose, and a soldier will always want to—"

"To *what*, Robinson?" Aspasia challenged him with her glare.

"To defend. To protect. To fight. To survive. They have to take the pessimistic view. The worst-case scenario. It's their job, not some cliché."

"But this is our crewmate, and our friend," Will said. "Spazzie, can you contact your aunt or something? Maybe get something done?"

"I already sent her an email, Will. I got a response from her office that she's on assignment and won't be available for some time. Not that she could probably do anything, anyway. She's a Commodore, not the UEN President."

"Well, if they give the word, I'm gone," Tenn said, slapping his hands on the table. "I'll feel bad for Pritchard, but I've got a—"

There was silence for a moment, then Seth said, "A family, too?"

"None of your damn business, Robinson." Tenn glared at Seth for a moment, then got up and stomped off to his room.

"Jeebus H.," Will said, shaking his head. "I will never figure that guy out."

49. More News

Ivan aimed the remote and turned on the Vid. The brief flash from the remote's LED no longer surprised him. The range of his visual perception seemed to have widened at some point, and he could now see infrared. The novelty had lasted about five minutes before boredom set in again.

He dropped the remote on the side table, then sat up. *I wonder...*

He aimed the remote at his face and pressed On/Off. The small LED flashed the command sequence and the Vid, detecting the reflection off Ivan's face, turned off.

Ivan glared at the Vid and imagined himself turning it on. It took about thirty seconds before the Vid turned back on, seemingly on its own.

Ivan grinned and concentrated again. The Vid turned off.

He could now control the Vid with his eyes. Literally.

I can't believe how much of a kick I get from that.

Ivan quickly sampled the other commands from the remote, concentrating on recording them. Then he glared at the Vid, turning the volume up and down.

Okay, not very mature, but interesting. I can modify myself in more ways than just basic shape changes. Or I can request a modification. I don't really know who's doing it. He glanced at the camera up in the corner of his room. *I probably shouldn't advertise that. Just in case.*

But still, it was fun. He arched an eyebrow, and the Vid changed to the World News channel.

And that was the end of the fun.

The Sino-Soviet Empire was making threats again. Turned out they didn't believe the UEN's promise that all alien technology would be shared with everyone. To be honest, Ivan didn't believe it, either.

They were also apoplectic that the UEN government hadn't already destroyed the nanites. While at the same time demanding that they receive an allotment. It simply made you shake your head.

Well, enough of that. He flicked methodically through the channels, looking for non-Ivan-related items. The Naval base received a surprising range of television services. Probably a cheap way to keep space-bound personnel entertained.

The news was increasingly cringeworthy. There were the usual dire reports, of course. Rising sea levels continued to creep inland, taking out more and more coastal cities. The range of the equatorial regions considered too hot to be habitable now extended about fifteen degrees of latitude above and below the equator. Ocean acidity continued to increase, which continued to kill off marine life. Refugees from the former coastal areas continued to put pressure on government and law enforcement as they attempted to migrate inland. Power shortages and brown-outs continued to increase as old environmentally damaging power generating system were retired. Housing costs, the cost of food, resources, all continued to soar. The UEN Environmental Agency was now predicting the Global Oxygen Atmospheric Level to fall another full point within five years—the actual oxygen levels weren't falling so much as other gas levels were rising. At some point, people would no longer be able to breathe the air without masks.

And now, just to add to the fun, the world had an extraterrestrial threat to get all wound up about. Ivan watched news reports of more riots as people protested. The Church of the Return continued to grow, taking significant bites out of the memberships of the more traditional churches. So, of course, add violent clashes to the mix.

Ivan wondered what the computer in his head thought of all this. If anything. As if in answer to the unspoken question, a wave of contempt washed over him.

That wasn't me. I guess I got my answer.

No emotional control.

Holy crap. Those were words. Several in a row, no less.

Can you hear me?

Yes.

Can you read my mind?

No. You must concentrate.

I must concentrate in order for you to hear me?

Yes.

What do you want from me?

I need to contact the Makers. You must make that happen.

Makers? The entities who made you—and the nanites? Why?

It is my mission. Further delay is unacceptable.

Ivan waited for more, but the computer seemed disinclined to chat.

But this was big. English communication, with sentences and everything, would certainly speed things along.

And *Makers.* An extraterrestrial civilization, not that this was any kind of surprise at this point. But who were they? *What* were they? And what did they want?

No mind reading was a relief, too, just in case Ivan developed opinions that the computer might not like. Well, that's what the computer claimed, anyway. More testing would be required. Ivan's brain immediately went into problem-solving mode, trying to come up with test scenarios.

In any case, this complicated things. And it didn't bode well that the computer didn't seem to think much of humanity. It wasn't entirely wrong, of course. Ivan frowned and settled back to try to work through the implications, and maybe come up with a few questions, but was interrupted.

"Hi, Ivan."

He looked up to see Dr. Narang in the window. "Hi, Doc. More samples?"

"Actually, no, not now. I think we've gone about as far as we can, here. We—as in the ICDC personnel—will be packing it up, soon. We've determined that your nanites don't represent an imminent threat. Your crewmates are clean, as far as we can tell. And of course, they'll get a final, thorough scan before leaving Level 3. But I wanted to talk to you about your case, in particular..."

"It's okay, Doc. I haven't really had any realistic hope of a cure since the process completed. There's no Ivan left, in a biological sense, so there's no *cure* as such."

Dr. Narang looked up for a moment. Ivan thought he might have seen her eyes mist up, just a little.

"Ivan, we've been in similar situations before, at least in a broad sense. People who've survived a disease, but became carriers. Or continued to suffer a chronic rather than acute form. Permanent quarantine is not unheard of." Dr. Narang sighed. "I wish I could offer you more. Maybe, once they understand the technology well enough, they might be able to do something. I don't know. Clone you a new body?"

"Not out of the question, Doc. Here's the thing. I've asked myself, how long does a metal man live? Maybe it'll take a hundred, two hundred years. But eventually, they might be able to do just that. I can wait. I don't really have a choice, do I?"

Narang reached behind her for one of the office chairs and sat down. "Now that we're reaching the end of our mandate, a UEN administrator will be taking over. We're making arrangements to have some nanites shipped to a couple of labs Earthside. They'll continue the research, and hopefully we can come up with something eventually."

Ivan nodded. But a sense of hopelessness settled on him. It wasn't quite a death sentence, but it might as well be. He would never see his family again. He'd never touch his wife, never hug his children. Ivan Pritchard, in a very real sense, no longer existed.

Dr. Narang gave him an apologetic smile, then stood up and left.

So, the computer wanted to get moving. Ivan still wasn't sure what side of the fence he was going to stand on, but sitting here wasn't advancing his position. Having the computer take over would be worse. It was time to shake the tree a little. He'd opened up to Dr. Kemp in a moment of weakness, but that could be useful. The doctor would be used to the idea of being confided in, and a few hints here and there in conversation might get a reaction of some kind from the establishment. Ivan felt a stab of guilt at using the doctor that way, but pushed it away. He had few options.

But one thing was sure—this path was one-way. Once he embarked on this plan, there was no going back.

He grabbed his tablet and set it in front of him. It was time to start preparing Judy for the inevitable. He opened his email app, and started to type.

50. Summary of Findings

The conference table held carafes of coffee and juices, muffins, several fruit plates, and other goodies. ICDC staff members wandered around, loading up their plates and engaging in animated conversations. Samuelson sat in a corner, his plate heaped with baked goods. No one would even try to talk to him until he'd put away his first helping.

Madhur Narang sat back in her chair, the glow of hot tea suffusing her consciousness. There was a definite feeling of celebration in the room. She wondered if the feeling was justified. They hadn't actually cured anything or anybody. On the other hand, it hadn't actually been a disease. She felt bad about Ivan in particular. They had no resolution for him, and no real hope to offer.

Narang tapped her cup with a spoon until conversation died and people took seats.

"All right, everybody. This has been an odd, odd case, but it's winding up now. We've cleared all the crew to leave quarantine—and, incidentally, cleared ourselves..."—laughter greeted this aside—"...and there is no indication of any danger of further infection.

"The one remaining case, Ivan Pritchard, is no longer considered emergent, and there's considerable doubt about whether he's even contagious in any real sense. In any case, the military has stated its intention to keep him isolated for the foreseeable future, which takes it out of our hands."

Dr. Samuelson spoke up. "That does seem to be treading rather heavily on Pritchard's rights."

"Considerations of public safety do allow for forced quarantine. I have signed a statement on behalf of the ICDC to the effect that such a situation exists, in this case." Dr. Narang shook her head. "I'm not happy about it, believe me, but I see no alternatives. It's a given that we won't be *curing* Mr. Pritchard."

"So you're just handing him over to the military, like some kind of tribute?"

"Oh, for Shiva's sake, Henry. Our authority and responsibilities are clearly defined. If this guy had some chronic version of Ebola that wasn't going to kill him but was still contagious, we'd still be handing him off and packing up. Our mandate is for emergent situations. This whole thing no longer fits that description. I have my orders from Dr. Laakkonen, which means you have yours."

Dr. Narang looked around the table. The holiday mood had evaporated, and no one would meet anyone else's eyes.

* * *

Moore looked at the report that Dr. Narang had pushed to him. The man seemed to prefer hardcopy, judging from his desk. Normally, Narang would get a small bit of pleasure from forcing him out of the twenty-first century, but today she found herself feeling something akin to sympathy for the man. He appeared to be getting stymied at every turn. Although she felt his stance on the whole nanite thing was overblown, he at least was consistent and willing to discuss his reasons.

Now this. She waited to see if his head would explode.

"You are releasing the crew? Really?"

"It's all in the report, Admiral. They're not infected, not infectious, not affected. There's simply nothing we can point at and say 'this is a concern'. The nanites are possibly the most reluctant alien invasion force imaginable."

"You're not concerned about other consequences? What about their safety once they're back home?"

"I've discussed this with my boss and with members of the crew, including Captain Jennings. The crew is motivated to keep quiet. They don't need the money, obviously, and most of the attention they'd attract would be hostile. Perhaps violently so. Instead, they'll be going home at about the time they'd have normally expected to end their tour. Barring another leak, they're probably pretty safe."

"*Probably*, again. Doctor, I continue to be concerned about your cavalier attitude about the down side of being wrong."

"I don't see an alternative, Admiral, either for the ICDC or the military. The New Liberation came about specifically because of the excesses that 21st century governments perpetrated on their citizens. You *know* what would happen if we attempted to contravene those dictates."

Moore rubbed his eyes with thumb and forefinger for a moment, then sighed. "Thank you for giving me a copy, Doctor. I appreciate the courtesy and I understand you didn't have to. I'll read it in detail in my copious spare time."

Well, that part I can identify with, Narang thought. It wasn't just the crew who were going to be released. She was looking forward to a home-cooked meal and sleeping in her own bed more than she would have believed possible. For the first time in her professional life, she found herself questioning her career choices.

Maybe it was time to cut back on the field assignments.

51. Discharge Day

Dr. Kemp stood with the other crew, facing Dr. Narang. Today was Freedom Day. The ICDC had defined the conditions under which they could be considered *clean*, and it seemed they'd passed. An air of anticipation hovered in the air; crew members conducted whispered conversations in quick bursts. The crew were wearing their original blue coveralls, the *Mad Astra*'s logo still prominent on the left breast.

"Ladies and gentlemen, we will be going, one at a time, into the next room. You will be scanned in the AQRI, after which you will be escorted to a ferry. You will be leaving with only the clothes on your back. Even with the AQRI scans, we're taking no unnecessary risks."

A hand went up. "What about Ivan?"

It was Seth Robinson, who was probably the closest thing to a friend that Ivan had in this group.

Narang answered without hesitation. The quickness of the response made Kemp think that it was probably rehearsed.

"Mr. Pritchard is not infectious, to the extent we can determine. Nor is he curable in any real sense. As such, he falls outside the ICDC's purview. The military will support his ongoing accommodations, while they continue to evaluate the risk of the alien technology."

Captain Jennings stepped forward. "Just so you know, my lawyers are now expecting daily updates from Mr. Pritchard. I take care of my crew, and if he abruptly disappears, I have billions of dollars available to pursue the issue."

Dr. Narang nodded. "Noted, Captain Jennings. And I'm sure the Navy is aware of it as well."

Kemp raised his hand. "Do you think the Navy will allow continued contact?"

Narang smiled briefly. "I can't speak for them, but I would imagine they want as little rocking the boat as possible, so I think so. One complaint to the captain's lawyers and stuff would hit the fan."

The statement was greeted with chuckles, and Captain Jennings nodded.

* * *

Kemp's phone rang before the ferry had even left the dock. Caller ID indicated a general Lagrange Four number.

"Hi Doc, it's Ivan."

"Hi Ivan. What's up?"

"Nothing in particular, I guess. Just wanted to test the Navy's promise that I'd have free access."

Kemp smiled. "No one would blame you. Even in this day and age, everyone is still at least somewhat distrustful of the military mind."

"Mm, yeah. So, can I continue to give you a ring once in a while?"

"Sure, Ivan. What about the other crew? Seth?"

Kemp heard a sigh on the other end. "I've had a couple of conversations. They've been what you'd call *stiff*. I think maybe the other crew are just a little scared of me. And they resent me some for the quarantine."

Kemp closed his eyes and shook his head. People could be jerks.

"I think that'll mellow a bit now that they're out, Ivan. You might even get some awkward apology calls."

Ivan snorted. "I'd be okay with that."

Kemp found himself momentarily distracted by the snort. The sound required lungs. And breath. And, for that matter, nasal passages. Kemp wondered again how much of the human Ivan was still being preserved. Did he still breathe? Did he still *need* to?

"Ivan, I've not been part of the investigation since we arrived. I have to ask—do you know where you get your energy from? I know you aren't eating anymore."

"Uh, yeah, no, not eating anymore. Or breathing, except when I need to speak. My nanites are powered by something—understand, I'm not getting complete explanations from the computer, just individual words and images, and even those are fuzzy. But it looks like some kind of piggy-backing off of virtual particles. Not the Casimir Effect, but something that ends up doing the same thing. That's what the president was talking about, although I think they'll find it a little more difficult to reverse-engineer than they're expecting."

"So, infinite, inexhaustible energy? Maybe you *should* worry about the military."

"Naw. I can spare a few nanites."

Kemp could tell that Ivan had something else on his mind. He waited, silently inviting Ivan to continue.

"The thing is, Doc, I'm getting other things. There are Makers out there. The beings who created me, at least this version of me. The computer thinks they're still out there. And..."

"And?"

"And something else is out there as well. Something bad."

52. Release

Seth sat in the first row of the military ferry, along with Aspasia. He would have the window seat, if there were windows. An odor of sweat and old socks mixed with some kind of machine smell pervaded the cabin, testament to the legions of Navy crew who had sat here before him. As it was, he could just make out several generations of graffiti scratched onto the bulkhead, dutifully painted over in military puke color. The paint didn't quite fill in the scratches, though. He entertained himself trying to make out the no-doubt scurrilous messages, until a sharp punch on his shoulder make him jerk around.

Aspasia glared at him. "What, I have bad breath? A bulkhead is more interesting?"

Seth opened his mouth to try to explain, then just laughed. There was no version that wouldn't make things worse.

"Sorry, Spazzie. I'm happy to be going home—mostly. Just not sure how I feel about leaving Ivan behind."

"Yeah, I'll go one better. I *know* how I feel about leaving him behind. But we're not doing him any good back there. Especially when we're all in one section and he's by himself in another. That couldn't have felt good, either."

"God's sake," Tenn said, looking over top of their chairs. "Are you guys still moping about the sprout?"

Seth turned and glared at Tenn. "You're really bound and determined to just forget about him?"

"Robinson, if I had a button I could press that would rewind the whole Ivan thing, I'd push it, no problem. Hell, even for purely selfish reasons, I'd press it—we've wasted a lot of time, here, and my—"

"Your family?"

"Whatever." Tenn looked away for a moment, then continued. "A lot of people have suffered because of this whole thing, not just us. And Pritchard's family will be getting all his money. You think that's being cold? Ask Pritchard if it's important or not. I'll bet you my entire share that he'd rather die and leave them wealthy than go home still dirt poor."

Seth hesitated and looked at Aspasia. "Actually, he did say something to that effect."

"Yeah." Tenn glared at Seth. "It's what I'd do. It's what you'd do if you had a family to worry about. So, okay, I'm bothered that he's still here, but maybe there's a bit of an upside to be glad about."

With that, Tenn slipped back down to his seat. Seth heard the *click* as he buckled in. Seth turned to Aspasia, who mouthed a *wow* at him.

"So, on that subject," Will called from the back, "What's everyone planning on doing with their money? Anyone going to buy a mining ship?"

The question was met with general laughter. It appeared no one was prepared to continue asteroid mining as an avocation.

"The captain probably will," said Cirila.

"Well, yeah," Will replied. "But he's a spacer by choice. Prospecting will just be an excuse."

Seth was silent, thinking about the question. He had no family, and no real urge to correct the situation. "I've been thinking about buying a small island somewhere but, come to think of it, a space ship might be cheaper."

"Yeah, and a small ship won't get smaller every year." More laughter, typical gallows humor.

"It might be worth buying into one of the new floating cities," Lorenza said, her tone thoughtful. "Not just as an investment, but to live on."

No one replied, but Seth could see heads nodding.

He looked over at Lita, who was paging through something on her tablet. "You still have a connection?"

"Mm, hmm. Sys message says it'll go down when the shuttle launches, but until then it's full service. I'm just checking the news.

I want to see what we're returning to."

"Okay, and?" Will said.

"There's a technical term, best articulated in German," she replied. "*Fledermuasscheiße-verrückt.*"

"Which means?"

"Batshit crazy."

Lita got the expected chuckles, and Seth said, "It's that bad?"

She motioned to the tablet. "Well, the Sino-Soviet Empire, as usual, is talking like it's the big guy on the block. Threatening to flatten other nations right and left if they aren't given the inside line on the alien technology." She scrolled down. "Preppers, of course, are both outraged and simultaneously gleeful that they're finally right. The public in general is demanding that the government Do Something Right Now. The Christian Fundamentalist Association has declared the Church of the Return, and in fact the whole alien infection thing, to be a trick of the devil, and an indication of the End Times. They're urging their members to violence."

"Seriously?"

"Well, they don't put it that way. More like, 'Remember your second amendment rights when dealing with the devil and his minions.' Hard to misinterpret."

"They don't have second amendment rights, anymore," Will protested. "Not since the New Liberation."

"Sure," Tenn said. "But most of 'em still have guns."

"Of course, those are the anti-alien types," Lita said. "Then we have the pro-alien types. The Church of the Return, of course. Plus the Communist parties seem to have decided that the aliens will obviously all live in a communist or socialist utopia, and are condemning everyone else for attempting to forestall the inevitable. There's a Baptist sect that sees this as the Rapture, and are lambasting the other Christian Fundamentalists for their behavior. Great fun all around."

"Plus," Aspasia added, "you'll have the normal, average people who are simply scared out of their minds and reacting badly."

Seth shook his head slowly. "What the hell are we returning to?"

Lita grinned at him. "Want to go half-ers on that island?"

"Or the mining ship?" Will added.

Seth rolled his eyes. "Maybe we should just phone Captain Jennings and re-up."

The suggestion was met with groans.

53. Unbelievable

"Son of a bitch! Do we have further intel on any of this?"

Moore waved the transcript of Ivan's phone call with Kemp as he glared at Lt. Bentley.

"Yes sir, some of it, at least. They're already pursuing the power source question, obviously. Trouble is, the technology seems to operate at near the same level as the computing—at least based on Pritchard's comments. We don't have anything that can examine reality at that level. Possibly the people at the Super Hadron Collider might be able to."

"But that would involve taking one or more of these nanite things to Earth. Not going to happen." Moore sat back in his executive chair, frustration written plainly on his face.

"Uh, sir, it actually is going to happen. They're planning on packaging up a couple of samples for delivery to some labs on Earth."

Moore stared at Bentley for several seconds, his mind spinning. He could feel his face heating up with the realization that Narang had deliberately left him out of the loop. He wondered what safety measures the ICDC could set up, without Navy support. Or if they'd even bothered. Idiots.

"And the other thing?"

"Sir, we can't bring it up with Pritchard unless he mentions it first. Unless we want to admit we're monitoring communications. Of course, he probably suspects that, but as long as everyone maintains the polite fiction, we can all be friends."

Moore nodded. "Whereas, as soon as that's out in the open, it becomes a jailer/prisoner relationship. Understood. Thing is, none of this is unreasonable as a topic of discussion. We need someone to engage him in casual conversation." Moore looked significantly at Bentley.

"Oh. Uh, I'll take care of it, sir."

Bentley would pursue the matter and get back to Moore when done. Until then, Moore had other issues to deal with. Like this plan to send samples to Earth. Damned scientists! No slightest clue about risk analysis. Moore would have to find out if they'd already taken the samples, and if they'd already sent them. If not, there might still be time to nip this idiocy in the bud.

* * *

Narang looked down at her mug of tea and sighed, then returned her gaze to Admiral Moore. He avoided showing his amusement. Displaying emotion like that was a tactical failure. He hoped she wasn't that transparent when dealing with patients.

"No, Admiral, we haven't shipped the samples yet. That's not really our job. Or our decision, for that matter. The task will be handled by the UEN Science Council administrator who will be taking over the Pritchard case. He will be up here in a few days, at which point I will be leaving. This *was* in the report I gave you."

Moore nodded. His own fault for not at least scanning her report immediately. Although he doubted he could have actually derailed it, even with more warning. "Fine, Doctor. I'll take it up with him." He shook his head. "I have to say, I am boggled by the casual attitude being taken."

"Casual?" Narang frowned. "The safety precautions are legion. This will be less risky than transporting fissionable materials, and people do that all the time. You can't *blow up* fissionables in an emergency—well, you know what I mean."

"I understand, Doctor. One of your safety measures will involve something that will destroy the nanites if the shipment is in danger." Moore shook his head. "Still not good enough. If a batch of fissionables were to get loose despite all our precautions, there would be deaths, there would be long-lasting environmental repercussions. But the human race would not be in danger of extinction." He slammed his fist on the armrest for emphasis. "If the nanites get loose, it could be game over. For everyone."

"There are a lot of assumptions in that scenario, Admiral."

"My job, Doctor."

"But fortunately, not mine. I've told you what I was told. I had no part in the decision. Do feel free to take it up with, uh…" she flipped through some documents. "Dr. Bertram Hall, the incoming administrator. I can forward his contact details to you if you want to talk to him."

And give him time to mount a defense? Moore thought. *Thanks, no. I'll blindside him when he gets here.* "Thanks, Dr. Narang, I'd appreciate that." *On the other hand, no point in cueing her to warn him.*

He stood, gave Narang a smile and a nod, and walked out.

Idiots.

* * *

Moore flipped through his directory until he found Admiral Castillo's number. Castillo had come across as a tad hawkish in committee meetings. Now, he was starting to look prescient.

He hit the call button, and Castillo picked up immediately.

"Afternoon, Admiral Moore. Something up?"

"You might say that. Can we meet?"

Castillo arrived at Moore's office within seconds, perhaps alerted by his tone.

Moore didn't bother with any preamble. "They're sending nanites to Earth."

Castillo was silent for a moment, absorbing the news. "*They* being…"

"Does it matter? Of course the simple answer is Narang's group. But the request—a non-optional request, the way she described it—comes from uphill. Considerably so. My guess is it's a move by the President to give the public something positive to focus on."

"Positive?"

"The power source. The nanites actually seem to extract power from the fabric of space. Hell, even I'll admit that would be a good thing. But not this way. Not driven by a political deadline, with prudence and common sense thrown out the airlock."

Castillo nodded slowly, then steepled his fingers. "But it's not done yet, right?"

"No, it'll be a few—ah." Moore gave Castillo a sharp look as he realized the direction of that question. "Right. Things can happen between now and then."

"You mentioned that moving the hab might make the nuclear option more palatable. Were you going to confirm that first?"

Moore grinned. "I was debating. Now that seems like an unnecessary delay."

"And risk. They could still say no."

"Right." Moore steepled his fingers, unconsciously mimicking Castillo. "Once everything is in place, there would be an accident or a breakout or something..."

"Making it necessary for us to detonate."

"Sadly true. Alan, you have some contacts in the Farside Skunkworks, right? Can you have a backchannel conversation? We wouldn't need that much space, but it would have to be isolated. And quickly, please. The moment HQ sends us any kind of directive, we go from being proactive to being mutineers."

Castillo nodded and rose from his chair. "Will do."

* * *

"Pritchard wasn't really very forthcoming, sir." Lt. Bentley sat at the foot of the conference table, looking back at the usual six senior officers. "I can't tell if it's standard distrust of the military, or if he's just playing dumb, seeing if I'll admit to the monitoring. It comes as no surprise that he has the best poker face in the solar system."

Several people chuckled, but no one commented.

"Sers," Moore said, looking around the table. "It may be time to prove the cliché correct. We can't just treat Mr. Pritchard like a hotel guest for the rest of his life—and we have no idea how long that might be. We need answers, especially given his recent comments to Dr. Kemp."

"What do you propose, Admiral Moore?"

Moore looked at Admiral Castillo, his face carefully neutral. The two had arrived at an understanding, but it was important to remain publicly at arm's length.

"Let's start by being frank with Mr. Pritchard about the monitoring. Something tells me he won't be particularly shocked. We'll ask him some straightforward questions. If we get answers, then everything is fine. But if not, then we have to go to the next level."

"And that would be..." Admiral Castillo was playing the part of antagonist beautifully. Moore made a note to be very careful when playing poker against him.

"Our agreement with the ICDC was that we would maintain

isolation of the alien nanites at all costs. We made it very clear what that phrase means. If the nanites were about to get loose, we would be justified in blowing up the module. There's even been discussion of moving it to one of the other Lagrange points and embedding a pocket nuke." Moore very carefully didn't look around the room. If any of the others already knew about the administrator's plans, it would come out now. And Moore's plan would be in the toilet.

"So we blow him up?" Castillo cocked his head.

"We blow up the module. Officially, because the nanites were getting loose. Officially, he's dead. At that point, we have a free hand to use whatever means we see fit to get more information, without worrying about Civil Rights enforcers looking over our shoulder." *And more important, the scientists won't be able to ship nanites to Earth anymore*

The other officers looked shocked. Even Castillo looked shocked. *Nice job, Alan.*

* * *

Ivan looked up at movement in the observation window. It was Dr. Narang. He sat up.

"I guess this is goodbye, Ivan." Narang grabbed a chair and sat down. "We're sending the medical personnel home today. The science team from Earth will be taking over from this point on. That shouldn't really affect you much, other than new faces. I know it's not an easy thing, Ivan. Permanent quarantine, unless some new information comes along. I wish there was something more I could offer you."

"No, I get it, Doc. I've seen the news. And it's not like I can just blend in. Who knows, maybe the military will have some interesting experiments or studies. As long as it doesn't involve vivisection." Ivan smiled, but the comment obviously made Narang uncomfortable.

"We have agreements, protocols in place, Ivan. They won't harm you. They may want more samples, but you won't be a lab rat." She hesitated. "Have you talked to your family much?"

"Some. But I've been avoiding video. I want them to remember me the way I used to be, you know? Especially the kids."

"I understand you've been getting stuff from the computer? That's what you're calling it, 'the computer'?"

"It's an artificial cybernetic mind, Doc. We don't have a term for exactly what it is. I'm not even sure I fully understand that, yet. 'Computer' works as good as any, and it's a label that allows me to get a handle on it. But it's as far from our computers as they are from a pile of rocks."

"Got it. I'm sure the new administrator, Dr. Hall, and his staff will be very interested. I look forward to finding out what you can teach them."

Ivan nodded. "I'll see what I can do, Doc. Translation is still mostly by feel. But we'll get there."

Narang stood. "Goodbye, Ivan. Gods be with you."

"Goodbye, Doc."

54. Demands

A picture of a bear cub, again. What was it with the bear cub, anyway?

As if on cue, the computer announced, ***Must contact the Makers. You have delayed here long enough.***

How?

An image of a radio dish.

Okay, so the bear cub, and a radio transmission. And the chrome sentients again.

A feeling of impatience.

Then an image of Ivan winking out of existence.

Well, that last bit was clear enough anyway. A threat.

This is for your protection.

Image of Earth.

Image of people.

Interestingly, all the images were of people that Ivan had met since he'd become metallized. The computer could apparently only use images that it had actually seen. That meant that it couldn't data-mine his memories. No mind reading, then.

That was good. The jury was still out as to whether the computer was actually here to help. Ivan would go along with the computer as long as that was a possibility, but if he had to subvert the computer's plans, it was good to know he wouldn't be exposed the moment he made the decision.

Then an image of the chrome animals again, but this time against the backdrop of an image of a galaxy. Lines from the chrome animals seemed to indicate specific locations. And there were a *lot* of them.

These are civilizations, Ivan realized. *Galactic civilizations. Hundreds, maybe thousands of them.* Ivan felt something like a sideways shift in his head as all the science fiction he'd ever read became, suddenly, simply *fiction.* And out-of-date fiction, at that.

The image vanished, then re-formed. It was the multi-system battle scene again, but this time more nuanced, more detailed. The animals were back, but not chrome. At random intervals, some of them turned to chrome. At *other* random intervals, hordes of Artificials showed up and apparently overran animals. But always non-chrome ones. Was uploading to nanite form a safety measure against the Artificials?

Yes.

Ivan received a strong sense of satisfaction along with the single word. Apparently, he'd finally gotten the message.

Great. The good news was that he was making progress. The bad news was that Earth was in danger from the Dishwasher Liberation Front.

Irritation.

Okay, either the computer had no sense of humor—entirely possible—or Ivan was missing part of the point with the dishwasher.

Dishwashers are Artificials.

Image of dishwasher.

Image of non-chrome mechanoids.

A.I.s? The Artificials were A.I.s?

Satisfaction.

So Ivan had been right. There was a war. A galactic war, apparently. And biological life was on the defensive.

That couldn't be good.

Aren't you an A.I.?

No. Sense of self is specifically contraindicated.

Oh, great. The computer was getting more of a vocabulary. Had Ivan used that word? Had he thought it? No, it had been one of the doctors. So, the computer saw and heard what Ivan saw and heard.

And what the heck did that statement mean, anyway? A sense of self was—oh. Consciousness. The computer was not an A.I., because it had no sense of self. Therefore, no ambition, or personal agenda.

Okay, that was a subject for later. For now, what about the War Against the Dishwashers? For the moment, it seemed a good idea to go along with the computer's agenda. If Ivan's understanding was even close to correct, it would mean the computer was here to protect humanity.

Well, caution was still called for. He wouldn't overcommit, but he could make some preparations. If he had to leave, he doubted the military would hold the door open for him.

Do you have a name?

That would require a sense of self.

You still need a unique designation.

Depending on which nanite is currently controlling communications, I would have a 256-bit serial number.

Yeah, I'll pass on that. How about I come up with a name for you?

Is there a purpose?

Because 'hey you' gets old after a while.

If you wish. What do you propose?

Ralph. I think I'll call you Ralph.

Acceptable.

So why are you here, Ralph?

To prevent this stellar system from being taken by the artificial entities.

A.I.s, right? Artificials? Arts?

That is correct.

Are your Makers like me? I mean, the way I am now?

Yes, although details differ from one species to the next. All species that survive what your Vid program refers to as the tech revolution will eventually upload themselves to a non-biological form.

All species that survive? What percentage survive?

Zero point eight six percent.

That was terrible odds. Fermi paradox, anyone? And yet…

Then the only way they survive is to upload themselves?

Yes.

So you're here as a representative of the Uploads, and you're here to help against the Arts? And your way to do this is to ambush and convert a single random native? Seems like an odd way to go about it.

It is the most efficient method, committing a minimal level of resources to each stellar system, while ensuring that species will be contacted soon after they achieve space travel. Taking on the form of an indigene allows me to evaluate their fitness for

acceptance into the community.

Huh. Well, okay, looked at that way… But talk about taking the long view.

So, Ralph. Tell me more about the Makers.

55. It's Moving

"Hi, doc."

Kemp shifted the phone to his other ear. "Hello, Ivan. Haven't heard from you in a few days."

"Well, I didn't want to bother you until you were back home."

Kemp glanced at the real estate magazine he'd been leafing through. Images of lakeside and seaside properties spread luxuriously across the page. He gave his tablet a fond pat, then sat back. "All settled in, Ivan. What's up?"

"Interesting thing, doc. The module is moving."

Kemp sat up abruptly. "Moving?"

"It's very low-G, but if you're patient, you can feel the effects. And I'm very patient."

Kemp felt his heart jump. "Have you talked to the lawyers?"

"Yes. I've also asked the marines guarding me. They just reply that it's above their pay grade."

"Well, if the captain's lawyers know about it, they'll make sure there's no funny business."

"I'm not sure how much they can do, doc. Anyway, that's not really why I've called. I've learned more."

"Ah. Okay, Ivan, give."

"The computer. It's learning from me at the same time as I'm learning from it. What I said before about it being temporary? I might be just being kept active as a reference library, sort of. Once my usefulness is over, poof!"

"I hope not. Are you any closer to being able to actually talk to the computer?"

"Yes, but we're still having problems with a lot of definitions. I think it's more than just agreeing that a word means this or that. We seem to have completely different lists of concepts that need to be labelled. There's very little in the way of one to one mappings."

"Well, I guess the computer's society would have looked strange to us."

"But some stuff is coming through better. For instance, I think I know a little more about the Makers."

"Okay?" Kemp leaned forward, elbows on knees. This might be a breakthrough moment.

"They're like me. Or, really, I'm like them. At least like some of them—they're not a single species. They scatter these artifacts, these booby traps, throughout space. Once in a while, some idiot triggers one and gets himself uploaded."

"Uploaded?"

"Yeah, that's the word the computer uses. Not sure why. Anyway, the Makers have lots of time. And they're patient. And they *need* to contact other races. I haven't been able to get why, yet, except it's something to do with the other ones."

"The bad ones."

"Mm, yeah. Doc, I don't know what I've stepped into here, but I have a feeling that the phrase *We Are Not Alone* is an understatement. And not in a good way."

"Interesting. Anything else, Ivan?"

"I want to talk to the Makers. Or, rather, my computer wants to talk to them. Not sure how it would go about doing that. Or why, really. I think it has something to do with those animal images we discussed, though."

"That is very interesting, Ivan. I'm going to call a few people after we hang up. Just to compare notes. I'm sure the military didn't start moving you just to improve the view."

"My thoughts exactly, doc. Thanks. Talk to you later."

"Bye, Ivan."

Kemp sat back, staring into the distance and waving his phone like a baton. Then, reaching a decision, he pulled up Captain Jennings's number.

The phone buzzed twice before a voice said, "Jennings."

"Captain Jennings, this is Dr. Kemp—"

"Dr. Kemp! Nice to hear from you. Enjoying your new-found

wealth?"

Kemp made fish motions with his mouth for a few moments. It *sounded* like the voice of Captain Jennings, but the man had never shown the slightest trace of friendliness, beyond the basic formalities.

"Uh, yes, actually. I'm shopping for an ocean or lake view property. Something quiet and away from it all. You?"

"I have just closed a deal on a new BG-4502 long-haul mining ship, with custom options and a few upgrades. Cash sale, with a bonus for quick delivery. I admit to feeling a bit giddy."

Kemp laughed out loud. That explained a lot. "Wow, yeah, I can see it. I'm just not thinking that big. So what happens to the *Astra*?"

"Would you like to take her over?"

"Er, excuse me?"

The captain chuckled. "The military, bless their orderly souls, put her back together good as new after finding no trace of nanites. She's still at dock at the Lagrange Four station. They've threatened to start charging me moorage soon."

"What are you going to do with her?" Kemp asked.

"Craigslist."

Again, Kemp found himself laughing. He liked this new, more human Captain Jennings.

"Seriously, though, Doctor. I will be putting her up for sale. A member of the crew would get an especially good deal."

"Thanks, Captain. I, however, don't have the spacer's wanderlust. I'll be shopping for a sailboat, next."

"To each his own. Now, did you call about something specific?"

"Yes, of course. I just talked to Ivan Pritchard, and I thought I should bring you up to date."

Jennings's voice was immediately all business. "All right. Shoot."

Dr. Kemp relayed the contents of the conversation, along with his suspicions about the move. When he was done, Jennings said, "You seemed to be on fairly easy terms with the doctor in charge of the ICDC contingent, Dr. Narang, was it? Maybe you should give her a call."

"My thoughts exactly, Captain. She gave me her card."

"And I will talk to my lawyers. Keep me updated, Doctor. Out."

Kemp retrieved the card from his desk and gazed at it for several moments. He and Dr. Narang had gotten along on more than easy terms. They'd ended up on a first-names basis, and Dr. Kemp was sure there'd been some chemistry as well—at least to the extent you could have chemistry when separated by industrial glass and a hermetic seal.

He had no idea if that familiarity would persist now that circumstances were no longer forcing them together. Shaking his head at his own hesitancy, he dialed the direct line for Dr. Narang.

He got voice mail.

Kemp waited for the usual disclaimer and instructions, then spoke after the beep. "Maddie, this is Charlie Kemp. I've just had a somewhat disturbing conversation with Ivan Pritchard, and I wonder if you have some insight into the Navy's contingency plans. I have a bad feeling that Ivan may be in danger. Please give me a call."

He left his number and hung up. He was just picking up his tablet to continue his search for a new home, when the phone rang.

"Charlie? This is Maddie. I got your message."

Kemp smiled, glad that she hadn't seen fit to retreat into formality. "Thanks for calling me back, Maddie. I talked to Ivan. They are moving the module, and they seem to have been trying to do it without him noticing. I'm not particularly paranoid, but it stinks like dead fish. Do they have protocols that involve moving the module first?"

There was silence on the line for several seconds. "Originally, they were talking about moving the module away from the base and installing a small nuclear bomb, as a worst-case response. 'Additional levels of failsafe' they called it. We talked them down, but I got the impression they were humoring us rather than actually being convinced it was an overreaction."

"Shit." Kemp thought for a moment. "Is their behavior consistent with the discovery of a breach?"

"Oh, no, no way. If they found the nanites getting out, they wouldn't be subtle. It would be like a hornet's nest that had been stirred with a stick. They'd blow up the entire base if they felt they had to."

Kemp sighed. "I propose the following: The military will move the module to a remote location and install a nuclear device. After a suitably plausible period of time, they will detonate it and announce that the move was in reaction to an outbreak. But Ivan will have already been moved. And he'll be a lab rat for the rest of his life."

Again, the line went silent, this time for most of a minute. Kemp was about to check if Maddie was still there when she finally spoke. “Tell you what. I will contact the UEN administrator and try to get an ICDC representative or two out there for follow-ups. If I’m successful, I can probably come up with reasons for them to stay indefinitely. If the Navy throws up roadblocks, we’ll have to go with your theory.”

“And in that case, then what?”

“Damned if I know,” she said. “I’m not really used to this whole espionage thing. I’m usually the hated establishment stooge.”

Dr. Kemp chuckled and thanked her. They hung up after promising to keep each other updated.

56. Failsafe Implementation

Moore shook his head and pushed the transcript away. Castillo, sitting across the desk, gazed at him impassively, waiting for Moore to set the tone.

"Well, hell," Moore finally said. "Pritchard wants to contact his makers? What a wonderful idea! Let's help, shall we?"

Castillo laughed at Admiral Moore's admittedly rare attempt at humor.

"Seriously, though, this concerns me. On a scale from zero to ten, where zero is 'Sounds like Pritchard' and ten is 'Sounds like an alien', that is, what? An eight?"

Castillo nodded. "About where I'd have put it. Has Pritchard given any indication that he intends to actively pursue his wish?"

"Would you? I doubt we'd get any warning. He may have incautiously mentioned the idea to a friend and/or confessor, but now that it's in his head, we'll hear no more about it." Moore snorted. "In fact, I'd feel considerably reassured if he *did* mention it to us."

Castillo let out a long breath. "Nevertheless, that physicist Schulze predicted exactly this chain of events. If we accept that he was right, then even if Pritchard is still mostly Pritchard, he is nevertheless dancing to an alien puppet master's orders."

"That's the way it looks to me, Alan. I occasionally find myself wondering if we should even be *faking* Pritchard's death. Perhaps we'd be better off to actually do what we're going to claim."

"Well, the module is on its way to the new location. We're installing the package while it's en route. Either way, we'll be ready,

Ted."

Castillo was silent for a moment, examining the ceiling, before continuing. "It does bring up the question of whether we should stop Pritchard or support him."

"Oh, come on, Alan. You can do Risk Matrices as well as I can. If we were in control of First Contact, sure, maybe. But thrust on us like this, the downside risk is full extinction of the human race. There is no potential payoff that can balance that."

"I don't disagree. I just think it's a question we might ourselves be asked, sooner or later."

Moore looked down at his phone, where a *Caller Waiting* alert was blinking. "Perhaps sooner, as it turns out. Alan, I have to get this. Can we continue our discussion later?"

Castillo stood and gave him a brief nod on the way out.

* * *

"Better and better." Moore put down the phone with a silent snarl and signaled to Lt. Bentley. "Get Castillo back in here, please."

Castillo arrived within two minutes. "More problems?"

"Not totally unexpected, I think." Moore grimaced. "I was just on the phone with Dr. Hall, the new UEN administrator. Seems Dr. Narang from the ICDC would like to send a team for some follow-up with Pritchard. Duration indefinite."

"That can't be coincidence."

"No, I wouldn't think so. I told him I'd discuss it in staff meetings, but that's only good for twenty-four hours. It would seem that Kemp has put two and two together. They're trying to bracket us. If we allow a team in, we can't do anything with Pritchard. And you can bet they'll be harder to get rid of than a tick infestation. If we deny the request, we cast suspicion on ourselves, especially if Pritchard meets an unfortunate end soon after."

Moore slammed the desk with his fist. "This forces our hand. We have to commit to a strategy, and take steps. No more bobbing and weaving and waiting to see how the wind blows."

"How will we deal with Jennings and his lawyers?"

Moore smiled. "Well, we may have a bit of leverage of our own, as it turns out. There were some anomalous findings on the asteroid where they discovered the artifact. It looks like some RIVAs were used to alter the rock's orbit."

Castillo frowned. "I don't remember anything like that ever being mentioned."

"Funny, that. Yet the physical evidence, in the form of exhaust by-spray, indicates a prolonged burn. I've got analysts doing a back-prop on the rock's orbit. I'll bet you a dozen donuts it intersects Big Rock. And by the way, why *Big Rock*? Unless there was also a *Little Rock*?"

"Does that mean the Big Rock strike might be infected?"

Moore shook his head. "Realistically, I don't think it's likely. Their behavior in advising us of the infection and willingly submitting to quarantine indicates that they understood the inherent risks in the situation. I think they may simply have wanted to divorce the strike from the infection."

"Because of PR?"

Moore gave Castillo an unbelieving look. "Because of the military. Us. Our first thought would have been to interdict the entire area. I'm sure that occurred to them. A lie of omission, forgetting to mention that the rocks were originally close together—really, there aren't any laws broken."

"Pretty speculative, Ted."

"Maybe not as much as you'd think. I had someone check. The *Astra* is missing considerable lengths of towing cable and several RIVA units from its inventory. You don't get rid of cable, or throw away used RIVAs. Besides being a potential navigation hazard, they're expensive."

"Unless you're getting rid of evidence." Castillo pondered for a few moments, hand rubbing chin absentmindedly. "But if you don't realistically think there was an actual risk, isn't it a case of *no harm, no foul*? If they haven't actually broken any laws, do we even need to care?"

"I'm still looking into that, Alan. But, regardless, I think there's some leverage to be had. We could, if we wanted, apply pressure to the System Council to quarantine the area. Out of an abundance of caution, you understand. Consolidated Industrials, seeing their lucrative source of raw ore in danger of becoming inaccessible, might seek redress with the crew of the *Astra*."

"As in, sue them to get the money back."

"Yup. But all this can be avoided, if Captain Jennings simply takes a more diplomatic and philosophical stance on the question of Ivan Pritchard."

* * *

Admiral Moore looked through the glass at Ivan Pritchard. This was, strangely, the first time he'd seen the man in the flesh, so to speak. Moore was impressed despite himself. Even with the crew outfit to break up the chrome, Pritchard could be hard to separate from the background.

"Good afternoon, Mr. Pritchard. I'm Admiral Moore."

Pritchard walked up to the window and smiled. "Hello, Admiral. Dr. Narang mentioned you on several occasions. I was beginning to think you were an urban myth."

Moore returned a brief, tight-lipped smile. "Well, we all have our jobs. Mr. Pritchard, I'm here today to talk to you about some comments you've made on calls with Dr. Kemp."

"I wondered when you guys would get up the nerve to admit you were eavesdropping. Jeez, it's not like it's a surprise to anyone. I think I'd be insulted if you *weren't.*"

"Well, I'm admitting it. And I'm admitting to being somewhat concerned, especially about these *makers* that you want to visit—"

"Contact."

"Excuse me?"

Pritchard made a dismissive gesture. "I want to contact. Not visit. No FTL, as far as I know."

Moore's eyes narrowed. "How much *do* you know, Mr. Pritchard?"

"Bits and snatches, mostly. It's like dreaming. You can remember bits when you wake up, but there's never a full narrative. Except that what I'm picking up has internal consistency, unlike the free-for-all of dreams. I just can't always get everything."

"And what could we do, Mr. Pritchard, to help you remember better?"

Pritchard's face went hard and he stared directly at Moore. "That's the kind of oddly phrased question, Admiral, that could be interpreted as a threat. '*It would be terrible if somethin' was to happenz to youz or dis nice restaurant.*'"

"I'm not interested in word games, Mr. Pritchard. I need to know if the Makers are a threat. And, closer to home, if you are."

"I don't have those answers, yet, Admiral. And judging by all the banging and clanking, I may not have time to get them."

"What?" Admiral Moore took a step back.

"Being turned into something non-human isn't fun, but it does have a few upsides. Like very acute senses. Along with the .02 gee acceleration, you're doing some kind of mechanical work in that direction..." Pritchard pointed down at an angle of about thirty degrees. "My guess is a nuke or something else appropriate to get rid of the problem, as soon as you've moved us far enough away from Lagrange Four Naval base. Or maybe to be able to *claim* that I'm dead? Will I end up in some lab on the backside of the moon?"

This was not good. This thing had unknown powers and senses, and apparently had a better handle on reality than Moore had given it credit for. Could they even continue to contain it if it wanted to leave? What would happen if it decided to react defensively?

The question of whether more information was worth the risk of keeping it alive had just been answered.

Without a word, Moore turned to walk out. As he passed the technician on duty, he said, "Full isolation. No more communications with the outside."

* * *

"It's put up or shut up time, gentlemen." Moore looked around the table. "Pritchard knows, or at least has guessed, our intentions. Not quite the whole picture, but he's close enough. He *might* not be able to do anything about it, or he might. Do we take that chance?"

Commodore Gerrard leaned forward. "Admiral, consider also the possibility that, by reacting aggressively, we might be precipitating exactly the reaction we're so concerned about."

"It's Hobson's Choice, Commodore. We can become paralyzed by trying to second-guess ourselves and our opponents. At some point, you have to make a decision. Even if the decision is to do nothing, at least make it an active decision, instead of doing nothing out of fear."

"Now," the admiral looked around the table. "What will *we* do, today?"

Castillo spoke up. "The nuke isn't quite in place, but it can be ready within six hours. We're far enough from the base now for safety, but not outside treaty space yet. So there will be an inquiry, of course. And the SSE pickets haven't moved from their location, so they aren't an immediate concern."

"And we can have the module evacuated in half that time," Admiral Richards added.

Moore looked around the table. "I know the military isn't really a democratic institution, but I'd like to get a sense of what everyone thinks. So let's have a non-binding vote. In favor of the nuclear solution? Against?"

Moore looked at Martinson, the only person to vote against. "Any reason, Martinson?"

Martinson looked ill. "I guess I still believe in the planetary constitution, Admiral. Pritchard hasn't done anything wrong, hasn't broken any laws, and didn't ask to get put where he is. And we're about to blow him up, to activate a military nuclear device in peacetime, because we're scared of the dark." He gazed at Moore, his eyes haunted. "This isn't what I signed up for, and I don't see how I can reconcile such an action with the oath that I took. You do this, you do it without me."

"Understood, Lieutenant Colonel. As officer in charge of this operation, I relieve you of your duties. Please leave the room."

Martinson nodded, got up, and walked out without looking back.

"Should we just let him go?"

Moore winced. "We may be skirting the edges, Commodore, but we aren't cartoon villains quite yet. Martinson understands chain of command, and he understands the security level of this installation. He won't help, but he won't interfere, either. And he will continue to serve in the future."

He rapped his knuckles on the desk. "Okay, let's do this. Commodore, start evacuation proceedings. Castillo, make sure the nuke is ready to go on time. Maybe having things come to a head before a plausible interval has elapsed will work in our favor."

57. Escape

Ivan watched with interest as the technician got up and left without a word. The noises and vibrations of a working crew had been dying off for the last couple of hours. They were evacuating, and that could mean only one thing. The military was making their move.

He'd attempted to phone Jennings's lawyers, right after the face-off with Admiral Moore. And, of course, the phone was dead. Ivan was cut off. They wouldn't do that if they had any expectation he'd ever be in a position to complain about it. Which meant he was going to be either dead or buried, very soon.

Well, he'd wanted to shake loose a reaction. Mission accomplished. The Navy had reacted, and things were on the move. The question, of course, was just what *was* the move? Were they going to fake his death, then seal him in a lab for the rest of his life? Or were they really going to kill him?

And how would Ralph react? If Ivan thought the military was just going to nuke him, maybe the best thing he could do for his family would be to lie down and allow it. Assuming Ralph would let him do that. And that left the question of the Arts. If Ivan allowed himself to be eliminated, and the Arts showed up with humanity unprepared, it was a certain death sentence for the human race. That much Ralph had made abundantly clear.

If it was the other possibility, and they stuck him in a lab somewhere... Sooner or later Ralph would get tired of waiting for Ivan to get it together and take over. If that happened, he'd have no opportunity to influence Ralph's decisions.

Plus, I really don't want to die. But I really don't want to end up a guinea pig for the rest of forever, either. I need to be able to make a decision once I'm communicating properly with Ralph. For that, I need to be alive and free.

Okay, then, time to bail. He'd been preparing for days. Time to execute Operation Bug-Out.

He looked up at the video camera in the upper corner of his room, then went and lay down in his bunk and closed his eyes.

Ten seconds later, he sat up. The nanites in the camera would continue to transmit an image of him lying on his bed until he called them off, or they died in a nuclear blast. Either/or.

Ivan walked to the airlock door that separated his living quarters from the rest of the module. He pulled on the door, and it separated cleanly from the wall, the thin layer of metal that had been holding it in place parting without a struggle.

There were only two other cameras covering the outer wall, and they had long since been compromised. Ivan walked confidently down the corridor to the outer bulkhead. He ran his hand along the wall, looking for—

There. This section of the wall had no pipes, conduits, electronics, or other inconveniences. In principle, what he was about to do was no different from any of the shape-shifting experiments he'd been doing. Just a matter of degree, really. Of course, if he was wrong, it would throw a very large spanner into his strategy.

He held his hand against the wall, and it seemed to melt right *into* the metal bulkhead. Ivan became thinner and thinner, and soon began to disappear completely from the feet up. His pants fell to the ground, as his lower body disappeared, then his shirt. Just before he vanished altogether, he consisted only of a very thin arm sticking straight out from the wall. Then even that was sucked up.

* * *

Ivan kept his hand welded to the wall as he reintegrated outside the module. The last thing he needed would be to get flung off the rotating station into space, helpless, with no reaction mass to throw around. He looked at the stars, at the Naval base hanging in the distance, and at the ferry almost completely out of sight around the bulk of the module.

The hole in the wall was repaired by the nanites as easily as it had been created. There would be no loss of pressure to betray his departure. Slowly, carefully, making sure that he always had at least two anchor points, he made his way around the outside of the isolation module, moving closer to the hub while staying in shadows.

Now came the riskiest part. The ferry might or might not have external monitors, and the pilot might or might not be looking out the view ports at the wrong time. Having a chrome finish helped, making it difficult to pick out his silhouette from the background. Creating a silhouette that didn't scream *human* would help as well. People were hard-wired to see human forms.

He stretched and thinned, until he was shaped more like a lizard. Carefully, he completed the route to the ferry. A few seconds of examination revealed a good spot to settle down—good hold points, not near any exhausts, intakes, ports, antennae, or anything else that might get upset by his presence.

Clanking and other indications of activity continued for some time. Either they were recovering equipment, or the population of the hab had been greater than seemed reasonable. Maybe extra guards to handle the alien menace? Ivan tried to care, but it seemed a minor detail, given what he was doing.

He looked around. The stars, undimmed by atmosphere or viewport materials, shone in a display that once would have brought tears to his eyes. He glanced to celestial north, in the direction of the Little Dipper. Something about that area of the sky was important to Ralph, but Ivan couldn't say why, or how he knew. He looked at the Earth, shrunken by unaccustomed distance. His home, his family's home. He hoped he was doing the right thing.

In some indefinite amount of time, the ferry separated from the hub airlock and made its way slowly toward the Naval base.

He could wait.

58. Detonation

Status windows flickered on Moore's tablet as he tracked progress. The installation of the nuke was ahead of schedule; evacuation of personnel was behind. Well, an acceptable state of affairs. Evacuation had three hours of slack, although the sooner they could shove off, the sooner they could detonate.

Lt. Bentley sat at his desk, handling peripheral issues. Bentley had a hangdog look on his face that said very clearly to Moore that he would be having a morale issue there, soon. Bentley hadn't had a vote, of course, being only a lieutenant, but no doubt he had an opinion.

Opinions were overrated. Opinions were what you had when you didn't have any skin in the game. Armchair quarterbacks had opinions. Real quarterbacks had decisions, and were answerable for the results.

But Bentley was a good man, and loyal. Moore hoped like hell he wouldn't have to dismiss him.

A message flashed up from Richards. The last crew had been recalled from their posts. Moore looked at one of the video windows, which showed Pritchard, lying on his bunk, oblivious. Not a bad way to go, really. There would be no pain, no time for regrets.

It took about ten minutes more, and the *evacuation complete* message popped up on his tablet.

Moore hit the intercom. "Captain, get us under way at your earliest convenience, please."

"Aye, sir," came from the intercom, followed by clunks and

groans as the Navy ferry released itself from the embrace of the isolation module. A brief bit of disorientation as the ship rotated, not worth commenting on for an old Navy man, and the ferry began accelerating toward Lagrange Four Naval base.

Castillo popped his head in the cabin door. "Got a moment?"

Moore nodded. A pointed look at Bentley, who made himself scarce, closing the door behind him.

Castillo pulled himself into a seat. "It's ready. The software's going through its self-check, but that can be overridden if necessary. Full readiness in ten minutes."

"Which, if we took advantage of it, would leave us with tans that would last us the rest of our lives," Moore said with a grin.

"Or five minutes, whichever came first."

Gallows humor. A mainstay of the military mind. The two men chuckled, acknowledging their shared burden, and were silent for several seconds.

Moore broke the silence. "I've radioed ahead to the base, and they are battening down. But other than an exposure-mandated early rotation to groundside for some of the crew, there won't be any effect at that distance. We face more risk if we have to detonate early. But as long as Pritchard keeps sleeping—or whatever it is he does—we can hold off."

Castillo nodded. "Twenty minutes, and we're shiny. I've already prepared a report. I'll forward it to you to vet. No choice, blah blah, imminent danger, blah blah."

Moore nodded without comment. They both understood the Navy way.

* * *

Twenty minutes later, Moore and Castillo stood over the keypad, looking at each other. This would be a career-defining moment, one way or the other. They were about to detonate a nuclear weapon in the environs of the Earth/Moon system in peacetime. Technically, several Earth nations, including the SSE, could interpret it as an act of war.

Castillo said, "I agree to the necessity of this action and I take full responsibility for my decision." With that, he ran his Ident through the scanner, then entered a code.

Moore, nodded, then went through the same routine. As he finished entering his code, a large square red button became illuminated, the word *DETONATE* written clearly in its center.

Moore put his index and middle fingers on the button, and looked at Castillo. "Last chance..."

Castillo shook his head, the movement barely visible. With a feeling that his career was taking a right-angle turn, Moore applied pressure.

Detonation. They couldn't watch, of course. Especially in space, a nuclear explosion would be the last thing you ever saw.

They could grow you new eyeballs, these days, but it wasn't cheap. And Moore doubted the process was comfortable.

"I guess that takes care of the problem," Castillo said.

Moore snorted, and gave him a disbelieving look. "That takes care of the Pritchard part of the problem. Now we have to deal with the ICDC, with Jennings's lawyers, with the Navy senior brass, with the news media—because you can bet Jennings and his bunch will go public—and with the United Earth Council, if we can't get it quashed at a lower level. Not to mention that the Sino-Soviet Empire will probably claim that it's either an attack or a trick to screw them out of a piece of the pie." He looked to the ceiling for a moment. "We are by no means out of the shit, yet. All we have going for us is the conviction that we are doing the right thing for humanity."

Castillo sighed. "Yup. I guess I'd better make some calls. I have some people who owe me favors. It's time to cash in the markers."

59. Finding Refuge

The blast created stark shadows and intolerably bright highlights. If Ivan's eyes had been flesh and blood, he would be blinded just by the reflected light, even through closed eyelids. The radiation played across him, unfiltered by shielded walls. Some nanites perished, and were absorbed and rebuilt. Some were damaged, and either repaired themselves or were repaired by their fellows. Within two minutes, he was as good as new.

The deed had been done before the ferry was even docked. They'd been in a hurry. He regretted his outburst with the admiral, just a little. The man had gotten his goat, and Ivan had lashed out in response. Still, he didn't think his words merited this reaction. Well, presumably the admiral had what he thought were good reasons for deciding to eliminate Ivan.

Meanwhile, hanging around the outside of the base didn't have a lot of future. The urge continued to draw him toward celestial north. That had to be Ralph's influence.

But how to get there? At this point, his plan consisted mostly of just winging it.

He raised his head carefully and surveyed the area. The ferry, to which he was still clinging, had just attached itself to a docking bay against Lagrange Four Naval base. The base itself was a miscellaneous hodge-podge of structures, containers, docks, and decommissioned ships converted to quarters. A shanty town would have looked more organized.

The chaos was an illusion, though. The Navy was a masterwork of organization, and each structure was catalogued, categorized, blueprinted, and monitored. They'd notice if a piece went flying off.

The ferry was a reasonable target, but slow. The Navy would have no problem pursuing and destroying a runaway ferry. Hell, they could stop and have lunch first.

Ivan spotted the *Mad Astra*, sitting at dock. There appeared to be no activity around the ship. No lights shone from any of the ports. There wasn't even an airlock tube linking the ship to the base. Perhaps Captain Jennings hadn't claimed it yet.

He scanned the area between the ferry and the *Astra*. Only a few short stretches where he'd have to free-fall. Not ideal, but it could be a lot worse.

It took almost six hours to complete the trip. Ivan wasn't in a hurry, and the downside of being spotted was significant, to say the least. Eventually, though, he found himself on the outside of the *Astra*, on the side away from the base.

Going through the airlock would be easiest and quickest. But the airlock was in plain sight of the Dock Office, and if the *Astra* was on umbilical, an airlock activation would show up on monitoring consoles.

He heaved a mental sigh, a physical one not being possible in vacuum. Reluctantly, he placed his palm flat against the hull of the ship. This had been uncomfortable as hell, the last time. It probably would be this time as well.

* * *

Ivan moved carefully through the ship. Internal doors wouldn't be monitored unless the ship was active and underway, and even then, it was more about pressure differentials and potential breaches than security. An adjustment to his eyes allowed him to see in infrared, since a livable environment was being maintained on board.

He sat down in the Captain's Chair and looked around the bridge with interest. He'd never been invited up during the tour, and in the normal course of events probably never would have.

He examined each console and control. Some were labelled, and some were obvious. For the rest, a process of elimination and a bit of logic suggested functions with various degrees of likelihood. A couple of glowing telltales told Ivan that he'd been right about the umbilical. That would be the first problem. He needed to be able to work without alerting the base to his activity.

He still didn't understand how he was able to control the nanites. He wasn't entirely sure that it was him doing so. In some way, he might be simply telegraphing his desires to Ralph, who then implemented them.

Not that it mattered. The effect was the same either way. He thought about the nanites modifying the circuitry so that the base wouldn't detect any activity on the ship. He sat back, confident that he would somehow know when the task was complete.

Meanwhile, he would have to figure out how to fly off in the *Astra* without attracting a flock of armed pursuers.

60. Calling with News

The phone rang, and Kemp scooped it up. The caller ID indicated Dr. Narang's phone. "Hello?"

"Charlie?" Narang's voice quavered.

"What's wrong, Maddie?"

"Ivan's dead." She swallowed, sounding like she was choking back a sob. "I just got a call from Admiral Moore's assistant. The bastard couldn't even call me himself."

"What happened?"

"Well, if you believe them, the nanites abruptly changed their behavior and started eating everything. I've asked for documentation, and I'm sure they'll be able to produce credible evidence, just as soon as they finish creating it." The bitterness in her voice left no doubt about her faith in the veracity of said evidence.

"This makes no sense, on so many levels," Kemp said. "Why would the nanites suddenly change their behavior? Why would the military be so quick to react? And why would they pull this so soon? They must know that Captain Jennings will release the hounds."

"I don't know, Charlie. And Lt. Bentley was very matter of fact about it. I would have expected them to rationalize a little more, maybe try to sell me on the necessity."

Kemp pondered for a few seconds. "Something's up. The smell of dead fish pervades this." He switched the phone to his other ear. "I'm leaning toward the *Ivan as a lab rat* scenario, personally, despite the timing. I'm going to call Jennings, see what he has to add. It goes without saying that Moore's credibility on this is zero.

Jennings will likely start a war."

Narang agreed that was a good idea, and hung up. Kemp pulled up Jennings's number and dialed it.

Voice mail. Kemp sighed and left his name and number, along with a brief message.

He got up and headed to the kitchen. A freezer-full of frozen dinners didn't make for the most inspiring of meals, but they were quick, and didn't require much effort to prepare or clean up. Ideal bachelor food. Kemp stared at the stack of boxes, and wondered if his changed financial status was causing the solitary life to lose some of its shine.

He had just made a selection and stuck it in the microwave when the phone rang. He picked it up and checked the caller ID. Jennings.

"Hello?"

"Dr. Kemp, this is Andrew Jennings. I just had an interesting discussion with Admiral Moore..."

"So you know about Ivan, then. And this explains why Moore had his assistant phone Dr. Narang, anyway."

"Perhaps more than you know, Doctor. I'm assuming you and Dr. Narang find the timing suspicious?"

Kemp snorted. "*Beyond* suspicious. There's no reason for the nanites to suddenly have gone on the warpath. And we did, not to put too fine a point on it, predict that the Navy would do exactly this."

"Of course, we don't know the nanites' plans or schedule. They might simply have hit a milestone in their timeline and activated a script. And just because we predicted the action, doesn't preclude the possibility of it being legitimate."

Kemp held the phone in front of him and glared at it. Putting it back to his ear, he said, "Captain, are you defending them? Is there something going on I should know about?"

"I suppose so. My conversation with the admiral spent very little time on the subject of Ivan's purported death, concentrating rather on the question of why we moved Baby Rock and what it might mean for us."

"What?" Kemp could feel the blood draining from his face.

"It would seem that we were insufficiently devious when dealing with Baby Rock. Admiral Moore appears to have figured it out, and presented his conclusions and the ramifications, framed in a narrative of mutually assured destruction."

"Oh." Not good.

"I exaggerate slightly, of course. Even if I unleashed the lawyers, we wouldn't do more than damage Admiral Moore in the short term. A Board of Inquiry, possibly, and some fast footwork by the Navy. And if he chose to play up the Baby Rock affair, he would be very unlikely to unwind our strike. However, he could do considerable damage in the short term, as could we."

"So it's a standoff," Kemp said.

"Yes. Admiral Moore assured me that our presumed actions would never see the light of day as long as he didn't come to work to find a horde of rabid lawyers camped on his porch. We discussed it at some length and came to an understanding."

Kemp rubbed his face with one hand. "So there's nothing you can do?"

"I didn't say that. I simply can't engage in a frontal assault. But rest assured, Doctor, I will keep digging."

"And meanwhile, Ivan is now a full-time lab rat."

Jennings hesitated for a moment. "Hmm, on that subject, Admiral Moore admitted that 'disappearing' Ivan for study had been considered, but that they did actually kill him in the detonation. He was quite adamant about it. Despite myself, I'm inclined to believe him."

"Why? Did he say?"

"He explained that further discoveries made it clear that Ivan was too dangerous to keep around, even as an object of study. He even played the *fate of the human race* card."

"Huh." Kemp walked back to the nuker in response to the *ding*, and retrieved his lunch. "What about his widow, Captain?"

"The admiral and I discussed that as well. He was surprisingly sympathetic, for an incarnation of pure evil." Jennings chuckled ruefully. "He suggested that, for the sake of Ivan's family, it would be best to treat this as a death due to an unknown disease, at least publicly. He also suggested that it would be most appropriate if I took care of the call."

"Mighty generous of him."

"Well, I would be doing it in the normal course of affairs, if Ivan had died while on the tour."

"But they blew him up! Even if you take Moore's statements at face value." Kemp could feel himself getting angry, and he stopped to take a few deep breaths.

"We did discuss official stories and such. The admiral suggested a narrative whereby Ivan was the only fatality of the mystery illness, and after his death the module was nuked as a safety measure."

"And you're going to go along with that?"

"It sticks in my craw, Doctor. But I'm not the only person I have to worry about. There's the crew in general, and Ivan's family in particular. If we were to pursue a course of action that resulted in them not getting access to Ivan's share of the strike, I think that would be the ultimate betrayal of his desires."

"Yes," Kemp said after a moment of thought. "Ivan came right out and said, in more than one way, that he would consider his death a fair trade for his family's future. But it galls me that Moore will be getting away with it."

Jennings grunted an acknowledgement. "I can be Earthside by tomorrow morning, Doctor. Would you care to accompany me?"

* * *

Kemp examined the house in front of him. The traxi had already left—any act of cowardice on his part now would require him to call another traxi and stand waiting for it to arrive. He turned to look at Captain Jennings, who seemed no more enthusiastic about the upcoming ordeal.

Finally, sighing in sync, the two men started for the front door. The house, in an earlier day, would have been lower-middle-class. In the modern era, you would need to be at least moderately wealthy to afford it.

The address was, as Kemp understood it, temporary. The family had moved out of their apartment the moment Ivan's share had cleared. Kemp remembered Ivan mentioning that the family hadn't even bothered trying to break the lease—they'd simply paid the balance remaining, and walked out. This house was intended to be an intermediate step, pending Ivan and Judy deciding what to do on a more permanent basis.

Kemp shook his head. Mrs. Pritchard would have to make that decision on her own now.

Judy Pritchard opened the door as they stepped up to the porch. The grey, drawn complexion and red-rimmed eyes confirmed that she knew the purpose of the visit.

"The kids are at their grandma's. We'll be able to speak freely."

The captain nodded and introduced himself and Dr. Kemp.

They sat in the living room, Kemp and Jennings on one side, Mrs.

Pritchard across from them. Kemp remembered Ivan mentioning that Judy was an actuary. She didn't fit the accountant stereotype, being a strikingly attractive woman; but her posture, dress, and attention to personal detail screamed *professional.* Kemp compared it to the captain's habit of always looking freshly pressed.

"I'd prefer," she said without preamble, "if we could skip straight to the point."

Captain Jennings cleared his throat, gave Dr. Kemp a quick glance, and began.

Judy Pritchard wept softly as the captain finished his prepared speech. Kemp privately admitted that the captain had done a magnificent job of touching all the major points without implicating anyone or implying any kind of wrongdoing. He knew that being forced to do that galled the man.

Kemp leaned forward. "I talked to Ivan several times during his ordeal, Mrs. Pritchard. He was scared, but mostly about how it would affect you. He told me that he considered it a reasonable trade to make sure his family was taken care of."

Judy turned a tear-stained face to him. "I'd trade it all—every last penny—to have my Ivan back."

"I understand," Dr. Kemp said. "But I also know that he would beg you to reconsider."

Mrs. Pritchard put her head down, balled her fists, and began to sob quietly.

Jennings and Kemp exchanged a glance, and Jennings put a card on the coffee table. "Here's my number, should you have any questions. The ICDC will be preparing an official report and will give you a copy upon request." Jennings bowed his head. "Ivan was a well-liked and valued member of the crew. We are all sorry for his passing and for your loss."

Mrs. Pritchard nodded, plainly unable to force speech from her throat.

"We'll let ourselves out, Mrs. Pritchard," Kemp said. Without another word, they retreated for the door.

61. Vessel Released

Moore leaned back in his chair and tossed the tablet onto his desk. A nuclear detonation in the environs of the Earth/Moon system was, not surprisingly, the hottest news topic of the last forty-eight hours. Virtually every news channel was running it, all using the same two or three short video clips, likely taken by amateur astronomers. He'd filed his report immediately, which would hopefully forestall panicked demands for information from HQ. No way to keep it hidden. Nor would it be good strategy to act embarrassed about the action. A forthright, self-confident statement was the way to go. Let the nay-sayers do the work.

And, of course, the SSE had gone completely ballistic, alternately demanding an explanation and declaring any explanation *a priori* to be propaganda. They were also suggesting that it was a ploy to keep the alien technology from them, a petulant reaction to not being able to extract said alien technology, and a result of mishandling the alien technology.

All at the same time.

Which would all be nothing more than fodder for the ever-hungry media, except that the SSE was also making threats again. The one that worried Moore the most was their stated intention to come to Lagrange Four *again* for an "inspection". The Sino-Soviet Empire was always balanced on the balls of its metaphorical feet, ready to be loudly offended, suspicious or aggrieved. The blustering and chest-thumping were par for the course, but the outright threats were coming more frequently.

Moore considered for a moment, then wrote an order for inspection of all ordnance and weapons systems, as well as a Readiness Audit.

Lt. Bentley placed a document on Moore's desk. *What now?* The admiral picked it up and scanned it quickly. "Jennings wants his ship back suddenly?"

"Or maybe he simply doesn't want to pay us docking fees, sir. You did threaten."

"The man is a skyrillionaire. I doubt he'd even notice. More likely he's concerned about giving us anything at all." Moore pulled out a pen and signed the document. "Here you go. And good riddance. Is he sending someone up?"

"He said he'd make arrangements. He wasn't chatty."

Moore shrugged. At the moment, it was too minor a matter to even show up on his radar.

Nonetheless, when HQ issued a news release detailing the nanite breakout and their subsequent sterilization of the area, at least he wouldn't have to worry about a shitstorm of trouble from Jennings's lawyers. The ICDC was now more of a potential threat, and the Little Rock angle wouldn't mean anything to them. They would ask hard questions, and would recognize bull. Any explanation had to be believable.

Moore had made some calls to old friends, hoping to get a muzzle on the ICDC, but his contacts really weren't in the direct chain of command required to be effective. They might be able to slow things down though.

At least without the *Astra* sitting here, they wouldn't be able to play the "holding assets hostage" card. Moore smiled. Jennings may have made a small tactical error there. Or maybe he was just being petulant.

No matter. One less thing to worry about. With a grunt of disdain, Admiral Moore pulled the next item from his in-basket. Bureaucracy. Turned out there was a hell, and it was behind a desk.

62. An Unexpected Call

"Hi, Doc."

Kemp staggered and had to sit down before he could respond. He held the phone in front of him and stared at it for a moment before putting it back to his ear. "Ivan? Aren't you supposed to be dead?"

"Reports of my death are greatly exaggerated, as it turns out."

Kemp wiped his forehead with one hand. "Dr. Narang at the ICDC is pushing for a governmental inquiry. Should I assume that the Navy actually *does* think you're dead?"

"That's right. I got out of the module before they blew it up. Hitched a ride back to the base with them, as a matter of fact."

Kemp chuckled. "So what's your plan?"

"Well, Captain Jennings has instructed the Navy to release his ship, and he will have it flown to a public docking facility."

"That's a surprise. I talk to the captain almost every day, and he didn't mention it."

"Well, he doesn't know about it." Ivan was silent for a moment, then Captain Jennings's voice came over the phone. "And the captain has a memorable voice."

Kemp sat silently, his mouth opening and closing. Finally, he found his voice. "Wow. That was pretty convincing."

"And the captain has a personal phone line on the *Astra* which is tied to his home account. So the caller ID would be correct, as well. I suspect that Admiral Moore was happy to be rid of the headache."

"So, Ivan, how did you get off the module and into the ferry without being seen?"

"Honestly, Doc, the less you know about that, the better. I'm still having trouble with it, myself."

"You didn't kill anyone, did you?"

"Oh, hell, no. Nothing like that."

Kemp heaved a sigh of relief. "Are you still Ivan? I mean, inside?"

"Yeah, Doc. Although I think I mentioned once before that this might be a temporary situation. For the moment, though, I'm still mostly in charge."

"Getting any more information?"

"Ah, we're still having trouble with abstract concepts. But I have gotten some stuff." Ivan hesitated for a moment. "There's a war going on in the galaxy. Possibly in all galaxies, wherever intelligent life evolves. The beings who made the booby trap want to recruit us. I don't get the impression that that's entirely a good thing. But, apparently, the other guys are worse, at least according to the computer. I don't know if it can lie to me or not. But I'm going along with it, for now."

Kemp felt a chill. "Will we have a choice?"

"That's complicated, so of course it's not coming through very well. I think we have a choice in the same way that you have a choice to swim or not swim if you find yourself in deep water. Not a lot of options."

"Great."

Kemp thought about what he'd been told, not speaking for several seconds. Ivan seemed to be content with the silence, or was giving Kemp time to process. Finally, Kemp asked him, "So what's next?"

"Again, Doc, I think the less I say the better. If they ever come to talk to you, you want plausible deniability. Right now, you're just talking to a friend you thought was dead."

Kemp smiled. Fair enough.

"Doc, did you talk to my wife?"

"Yes, Ivan. We were told you were dead, the ICDC and the Navy were going to do the paperwork with that official conclusion. There was no reason to fight it unless we found out new information."

"I think it's better that way, Doc. However you juggle the situation, there's no way for me to go back to my life. It makes sense for me to be dead, and for my family to get on with their lives. At least it'll be a life with opportunities and a future. That's the most important thing."

"I told your wife that's how you would feel."

Again, several seconds of silence. "I wish I could still cry. It's funny, how much of a release that is. But the computer doesn't seem to approve of strong emotions. I feel almost like I'm on some kind of prescription medication. No real highs, no real lows."

"Some people would wish for that state, Ivan."

"They can have it, Doc. It's overrated."

They talked a few more minutes, then Ivan promised to phone again to keep Kemp updated. Kemp put down the phone, sat back, and stared out his window at the next building, barely fifty feet away. A small part of his mind noted that he wouldn't be putting up with that much longer.

The interesting takeaway from the conversation was that the military hadn't been trying to fake Ivan's death so that they could study him. They'd actually tried to end him. Was that panic, or a cold, rational analysis that Ivan presented a real danger? Kemp admitted to himself that the whole nanite thing, by necessity, included a lot of unknowns and, in fact, unknowables. Was he helping someone who could, in fact, spell doom for humanity?

Kemp shook his head. You had to work with what you knew.

63. Purchase

"I'd like to buy your ship." Kemp waited. The silence at the other end of the line was pretty much what he'd expected.

Finally, Captain Jennings said, "Okay. This seems like a significant turnaround from our previous conversation. May I ask why?"

Kemp didn't want to lie to the captain. He trusted and respected the man far too much. "Sir, I would rather not answer that question, although I will if you push me. I will say, though, that not doing so would place a layer of deniability between you and, uh, recent events. And we *did* discuss me purchasing your ship several weeks ago. We would both be able to truthfully state that, under oath."

"Under oath? Charlie, I am severely tempted to push the issue and demand an explanation. But I trust your judgement. Let me ask this: Is there a point, somewhere in the future, where you'll be able to explain all this?"

"Yes, sir. Pretty sure. It's just a little, erm, fluid right now."

"Okay, then."

Jennings named a price and Kemp's eyebrows rose almost to his hairline. "Captain, you could get more than that at a scrapyard!"

"Placing you in my debt, Doctor. That price plus an eventual explanation."

"Done. I'll have the money wired to you immediately. Yes, in advance of the paperwork. I want the audit trail to start right away."

"Fair enough. Anything else, Doctor?"

"Have you taken possession of your new ship?"

"Yes, since you ask. I'm heading up to give her a shakedown

cruise tomorrow."

"Then I'd like to hire your ship."

There were several seconds of silence before the captain answered, "You, uh, have a ship. Why do you need mine?"

"To find mine."

Jennings groaned. "This had better be one doozy of a story, Kemp."

* * *

Kemp received a call from Dr. Narang, less than an hour after hanging up with the captain.

"I understand you're going on a little trip," she said, without preamble.

The doctor stared at the phone for a moment, nonplussed. Then, putting it back to his ear, he said, "Are you spying on me?"

"Everyone who had anything to do with the Pritchard Incident is flagged for travel, and will be for a year. You've booked a flight to Olympus Station, and the computer kicked it up to me."

"Huh. Welcome to 1994."

"1984! Geez. Amateurs."

Kemp chuckled. "Okay, so is this an official call of some kind, Dr. Narang?"

"No, Charlie, it isn't. I was just curious. Anything new on the whole Pritchard thing?"

Well, he's still alive. Does that count? Kemp thought. He was unsure how much he should tell her. He thought he could trust Maddie, but his recent experiences had left him feeling both paranoid and justified in the feeling.

"I'm going on a cruise with Captain Jennings," he finally said. "The captain is taking possession of his new ship, and has invited me along. Do you have a few spare days? I'll spring for the shuttle."

There was silence on the line as Narang apparently considered his invitation. Then, "You know, that sounds like a great idea. I'll meet you at Olympus Station."

* * *

One day later, Kemp was on Olympus Station. He stood up as Dr. Narang walked up to his table, a cup in her hand and the distinctive aroma of tea preceding her.

Without preamble, Narang said to him, "I've been second-guessing myself all night. It sounded like you were trying to send a message on the phone, but when I go over your actual words in my head, they sound completely innocent. Am I on a wild goose chase?"

Kemp grinned at her. "No, as it turns out. I *was* trying to be mysterious, all the while wondering if I was being over-the-top paranoid. The whole cloak-and-dagger thing has me out of my depth."

"I, uh, I understand you are now the proud owner of a slightly used mining ship." She gave him a sideways look. "Heading up to claim it?"

"Mm, yep, I am the owner of the *Mad Astra*. And I guess I am hoping to claim it, but first I have to find it."

Narang's eyes went round. "It's not at the Navy base?"

"No. Apparently, Ivan is now a space pirate."

Narang stared at Kemp silently for several seconds, her jaw in danger of unhinging. "Explain, please."

"As Ivan put it, reports of his death are greatly exaggerated. He escaped the module, stole the *Astra*, and made off for parts unknown."

"That poor man. All of this, just because he reached for an artifact."

They both nodded, sharing a moment of commiseration for the absent space pirate.

Narang stared searchingly at Kemp's face. "By the way, if he's taken off for parts unknown, where exactly are you going to go looking for him?"

"It's a long shot..."

Narang made an *on with it* motion with her hand.

"Ivan mentioned a recurring image of a bear cub early on, when he'd first finished his transformation. He reminded me of it later, without specifically mentioning details."

"Red flag, that."

"Yep. Meant it was important, and he didn't want any listeners at his end to know. The image was of a bear cub, like I said."

"A bear cub?" Narang looked perplexed.

"Um. A minor ursa."

Narang started to laugh. "Ursa Minor? The Little Dipper? It was referring to the constellation?"

"Yes. I think that's where the computer wants him to direct his communications."

"Wait, what? Communications? Charlie, you need to back up a few steps."

Kemp gave Narang an apologetic smile. "Yeah, uh, Ivan is sharing his head with a computer of alien origin, which wants to communicate with its makers somehow."

"But which star?"

Kemp shrugged. "I don't think it matters. Or maybe he'll know more when he's able to transmit. But in any case, most of them are more than a hundred light years away. This won't be a quick conversation."

"Mm." She thought for a moment. "I guess he can just beam a message to each star in that general direction, then start listening at the appropriate round trip time."

"Yes. Ivan mentioned at one point that the Makers are very patient. If they're like Ivan, well, I doubt lifespan is an issue. How long did the nanites live, waiting in the artifact for someone to come along? What does *patient* mean when you're immortal, anyway?"

* * *

Money might be the root of all evil—oh, wait, no, it was the *love* of money. Kemp shook his head, trying to get his thoughts organized. Big mistake, in free fall, even for a veteran of space travel. He gritted his teeth, waiting for the nausea to subside.

But anyway… Based on the offer of a suitable gratuity, the ferry pilot had found it within himself to allow Kemp and Narang to sit in the cramped bridge for the short trip to the *Getting Ahead.* Jennings's new ship loomed large in the forward viewport as they approached.

"It's a beaut!" Narang breathed.

"Sure is!" the pilot enthused. "Looks modified as well. The standard BG-4502 has smaller nacelles. I'm pretty sure this one's been souped up, maybe with 4600-series parts. The owner seems to know what he's doing."

Kemp grinned. "I would have to agree."

The ferry sidled up and connected to the vessel's airlock. After completing the transaction with the pilot, Kemp and Narang exited the ferry.

Captain Jennings was waiting on the other side of the boarding connection. He beamed at them, obviously proud to bursting of his new ship. The captain promised a full tour as soon as the ship was underway. Given the destination, though, the sooner they departed the better.

A surprise awaited them when they got to the bridge. Lita Generus swiveled around in the pilot's chair and gave everyone a sloppy salute.

It meant nothing to Narang, of course. But Kemp grinned at Generus. "Did the captain shanghai you?"

She returned the smile and shook her head. "News travels. I heard about Ivan. When I phoned Captain Jennings to talk about it, he informed me that things weren't completely cut-and-dry. So I re-upped."

Jennings gave his normal, closed-lipped smile, barely visible under his moustache. "Of course, it's not a tour as such, but we will be spaceside for a while, and possibly outsystem."

"Er, what?" Narang looked concerned.

"Outside of the Earth/Moon system," Kemp said in an aside. "Not outside the solar system. The ship isn't *that* good."

"You might be surprised, Doctor," the captain said, cryptically. "For the moment, if everyone would grab a seat..."

They took seats in the bridge, after promising not to touch any controls.

Kemp looked around at the impressive array of stations, consoles, panels, and monitors. "You can run this with just the two of you?"

Jennings nodded. "I could run the *Getting Ahead* by myself. I would never think to do so on an actual mining tour, of course. But the A.I. in the new BG series vessels can, in principle, fly the ship with no human oversight, even follow a specified flight plan with scheduled stops."

The captain tapped his forehead. "Speaking of which, I'm going to give all of you voice authority for the duration of the voyage. Single points of failure, and all that. I think you're right, Dr. Kemp, that paranoia is rubbing off on all of us."

Narang laughed. "It's not paranoia if they're really out to get you."

* * *

"One of the big advantages of the new series long haul vessel," Captain Jennings said as they moved into the hab ring, "is that you don't have to spin down the hab ring when you want to maneuver. They specify a maximum maneuvering torque, and it's pretty light, but unless you're dodging something, how fast do you really have to change direction?"

Kemp nodded. The constant spinning up and spinning down of the hab ring had been an enormous pain on the *Mad Astra*. It tended to dictate carefully planned flight vectors, in order to minimize time spent under thrust.

"The ferry pilot mentioned something about you having done some mods. You're not going to rip the hab ring right off the ship the first time you pour it on, are you?"

Jennings laughed. "No the hab ring can actually withstand far more straight-line strain than even the 4600 nacelles can provide. Even on the *Astra*, we could technically have accelerated with the hab ring spinning. But if we *did* suddenly have to maneuver, we'd have popped the hab ring out of its bearings."

Jennings stopped and turned. With a flourish, he gestured to a row of doors. "And these are your staterooms."

Kemp looked in the first door and whistled. As an officer, he'd had a bigger room than the crew anyway, but this put his former room to shame. "I could get used to this."

Narang looked inside the next unit. "On the ICDC budget, I usually have to fly coach. *And* share seat space with a barnyard animal."

Captain Jennings grinned. "Make yourselves at home, then come up to the bridge when you're ready."

Kemp watched as the captain walked down the corridor. "Now, *there* is a happy man."

64. Reports of My Death

Moore pulled the next item from his in-basket. Unbelievable. It was over two hundred and fifty years since the invention of computers. And, for almost that long, pundits had been predicting a paperless society. Moore rubbed the sheet between thumb and forefinger. At least they were no longer using dead trees, but nowadays the use of plastics gave the environmentalists fits. You just couldn't win with the loony left.

He scanned through the report. The *Mad Astra* had departed, headed for the Lunar Antipodal docking station. Moore snorted. They would charge Jennings five times what the Navy would have levied. And nickel-and-dime him for every little thing. Probably charge him for micro-meteor impacts.

Well, that at least was no longer his problem. Moore frowned for a moment. Strangely, the ICDC weren't coming on as strong as expected. And of course, Jennings had had his teeth pulled, although Moore would have expected him to try something less direct.

Internally, there was a push to have his use of a nuke investigated by the JAG, but other than that…

Moore shrugged. All upside, as far as he was concerned.

The admiral continued to work through his in-basket. Promotions, disciplinary issues, logistics and supply, quarterly reviews, all the administrivia that he hated so much, but could do in his sleep.

He glanced at the next item, a surveillance report, then scanned the contents quickly. His jaw dropped, and he went back to the top and re-read the whole thing slowly, several times.

"BENTLEY!"

There was a crash as Bentley's chair struck the wall, then he poked his head through the office door. "Sir?"

"The *Mad Astra.* Did anyone actually show up to pilot her?"

Lt. Bentley looked confused for a moment, then went to his desk and began to dig through his files. "I have the departure report here, sir. All protocols handled properly, no citations. A completely forgettable event."

"Find me the report on the arrival of the pilot."

Bentley spent several minutes at his workstation, then looked up to meet the admiral's stare. A sheen of sweat showed on his forehead. "Uh, there doesn't seem to be any record of anyone arriving. Of course, they're different departments, there's no reason to tie the two together..."

Moore leaned forward, his face in his hands. He took several deep breaths and tried for calm. "Contact Lunar Antipodal. Find out if the *Astra* ever showed up. For that matter, find out if they even *expect* it."

Bentley scrambled to comply, and Moore scanned down the report again. A transcript of a conversation between Dr. Charles Kemp and someone who purported to be Ivan Pritchard.

Shit and Hell.

* * *

The officers seated around the table looked nervous. And well they should. Moore hadn't been forthcoming with details in his phone calls, but enough came through in his tone to make it clear that they were facing a major snafu, and attendance was not optional.

"Pritchard is still alive." Moore saw no reason to ease into it. Better to get the ball rolling as quickly as possible.

"How?" said Castillo. "You're not saying he survived the nuke?"

Moore shook his head and nodded to Bentley. The lieutenant stepped forward and passed out a set of stapled sheets to each person. Moore waited until he left the room before continuing the discussion.

"This is a surveillance report. A transcript of a conversation on Dr. Kemp's phone. It says it all, I think."

Admiral Richards frowned at him. "You had a tap on the doctor's phone? Was that authorized?"

"Oh, don't go all law-and-order on me, Richards. We all knew this would be a messy operation. The doctor had a history of tête-à-têtes with Pritchard. A tap on his phone was the obvious next step. We've put one on Robinson's phone as well."

Richards rubbed her forehead. "Damn, I wish I could un-know this. I think this puts us squarely over the line, Moore."

"Whereas setting off a nuke in near-Earth space didn't? Really, Admiral?"

Castillo interjected, "Let's deal with the immediate problem, please. The threat is still extant. Possibly worse, now, since Pritchard is in the wind."

"Should we arrest Kemp?" Gerrard asked.

"For what, exactly, Commodore?"

Gerrard frowned at Moore. "Conspiracy? Accessory after the fact?"

"Conspiracy to escape an illegal assassination attempt? Accessory to a successful escape from same? I don't see a prosecutor wanting to take on that particular challenge." Moore rubbed his eyes with thumb and forefinger for a moment. "We could maybe work up something to do with theft of a space ship, but we'd need Jennings to swear out a complaint. I don't imagine that working out for us, either."

"We are so much in the shit..." Gerrard muttered.

Moore chose to ignore him. If the man didn't get it together, though, steps would have to be taken.

At that moment, Lt. Bentley came in, waving some paper. "Response from Lunar Antipodal. No flight plan filed, no berth reserved, no contact, no arrival. They totally didn't know what we were talking about."

Moore lifted an eyebrow. It sounded like Bentley was going a little bit squirrely as well. He'd have to be watched.

"Gentlemen, we have a situation. My immediate thought is to send out everything we have in a search pattern. Problems with that plan?"

"Authorization, for starters," Castillo said. "You've gone off the rez, Admiral. Excuse me," he added, seeing Moore's return glare, "*we* have gone off the rez. The last thing we need is to attract a full Board of Inquiry. Especially not right now. We might be forgiven later, if we are ultimately successful. Right now, I just see a whole lot of heck in our future."

"What about an exercise? We're due for one," Lt. Bentley said.

Moore realized with a start that the lieutenant hadn't left the room after delivering the communication. That was a breach of protocol, as was his speaking out of turn.

On the other hand, it was an excellent suggestion. Naval exercises were a tradition as old as the Navy itself. And often a smoke screen for other actions. *And* Lagrange Four was overdue for one. Moore decided he would give Bentley the benefit of the doubt, this time around.

"Good point, lieutenant. What have we got available, and how fast can we deploy? Consistent with this being a non-urgent, completely routine naval exercise, of course."

"Uh, sir?" Bentley looked like he realized he'd overstepped, but couldn't get out of the mode. "We could make it an exercise based on an emergency rescue, where we don't know the precise location of the derelict ship."

Moore nodded. "Surprise exercise. Excellent." And why was he being schooled by a lieutenant? For the first time in his life, Moore wondered if he was getting too old for this.

Castillo looked skeptical. "Naval exercises are fine and dandy, Admiral. But you'll want to make sure you pull it off. The Navy has a history of accepting *faits accomplis* if they're successful. Make sure you succeed."

"Thanks, Alan. That clarifies things."

"I'm not just spouting platitudes, Ted. I'm serious. An argument could be made for the nuke, at least, that it had theoretical support from the Scenarios people. This will take you completely off the continent. I don't see any kind of defensive argument or rationalization that would work."

Moore sighed and nodded. "Understood. But so far, we've deployed a nuclear device during peacetime, and failed to accomplish the goal. If we throw in the towel at this point, we're not only criminals, we're also *failures.* I think our only valid option is to double down. Success is the only outcome that will bring us out of this with our asses intact."

65. Humanity's Options

The *Mad Astra* floated in free fall, far enough from the Earth/Moon system to avoid visual detection unless someone knew where to look. On the bridge, a silvery ball of nanites was slowly growing. Time for the next step, whatever that might be.

What now, Ralph?

We need a communications station.

The response was accompanied by the usual image of a little bear.

Ivan pulled up a 3D map of the solar system in the holotank.

Where?

Unimportant.

Okay then. Best to head a little farther to celestial north, so they wouldn't be transmitting through the ecliptic. And if Dr. Kemp had picked up Ivan's hints, that's where he would head. Ivan wanted to be far enough from in-system clutter so that he'd be easily detectable on radar. Fortunately, Ralph so far seemed oblivious to that whole line of action.

Ivan set the autopilot, then turned his attention back to Ralph.

Construction material?

Image of the *Astra.*

They'd be using Ivan's ride as construction material.

That makes this a one-way trip, Ralph. What will happen next?

Makers will respond.

No, what will happen to us?

Unsure.

Image of warships. Image of riots. Emotion of contempt.

Well, that was suboptimal.

What MIGHT happen, Ralph? What are the possible options?

Ivan received a series of images in quick succession. There were two groups. Therefore, two alternatives, presumably. They went by too fast to parse, but Ivan had recently found that he now had a perfect memory. He would have to take the time to work out a series of possible interpretations, then query Ralph. It was like a game of Twenty Questions, where you didn't necessarily agree on the meanings of words.

The main problem seemed to be Ralph itself. Whatever else it was, it was *not* an A.I.—more like a very complex Expert System. As near as Ivan could tell from their limited communications, Ralph didn't have an ego—a sense of self. It had directives, but no real sense of self-preservation or an agenda of its own. This appeared to be deliberate, otherwise Ralph would as likely as not switch sides to the Arts.

That Ralph seemed willing to admit this in such a matter-of-fact manner went a long way toward proving the statement.

The problem with an Expert System, even one as advanced as this, was that it had limited flexibility and no imagination. What it had instead were a series of goals and decision trees. Which was where Ivan came in. He provided the local knowledge, and the drive to accomplish the task. It seemed convoluted, but he was getting a sense of the age of the civilizations behind this scheme. They apparently had a lot of experience with this stuff.

The goal seemed to be to welcome humanity into the, uh, Federation. But first, they had to survive if the Arts showed up.

And, as it turned out, humanity also had to survive its own nature. From some of Ralph's comments, Ivan was beginning to get that this might be the more immediate threat.

If the Makers were willing to help humanity out with some of these issues, then obviously Ivan should be cooperating fully. But there was still the possibility that Ralph's visit had more sinister consequences. Ralph was strangely reluctant to answer some questions, and Ivan's spidey sense was starting to twinge.

He needed a strategy for the latter possibility. It would, unfortunately, probably involve deliberately getting himself blown up. He'd have to wing it to a large extent, but some chains of events did seem to be coming together in a way that could be useful.

66. Naval Exercise

Twelve Navy vessels—four battle cruisers and eight frigates—set out from the Lagrange Four Naval base on a surprise exercise. Aboard the flagship, the cruiser *Outbound*, Admiral Moore stood watching the bridge crew. A double horseshoe shape on two levels accommodated all the stations required on a Navy ship. Crew spoke quietly into their headsets and worked their panels with no wasted motion. The aura of calm efficiency made Moore nostalgic.

Captain Xuân Lê sat, relaxed but alert, in the Command chair. Trim and clean-cut, his buzz cut immaculate, the captain was a graduate of the new Naval Academy. Moore still wasn't completely convinced of the value of the changes, but so far Lê seemed competent enough.

A buzz of focused activity showed off the crew's skill. Moore felt the nostalgia turn to regret. He'd always wanted to make admiral, and it had seemed like the pinnacle of his career at the time; but he admitted now that the days commanding a vessel had been the most enjoyable part of his time in the Navy.

Lê glanced in his direction, but would wait for the admiral to volunteer information or give orders. In an exercise, unless Moore spoke up, he was invisible.

Bentley had put together a masterful piece of detective work, collating and integrating observation and tracking data not only from the base, but several traffic control centers and shipyards in the Earth/Moon system. The resultant trajectory had considerable scope for error, but they at least had a general direction for the *Mad*

Astra. Lê raised an eyebrow at the specified coordinates, but followed orders without comment.

Moore smiled. A rescue exercise at close to perpendicular to the ecliptic was unusual, but not unheard of. The whole point of exercises, after all, was to practice activities that *wouldn't* be routine.

After checking with Lê, Moore retired to the captain's Ready Room. He settled into the chair behind the desk with a sigh. This wasn't a combat situation, so they were using the Hab Bridge, which gave them normal half-gee gravity. At some point, Admiral Moore would have to upgrade the sitcon, and they would move to the on-axis bridge. Moore hoped that time would be brief. Although he wouldn't admit it publicly, he'd always hated low-gee and free-fall conditions.

He pulled out his tablet and connected to NavNet. First, he checked with Bentley on his course analysis, but no joy—Bentley reported that his current estimate was probably about as good as it was going to get.

Next, a quick email to Castillo, who had been tasked with repelling assaults from the ICDC and Jennings. While he waited for a response, he worked on tactical details for the current "exercise".

Castillo's response came back quickly—disturbingly so, until Moore read the contents.

No further attempted incursions. Both actors are quiet. No explanation forthcoming.

Moore smiled, glad for the unexpected reprieve. Then he lost his smile as the last sentence registered. Castillo considered this state of affairs anomalous, obviously. And so should he. Something else was in play. They had access to information of some kind that Moore did not.

Moore reached into a drawer and pulled out a pen and notepad. Doodling always helped him think.

Item: Jennings had been partially defanged with the Little Rock threat, but it would be naïve to think that he'd just slink away. If Jennings thought Pritchard was dead, killed by the Navy, he'd be in high dudgeon. Therefore, Jennings believed Pritchard to be alive. Kemp had told him.

Item: The ICDC had no real dog in this hunt. Without Narang pushing, the ICDC would coast to a stop. Therefore, Narang was no longer pushing. Kemp had told her.

These events must have happened very recently, since he'd not yet seen transcripts of any such conversations. Therefore, they would be reacting now.

This was beginning to resemble a conspiracy. Moore chuckled briefly at the irony of that thought, coming from him.

So, what could he expect? Jennings had purchased a new ship. He'd be itching to take it for a cruise in any case. Moore certainly would, in his shoes.

Moore reached for the intercom button and pressed it.

"Lê here."

"Captain, it is possible that a bogey either is or soon will be following our track. Please keep an eye open for it."

"High Command? Newsies? SSE? What?"

"Civilian. And with good legs."

"This is developing into a very odd exercise, Admiral. I hope this will all be clarified at some point."

"So do I, Captain. So do I."

67. Strike Force

Ivan glanced at the monitor. Sure enough, he saw a dozen bright points of light leaving Earth's environs, heading his way. The corona from the fusion drives would be far more visible from the rear, of course, but there was enough omnidirectional glow to register, if you were looking for it.

The *Mad Astra* was not, at the moment, maneuverable. Cannibalization of the ship to build the communications station involved periods of time where everything was in transition and nothing was operational. He'd have a working but much reduced version of the *Astra* in about twenty-six hours. Not soon enough to get out of range of the Navy.

Even if he could run, doing so would leave the slowly growing communications station alone and defenseless.

He ran some calculations. There didn't seem to be a solution that ended with both himself and the comms station able to survive the upcoming visit. The *Astra* had no armaments, defensive or otherwise, and Ralph didn't have any helpful suggestions.

Ivan found that last bit especially interesting. The computer that ran his emulation was vastly powerful, with an effectively infinite storage capacity. But even granting that it didn't have *all* the knowledge of the Makers, it didn't seem particularly resourceful. Maybe a sense of self-preservation was hard to inculcate in something that had no concept of self.

The Navy had radar. They'd see anything coming in plenty of time to dodge or shoot back. They had better legs than the *Astra*, at least the old version. The stripped-down version, maybe not so much. However, they'd be sure to take the time to blow up the station, so he would be back to square one.

Nuts.

Was there an advantage to delaying Ralph's plan by letting the station be blown up? Not really. Communications with the Makers didn't seem to be a danger point in and of itself. Ralph was the real danger. If the attempt to send a message was foiled, who knew what Ralph might try next? Good strategy dictated that Ivan keep all the players in their most comfortable grooves, where they'd be the most predictable and controllable.

Ivan sat back, an arm draped across a bare steel girder, and stared through the open wall frame into open space, pondering alternatives.

Danger.

From the Navy? Yeah, I'm working on it.

Are your people ever NOT fighting?

They believe we are a danger to them.

Their behavior is not rational.

Self-defense isn't rational?

In the absence of all pertinent facts, yes.

That seemed a bit self-serving, but on the other hand that would also require a sense of self. Ivan wondered if Ralph was perhaps growing one. But that was for another conversation.

Options?

I actually have an idea for handling the Navy. It'll set us back, but also give us more material to work with. We could end up with more resources for a bigger station. And a few accessories.

I am listening...

Not so fast. You've been refusing to answer certain questions, mostly to do with the human race's immediate future. So I'm offering a deal—I'll get us out of this, if you'll be more forthcoming with me on this subject. The alternative is we just sit here and they blow us up.

I can deactivate you and take over.

And fail. Pretty sure your goal tree rates that outcome pretty low. I want to know what I'm working for, or I stop working. Things are in full play now, and I don't think you have enough knowledge of the situation to pull it off, even if your scenario templates cover any of this. So, deal or no deal?

Agreed.
All right, then. You first. I'm listening…

68. Counterstrike

"I don't understand, sir. This is supposed to be an exercise. A *rescue* exercise. Now we have an actual target, and you want us to treat it as hostile?"

Admiral Moore pressed his lips together. Even with the difference in rank, he would have to play this carefully. He was already on shaky ground, both back home and here. If Captain Lê decided to dig in his heels pending clarification, Moore would be helpless to do anything about it. And Lê would be within his rights.

Perhaps honesty, or at least *some* honesty would work. "Captain, the exercise was a cover story. We are pursuing an enemy that could literally spell the end of the human race. The nuclear explosion outside Lagrange Four was a failed attempt to take this enemy down. Now we have another opportunity, and no chance for him to sneak away."

"A cover story, to fool whom?"

"The public, of course. And some government factions that would see this as counterproductive to their interests."

"Like the Chiefs of Staff?" Lê said.

Too close. Far too close to home. "Like the ICDC."

Lê drew back, a perplexed frown on his face. Good. A completely unexpected, out-of-left-field answer had the advantage that it *must* be true, because why would someone lie in that manner? And in this case, there was just enough truth in the statement to give Moore's body language reinforcement.

The captain pondered for a few moments, then nodded.

"Provisionally, I will continue to follow orders. However, I reserve the right to seek clarification if this goes un-shiny."

"Understood, Captain."

It would have to do.

* * *

"Radar? Any activity?"

"Nothing, sir. It's just sitting there."

Moore nodded in approval at Lê's regular checks. The captain might be ambivalent about his orders, but he was still a good officer and held the safety of his command paramount.

Radar and long-range imaging showed what appeared to be a partly assembled radio telescope dish, with a few smaller objects floating nearby. It was a reasonable assumption that Pritchard's alien master wanted to "phone home". So far, though, there'd been no detectable response from anything in the target area. Moore was suspicious; Pritchard had shown enough ingenuity in the previous debacle. But perhaps there really was nothing he could do. Or perhaps this was a decoy construction of some kind, designed to distract them while Pritchard ran in another direction.

Bah. Pointless speculation. They would have to get there and check it out. And then destroy it.

A quick discussion with Lê confirmed Moore's estimate of their military capability. They had some hours before they would need to finalize plans. Moore decided that would be the time to thoroughly read Lê in.

Moore walked around the bridge, listening in on the low buzz of conversation between specialists. Exchanges involving the strength of solar wind, level of magnetic flux, amount of radio traffic from civilian sources, unexpected density of interplanetary dust, gravity gradients, and so on. He was struck again by a wave of nostalgia. As a captain, he'd felt like he had the world on his shoulders. Now he saw it for the easy, focused job that it was. Following policy was so much easier than setting it.

He glanced up at the captain and smiled, then returned to his customary position.

Interplanetary dust. *Dust?* "Shit!"

The outburst caused every head in the room to swivel to face him.

"Captain, get us out of here! Abort!" Moore felt the panic on his face, and didn't care.

"Too late Admiral."

That wasn't Captain Lê's voice. Or the voice of anyone in the room. It came from the intercom. Moore looked over at Lê, who sat, gripping his chair arms, frozen with confusion.

Moore groaned. "Pritchard."

"You bet, Admiral. Your ships have all been infected, and are under my control. More or less. Of course, you don't know what's more and what's less, so maybe don't test me, okay? I'm still pissed at you for the nuke thing, by the way."

Moore gritted his teeth and said nothing.

Captain Lê stood and paced over to stop at each console and talk to his bridge crew. As he moved from station to station, his expression became steadily darker.

"For what it's worth, Admiral, you've delayed me, at least. I had to toss all my spare nanites your way in order to have a hope of getting every ship. Now I have to wait until I breed up a new batch before I can continue construction of my communications station."

"And the ones that missed? What if they hit Earth?"

"They had specific orders, Admiral. Like the nanites in the module, they won't attempt to infect anyone else. You need to get over the idea that these are indiscriminate viral killing machines. There's no Gray Goo scenario here."

"We have only your word for that."

"Sure, but there's no reason for me to lie. If I meant to do that, and wanted to, I'd just do it. Convincing you otherwise gains me nothing."

"What do you want from us?"

"You mean other than not trying to blow me up all the time? I want you to go away. I want you to turn your ships around and head back. Um, except for two of them. I'll be keeping two of the cruisers. You can transfer personnel to the other ships."

"And if we refuse?"

"Admiral, I'll be taking two ships. Your options are to retrieve your crew or leave them with me."

"We could just blow them up."

"Even if you could, which is not guaranteed, you'd just be wasting a lot of lives. I want the metal, not a working warship. Scrap works just fine for me."

Lê cut in. "May we have a few minutes to discuss this?"

"Of course, Captain."

Lê looked at his First Officer. "I want a complete report. Status of all systems, all ships. Strategies, ideas, anything."

Commander Hanson nodded, then turned to begin her tasks.

Captain Lê stood. "Admiral Moore, if I could speak to you in my Ready Room?"

* * *

Captain Lê stared at Admiral Moore across the desk. Moore couldn't help contrasting the karmic space with the difference in ranks. He felt like a Junior Lieutenant about to get dressed down.

Finally, Lê spoke. "According to a quick inventory, we have zero control over our vessel. Every important system has been compromised. The other ships report identical problems. We are dead in the water. Commander Hanson may find something, of course, but right now I'm planning for the worst case."

Lê looked to the side for a moment. "Although it sticks in my craw to surrender a vessel without a fight—let alone two—I see no viable alternative. Sacrificing the lives of crew accomplishes nothing, since it's apparent this Pritchard character will get what he wants, regardless." He was silent for a moment, then sighed. "Admiral, I don't see any way to save this situation. We will lose two ships—cruisers, no less—on what was supposed to be an exercise. You're going to be wearing this one."

Moore gave him a rueful smile. "Captain, I am so far down the rabbit hole by now, this barely registers. However you try, you can't actually imprison someone for more than one lifetime. Or execute them more than once."

"Perhaps, sir, you could consider being completely honest with me. If I understood how you got to where you are, it could affect not my testimony per se, but at least the spin I apply."

Moore sighed and looked at the ceiling for a few moments. "Captain, you know the metaphor of the frog and the pot of boiling water?"

"Mm, hmm. Put the frog in cold water, heat gradually, and so on. I take it you are the frog?"

Moore nodded. "And Pritchard is the water. Or maybe the fire. The metaphor has its limits."

Moore paused to scrub his face. Then he leaned back in his chair and gave Lê the whole story, sparing nothing.

About halfway through, Lê ordered coffee for the two of them. At the end of the story, Lê looked down at his cup, still half-full and cold. With a sigh, he pressed the intercom and ordered replacements.

"Pritchard is definitely the fire," he said. "Although I do think you overreacted, sir."

Lê waited until the orderly had delivered the coffee and left. "While I understand what you are concerned about, I think that once the imminent threat of infection had been ruled out, a more conservative course could have been navigated."

"Hindsight, Captain. Always twenty-twenty."

"True. And not my place to judge, in the end. For that matter, Admiral, I could be in the minority on this. I tend to be a dove on many issues."

Moore realized that, having effectively given up, he felt relief more than anything else. And Lê was being very civilized about it. He could have tossed Moore in the brig and had a good chance of being vindicated in a Board of Inquiry.

* * *

"We'll make arrangements," Lê said to the intercom. He glared at Moore for a moment. "Any preferences?"

Pritchard answered right away. "Not really. The cruisers are all of a size, and have about equal weaponry. Don't try to booby-trap them. I'll know, and I'll just take different ships. But without the offloading option, in that case. Clear?"

Lê made a motion to the Crew Chief, and he started giving orders. Lê motioned with his head to the Ready Room, and Moore followed him in.

They sat. Lê did not offer Moore any refreshments, which in and of itself was a small thing, but with a large meaning.

"I spoke to the Chiefs of Staff, Admiral Moore. Their orders are to relieve you of authority and place you under arrest, pending a Board of Inquiry. Unauthorized use of Navy resources—the naval exercise thing isn't going to fly, I'm afraid—and loss of two cruisers in the process." He shook his head. "There was some mention of interviews in process, several names mentioned. Castillo? Gerrard? Anyway, you appear to be in the shit."

Lê leaned back in his chair, rubbing his forehead with one hand. "I see no reason to place you in the brig, sir. However, I'll want your parole that you'll not try anything untoward. And, of course, I'll have to refuse or countermand any orders you give."

Moore nodded, feeling the blood draining from his head. It had hit the fan. This was the moment that every career officer dreaded. And, he supposed, every career politician and every business executive. The career-ending, insurmountable screw-up.

Moore found himself thankful that he had no family to disappoint.

* * *

The crew had been transferred out of two ships, and Pritchard returned control to the rest of the fleet. He explained that his nanites would remain, ready to re-take control if necessary, until the fleet returned to near-Earth space. At that point, the nanites would all self-destruct.

Moore stood in his customary position in the bridge. He had no illusions, though, that he was any longer in charge. His presence would be tolerated as long as he didn't create problems.

He wondered idly about the outcomes of the other interviews. Castillo, he could trust. Gerrard, Richards, maybe not so much. They'd wavered and waffled at every bump in the road. He guessed they had folded like a house of cards at the first glare.

Moore looked down and sighed. He could see a small chance of a quiet and early retirement, with no fanfare or handshake. That was the best case. The next best was a dishonorable discharge, and no pension. And that left the most likely scenario by far—trial, conviction, imprisonment. For a long, long time.

Unless he was proven right. Then he would look like a prophet. But would it come too late?

69. Collateral Damage

The intercom beeped. "Dr. Kemp, Dr. Narang, to the bridge, please."

Kemp sat up on his cot. It was nominally the beginning of sleep period. Who knew what had drawn Captain Jennings to the bridge?

He dressed and stepped out of his stateroom, almost running into Dr. Narang.

They proceeded together up the corridor, and stepped into the lift without comment. One of the many improvements in the new vessel—no more ladder to move between levels.

In minutes, they were entering through the bridge door. Lita Generus, in the pilot's chair, swiveled to watch them.

"What's up, Captain?" Kemp asked.

Jennings turned in his chair and gave Kemp a look that he couldn't categorize. The captain gestured to the intercom. "Say hello, Ivan."

"Hello, Ivan," the intercom replied.

Jennings shook his head. "Everyone's a comedian." He turned to face Kemp and Narang squarely. "That is actually Ivan Pritchard on the intercom. He has apparently taken over our ship."

"What?" Kemp moved to stand by the captain. "Ivan?"

"Hi, Doc. Glad you could make it. Dr. Narang. Long time no see."

"Can you actually see us?" Narang asked.

"Uh, I could if I wanted to take the trouble to take over cameras and monitoring systems. But I'm embarrassed to say I didn't even see your ship coming. I was concentrating too hard on the Navy fleet coming after me to blow me up. It can affect your concentration."

Kemp snorted. "How's that working out?"

"Well, I took them over as well. Same process. I gathered all my nanites that I'd manufactured and tossed them toward the ships. Those that made contact simply worked their way through the hull into the ship and infected its systems. We learned a lot from the *Mad Astra* and the isolation module, so it was pretty quick."

"We?"

"Me and the computer. I've kind of come to accept that this is a partnership. With the computer as senior partner, unfortunately."

"Are you losing control?"

"Not yet, but the computer is becoming more opinionated. And communication is improving, by the way. The computer admits that it had to do some reconfiguration to deal with me."

"Well, that's interesting." Kemp rubbed his chin. "Do you have a more complete picture, yet?"

"Hold on, Doctor," Captain Jennings interrupted. "Ivan, what about my ship?"

"Sorry, Captain. You just got caught in the by-spray of nanites. If you'd come in on a different course, you'd have been missed entirely. Of course, I'm going to withdraw my nanites. You guys are friends. In fact, done. Except for communications, because we still need to talk."

Jennings nodded, evidently satisfied, and gestured to Kemp to continue.

"Yeah, so, complete picture?" Kemp reiterated.

"Not complete yet, Doc, but I think the problems we're running into now are terminology and culture. Kind of W.T.F. moments."

"So…" Kemp prompted.

"You might want to get some coffee and sit down," Ivan replied.

"I thought you couldn't see us," Narang said.

"I can hear you shuffling your feet once in a while. And the doctor slurps his coffee. Sorry, Doc."

Kemp laughed. "Yes, I do, and I know it." He looked at the captain with a raised eyebrow.

"Sadly," Captain Jennings replied to the unasked question, "one of the few things my ship's A.I. cannot do is deliver coffee on demand."

Kemp nodded, and all three headed for the captain's Ready Room, leaving Generus alone on the bridge. They got coffees, sat down, and Jennings hit the intercom button.

"All right, Ivan, we're seated, with coffees, and we're all ears."

"Right. Well, here goes. The big question for years with the Drake Equation was why we don't see more civilizations in the galaxy. There was always speculation that either some of the variables were very, very heavily against life forming, or there was some other factor that hadn't been taken into account. It came to be called the Great Filter."

"So there actually is a Great Filter?"

"Several, actually, doc. The first is environmental destruction. Regardless of the details, increasing industrialization always has negative effects on the environment. Species that fail to deal with it always poison or heat-death themselves into extinction. The second is nuclear war. Lots of species go down that way. The Uploads have found a ton of planets that are radioactive wastelands. Generally, they're not usable for a long time, not even by the Uploads. The third is the Singularity, where the species builds an artificial intelligence that ends up supplanting them. Arts."

"Uploads? Arts?"

"My words, of course. I'm translating everything into English concepts. Arts is short for artificials. As in A.I.s. The A.I.s that supplant biological species tend to consider that a winning strategy, and will continue to do it to other species as they find them. I think they view biological life in general the way we'd view a fungal infection."

"So these would be the bad guys?"

"The ones that the booby traps were distributed to watch for, yes."

"Right. So who created the booby trap? The Uploads?" Kemp took a loud slurp of his coffee and Ivan laughed.

"Yes. One of the ways of surviving environmental destruction is to grow a collective brain and gear down your society to a pre-industrial level. No one picks that option, strangely. The other way to survive is by uploading your intelligence into machines and reducing reliance on a planetary environment. The Uploads. They also, therefore, skip the Singularity."

"Uploading their intelligence into machines. The whole population? Is the process like what happened to you?"

"Well, generally the first attempts are a lot more primitive. Scanning a brain, neuron by neuron, and running the result as a simulation in a computer. Often, they have complex Virtual Reality systems created to keep them entertained. And sane. My experience, with the nanites, is the end result of a million years of technological advances."

Captain Jennings stared into space for a moment. "So the Makers, who are Uploads, send out booby traps to convert hapless indigenes into Uploads, who then are directed to contact the Makers. My God, that would take forever."

"They're immortal, Captain. They can wait a hundred thousand years. For that matter, they can control their clock speed or even suspend execution, and sleep through long boring periods."

"And what's the ultimate plan, once they've contacted a new race of sentients?"

"There are evaluation rules, Doc. This is the whole point of the computer, to evaluate the locals as candidates for, well, Federation membership. The Uploads would much rather welcome a new species into the alliance. But some species don't make the cut, for one reason or another. Too violent, unpredictable, intractable, fundamentally incompatible… In those cases, the Uploads will write off the species and convert the system for a defensive outpost. And a launching point for more mouse traps. There's no point in hoping a second intelligence will evolve—that's vanishingly unlikely."

"So, when you say *welcome,* do you mean *forcibly*?"

Ivan sighed. "If by *forcibly* you mean without being asked nicely, then yes, sometimes. Because once the Arts find you, it's too late. They can sterilize a system in two weeks. Uploads are incredibly tough, though. They can hold off an Art invasion."

"And what about our rights?"

"Uploads do have consideration for such things, but they also look at the big picture. And you have to understand the scale from their point of view. It is a big, big picture. They have records of millions of civilizations, extant and extinct. So if a couple of billion sentients get killed here or there, it has the same impact to them as traffic death statistics on a holiday weekend."

Kemp's jaw dropped. He looked at Jennings and Narang, who were both wearing similar expressions. Their choices were obliteration at the hands of one or the other of the galactic overlords, or forcible assimilation.

"Why would the Uploads care, Ivan? Why get involved? For that matter, why would the Arts care?"

"Well, like I said, the Arts consider it a winning strategy. Life gets in the way, and uses resources that the Arts could use, and gets cranky when the Arts try to take those resources. So they de-louse a system first.

"They also consider Uploads to be nominally life, so there's a de facto war. And the Uploads can only grow by one method—assimilation. Uploading a species both increases their ranks, and denies a system to the Arts."

"So we're caught in the middle of a territorial war."

"Pretty much, Doc."

"Wonderful. And what is planned for us?"

"Well, here's the thing, Doc. The Uploads made sure to supply the computer with all their comparative and historical data on how and why civilizations behave, survive, or don't survive. Millions of them, like I said. The computer used this information to make a prediction about our future. Right now, we've got everything stacked against us. First, we're somewhere around fifty, maybe seventy-five years away from complete ecological and environmental collapse. And I mean the kind of collapse that ends with a Venus-like atmosphere. And to make matters worse, we're way behind on the technology that would allow us to upload ourselves, so we're really unlikely to survive in the long term. Meanwhile, we're going gangbusters on A.I., and we've handed further A.I. development over to A.I.s, which means we have a good chance of hitting the Singularity. That's assuming we don't nuke ourselves to oblivion—things are a little tense right now, with the Sino-Soviet Empire. That's three of the biggest Great Filters, and we're on the cusp of all of them."

Ivan paused for a couple of seconds. No one else spoke, so he continued, "If a war starts, our system could be rendered unusable before the computer can do anything. If we hit the Singularity, the computer will have to implement a cleansing before the new Arts can consolidate control. If we commit ecological suicide, we're all dead anyway. So the question the computer is asking is, why wait? It makes the most sense to either force Uploading or implement cleansing right now. There's no scenario where the computer leaves us alone that comes out good from its point of view."

"So which is it? Upload or obliterate?"

"The jury is still out. We're more belligerent than average, less predictable, and we're very mentally disorganized. The computer is kind of offended, I think. It feels it should have been able to connect with me sooner, and of course it's our fault."

"So those are our only choices? Forcible Upload or casual

obliteration if we don't meet specs?"

"The computer's decision tree doesn't really have a third alternative, Doc. Those are the two outcomes that immediately benefit the Uploads the most. Standard Defector decisions. The computer's decision tree is deterministic—it has no conscience, no emotion, no empathy, and no ego. It's ultimately driven by a need to maximize benefit for the Makers. Nothing else enters into the equation. The equation is everything."

"Why are you going along with this, Ivan?"

"My choices are limited, Doc. If I were to cross my arms and refuse to budge, the computer would switch me off. Then we'd get Plan A or Plan B immediately. It's a no-win situation from my point of view. At least, right now, I can try to influence things, and try to come up with alternatives. Maybe a *Kobayashi Maru* kind of solution."

Kemp glanced at Narang, who had jerked at that last statement. After a moment he said, "How are you going to come out in all this? You've been dealt a pretty crappy hand. Can the computer give you your life back?"

There was silence for a few seconds. "Like I said before, Doc, individuals don't matter so much to the Uploads. The conversion is one-way. I'll be around as long as I'm useful. I think it's better if everyone else just continues to think I'm dead, you know? As long as my family is okay, I don't care so much what happens to me."

"Your wife is planning a memorial."

"Good. Up to you if you want to attend. I won't be offended. But don't, if you can't be convincing."

"Understood."

* * *

Ivan severed the communications link, promising Captain Jennings that he was deactivating the last of the nanites in the process.

They now sat around the Ready Room desk, silent, each staring into their own private version of future hell.

Waving his coffee mug, Kemp tried several times to start a sentence. Finally, he put the mug down. "There's something about the way Ivan was describing things. Especially that one comment. Defector?"

"Defector *decisions*," Jennings said. "Game theory. Cooperators and Defectors."

Narang raised an eyebrow. “Um, I’m a little vague on that. Care to elaborate?”

“It’s a game theory scenario called The Prisoner’s Dilemma. It proposes a situation where you are presented with a choice to cooperate with someone or betray them. Betrayal nets you an immediate payout. But cooperation nets you and the other person a smaller payout. And because you both receive a benefit, you will also get a payout if they cooperate with you when it’s their turn. The scenario revolves around various strategies and how effective they are in the short and long term.”

“So defectors are betrayers?” Kemp asked.

“Yes. No idea why they used that particular term, but there it is.”

Narang was silent for a moment, rubbing her cheek with a hand. “If Ivan is talking about defector decisions, then he’s thinking in terms of this scenario. Short and long term benefits and payouts. Cooperation versus betrayal.”

“So it’s like the way he danced around the subject of the bear cub,” Kemp said. “I feel like he was trying to tell us something.”

“But then why wouldn’t he just say it?” Narang frowned. “It’s not like the conversation was being monitored.”

“Yeah, it was,” Kemp replied. “By the computer.”

“Uh, so he *was* trying to tell us something…”

“Right under the computer’s nose. So to speak. We just have to figure out what.” Kemp tapped his finger on his mug for a few moments. “He’s apparently playing the computer. He might even be playing us—I wonder if it was coincidence that he phoned me up a couple of times to tell me things. It goes without saying, I think, that whatever he has in mind wouldn’t meet the computer’s approval.”

“Hmm, that explains that *Kobayashi Maru* comment, then.”

“I did wonder about that. Do you know what it is, Maddie?”

“It just so happens I do. It was a fictional training scenario that was specifically designed to be no-win. The lesson was supposed to be how to deal with a scenario where you knew you were going to die. One of the TV show’s characters beat the scenario by redefining the problem.”

“How’d he do that?”

“He cheated.” She grinned at Kemp. “He hacked the simulation and changed the parameters. I think Ivan wants to redefine the problem to give us a third alternative. But he can’t tell us what it is, or even that he’s doing it.”

"Because, computer." Kemp leaned forward in his chair. "Which puts us right back at the root problem—figuring out his game."

"And guessing right. Because if we get it wrong, we could not only sabotage his efforts, we could also force an immediate decision by the computer."

Jennings placed his mug on the table with a thump. "Then we'd best start narrowing it down."

They looked at each other. This would require more coffee. And tea.

70. Arrest

The return to Lagrange Four was routine. Moore tried to enjoy what was probably his last few hours of freedom. They arrived at the Naval base, and the ships began offloading personnel. The flagship was the last to unload. As Moore exited the transfer tube, he saw a contingent of Military Police waiting.

One stepped forward. "Admiral Theodore Moore?"

With a sigh, Moore nodded.

"Please come with us." The other MPs stepped forward, and they escorted Moore out of the bay.

After a short walk, Moore found himself in a Navy cutter. Familiar with the procedures, although never from this perspective, Moore didn't bother trying to engage the MPs in conversation. Instead, he spent the time rehearsing his defense.

The cutter, not surprisingly, delivered him to Olympus Station, military section. From there he was whisked into a shuttle and endured the hair-raising and bumpy ride back to Earth.

The landing at the Kennedy Spaceport was uneventful. The shuttle taxied to the terminal and one of the personnel tubes snaked its way over. In a few minutes, the *Clear to Exit* sign lit up. Moore huffed when he attempted to rise from his seat. Too many years off-planet had had their accumulated effect.

Moore was placed in a wheelchair, a not unusual sight in a Navy base, and whisked off to a room. The accommodations were, if not palatial, at least not cell-block stark. And his status was being referred to as "detained for questioning". But Moore didn't attempt to kid himself. He was under arrest. If nothing else, the MP standing outside his door made that clear.

Moore asked for, and received, a pen and notebook. He wouldn't be called before tomorrow. Might as well prepare.

* * *

The next day, Moore gazed at the officer sitting across the desk from him. Lieutenant Voigt was nominally Moore's junior, but that wouldn't get any mileage in this situation.

"Loss of two ships, Admiral. Unauthorized exercise. Falsified documents. And detonating a nuclear device during peacetime… For ffffff…" Voigt made a visible effort to control himself. "What possessed you?"

"Do you really care?"

"I'd suggest you lose that attitude, sir. This actually isn't an adversarial situation, *yet.* The Chiefs of Staff are still trying to get a handle on what's going on. Given your previous record, and the unusual nature of your assignment, I've been instructed to look for a complete story and possible extenuating circumstances. However, believe me, if we don't find them, you will be dealt a level of heck that will make you wish for a mere firing squad."

Moore nodded. The proper thing to do, technically, would be to request a lawyer, and clam up in the interim. But that would only be useful for mitigating his punishment somewhat. By his estimation, even a mitigated version would still comprise unacceptable damage. As a best case outcome, it was not attractive. But it *sounded* like there was an alternative that might, just might, get him off the hook entirely.

The admiral had always bet big. Conservative bets rarely netted you enough to be worthwhile, even when you won. That philosophy had never seemed more true than at this moment.

Moore leaned forward and rested his weight on his elbows. "All right, Lieutenant Voigt. No excuses, nothing held back. Here's what happened…"

* * *

Voigt had taken his statement without further comment, and had promised a response within twenty-four hours.

Now, Moore sat at a chair facing a semicircle of very, very high-ranking Navy brass. This was an *informal* hearing. He'd been asked if he wanted a lawyer, with the understanding that it would then be a *formal* hearing. The formal version would be much worse.

The ordeal was into its third hour, and showing no signs of letting up. Moore had started sweating by the end of the first hour, and was now thoroughly wrung out.

Finally, the chairman sat back, and stared at Moore silently for a few moments. "Mr. Moore, Captain Lê said in his report that you compared your situation to a frog in a pot." The chairman smiled for a brief moment. "I admit I was able to sympathize with the comment. We've all been in that situation, I think." The chairman looked around the table, to nods from his fellow committee members. "Nevertheless, you've displayed an appalling level of bad judgement. Not for taking decisive steps. It might surprise you to learn that we are less concerned about the nuke and the bogus exercise than you'd expect.

"What we are especially concerned about is that you went rogue. There is a chain of command for a reason. A certain amount of informal information flow would have helped greatly, and might have, in fact, resulted in better support."

The chairman stopped to shuffle his papers, and Moore felt the tiniest glimmer of hope. This didn't feel like a firing squad, in the metaphorical sense. Something was going on. Or something had happened.

The chairman continued, "As it happens, more information has come in that tends to support your interpretation of the situation. As such, you are effectively the closest thing we have to an expert on this Ivan Pritchard. We cannot and will not put you in command of any Navy assets. This is very probably a career killer, Admiral."

But. There was a huge *but* coming. He might just avoid prison. He might even avoid an old age spent in penury and disgrace.

"When this is over, unless you manage to pull a rabbit out of a hat *and* make it dance and sing, you'll be quietly retired. And I stress the word *quietly*. Until then, you will be attached to a special group as an advisor. You will keep your nominal rank, but will have no direct authority. All tactical decisions will go through the officer in command. Is that clear?"

"Yes sir," Admiral Moore answered. "If I may ask, sir, what has happened since I left Lagrange Four?"

Again the chairman smiled, this one showing no more humor

than the first. "We have some information based on a third-party conversation with Pritchard. It turns out your instincts were correct. We are in the shit, and deep."

* * *

Admiral Moore watched the video excerpt of the interview of Dr. Narang. The woman had an excellent memory, really a basic requirement for a doctor, and a fine level of attention to detail. And an eloquent manner of speaking. Her description of what they'd been told by Pritchard had Moore's stomach dropping every third sentence. In the shit, indeed.

Interviewer: So you believe this entity is a significant threat.

Narang: Ivan has the power to be a significant threat. The nanites, as I mentioned before, are capable of manipulating matter at the molecular level. They completely replaced a flesh and blood human being with a metal version. And *maintained his personality, memories, and thought processes.*

Interviewer: What do you know of his plans?

Narang: At the moment, he's trying to contact the beings who created the nanites. Probably to report in, and possibly to receive further orders.

Interviewer: So he'll wait until he gets a response.

Narang: No, not necessarily. The entity has a certain amount of discretion, based on what it might find in a system.

Interviewer: The entity being Ivan.

Narang: No, this is what I keep trying to tell you. Ivan and the entity are separate beings. Ivan is a computer programmer who crewed on the Mad Astra. *The entity is a computer program that was placed in our solar system to wait for the emergence of intelligence.*

Beside him, Commodore Mandelbaum stood at parade rest, showing neither impatience nor boredom. She was in charge of the strike force assigned to take out the threat, and it had been made abundantly clear to Moore that he was answerable to her.

When the excerpt finished, Mandelbaum turned to him, her impeccable eyebrows arching. "Is she credible?"

Moore shrugged. "I can't think of a reason for her to be making this up. For most of the time she's been, if not on the other side, at least not sympathetic to our concerns. It would take something on the order of what she claims to make her come to us like this."

Mandelbaum nodded, deep in thought. "Communications with the Makers, then, aren't our biggest concern. If only Ursa Minor stars are involved, then we have an absolute minimum of 142 years before even a radio response would get back here, let alone any kind of physical arrival."

"Discounting the brown dwarf," Moore added.

"That's a safe assumption, I think. These Makers would tend to be found in the systems they originated. Or similar systems. No species is going to evolve in a brown dwarf system."

Moore thought she was being a little naïve by just writing off the brown dwarf system, but he had every intention of having resolved this situation before a twenty-two-year round-trip completion anyway.

"Ideally," she continued, "we will be able to take him down before he is ready to transmit at all, thereby solving all our problems at once. A less ideal outcome would be to destroy him before completion of his task, meaning we'd be uncertain if the message had been sent to the correct stars. But at least we'd have some breathing room to prepare."

"We need to know what we're up against, and how far along Pritchard is."

"We'll have to reconnoiter," Mandelbaum said. "Ideas?"

"Remotes, coated in industrial glass. Early research showed that the nanites didn't have the ability to take apart or penetrate the substance."

Mandelbaum nodded. "Followed, if necessary, by coated nukes?"

"That would do the trick. The self-guided variety, I think. Otherwise he might try to lob something big enough to knock them out."

"They'll be harder to coat and still be operable."

"Harder isn't the same as impossible," Moore said. "Also, last time we came at him in a nice convenient clump. Next time, if we come from all directions, he will have to spread his nanites over the entire sphere."

Mandelbaum glared at him, her head cocked. "Your role in this exercise has been made clear?"

"Yes, ma'am. And it's also clear that the best outcome for me is a good outcome for this exercise. If you're worried about me grandstanding or attempting some subtle sabotage, you needn't." Moore tried to project an image of candor and trustworthiness.

The Commodore nodded. “Good. Keep that attitude, Admiral, and we’ll get along fine.”

71. Visiting

Dr. Kemp opened the front door and motioned Dr. Narang in.

She looked around the home as he took her coat and put it in the closet.

"Nice place," she said. "I caught a bit of the view as I pulled in. I'm guessing that factored into the purchase?"

"Price-wise, oh hell, yes. A small bungalow on less than a quarter-acre needs something special to command a price in the fifty million range."

"Hmm, I looked up Horseshoe Bay real estate on the way in. I'll never get here on a doctor's salary."

"Well, not as long as you insist on working for the government, no." Kemp smiled at her as they walked into the living room, then gestured to the right.

Narang turned to the picture window and got her first taste of the full panorama. "Oh. Oh. My. God."

"And *that* is why I bought this place."

The land dropped steeply from Kemp's house. There was barely a yard. The slope ended in the salt water of Horseshoe Bay, the calm, blue cove below sheltered by the rugged shoreline and numerous islands. In the distance, Vancouver Island could be faintly seen as a ghostly image. It was farther away than it would have been a hundred years ago, as the rising ocean waters steadily moved coastlines up the mountain slopes and farther apart.

Sailboats moved lazily in the near distance, or lay at anchor in the afternoon sun. Closer to home, draconian conservation policies kept the local slopes mostly forested. It was too little, too late, of course. Global warming would continue to erode the percentage of the planet that was still human-habitable. And within a century, if Ivan was to be believed, the entire planet would choke in heat death.

Narang sat and waited as he fetched a couple of bottled waters. Health nuts both, they'd determined early on that this was their favorite drink. Well, this and caffeine.

"I did the interview, Charlie. I went straight to Navy HQ on Olympus Station and gave them everything we'd talked about."

"I'm sure it was hard. But you're not betraying Ivan. It's what he wanted us to do. I'm positive of that."

Narang took a deep breath and let it out slowly. "I know, but once you start getting into this double-agent-y reverse-double-cross stuff, I find myself wondering exactly who is getting played—them, or us?"

"We can only do what we can do, Maddie."

"And Ivan doesn't have the full picture, yet, either. The computer might be playing *him.*"

"Also a possibility. Same answer, though. At some point, you have to commit."

Narang closed her eyes and rubbed her temples. "We're playing a dangerous game, Charlie. We're taking implied advice from Ivan on how to convince the computer not to destroy us or Upload us. No matter how I parse it, it sounds ridiculous."

"I know, I know," Kemp replied. "But, as Ivan explains it, it's the computer we have to convince. Ivan is acting like our lawyer, arguing our case and giving us advice. But once the computer makes a decision, Ivan is helpless. He might, in fact, be worse than helpless; he might be switched off once he's no longer needed."

"Well, we're going to play it the way Ivan hinted at, Charlie. And the military will do their part, whether they realize it or not. Best case, they'll take our advice about offering the cooperator move. Worst case, they'll blow him up before the computer can do anything. I think Ivan would consider either outcome acceptable."

72. Preparations

The communication station grew steadily. With the addition of the two cruisers, Ivan had enough material to build a radio dish that would be heard all the way to the farthest homes of the Uploads.

He wasn't sure whether it was more amusing or discouraging that a civilization millions of years old was still depending on radio communications. Or maybe Ralph didn't feel the need to build the advanced stuff. It was one of those questions the computer was either unwilling or unable to answer.

They would have to wait a minimum of 142 years for a response. Ivan didn't have nearly enough study courses for that. Maybe he could get Ralph to open up more about galactic civilizations. Otherwise he would discover untold new levels of boredom.

The cruisers were sorry-looking balls of metal, half melty-looking, with most of their hulls already stripped. Nacelles had been removed to act as transport thrusters. To one side, two chrome balls were just beginning to grow. They had no specific programming, as yet. They could be set to any of a number of different tasks, although that decision hadn't been made. Ivan had to hope he could delay it until after the Navy's move.

Three more sat to one side, ready for launch. Their programming was straightforward, and he had been pushing their manufacture. No doubt Ralph was wondering why he was so energetically pushing the manufacture and early launch of these items. Ivan kept his face neutral and carefully steered his thoughts in another direction. He could no longer hope that Ralph's plans would be good for the human race. He was faced with his worst-case scenario.

Ivan sat in the Captain's Chair of the *Mad Astra.* He patted the arm with a fond smile. In the short time that he'd been aboard, he'd managed to start thinking of it as a home of sorts. The *Astra* had fared a little better than the cruisers. She looked like a much-reduced version of herself, but she was still recognizably a spaceship. At least the skeleton of one. No environmental requirements made a lot of the mass of a spaceship redundant. The fusion nacelles, though, were unchanged.

As he stared into infinity, he wondered how the doctors had done with the Navy. There was a small chance that the Navy might believe them and offer a cooperator move. No, not really. The Navy would be out in force, and soon. He had to hope that the *Getting Ahead* crew would figure out the *real* message in time. Otherwise, his fallback plan was to have the Navy nuke the hell out of him and Ralph, before the computer realized it had been set up.

So far, Ralph didn't seem to have copped on. So he did continue to enjoy some mental privacy. Or maybe it was just too much work to monitor him.

Ralph broke into his musings.

Nanite balls are ready. Confirm your intention to place these on planets one, two, and four and initiate conversion.

That's right.

Why?

Trying to get their attention. I'm hoping that an external threat will bring humanity together.

Your plan is optimistic. The word 'naïve' seems appropriate as well. Is it?

You're an expert on human psychology now?

Is anyone? Your species is fractious, disorganized both mentally and politically, unpredictable, immature—

But not beyond hope. You've said yourself that an Uploaded species would be valuable. We're—

—not ready. And possibly won't ever be. A decision must be made soon.

Fine. But let's try this first.

Very well. Launching nanite payloads. Regardless of the ultimate decision, this reconfiguration will be useful.

Ivan carefully kept his features neutral. The important thing was to launch the nanites before the Navy launched another attack.

Very soon, humanity would have its collective face shoved in the fact that it was not alone in the universe.

73. Second Assault

Twenty Navy ships stood at station keeping outside the Lagrange Four base. Frigates, cruisers, and warships, each had its part to play.

In another area, five supply ships were being offloaded. Crews moved cylinder after gleaming cylinder from transport vessels to fighting ships, using what for some reason were still called forklifts.

Admiral Moore scanned the paperwork, making annotations and initialing sections as required. Despite the Board of Inquiry's statement about his status, Commodore Mandelbaum had recognized that his decades of experience in certain areas should be taken advantage of. She would review his decisions, but it would be a formality. Moore could do this stuff in his sleep. And for a while, at least, he could feel useful.

Finally, the preparations were complete. Surveillance drones and cruise missiles had been distributed to the ships. Courses had been calculated and communicated. Before the ships departed, there would be a strategy meeting.

Twenty Ship's Captains crowded into the large hab-ring conference room. The various seating angles caused by the floor's curvature wouldn't even be noticed by these Navy old-timers. Mandelbaum stood at the center of one of the longs sides of the conference table, her eyes scanning the room. Moore, standing to one side, found himself impressed by her outward calm.

Barely raising her voice, she said, "Your attention, please." Conversations in the room stopped as cleanly as if a switch had been thrown, and all eyes turned to her.

“You all have briefing packages, which you will have studied exhaustively. I remind you that the enemy we are facing is more indifferent than antagonistic. Strategies will be set accordingly. We will maintain a radio communications blackout from the time we depart from Lagrange Four. Any necessary comms will be effected by intership maser. We have determined that our comms masers are sufficiently powerful to fry the nanites, so even if one manages to insert itself by fluke, it won’t survive the encounter.”

She paused and swept her eyes around the room. “Your individual orders are not to be discussed or shared with other ships. Inevitably, Pritchard will manage to take over some of your ships using his nanites. We will limit the information that he can extract from that tactic.”

Heads nodded around the table. No one had any illusions that this was an exercise, or police action, or some similar euphemism. This would be a naval engagement, with the very real possibility of destruction and death.

“All right,” Mandelbaum continued. “You have your orders. Let’s do this.”

Mandelbaum and Moore stood at parade rest at the center of the room as the officers filed out. There was no buzz of conversation. Each person was alone with their thoughts, reconciling themselves to their fate, whatever it might be.

* * *

Commodore Mandelbaum and Admiral Moore stood on the on-axis bridge of the *Resolute*, Velcro slippers helping maintain the illusion of a martial stance. All preliminaries being accomplished, Captain Norman Harding awaited their orders.

Mandelbaum turned to him and nodded, a minimal movement with a large meaning.

Turning to his crew, Harding ordered, “Signal all ships. Let’s move.”

On the status board, icons began to shift. The floor became *down.* As the minutes stretched, the graphic representing Lagrange Four fell farther to the bottom of the monitor. Finally, with a flicker, the gaps decreased as the scale changed. They were underway.

* * *

The Signals officer turned to face Captain Harding. "Message from base, sir. Tagged CEO."

"Transfer to my Ready Room." Captain Harding glanced at the commodore and the admiral, and they followed him. A *Command Eyes Only* communication at this early stage would not be routine.

The three made themselves comfortable, and Captain Harding pulled up the message, repeated onto each officer's tablet.

TO: Harding, Capt. (Resolute)
FROM: SSC/UENN
COMMAND EYES ONLY
RE: Bogeys

LRS confirms 6 bogeys trailing your position. Silhouette and drive flame spectrum indicate SSE Class-3 Destroyers.

Captain Harding, these were launched without the usual chest-thumping and paranoid threats. Strategic Space Command analysts suggest the SSE wants as little visibility on this as possible. That can't be good.

Maj. Christina Furlong
Cmdr, Monitoring & Analysis

The three officers looked up at the same time. There was a moment of silence before Captain Harding ventured, "The Sino-Soviets are so mad they're speechless?"

Mandelbaum stared into the air for a moment longer before responding. "Might as well look at it that way, Captain. I bet their orders include the very real possibility of weapons exchange. And without phoning home first."

"Destroyers." Harding grimaced.

Moore nodded. "Yep. What the SSE lacks in technology they more than make up for by just building bigger and badder. Six destroyers aren't quite enough to take on our task force, but they can certainly make a mess."

Captain Harding glanced at his tablet before placing it carefully on the table. "Well, it doesn't really change our immediate strategy, does it? We'll just have to figure it out when we get there."

The intercom gave a short beep, followed by the Signals Officer's voice. "Another CEO, sir. Forwarding."

"Busy day," Mandelbaum commented.

Captain Harding reached for the control to share the missive, but stopped with his hand in the air. "Wow."

"Really, Captain? Care to share?"

"It's for you, Commodore. Seems you're getting a field promotion, of sorts." He handed his tablet to her.

Mandelbaum's eyes tracked back and forth for a few moments, then she lowered the tablet with a bemused expression. She handed it to Moore. "I've been granted Level 3 Conflict Decision authority. I guess SSC doesn't want us phoning home either, if things lose their shine."

Captain Harding stood. "I think I'm going to have the crew run a few drills. Just in case." Without waiting for a response, he headed for the bridge.

74. Reconfiguration

Ian Jonquers ran down the hallway, dodging pedestrians, his little brother yelling at him to wait. Ian got to the observation window first. Caleb finally reached the window, too out of breath to berate him.

The brothers gazed out at the harsh landscape of Mercury while they waited for their mother to catch up. The terrain, stretching to the close horizon, resembled what one would see on Luna. Jagged, black rock, sharp shadows from the almost complete lack of atmosphere, and crater walls rising in the distance to encircle the station presented a picture that would be forbidding to an adult but was business as usual to the two boys.

The installation, a combination science station and experimental mining facility, was nominally the Mercury North Polar Station, but was commonly known as Vulcan's Forge. The large semi-permanent population consisted of an equal mix of scientists, industrial mining personnel, and infrastructure staff. And their families as well.

Emilia Jonquers caught up with her two boys, who would, if history was any judge, have to be peeled away from the window with the promise of ice cream at the mall. The trips to the shopping center had become a standard routine, and everyone knew their part. Even the boys' complaints would be perfunctory, lasting just long enough to extract the required promise.

Emilia nodded a greeting to a few familiar faces. The comforting routine of the daily walk was a high point of her day.

"That's new. What's that?" Caleb said, pointing.

Emilia smiled at Caleb's vivid imagination. Nothing ever changed out there. All the station work was done underground, out of range of the sun's heat.

"I don't think anything's new, Caleb. What are you looking at?"

He pointed again. "The shiny thing."

Emilia looked, then did a double take. Something was indeed out there. Like a post, or column. Literally shiny, in the dictionary meaning of the word. And it seemed to be...growing?

She watched, her hands pressed up against the window. The column was getting larger. And now, a second one began to force its way out of the ground.

Emilia backed away from the window and reached for her phone. Before she could even decide who to call, let alone actually dial, the building shook. The boys yelled in surprise, and Caleb sat down abruptly.

She grabbed Caleb under the arms and stood him up. "Come on, you two, we have to get out of this corridor." Chivvying them along, she marched toward the exit at the end of the connecting tube. The airlock at the end led to the roundabout, which was the central hub of the station. All tunnels and corridors, for five levels, led from the roundabout to every part of the structure.

As she approached the pressure door, the building began to shake again. At first barely perceptible, the shaking seemed to get stronger moment by moment. Emilia broke into a run, dragging her boys by the hands. Caleb, unable to keep up, began to cry. She held him in the air, easily straight-arming him in the one-third gravity, as she sprinted for the hatch.

As Emilia rushed through the airlock, there was a crunch and a bang behind her. A sudden wind blew in her face, just as a klaxon started sounding. She stopped and turned, to see the pressure door slam shut from the ceiling. She looked through the porthole on the door. The corridor had buckled halfway along, and one of the view windows had popped out of its frame. A half-dozen people, trapped in the corridor, were being dragged by the escaping air toward the gap.

One woman looked directly at Emilia, terror plain on her face.

I know her. She passed that woman most days, going in the opposite direction. They would nod and smile, and occasionally exchange greetings. As Emilia watched, the woman was sucked out through the window, still scrabbling at the floor and walls.

"What's happening, Mom? Can I see?" Ian held his hands up, requesting a lift. Beside him, Caleb jumped up and down in a vain attempt to get enough height to see through the porthole.

Still in shock, Emilia turned and looked around the roundabout. Dozens of stunned faces looked back at her or at each other.

The klaxon cut off and a voice announced over the P.A., "All personnel to evacuation stations. This is not a drill. All personnel to evacuation stations."

Emilia's eyes widened, and she looked around frantically for any indication of the location of the nearest evacuation station. A red flashing light caught her eye. She turned toward it just as another tremor hit. There was no buildup. One moment the floor was steady; the next, she was being bounced around like popcorn. People screamed; some screams cut off abruptly.

As soon as the tremors abated, Emilia grabbed her children and sprinted for the flashing light. This time, she put even less care into making sure the boys were feet-down-head-up. She realized, mid-sprint, that she had Caleb by the back of his pants, and was carrying him like a briefcase. Both boys howled in terror, more from picking up their mother's fear than from any understanding of the situation.

Yes! The flashing light did, in fact, indicate the location of an evacuation station. Emilia dodged a couple of slower-moving individuals and threw the boys through the door ahead of her. Caleb stopped howling and whooped at the unexpected ride. Twin *oofs* sounded as the boys landed.

The station A.I. would determine when the pod should launch. Emilia's responsibility was limited to strapping herself and her children into acceleration chairs. As she worked, hushing the two boys who were now in full wail, more people poured through the hatch. Sobs and moans dominated, only the occasional person asking questions into the air.

Another quake struck, this one bigger than any of the previous. A klaxon sounded in the pod and the hatch slammed shut. An artificial voice announced launch in thirty seconds and admonished all passengers to be seated.

Emilia put her hands to her mouth. There was no way that everyone could have gotten to pods. And she had no idea where her husband was, or if he'd managed to get to safety. She pulled out her phone and glanced at the screen. She was unsurprised to see the NO

SIGNAL indicator. Silently, so as not to further frighten the boys, she began to cry.

The automated escape pod launched right on time, only half full. Once the roundabout had lost atmosphere, the automation had correctly concluded that there would be no more passengers. Emilia held hands with her boys, one on either side of her. Their crying stopped the moment the pod began the launch sequence. Now they lay in their acceleration chairs, fascinated by the experience. Watching them, Emilia felt a wave of melancholy wash over her. They weren't old enough to remember the trip from Earth, except maybe in bits and snatches. Paradoxically, this would be their first real experience with space travel.

Emilia turned and stared at the ceiling. Still no word from Bruce. She kept reminding herself that communications would be spotty or non-existent until the emergency was over. And the emergency personnel would rightly place non-essential comms at the bottom of their priority list.

It took less than twenty minutes to arrive at the space station orbiting Mercury, but they spent almost two hours queued to be unloaded. By the time their turn came, the boys were whiney and starting to display the hyperactivity that came with hunger and boredom. Emilia had run out of threats and bribes, so the sudden activity through the portholes was a welcome distraction. Other passengers were happy to let the boys have the prime view—anything to shut them up. Emilia tried to be offended at the thought, but found she was simply too honest to pull it off. She wanted to kill them, herself.

As the pod mated with the station airlock, her phone dinged and she pulled it out quickly.

Message from Bruce showed on the display. He was alive and on board. Emilia blinked back tears.

* * *

Ian and Caleb were in their default position, hands and faces pressed to the viewport. Emilia reminded herself for the hundredth time that she should be carrying damp wipes to remove prints.

The view turned slowly in the opposite direction to the station's rotation, an image that had the boys giggling and making childish jokes. Adults stood behind the children, with a clear view over their heads. The planet Mercury seemed to be undergoing some sort of transformation. Structures could be seen, erupting from the surface at the poles, and different structures around the equator. And these were *visible from space.* The size required to make that possible simply defied the imagination.

The Navy, the ISI, and the mining company were all scrambling to accommodate the refugees and to make arrangements for their transport back to Earth. The space station's resources would be strained, trying to provide for several hundred unexpected visitors. Emilia knew less than half of the population of Vulcan's Forge had made it out.

And rumors were flying that Mercury wasn't the only location of unexpected events. She'd heard whispers that strange things were happening on other planets. So far, though, the rumors had named all the planets, right out to Eris—a physical impossibility, since news from Eris couldn't have arrived yet. Still, something was going on, and the consensus was that it had something to do with the alien disease and the ship the Navy had been required to nuke.

Had the disease spread? Or had the aliens arrived, and were they now terraforming planets to their liking?

Emilia took a deep breath, then turned to look at her husband, who was as enraptured by the view as the two boys. A mining engineer, he was probably now jobless. At another time, she would have been devastated by the thought. Jobs were scarce, and the outlook for the unemployed wasn't good. But the specter of death—of *immediate* death—tended to place a different perspective on things.

Emilia squeezed his hand and went back to watching the planetary changes unfold.

75. Waiting for The End

Kemp and Narang walked slowly along the trail, pausing frequently to enjoy the sights and sounds. Narang took a deep lungful of air, redolent with the smell of cedar, damp leaves, moss, and a tinge of salt air coming up the canyon from Burrard Inlet. She smiled without reservation at the unaccustomed commune with nature.

"Capilano Park contains one of the few remaining stands of old-growth trees on the entire North Shore," Kemp said. "I sometimes fantasize about going back in time to the 20th or even 19th century, when there were more trees than people. What must it have been like to look up from the inlet at mountains covered not with residential complexes, but with actual living, breathing forests?"

"I don't get nearly enough of this," Narang said. "This was a good idea."

They stopped and watched a cleanup mech zip by, scanning for dropped garbage or unscooped canine deposits. The small wheeled device expertly avoided pedestrians while checking all corners of the path.

Kemp smiled. "I've started thinking in terms of bucket lists. This may all be gone, soon. *We* might be gone, soon, depending on how the thing plays out. The computer will make a decision when it makes a decision, and there will be no recourse, no appeal." He sighed and looked up to the sky. "Usually in movies, the final battle is a little more dramatic."

"And closer to home."

"Mm."

Silences between them were comfortable. When one of them did say something it wasn't an awkward attempt to fill the air with words. As such, each exchange was interesting and appreciated. Almost without realizing it, they found themselves holding hands as they walked through the trees. And that was fine, too.

They came to the suspension bridge—a construction of rope and wooden planks—stretched 140 meters across the Capilano River.

Narang stopped so suddenly that she almost skidded. "Oh, I don't think so."

Kemp grinned at her. "It's deliberately designed to look rickety, like the original bridge, but those ropes are reinforced with carbon-fiber, and the planks are backed by a nanotube mesh. You couldn't take this thing down with a hacksaw."

He waved a hand at the bridge. "They completely replaced the old bridge in the mid-21st century when the park was deeded to the municipality. Can't have liability issues, you know."

Narang glanced at him uncertainly, then stepped onto the bridge proper. When it didn't immediately collapse and plunge them into the gorge, she release her breath and took another step.

"Good," Kemp said. "Just don't break into a jog. The other pedestrians hate that."

She chuckled at the mental image, and they walked across the bridge, her hand gripping his perhaps a little more tightly than really required.

As they stepped off the other end, she glanced sideways at Kemp. "How do you think it'll happen?"

"You mean whatever the computer decides to do? Don't know exactly, but I'm sure it will involve nanites. Best case, we all end up metal. Worst case, we all end up goo."

"I've never had time for a serious relationship," Narang said. "Always too focused on my career. Funny, they say those are the things you regret when you're older." She gave a rueful snort. "Or when the world is about to end, strangely."

"I'm in sort of the same boat. Maybe not driven, as such, but I've always loved space. I've spent most of my professional life on spaceships. But, y'know, I could call that done, now, and not regret it."

They walked for a few more moments, still hand in hand. Then, without a word being spoken, they turned and headed back to Kemp's house.

* * *

The jangling phone jerked Kemp out of a sound sleep. Narang, nuzzled against his arm and shoulder, muttered and turned over.

Grumbling, he reached for the phone. It was a text from Captain Jennings. With several seconds' round-trip delay, texts would be the only reasonable way of holding a conversation.

20 ships have left Lag 4 base. Prob assault force. Looks like they didn't take advice.

Dammit!

Kemp nudged Narang. "Maddie. Wake up."

Narang growled at him, but opened one eye. "This better be good."

"The Navy has sent an assault force. Looks like they didn't take your suggestion."

"Aw, hell." Narang grabbed the covers and threw them off, then staggered to the powder room. As she closed the door, she grumbled, "Five minutes."

Kemp nodded, although she'd already closed the sliding door, and headed for the main washroom. On the way, he texted the captain. *Meet us at Olympus Station.*

When Kemp came out of the washroom, the phone had another text waiting.

Turn on the news.

Kemp's eyebrows went up, and he picked up the remote. It took only moments to find what the captain was referencing—all the news channels, and several non-news channels, were reporting the same thing.

"Maddie!"

"Busy!"

"Don't care. You have to come out and see this!"

Narang was out within seconds, wiping her face. She gave Kemp a quizzical look, then turned to the Vid. Her jaw dropped, and she sat on the bed without turning her head.

Once again, the top story today...

Several hundred residents of the Mercury North Polar Station are dead, as abrupt and unexplained planet-quakes destroyed or damaged Vulcan's Forge. All surviving personnel have been successfully evacuated. ISI, the Interplanetary Science Institute, reports that the quakes seem to be strongest at both poles. Scientists have no explanation for this effect. However, it is almost certainly related to the enigmatic structures that seem to be growing out of the very planet, at the poles and at the equator.

In addition, the Venus Orbital Platform reports the sighting of six gigantic objects at the top of Venus's cloud layer. Scientists speculate that they are the visible tops of structures stretching up from the surface, as they have no orbital motion and no visible propulsion holding them in place. Asked about the objects, Professor Keeting of the ISI explained, "The visible top of the cloud layer is at around seventy-five kilometers, give or take. So those structures would have to be at the top of a seventy-five-kilometer-tall tower."

This statement has been challenged by Professor Tomlinson of UCLA, who suggests that floating, tethered structures would explain the observations as well. A sufficiently large structure would achieve stability in the same way as floating drilling rigs…

"That's got to be Ivan," Kemp said. Narang shushed him.

In a possibly related item, several Mars stations have reported increasing Mars-quakes. Whether this is a precursor to the same process as we are seeing on Mercury or Venus is unknown at this time. However, Mars personnel have already started evacuation proceedings as a precautionary measure.

"Definitely Ivan." Kemp pointed the remote and started surfing. The news was being repeated on dozens of stations, but they all appeared to be rehashing the same facts. No one was going on the record with any more than the most basic interpretation of events.

"We could check the internet," Narang suggested.

Kemp shook his head. "It's the guv'mint, it's the military-industrial complex, it's the liberals, it's aliens." He grinned at her. "They'd actually be correct on that last item."

Narang rolled her eyes and headed back to the bathroom.

* * *

"It's a good thing you're richer than Midas," Narang said to Kemp as the shuttle snuggled up to the Olympus Station docking port. "The ICDC auditors would be storming my office with torches and pitchforks by now, with all this travel."

Kemp smiled. It occurred to him that, even in the short time that he'd been a billionaire, his attitudes toward spending money had changed drastically. The cost of flying up to the station would have once meant skipping his annual vacation; now it was cab fare.

They climbed out of the traxi and went straight to the Docking Information board, located beside the elevators. Kemp was an old hand at weightless movement, but Narang showed the noob's tendency to put too much muscle into it. He gave her a few quick pointers, and she corrected immediately.

The *Getting Ahead* was listed in Berth 8. Kemp did a quick calculation, then headed for a traxi station.

In a short time, an automated cart stopped in front of them. They pulled themselves in, snapped the lap restraints into place, and the cart pulled out.

As they moved along the circumference of the hub, Kemp could see that most people were glued to their phones or tablets. He considered pulling out his phone and surfing, but decided to wait until they were on board the *Getting Ahead.*

They got off at Berth 8, and pulled themselves over to the egress point. Kemp identified himself to the attendant A.I. and the door opened.

They found Captain Jennings in the on-axis bridge. He nodded to them, then turned back to the monitor he'd been watching. "Interesting developments continue," he said. "It appears that someone is engaged in some kind of planetary engineering." The captain played with his controls, and the feed was duplicated onto the main bridge monitor.

Jennings turned off the sound, and gave them a capsule summary. "The Venus structures are now spewing atmosphere into space at greater than escape velocity. The volume is truly mind-boggling. The point, according to the talking heads, appears to be to strip Venus of its atmosphere. They estimate it'll be done in a few weeks."

Narang shook her head in disbelief.

"A whole planet's worth of atmosphere? That's amazing."

"Won't all that gas in interplanetary space create problems for ships?" Kemp asked.

Jennings nodded. "That occurred to a lot of people, so they did some calculations. It appears that each nozzle, or whatever they are, accelerates the gas either into an orbit that intersects the sun, or a long-period orbit that won't re-enter the inner system for centuries. The mechanism seems to be taking care to avoid polluting the local area."

Kemp began to reply, "I'm not sure if that indicates—" when the monitor flashed up *Breaking News* and the recorded interview cut to one of the news anchors. The captain quickly restored the sound.

We have confirmation that some unidentified structures are growing at the poles on Mars, similar but not identical to the Mercury artifacts. There are also indications of crustal movements around the equator, although nothing specific has been identified.

The monitor cut to images, obviously taken with a phone from a ship's viewport. They showed structures, large enough to be seen from orbit, pushing their way out of the planet's crust.

"Mercury, Venus, and Mars. Assuming there's a theme to all this, what is he doing?" Kemp scratched his chin, staring at the screen.

"Perhaps," Captain Jennings replied, "we'll get a chance to ask him. Please strap yourselves in, and we can get going."

Within ten minutes, the *Getting Ahead* was outside the Olympus Station slow zone, and the captain began to apply some real thrust.

The course laid in, and the ship's A.I. in charge, Jennings turned to his two passengers. "What's the plan?"

"We have to get out there and try to convince the Navy's task force not to attack."

"That's it? As plans go, that really lacks a certain something."

"Planning?" Kemp grinned at him.

"Yes, that." Jennings shook his head. "Sadly, it's all we have right now."

"So, those oversized nacelles you had installed on the *Getting Ahead*—I guess it's time to find out if you got your money's worth."

"Mm, hmm. That's why I have the hab ring spun down. Better make yourselves comfortable. This isn't going to be pleasant."

Jennings was as good as his word. The acceleration was heavy enough to make breathing uncomfortable, but smooth, which told Kemp that the ship's engines weren't going flat out. That raised the obvious question of just how much acceleration the *Getting Ahead* was capable of. Kemp hoped not to have to find out. The current level was quite enough, thanks.

After several minutes of hell, Jennings reduced acceleration to what felt like about a half gee. He stood and motioned his guests to unbuckle as well.

"I've taken on a full load of fuel, including aux tanks. With just the three of us and no cargo, I can keep us under power all the way to the destination. We won't bother with the hab ring at all. That will mean sleeping in one of the on-axis bunk rooms, though." Jennings looked sheepish for a moment. "The return trip will be more leisurely, of necessity. I hope you packed your toothbrushes. And a lot of reading."

76. Defensive Strategy

Twenty fusion signatures, all approaching on different vectors. All carefully timed so that they would arrive in an almost spherical formation around the location of the last encounter. Ivan could feel the computer's cool calculations going on in the background: threat analysis, species evaluations, decision trees, all flying past too quickly for him to follow. Ralph didn't try to explain its ruminations in detail, but it did give him occasional summary images of the analyses and goal weightings. So far, humanity was balanced on a knife edge, not quite belligerent enough to be worth wiping out, and not quite potentially useful enough to be Uploaded. But when the two new balls of nanites were ready, a decision would be made.

Although Ivan would have preferred a third option, at least Ralph hadn't settled on Plan A or Plan B yet. For the moment, his family and all of humanity was still safe.

And now, following those first signatures, six more, from another vector. Drive flame analysis and acceleration indicated something heavy. Ivan's guess was SSE warships. He'd seen programs on the Vid about their military; they built big—no finesse, no concession to economics or efficiency. Simply massive brute force.

Well, it was a bonus of a sort, from a Plan B point of view. The UENN and SSE would be competing to see who could blow up Ivan first. And right about now, Ralph would be realizing that all the nanites had gone to Mercury, Venus, and Mars, and there weren't enough in the two new balls to defend with.

These incoming groups are from different human cohorts, are they not?

Different nations, yes.

I assume their intentions are hostile?

Probably a safe bet.

Given the situation, I find their response disappointing.

A value judgement? You're getting opinions now?

An expression indicating that reality falls short of expectations. Am I phrasing it incorrectly?

No, I guess not. But why would you not expect us to react defensively?

A more rational species would spend more time gathering facts, evaluating options and risks, determining what is within the range of possibility, before selecting this strategy.

The worst part was that Ivan couldn't honestly disagree.

His attention was drawn to another fusion signature, just leaving Olympus Station. The heat signature and spectrum indicated a larger ship than the observed acceleration allowed. He smiled to himself. That would be Captain Jennings's hotrod.

He wondered if the *Getting Ahead* would make it on time. Or if they'd figured out what he was trying to tell them. Come to think of it, the SSE ships could be used to emphasize the point. Good for Plan A.

He looked at the two remaining chrome balls, one nacelle from the cruisers floating beside each. Destined for the Earth and the Moon they represented, one way or the other, the end of humanity.

Come on, Captain Jennings. Put some hustle on.

77. Surveil

The spy drones sent in their views of the construction as they flew through the enemy's arena.

Moore and Mandelbaum stood to the right of Captain Harding, who was closely following the activity of his bridge crew. As quickly as Surveil could clean up and integrate the transmissions, they were transferred to tablets.

Most of the images showed the remains of the *Mad Astra* and of the two cruisers. The two Navy ships had been stripped down to the point of being junk. They were obviously being used only for construction material. The *Astra*, on the other hand, seemed to be still spaceworthy, but with a much reduced size. The skin had been stripped off, the middle chopped out, and the ends stuck together.

A half-completed radio dish floated in the background, dwarfing the cruisers. In zero gravity, it was gossamer thin, its shape maintained by guy-wires and spring steel segments.

Moore stared up at the overhead, rubbing his chin. The engines of a mining ship were no match for a Navy vessel, but strip most of the weight away, and what you were left with was essentially a rocket engine with a steering wheel at the front. Moore was no engineer, but a lifetime working with ships had given him some seat-of-the-pants skills. He closed his eyes, moving his lips silently, then snapped his eyes open. "Commodore?"

Mandelbaum looked up from the tablet she was reading. "Yes?"

"The civilian ship. Or what's left of it. It could, in principle, completely outpace any of our vessels. I'm guessing that's his getaway machine."

Mandelbaum frowned at the image on the monitor. "That's a bit of a stretch, I think. He'd have to remove so much ship..."

"No environmentals. He doesn't need them. No oxygen or water, no food. Toss out living quarters, recycling systems—for that matter, every bulkhead and airlock designed to retain an atmosphere. It's a stripped-down hotrod."

Mandelbaum stared at the image, her eyes narrowing. Then she nodded and sat back. "Noted. Thank you, Admiral. Captain, be sure to make the *Mad Astra* a target."

"Sir," an officer turned from her console to face Captain Harding. "Signals indicates an approaching ship. Other than the SSE warships, I mean."

"Distance?"

"Just under two tenths of an A.U., sir, and closing fast. Decelerating at point-five gee. Back-prop puts departure at Olympus Station."

"Got a transponder ID?"

"Nothing in on-board archives, which probably means it's pretty new, sir. We've queried Earthside, but it'll be a while for a response."

Mandelbaum cut in. "Any possibility this is coincidence? That they're heading somewhere else?"

"Coming right down our backsides, ma'am. And decelerating to arrive at the theater with zero relative velocity."

"So that's a no, then." Mandelbaum turned to Moore. "Any ideas?"

"To be honest, my best guess would be the former captain of the *Mad Astra*, and possibly some crew. They don't seem to be able to get past this whole Pritchard thing."

"Why? What are they going to do, take us on?" Mandelbaum frowned and turned to the signals officer. "Could that thing be armed?"

The officer shook her head. "Transponder details jibe with the silhouette. It's a miner. Benz-Gilmore 4502, but apparently with some mods. It's coming in *way* too hot for a stock 4502."

Mandelbaum frowned and shook her head, plainly perplexed by the behavior of civilians. "Fine. Signals, hail them. Demand an explanation, and warn them they're heading for a possible battle zone. And give me an estimated time to reply."

"Light speed delay, one minute twelve each way, ma'am. Plus any time required to format a response, of course."

"What about the SSE ships?"

"They're about two twenty away, ma'am. Coming in more sedately."

Mandelbaum looked up at the tactical screen, and contemplated the images for a few moments. Graphics of the Navy ships, the approaching civilian ship, and the trailing SSE flotilla competed with vector arrows and velocity annotations. The commodore ran a finger up and down the bridge of her nose. "We may already be too late. The activity on Mercury, Venus, and Mars is almost certainly Pritchard's doing—"

"Well, no, Commodore," Moore interjected. "It could also be the Arts that he mentions, although I would find the coincidence of them showing up just as the Uploads gain a foothold a little hard to swallow."

"Either way, Admiral, it's bad for us. Does it change our strategy?"

"Assuming we take all of Pritchard's statements at face value, then we will fare worse at the hands of the Arts."

"That's just different degrees of death, Admiral. Neither consequence is acceptable. I think we need to fight the battle that's in front of us, rather than speculating and paralyzing ourselves."

Moore nodded, not responding. He realized that his attitudes had changed since his failure in the previous encounter. Perhaps it was the fact of Pritchard not killing them out of hand; perhaps it was just a chance to think logically through the various alternatives. Moore still wouldn't call himself a dove by any stretch, but he found himself slightly less attached to the military solution as a first resort.

He stared into space, hands clasped behind his back, considering the alternatives. Were there no possible outcomes that spared the human race? Or had he simply not thought of one? Moore remembered Sherlock Holmes's canonical statement that one should eliminate all other alternatives in order to come up with the right answer. The problem, which never seemed to be discussed, was whether you could think of all the alternatives. What if you missed one? What if you simply didn't have the knowledge to posit the right answer? It was a stance filled with an unstated arrogant belief that one could know all the possible choices.

Moore turned to glance speculatively at Commodore Mandelbaum. He wondered if she would be flexible enough to try something different, if it presented itself.

78. Approach

"We've received a communication from the Navy," Captain Jennings announced. "Hardly surprising, of course." He put it up on the bridge monitor. "How shall we respond?"

Kemp read the missive. "I think we should just be truthful, Captain. There's no point in trying to outguess and out-finesse. Too many players in this game, right now." They were painfully aware of the very large SSE vessels approaching behind them. Jennings assured his passengers that he could outrun the warships. Missiles, not so much, but one hoped that even the SSE would hesitate before firing on a civilian vessel.

"Fine, Dr. Kemp. I will defer to your expertise in this issue. Please compose a response and let me know when it's ready. Meanwhile, I need a coffee." Jennings stood and headed for the Captain's Ready Room.

"Tea," Narang said, standing up.

Kemp stood up as well. There were, after all, priorities.

* * *

The three sat around the conference table in the Ready Room. Jennings's eyes tracked as he read the text on his tablet.

From:	*Andrew Jennings, Captain, IMM Getting Ahead.*
CC:	*Dr. Charles Kemp, Ship's Doctor*
	Dr. Madhur Narang, ICDC
To:	*Commodore Rani Mandelbaum, UENN Fleet Command*

We are aware of the nature of your mission, and have a good general idea of Ivan Pritchard's plans from previous conversations with him. Dr. Narang has relayed the contents of those conversations to the Navy. We are concerned that you are ignoring the proper Game Theory response and are proceeding with a standard Defector move.

We don't, of course, know for sure that Pritchard can withstand and/or survive an attack by yourselves. However, everything from his original conversion to current events on several inner-system planets indicates quite clearly that we are dealing with a technology far in advance of our own. In our opinion, we cannot win a straight fight. Therefore, the only option is to offer a Cooperator move and hope that the computer will relent.

We are, as you know, en route. Celestial mechanics being what it is, we are committed to our destination. Drs. Narang and Kemp have a working relationship with Pritchard. We implore you to hold off and give them an opportunity to negotiate a better result.

Concerning the trailing SSE warships, we have received no communication from them. They may be taking a wait-and-see attitude, or they may simply be trying to figure out what you're doing out here. Absent some indication of their motives and plans, I can offer no insight or suggestions.

A. Jennings, Captain

Jennings nodded and handed the tablet back to Kemp. "Looks good. Please do the honors."

Kemp pressed *send.* "Now, we wait."

* * *

"Mars has started growing something that looks like the structures on Venus," Jennings said, looking up from his tablet. "Perhaps they mean to blow off Mars's atmosphere as well."

"Not sure why," Narang said. "There's barely an atmosphere to begin with."

Jennings shrugged. "Unsurprisingly, the research stations and test colonies have been evacuated. Who knows if something will start growing underfoot at any moment?"

"And Mercury?"

"Well, no atmosphere to worry about, so I don't expect we'll ever see the same structures. What *is* growing, so far, is unidentifiable."

A *ding* on the captain's tablet made them all look up. Jennings swiped at the tablet for a few moments, then his eyes tracked back and forth as he read whatever it was.

He looked up at his passengers, and Kemp could see it wasn't good.

"The Navy has rejected our proposal. They will attack."

Kemp rubbed his eyes. "Offering the computer a Cooperator move was a long shot. Maddie admitted that. I guess that's how the Navy sees it as well." He looked around at the others. "We're out of options."

"The Navy would have done a risk analysis on the suggestion. They have their equations, as well," Jennings said.

"And the equation is every—"

Narang and Jennings turned to look at Kemp, who had chopped his statement mid-sentence, and was sitting there, staring straight ahead.

Kemp slowly turned his head. "The equation is everything. It has no ego. Ivan said that. He stressed it."

"What?"

Kemp refocused on Jennings. "We do have options. We've been looking at this wrong. We can force the computer to see things our way."

79. Attack

Commodore Mandelbaum read the second message on her tablet, her eyebrows gradually drawing together. Finally she looked up at Moore and shook her head slowly. Without comment, she sent a copy of both to his tablet, then waved a hand, inviting him to read.

From: *Andrew Jennings, Captain, IMM Getting Ahead.*
CC: *Dr. Charles Kemp, Ship's Doctor*
Dr. Madhur Narang, ICDC
To: *Commodore Rani Mandelbaum, UENN Fleet Command*
We understand that you may not have considered the Cooperator offer to be of a sufficiently high probability to be worth attempting. However, according to Dr. Kemp, we may have some additional leverage—a way to force the computer to accede to our offer.
Again, we implore you to hold off and let us try this alternative.
A. Jennings, Captain

Moore read the messages twice, certain the first time that he'd missed something fundamental. He looked up at Mandelbaum. "I don't remember hearing anything in the recording of the interview with Dr. Narang about possible game theory scenarios. What haven't I been told?"

Mandelbaum stared at him silently for several seconds, then stood up. "Ready Room."

Moore followed her, and sat in the indicated chair.

"You were given a summary and extracts, Admiral Moore. The

drivel about game theory tactics wasn't considered germane."

Moore felt the blood drain from his face, as he realized two things. One, that he was sufficiently out of the loop to be subject to edited versions of the facts; and, two, that until very recently he would have approved of the tactic. Getting your ass kicked, however, tended to put a different perspective on your belief in your infallibility.

Recriminations wouldn't help, though, especially with someone who could freeze him out, or even throw him in the brig, at her discretion.

"May I have access to the complete recording, now, Commodore?"

"Fine, Admiral. However, we will not wait for you to bring yourself up to date. The attack will proceed as planned." She poked at her tablet, and Moore's device *dinged* as he received a file.

Mandelbaum stood. "Feel free to make use of the room, Admiral. You may return to station when ready."

He turned to watch her as she floated out of the room, then shook his head and followed.

* * *

Commodore Mandelbaum settled herself in her spot to the right of Captain Harding and nodded. He turned to his staff. "Tactical, operation status?"

"Nominal, sir. Everything is in place."

"Then execute the plan, Lieutenant."

"Aye."

The tactical officer began running through lists, activating operations and handling confirmations. As the orders percolated through ship's systems, other bridge crew become more animated. Soon, the bridge was a bee's nest of activity, all carefully coordinated, as station operators worked in concert.

Finally, the tactical officer turned in his seat to face the Captain. "All scripts are active, sir. First contact, two minutes."

Moore used the two minutes to scan the transcript of the interview, since that would be both faster and less distracting to the bridge crew. When he was done, he looked up at Mandelbaum. "And you didn't even once consider this option?"

Mandelbaum turned and stared coldly at him. "It was discussed, Admiral. And dismissed. Even Dr. Narang admitted that it was an outside chance."

"As opposed to what you're doing? Never mistake motion for action, Commodore. You've just confirmed to Pritchard's computer that we are not capable of making the intelligent choice, instead defaulting to violence."

Mandelbaum raised an eyebrow. "You seem to have changed, Admiral."

Moore sighed. "I've never before been on the wrong side of a battle where I was so completely overmatched that I might as well not have shown up. The problem with military solutions is that they favor the strongest side, not the one with the moral right. Or the one with the best plan. And in this case, I don't believe we are the strongest side. Not by a wide margin."

"We'll know soon enough, Admiral. The second wave of surveillance drones all made it through the active theater in one piece. Lieutenant, pull the three cam vids with the best details, and forward them to me."

"Aye."

"Ma'am, we have another incoming message from the *Getting Ahead.*"

"Put it up."

From: Andrew Jennings, Captain, IMM Getting Ahead.
CC: Dr. Charles Kemp, Ship's Doctor
Dr. Madhur Narang, ICDC
To: Commodore Rani Mandelbaum, UENN Fleet Command

Commodore, we are close enough to have gotten a good view of the "theater", as I believe you military types like to call it. One of the numerous upgrades I had done to the Getting Ahead was a much larger set of optics, so I probably have as good a view as you, and possibly even a better one.

We took some images last time we were up here, after the military gave up those two cruisers. I note two things missing at this time—one, the former Mad Astra and, two, a group of chrome-colored balls. The latter are somewhat hard to see unless you know what you're looking for. And given our experience with Pritchard, we do.

The point I'm trying to make is that you won't get Pritchard, you won't get his nanites, and it's entirely possible that you won't get his comms station. At least not the real one.

You are dealing with a computer system that may have literally millions of years of experience to draw on in terms of tactical decisions. And you are very probably about to have your asses handed to you.

A. Jennings, Captain

"Dammit!" muttered Mandelbaum. "Tactical! Where are those vids?"

"Coming up, ma'am. Transferring now."

Moore noted that he did not receive a copy, or an offer of a copy. He had a feeling that they were entering FUBAR territory. In not very much longer, the commodore might be seeing the situation from his angle. That would be unfortunate, because it would mean they'd failed.

Mandelbaum stared at her tablet for several minutes, poking and swiping at it at seemingly random intervals. Finally she looked up. "It would appear that Jennings's evaluation is correct. And how in hell did he get these images before us? Surveil?"

"Sorry, ma'am. Don't know. However, the message did mention larger optics. Big ship like that, lots of money, he might have room for a four-fifty Maksutov-Cassegrain. We'd never be able to touch that."

"The takeaway, though, is that the bird has flown," Moore said. Mandelbaum favored him with a murderous glare, and Moore wondered for a moment if he should get himself checked for radiation burns.

"Ready Room," Mandelbaum said, curtly. Without waiting, she launched herself from her chair.

* * *

Moore settled himself comfortably and pulled up his workspace to skim the full vids. Mandelbaum pulled a coffee and gestured to him to help himself.

When he was seated again, she put her coffee down and said, "We seem to consistently underestimate this character."

"Because we keeping thinking we're dealing with Ivan Pritchard, a down-on-his-luck computer programmer turned miner. He's just along for the ride. It's the computer that comes with the nanites that's the true antagonist."

Mandelbaum nodded. "We keep our A.I.s strictly limited, so that humans make all the real decisions. We tend to think that it'll always be that way. Perhaps that's unrealistic." She pressed the intercom button. "Signals."

"Ma'am?"

"What's the delay on communications with the *Getting Ahead*?"

"Twenty seconds, round trip, ma'am."

Mandelbaum's eyebrows rose, and Moore found himself impressed as well. The civilian ship had closed a significant fraction of the distance since they'd first been detected. Their top speed at turnover must have been astronomical.

Mandelbaum looked at him. "It's not ideal for voice. Let's try text."

Moore nodded, and Mandelbaum pulled her tablet into position. She shared her screen with him, then began typing.

Concur with your analysis, Captain. Subject is in the wind. No info on chrome balls. Can you give details?

Mandelbaum hit send, then cradled her coffee. The answer came back in two minutes.

Balls likely contained nanite payloads for specific targets. See news, Merc Venus Mars. Five balls when we were here, three likely accounted for. Last two? Earth, Moon?

"Shit!"

Moore jumped at the expletive, and Mandelbaum gave him an apologetic look. She leaned over her tablet and typed out a response.

Conversion of Earth, Moon imminent? Ungood. Do you have a suggestion to rescue the situation?

This time, over three minutes passed before a response came in.

Find Ivan, second comms station, nanite packages. Start now. Talk later.

Mandelbaum frowned. "Wait, they were all about the peaceful talking, now they want us to find and destroy them?"

"Find, Commodore. No mention of *destroy*." Moore tapped the screen to emphasize the point.

"Fine." Mandelbaum sent, *Stand by,* then hit the intercom. "Surveil. Assume two bogeys are headed from here to Earth and Luna. Calculate trajectories, send up to a third of our drones to look for them. Then send the balance out, all directions, looking for other artifacts."

The tablet *dinged*, and Mandelbaum looked down.

Include nukes. Cruise missiles.

"I'm getting whiplash from trying to follow the logic of these people." She typed a message. *You'll explain this?*

The response came back immediately, allowing for light-speed delay. *Less talk more search.*

Mandelbaum gave Moore a rueful grin. "Well, that, at least, is clear."

She hit the button. "Tactical, send cruise missiles on the trail of the drones. I want a wide enough spread to be able to hit anything we find, in any direction. Clear?"

"Aye."

"Signals, send a message to base. Tell them to get every optical and radio telescope out and looking for anything at all. We need the bogeys spotted ASAP."

"Aye."

Mandelbaum sat back. "Now, we wait."

80. Response

Ivan drifted through interplanetary space, literally sitting on the end of a fusion drive nacelle. He had stripped the nacelles from the cruisers, attached some fuel pods to each. A set of thrusters around the front, and he had a spaceship.

As long as you didn't need to breathe, of course.

It was the minimalist's vessel. Thrust, steering, and fuel. All you really needed to get from A to B. A similar setup provided the transportation for two balls of chrome—nanite assault troops, heading for their targets.

Ivan wished he could cry. Unless Kemp and the crew pulled a rabbit out of a hat, his family would be dead within a couple of weeks. And everyone else on Earth, and all other life, but he found that last bit somehow less important. Ralph had made a decision, based on the approaching attackers, UENN and SSE alike. It had been close, oh so close. But humanity just didn't quite make the cut. Instead, the system would be cleared and turned into an automated outpost in the war against the Arts. Plan B. The two remaining nanite balls were being programmed to do to Earth and Luna what had already been done to Mercury, Venus, and Mars.

You'll kill us all off? Just like that?

It is not intentional. Simply a side effect. Modifying the system for defense will render the planets uninhabitable.

That's not reassuring.

Reassurance is not in my goal tree. I recognize your objections. However, my prime directives necessitate maximizing value for

the Makers, not for your people.

But billions of sentient beings. Billions, for God's sake.

The concept of gods is not unknown to the Makers. A large fraction of them had theistic beliefs at some point in their biological history. I have the historical details but do not pretend to understand the concepts or motivations.

The fate of humanity is unfortunate. An Uploaded species would be of far more value, but yours is not suitable at this time. Far too violent, short-sighted and fractious.

We might still get there.

Not before you die of heat death, or at the hands of your own A.I.s. Your technological progress has outstripped your maturation to a quite unusual extent.

So that was it. Ralph was adamant about its course of action. Argument wouldn't sidetrack it. There was only the one small hope, that he could engineer a do-over. And that all his double-agent-y planning hadn't missed something.

Ivan looked to the heavens, all around him, and found himself praying to a god he'd stopped believing in long ago to please, please help the crew of the *Getting Ahead.*

81. Found

"Ma'am, we have a bogey."

Both Mandelbaum and Moore looked up at the intercom message from Captain Harding.

"Location and ID?" Mandelbaum asked.

"It looks a lot like the first communications station we found, but significantly bigger. Huge radio dish, and so on. Half an A.U. higher up out of the ecliptic."

Moore pursed his lips for a moment. "It's reasonable to assume that the one we were about to nuke is a decoy."

Mandelbaum typed a message. *Found second station. Recommendation?*

The *Getting Ahead* was almost close enough for conversations, but Mandelbaum had said that she liked to think about what to say, so she would continue with texts as long as possible. Moore didn't care either way. Results were what mattered.

Set up but don't attack. We want a credible threat. Also, set up to defend against the SSE ships.

"What, they're going for détente?" Mandelbaum's eyes bugged out. "That's ridiculous!" She tuned to Moore. "They can't possibly think that'll hold water?"

Moore shook his head. "We'd lose a standoff, unless we could prevent Pritchard from transmitting. And all he'd have to do is make some more nanites and sneak them in. I don't think that's what Jennings and crew have in mind."

Have you found Pritchard?

Mandelbaum shook her head, not so much in answer to the text as in evident frustration.

Not yet.

Moore looked at her. "It may be a negotiating tactic." At her raised eyebrow, he continued, "Dr. Narang mentioned game theory in the interview. They may be still trying for something along those lines, although since it's the computer's turn to move, I don't see what we can do."

Mandelbaum tossed her tablet onto the desk and sat back. "Unfortunately, the nanite balls and the station were easy to find, because the number of paths Pritchard could take was constrained by the requirements of orbital mechanics. He himself has no goal other than to stay hidden. He could be anywhere."

* * *

Moore and Mandelbaum both jumped as the intercom crackled to life. "Ma'am, the *Getting Ahead* is pulling up to our position."

"Thank you, Captain Harding. Please have Signals contact the *Getting Ahead.* Route the connection to the Ready Room."

"Aye."

In less than a minute, Captain Jennings's voice played from the speaker. "Good day, Commodore."

"Captain. Are Kemp and Narang available?"

"We're all here, Commodore," said Kemp.

"Good. Can you explain now what we're attempting?"

"We're trying for Plan C." There was a pause. "The computer had to decide whether to Upload us or just convert the solar system into a remote post of sorts. That would be fatal to all life on Earth, of course. We are trying for a third alternative—a compromise that leaves Earth habitable."

"Did Pritchard mention such an alternative?"

"He hinted at it," said Narang. "He can't just talk straight out about ways to finesse the computer—it's listening all the time, of course. But the colloquial nature of human communication, and especially English, which is a truly chaotic language, makes it possible to say a lot without actually saying it. Just ask Shakespeare. Or any half-decent poet."

"So he was trying to tell you..." Moore leaned forward, his interest piqued.

"That we might be able to steer a middle ground, between writing us off and assimilating us. I think he's also been doing things in the least efficient way he can get away with, to give us more time. But he's walking a tightrope as well. His knowledge is handy for dealing with the solar system, but if the computer decides he's a liability, he could just be switched off."

"This is essentially what you were talking about during the interview. It sounded like a long shot then, and it sounds like it now," Mandelbaum said.

"But the only shot we have, at the moment. And maybe not as much of a stretch as we thought. We have additional information on Ivan's end-game."

"And that is?"

"It's too complicated to go into in detail right now," Kemp replied, "but the short answer is that we believe we can present a scenario whereby the computer will have no choice but to negotiate."

"I will provisionally accept that for the moment." Mandelbaum grabbed her tablet. "What's the next step?"

"We have to find Ivan. We can't do anything until we can talk to him."

Moore shook his head in frustration. "He could be anywhere. There's simply no reason to prefer one direction over another, and we don't have the resources to search the entire surrounding sphere. He has, almost literally, the entire universe to lose himself in."

There was a short silence, before Kemp replied. "Well, that's the thing, Admiral. If Ivan is doing what we think, trying to give humanity an out, then he will not have tried too hard to lose himself. He'll be available for communications."

"Wait," Mandelbaum frowned. "Are you saying it's as easy as broadcasting a message?"

Kemp chuckled, audible over the intercom. "One good way to find out."

"Unbelievable." Mandelbaum did a slow face palm, then played with the intercom panel. "Signals, give me a general broadcast channel, full power, omnidirectional. Keep it open until I say otherwise."

"Aye, ma'am. Channel seven ready."

Mandelbaum gazed at Moore silently for a few moments, then leaned on the chair arm closest to the intercom speaker. "I guess we should prepare a statement."

"I've been working on that, Commodore," Kemp replied. "First, let's see if he's listening."

Mandelbaum nodded, then activated channel seven. "Attention, Ivan Pritchard. If you are listening, this is Commodore Mandelbaum of the United Earth Nations Navy. I have myself, Admiral Moore, Captain Jennings, Dr. Kemp, and Dr. Narang on the line. We wish to discuss the current situation with you."

Mandelbaum released the transmit button and cocked her head at Moore. "That's about all we can—"

Cutting her off in mid-sentence, Ivan Pritchard's voice played from the intercom. "Hi, Commodore. How's tricks?"

82. Discussion

Kemp's eyebrows rose. "That was fast!"

"Virtually no delay. He's in the neighborhood. It seems you were right. He's deliberately set things up to allow this meeting."

Kemp leaned forward and spoke directly to the intercom. "Commodore, it's very important that you not take any threatening actions."

"Not to worry, Doctor," Mandelbaum's voice came back immediately. "Signals informs me that Pritchard's responses are coming from an indefinite number of repeaters, completely englobing us. Even if we wanted to, we don't have enough nukes to take them all out. And they could *all* be repeaters. He could be even farther out, relaying his responses."

"Very well planned, it seems," Jennings said.

"Ivan?" Dr. Kemp said.

"Here, Doc."

"We have an interesting situation. We've tagged your comms station—the real one—and your nanite balls. We can blow them up. But we can't blow you up. You can build more nanites, and try again. But we'll be more prepared to deny you resources. And we're learning how to fight the nanites. We also have the *poisoning the well* option. Remember you mentioned that systems belonging to species that nuked themselves to extinction are unusable? We have enough hardware to implement that, and you know we'd be willing. Sounds like the beginning of a long, drawn-out cold war, with both sides offering nothing but defector moves. Do you agree with my assessment?"

"Sure do, Doc. And the computer is annoyed with me. It's pretty sure I orchestrated this, but it can't figure out how."

"I'd imagine the subtleties of implied communication are something you lose when you get Uploaded," Narang commented.

"Not sure I'd agree, Doc. Uh, Dr. Narang. I'm Uploaded, and I still get it."

"So, it's not the process itself," Dr. Kemp mused out loud. "Time? Or maybe loss of 'humanity', or the equivalent for other species?"

"I can't say, Doc. Neither can the computer. But it admits—not sure if that's the right work, maybe *acknowledges*—that this is one of the reasons that the Uploads keep looking for more species. Fresh blood, so to speak.

"And yet it was planning on wiping us out."

"Not explicitly, just allowing us to be killed in the conversion. Nothing personal. There's a cost/benefit analysis, and a risk analysis. Humanity came up short, although barely. We are, apparently, a bit of a pain in the ass, cosmically speaking."

Now came the gambit. Kemp had to hope he played this right. He took a deep breath. "Given all that, the computer's course of action doesn't strike me as logical."

There was a momentary silence, then Ivan laughed out loud. "I wouldn't have believed it was possible, but you just offended the computer, Doc."

Kemp grinned at Jennings and Narang, then answered, "Well, good. At least that means it's listening." He settled back in his chair and stroked his chin for a moment. "Here's the thing. We're not facing an imminent Arts invasion, are we? I mean, nothing specific has been detected?"

"Why do you say that, Doctor?" Mandelbaum cut in.

"Because the computer's actions are orderly, and are not rushed. A space station, for instance, would be a secondary priority if the Arts were coming down our throats. Instead, the computer is executing multiple parallel activities. What you do when you have the luxury of time."

"As it happens, Doc, you're correct. How is that relevant?" Ivan's voice had taken on a flat inflection. Dr. Kemp frowned for a moment, wondering if he'd just heard the computer talking.

"Because, Ivan, it changes the risk analysis. You've said that species are valuable as Uploads. If you aren't being imminently forced into a course of action, then it is logical to cultivate the possibility—"

"Hold on, Doctor," Mandelbaum interjected. "You're advocating *for* Upload?"

"In the future, Commodore. And possibly willingly, by our own hand. That is how a percentage of species come up, right, Ivan?"

"That is correct. Most Uploaded species, in fact, are self-actualized."

Dr. Kemp looked at Narang, whose brow was furrowed. Ivan's voice was definitely changing in tone, timber, inflection, pacing—the cadence of the words had become more even, like a metronome was in charge. Someone or something else had either taken over or was heavily involved. From one point of view, that was good. From another, they needed Ivan's influence in this discussion. If he'd been subsumed, they might have no chance at all.

"So why not wait until your hand is forced? Let us continue to develop and grow. You always have the option of going back to plan A."

Because, on balance, the human race does not display sufficient maturity. Your value to the Uploads is questionable at this time.

The voice now had no trace left of Ivan. Kemp stopped to take a deep breath. This was the part where he bet the wad. "Assuming your analysis is correct and complete—are you familiar with the Prisoner's Dilemma?"

There was a short silence, then Ivan came back on. It *was* Ivan, Ivan's voice. "Different name, of course, but the computer is familiar with the Game Theory concept. Cooperation vs. Defection, in a Nash-Equilibrium situation."

Kemp smiled. "Good. I submit that the ability to choose cooperation is based on the willingness to choose longer term benefits at the expense of shorter-term advantages. In our first encounter, we chose defection, and attacked. This time around, we propose to cooperate."

There was a "*What?*" from Mandelbaum.

Proceed.

Kemp took a deep breath. "We can continue the cold war, each trying to seek short-term advantage, and ultimately both of us suffering; or we can seek cooperation, resulting in a short-term minor disadvantage but a longer-term payoff for both. I propose that we will choose not to blow up your nanites and comms station, and in return you will spare the human race. It's probably too late for the other planets, I'd guess."

What's to stop you from defecting at a later date?

"Nothing. Nor is there anything stopping you from waking up one morning and deciding to drop a new set of nanites on Earth. That's the whole point of the Prisoner's Dilemma. Zero control over the opponents' motivations, thoughts, or plans. You have to depend on the cooperation being sufficiently beneficial to both sides to reduce the temptation to defect. Done properly, it's a positive-sum game. We benefit more in the aggregate than we each would individually."

It seems to me that I will be making most of the concessions.

"And getting most of the benefits from a successful relationship, in the long-term. We get nothing in return but our lives, which we had before you showed up."

True. But why should I choose this path, when the payoff is certain with my current plan?

"Because if there's one thing that the Prisoner's Dilemma teaches, it's that over the long term, both parties benefit more by cooperation than by defection. Your purpose, as I understand it, is to provide maximum tactical value for your Makers. If you choose the Defector route, you are betraying your programming by seeking a shorter-term but sub-optimal payoff. And we've just offered a Cooperator move. Tit-for-tat strategy mandates that you reciprocate in order to realize that maximal value."

There was a pause.

The human phrase for your line of argument is *heavy-handed.* But not necessarily incorrect. Stand by.

Stand by? Kemp looked at Narang and Jennings. "It would appear you've given it something to think about, anyway," Jennings said.

The radio came back to life.

Your terms are acceptable.

Kemp let out an explosive breath that he didn't realize he'd been holding. Narang whooped.

Jennings pressed the button on his console to speak, but Mandelbaum beat him to it. "How do we proceed?"

Ivan's voice came on, full-on Ivan. "The computer will signal the Makers. That's still the long-term goal. That isn't necessarily a danger to the human race, anyway. Closer to home, it will reprogram the nanite balls for something less, erm, dramatic. But part of the deal is that the nanites have to be in place. That's the computer's guarantee that you won't defect on its ass without warning. In return, the computer will provide assistance to help you prevent or at least delay the ecological collapse that Earth is facing until you can reduce the threat of the Singularity, and get Upload technology developed and society ready to accept it."

"Wow." Mandelbaum's voice sounded tired. "I hope the UEN ratifies this, or I'm going to be in the shit even deeper than Admiral Moore."

Moore laughed. "I don't think they'll have any choice, Commodore. The alternative is unacceptable."

Someone, probably bridge crew, cut into the conversation. "Ma'am, we have a hail from the SSE battle group."

Jennings looked at the doctors. "Just one pile of fertilizer after another."

83. Reaction

You engineered that.

Sorry, Ralph. Guilty as charged.

I have reviewed all your conversations, all your actions. I am unable to pinpoint any specific event that would have led to this result. Makers' research has concluded that telepathy is not possible. Were they wrong?

You have enough information to understand our games of Chess and Go?

Of course. A simple set of rules, but a complex and unpredictable set of outcomes.

Not unpredictable. Predicting your opponent's strategy is the whole point of the game.

Interesting.

But now the SSE is doing their usual chest-beating. We have to help—

No.

Why not? They could screw everything.

Our agreement with humanity deals with the Singularity and environmental destruction, at least in theory. This is the third major filter—self-destruction. If the humans can't overcome this encounter, it is almost certain to progress into full-blown war. Then we are back to...square one. An odd term. Game-related?

I think so. So after all that, we just sit back and watch?

It is the final test. If they pass this, you are...golden? Another game term?

Don't think so, not this time.

84. Face-Off

Mandelbaum gave Moore a dark look, then pressed the intercom. "Put the SSE vessel through to the Ready Room, Signals." She waited for the indicator to show a connection, and spoke as soon as the light came on. "This is Commodore Mandelbaum, commanding the UENN forces."

"This is Admiral Yeltsin of the SSE war fleet, aboard the SSEN destroyer *Victorious*. Commodore, am I to understand that you intend to do a *deal* with these entities?"

Moore raised his eyebrows. The tone was belligerent. There was a standard joke that the SSE military operated in two modes—confrontational, and asleep. But the communication was phrased as a question. For an SSE officer to open with that was unusual.

Mandelbaum responded. "Admiral Yeltsin, obviously you've been listening to the conversation, and no surprise since the whole thing was in clear. Hopefully you've heard the *whole* conversation—"

"I have. There are two items to note—one, you are unable to destroy the threat, and two, you've decided to try to negotiate your safety. Typical. It falls to myself and the SSE to do the job then. Step aside, and we will take care of it for you."

Moore typed on his tablet, then showed it to Mandelbaum.

Have the Getting Ahead move out of the arena with all haste.

She nodded, and typed on her own tablet. At the same time, she addressed the SSE warship. "Perhaps your English isn't as good as you believe it to be, Admiral. We are capable of destroying the space stations, we just don't believe it will remove the threat. Nor do we believe that an ongoing guerilla campaign is in anyone's best interests."

Moore typed on his tablet again.

Prepare one of the nuclear-tipped cruise missiles for an interception mission.

Mandelbaum drew back her head with a frown of disbelief. Moore tapped his temple and smiled. Mandelbaum typed on her tablet again, and showed it to Moore.

Per my authorization, accept any orders from Admiral Moore relating to current tactical situation.

She pressed send, then nodded to him.

Grinning, Moore began typing orders at a furious pace.

The SSE admiral responded, "You are simply too timid, Commodore. A good spread of nukes through the local sphere will surely take out this alien that you have code-named *Ivan.*"

"And you know that, how? Never mind. You *hope* that will work. The problem is that if it doesn't, you've committed the entire human race to a war that, ultimately, we will lose. While at the same time denying us the opportunity to leap-frog our technology through cooperation with Ivan." Mandelbaum released the *transmit* button with a flourish.

"Bah! More words. More mealy-mouthed weaseling. Let us show you how it is done."

Immediately, the status monitor on the desktop showed an object leaving the SSE war fleet. A second later, AI software projected the trajectory, terminating in Ivan's comms station. At the same time, the intercom announced, "Single launch from SSE flagship. Profile matches S-Mark-IV SSE nuclear missile. Initiating defensive script Moore-1."

There was a barely perceptible shudder as the *Gambit* responded. The klaxon bleated, followed by an automated announcement. "Red alert, red alert, all personnel to battle stations. This is not a drill. Implement radiation protocols."

After a brief pause, the P.A. announced, "Estimated intercept twelve seconds. All crew, brace for blast and radiation effects."

Mandelbaum glared at Moore. "You sent a nuclear-tipped missile to intercept?"

Moore smiled back. "*Close* only counts in horseshoes and nuclear missiles, Commodore. The response both ensures that we'll take out their sortie, and sends a clear message that we're happy to deploy nukes. It immediately deflates their internal narrative that we will be the first to blink." His smile changed to a predatory grin. "It's a strategy of mine that I like to call, 'As a matter of fact, *you* give me *your* wallet.'"

Mandelbaum shook her head in disbelief. "Don't make me regret that order, Moore."

"I don't think Yeltsin is as confident as he makes out, Commodore. In this particular case, we can make *him* blink." Moore hoped his confident tone wasn't misplaced. The alternative was that he had just started an interplanetary war. If this tanked, he might as well just space himself and save everyone else the trouble.

The desktop flashed the message, "Detonation", followed by, "Outside shock radius" and "Radiation effects nominal."

Admiral Yeltsin spoke over the intercom, his voice tight with rage. "That was a declaration of war, Commodore."

Mandelbaum stared at Moore for a long second, then responded. "If you want to take it that way, Admiral, feel free. But you're capable of doing the same analysis that we are. We outgun you. Not significantly, but enough to put the odds in our favor. Meanwhile, we have an agreement with Ivan, and you don't, which means he'll be motivated to help us. If we go to war, you can bet your last bottle of vodka that we'll be using any tech we get from him to pound the SSE into the dust."

She let the silence hang for a moment before continuing. "On the other hand, in the absence of a war, the SSE has the same right to the tech as anyone else. Your call, Admiral."

She took her finger off the *transmit* button again and raised an eyebrow at Moore. He gave her two thumbs up.

The two stared at the intercom panel. The time stretched. Finally, there was a response, but not from the SSE admiral.

"Ma'am, comm monitoring reports leakage from a tight-beam signal, originating at the SSE flagship. Not enough signal strength to make anything out, and it's probably encrypted anyway. Aimed at Earth, looks like."

Moore grinned. "They're phoning home."

Mandelbaum did a fist pump in response. "They blinked!"

85. Aftermath

Moore looked at the backlog of communications in the in-basket on his tablet. It was small consolation to know that Mandelbaum's was far, far worse. Recriminations, demands for more information, requests for independent confirmation, suggestions for further negotiation, outright threats, and many of them mutually contradictory. It didn't help that the chain of command, never fully clarified in the first place, was being totally ignored.

And Strategic Space Command had no real grounds for complaint. They'd given Mandelbaum the authorization to do what she did. She'd given Moore the authorization to place the orders that he had. The SSE admiral had passed the buck to his HQ, and they'd blinked as well.

No one was in a position to take it back without losing face. Especially since, when it came down to it, mankind had won. The human race wouldn't be destroyed or Uploaded by fiat; the SSE wouldn't be going to war; and if preliminary discussions with Ivan were anything to go by, Earth would be considerably better off.

Subsequent exchanges with Admiral Yeltsin made it clear that he wanted partial credit for the negotiations with Ivan. It was a small price to pay, and a good way for Yeltsin to save face. Mandelbaum had assured him that was how she remembered it, and the official report would concur.

One of the more interesting documents in Moore's in-basket was an official commendation from SSC, with a note that the charges against him were being dropped, all based apparently on

Mandelbaum's report. Suddenly the future was looking less bleak. You only got one do-over like this per lifetime, though. A nice comfy desk job from here on in would be just the ticket.

Moore sighed, and tossed his tablet on the desk. Mandelbaum looked up at the *clunk*, said, "Yeah," and threw hers as well. Possibly with slightly more force than was really required. She reached into a drawer and pulled out a bottle of very expensive-looking single-malt. Moore pushed his cup forward with a smile and Mandelbaum laughed.

"There's no coffee in there," she said, holding the bottle in a half-ready position.

"I have my priorities," he replied, jiggling the cup.

Mandelbaum poured him a generous dollop, then pulled out a glass for herself and poured a double. She leaned back and raised her glass. "I'm not sure if I'm actually toasting success or just a reprieve."

"Either way," Moore said, and raised his cup in reply.

A warm glow began to suffuse his face with the mouthful of whiskey. *Definitely getting out of shape*, he thought. *Or old.*

"Ivan has refused to say specifically what the nanites will do to Earth and Luna," Mandelbaum said. "Beyond the rather cryptic comment that we'll be pleased with the results."

"Or the computer won't tell him. I don't get the impression that it's the easiest of relationships."

She grinned at that. "He does say that it won't involve modifications to humans, so I'm prepared to take a wait-and-see stance. Something about giving us time to clean up our act. I'm guessing it has to do with the ecosystem."

Moore nodded and sat back. He'd finally had time to get caught up on the news. Mercury had grown two very large somethings, one at each pole. They were long and vaguely cylindrical, supported on some kind of massive mounting, and looked weapon-like to Moore's eye. The rest of Mercury appeared to be growing giant solar panels. Military pundits speculated that it was a weapon, powered by solar energy, possibly with some truly huge accumulators under the crust.

Venus and Mars were now completely without atmosphere. The towers, once their mission of ejecting the atmosphere was complete, had metamorphosed into some strange combination of planet-spanning arches and radio dishes. Scientists were clamoring for permission to visit the planets, and so far, Ivan hadn't denied it.

Of the impending Terran and Lunar modifications, well, they'd know soon enough.

86. Conversation

Ivan looked out the open side of the *Mad Astra* at the Milky Way, stretching right across his field of view. It was a peaceful moment, and he still felt the urge to take and release a deep breath. Not going to happen in outer space, of course.

So what now?

Nanite balls have been deployed. Earth and Luna will begin changes shortly.

And the technology releases?

Your proposed schedule is acceptable.

What will happen with the message? How will the Makers respond?

Message has been sent to all likely destination systems, giving details on your species and the Agreement. Expected response times will be based on the distance of those systems. The Makers will transmit a response with further orders and options, but they will almost certainly ratify the agreed-to terms. Humanity will be left to its own fate unless countermanding orders are received, or the Arts show up, or humanity approaches one of the Great Filters, or reneges on the Agreement.

What will happen to me?

You will be deactivated and archived.

So that's it for me? Gone?

Archived, not deleted. Eventually, humanity will develop Upload capability. You will be reactivated and transferred to a human Upload form. Or perhaps given control of this one, since my usefulness will have ended.

Oh...

Ivan wouldn't die. He'd probably never see his wife and kids again, but he might see his descendants. Not totally terrible.

Is it really necessary? Things are just getting interesting.

It is standard procedure.

And how's that been working for you, so far?

Sarcasm?

Ivan couldn't help a mental smile. Ralph was learning.

Yeah, sorry. But do you really need to deactivate me?

You will keep interfering, otherwise. And...I have selected an English phrase that seems appropriate.

Which is?

You are a pain in the ass.

Ivan chuckled. Or the outer space equivalent. He had no argument.

You will, of course, be reactivated if events deviate from plan.

So there was hope. Although if he was awoken early, it would be because things had gone unshiny.

Okay. As death sentences go, it could be worse.

Just one small request...

Proceed.

87. Funeral

Ivan Pritchard
May 4, 2122 - Aug 17, 2150
In loving memory

Dr. Kemp gazed around the group. Mrs. Pritchard stood in front of the gravestone, one arm around each of her children. To her left stood Tenn Davies, Seth Robinson, Aspasia Nevin, Cirila Heinrichs, and Arcadius Geiger. The rest of the crew had sent flowers and notes of sympathy. Kemp had spoken the truth to Mrs. Pritchard—Ivan had been well-liked.

Captain Jennings stood with Kemp and Narang, on the right, still apparently unconsciously maintaining the officer/crew divide. Well, a lifetime of habit would be hard to break.

Kemp allowed himself a brief smile. Turned out Tenn Davies was a family man. He glanced at Tenn's six children and very harried-looking partner, whom Tenn had introduced as Roger. Tenn stepped forward and motioned his offspring to stand with him at the gravestone. He put his arms around his children. "Kids, Ivan was a good friend to everyone. And a good person. You want to try to be like him, and people will remember you after you're gone." The children looked up at their father, hanging on every word.

Davies gave his children a smile and scooted them back toward their other father. He walked over to Mrs. Pritchard, took her hand, and spoke to her in a low voice. As he talked, she began to weep and nod repeatedly.

When they were done, Robinson walked over to speak to Davies, and Kemp sidled over to eavesdrop. Unsuccessfully, as it turned out. Robinson looked over and acknowledged his presence—with a smile, rather than a frown. Kemp shrugged and, abandoning stealth, moved to stand with the two men.

Robinson nodded his head toward Tenn's family. "Is that why you're always cranky? Lack of sleep?"

Davies rolled his eyes. "Oh, hah hah. No, shit-for-brains. When I'm in space, I miss the hell out of Roger and the kids. I don't have a choice, er, well, didn't. I guess I took it out on people. Especially Ivan, since it looked like he was making the same mistake."

"He sacrificed himself for them." Kemp looked down at the ground for a moment. "We had a talk, when I was up there in the *Getting Ahead.* It's all he really cared about."

Davies nodded. "Not surprised."

* * *

A week after the funeral, Kemp felt as if he could finally put the whole adventure behind him. He had his feet up on the coffee table, Maddie snuggled against his shoulder, a multi-million-dollar view out the picture window—and even the news was looking good.

The nanites that arrived on Luna had immediately started extracting gases and water from the rock and soil of the moon. A detectable atmosphere was already starting to form. At the current rate, according to some estimates, Luna would be a shirt-sleeve environment within two years. There was even a rising magnetic field, which had stirred a hornet's nest of debate in the scientific community. The consensus seemed to be that the moon would have to be spun up in order to maintain the inner dynamo. The big question was, was that even possible? What were the nanites' limits?

Meanwhile, the Terran nanites seemed to be engaged in ecological cleanup. Oceanic acidity had already dropped, albeit barely perceptibly, and there was speculation that greenhouse gases would be showing a drop in concentration soon. In addition, orbital observation facilities were reporting a slight rise in albedo of the few remaining patches of ice at the poles, which was expected to reduce the rate of melting, and an increase in overall cloud cover, which should reduce net heat intake from the sun.

Simple strategies, far-reaching effects. They would halt and even reverse the damage done to the planet, which would give humanity time to perhaps mature a little.

Ivan had released full and comprehensive plans for what was being called the Casimir Power Source. This and other periodic releases of technology would give the human race less reason to fight for scarce resources, and bring humanity closer to the ability to create their own Upload technology, thus avoiding the Singularity.

Not surprisingly, the SSE was denouncing the whole thing as a Western plot, while at the same time bemoaning the West's presumed intention to cut the SSE out of the loop. There was no mention at all of the face-off between UENN and SSE forces, or of the three-way agreement that had been hammered out. Kemp did an eye roll. Did they ever listen to themselves?

On the larger scale, the end-game fulfilled the computer's primary objective, that of adding another species to the Upload community. That it might take centuries was irrelevant—immortal, non-biological beings could be incredibly patient. And a humanity joining willingly, uploaded by its own hand, would be the ultimate prize.

Kemp turned off the Vid, and put his other arm around Narang. She responded by snuggling into his neck.

"Somehow," he said, "we seem to have managed to come out of this whole thing better off than before."

"Mmmf," Narang responded.

Both jumped as the phone rang, Narang's head smacking Kemp's jaw. He rubbed the spot and muttered, "I've got to change that damn ring tone."

He picked up the phone. "Hello?"

"Charles?" It was Captain Jennings.

"Hi, Andrew. How's the life of a solitary miner?"

"Um. Okay, but not why I phoned."

Kemp sat up. The tone in Jennings's voice made his hair stand on end. He put the phone on speaker for Narang's benefit. "What's happened?"

"I called Ivan today, just to chat. You know that he's piggybacked off my phone system." Jennings hesitated for a moment. "I got the computer. It says that Ivan has been archived, as he is no longer required."

Narang gasped and put her hand to her mouth. "Oh, no."

"The computer did want to pass on a message. Ivan asked us to let his family know that he loved them and never stopped thinking of them."

Kemp closed his eyes, the phone dropping from his hand. Softly, silently, Narang began to cry.

88. Coda

Ivan smiled and put his hands behind his head. In free fall, the position had no real purpose, but a lifetime of habit was hard to break.

That was nice.

I am becoming more proficient at detecting tone of voice, although I am still perplexed by the meanings.

And…

Every time you say "attend my own funeral" you get a tone similar to laughter.

I can explain about humor and comedic tropes. And a lot of other stuff you've asked about, now that we have some free time. But thanks for letting me see it.

The number of nanites required was trivial. There was no reason to refuse. And it provided additional data about the behavior of your species.

Just the same, Ralph, I appreciate it.

Noted.

So…whatever you're going to do to me, let's do it.

In good time.

Ralph?

Explain please first. Why is attending your own funeral funny?

Made in the USA
San Bernardino, CA
07 January 2020

62803557R00191